THE SALMA OPTION

JAMES McGEE

ALSO BY JAMES McGEE

1

ISBN 9798354152995

THE SALMA OPTION

1

Chad, North-Central Africa.

It was an hour before dusk when the horsemen rode into the valley, their clothing caked with dust and flies, their lower faces concealed by their keffiyehs, their bandoleers and Kalashnikov assault rifles strapped across their backs.

The ride from Kutum had taken thirteen days. The arid desert land through which they had travelled had provided little shelter but the men were familiar with the country and knew the safest places to bivouac and which wells were free of contamination.

The unclean wells were those located closest to the burned-out villages, destroyed during government-sanctioned raids. Their contents were still tainted by animal remains and, in some cases, by human corpses that had been left to rot in the years since the settlements' destruction.

The clean wells were known to the horsemen because they were the more isolated ones they'd protected during the war, while they were poisoning the villagers' main water supplies in an effort to root out members and supporters of the People's Liberation Army.

They rode slowly, cautiously, and in single file; four slender, dark-skinned men with hollowed-out cheeks and watchful eyes, mounted on wiry horses bred for speed and agility by descendants of the Rizeigat, fighters born to the saddle, whose lineage could be traced back through generations of Bedu tribesmen.

The animals' hooves clattered as they picked their way across the stones and loose scree, until, eventually, the earth and rocks gave way to a fresh landscape consisting of open savannah and clumps of acacia and scented thorn, which, while not thick enough to be called woodland, were, nevertheless, of sufficient density to provide shelter for the night.

The lead rider, whose name was Jaafar, drew his mount to a halt and lowered his scarf. Eyes narrowed against the glare from the setting sun, he gave the order to make camp. Dismounting and removing their saddles and equipment, the men tethered the horses and after seeing to the animals' feed, they set up their net shelters and spread blankets on the ground beneath them before collecting wood for a fire.

When the sun had dipped behind the trees, the men performed Maghrib and when their prayers were concluded they used a kettle made from an old ration tin to brew tea using water from their canteens, and a round metal pot in which to prepare a stew using strips of dried goat meat they'd acquired from a fly-infested roadside stall three days before. Stored between their saddle cloths and their horses' flanks, the meat had softened during the ride but was still tough and stringy and on the turn, so they masked the taste with some sliced red peppers, onions and crushed garlic and ate the result with a mash made from corn porridge, fashioning cones out of fresh-baked durra bread to use as spoons.

When they had eaten, Jaafar's companion, Faheem,

took a handful of ground coffee beans from his pack and dropped them into the kettle with some fresh water. When the water boiled he added ginger slices and crushed cardamom pods to the brew which the men sipped from battered tin cups.

As the evening wore on, with the air reverberating to the whine of cicadas, the men passed around a small pot of toombak, smearing the mix of finely ground tobacco leaves, sodium bicarbonate and water along the inside of their mouths between cheek and gum.

Despite being warmed by the fire and with their bellies full, the men knew they could not relax their vigilance. Predators stalked the darkness, which meant a watch had to be kept and the fire fed. To that end, they checked and cleaned their weapons as they conversed.

The talk was of the coming days. If all went well, the money they would make would put food on their tables for several months. It was even possible they would earn enough to mend the corrugated roofs on their houses or, if they were very lucky, to buy a pick-up truck. In a country blighted by war, famine and pestilence, it wasn't the size of your house that marked you as a man to be respected, it was the third or fourth-hand Toyota parked in the dirt alongside it.

From out of the darkness and the open grassland that lay beyond the trees there came a sudden explosion of hoarse barks. It was followed by a chorus of high-pitched squeals and then by a series of wheezing howls which, to an untrained ear, might have been mistaken for car engines being turned over or the whirr of electric drills with the switch set to high. The harrowing sounds persisted for several minutes before fading into the night. Guns held across their knees, the

3

men stared off in the direction of the commotion. Shadows played across their faces, illuminating the whites of their eyes as the fire crackled, sending sparks spiralling into the star-studded sky.

When their weapons and equipment had been prepared for the morning and lots drawn to determine the watch rotation, Jaafar's companions retired to their shelters, leaving him by the fire. Wrapping his blanket around his slim shoulders, he poured the last of the coffee dregs into his cup and with his rifle propped against his thigh, he made himself comfortable.

Not that any of them would be able to enjoy an uninterrupted sleep. The small hours prior to the dawn would be the most taxing. By then, the sense of anticipation would have become almost unbearable.

For tomorrow the hunt would begin.

The men were awake and up before the sunrise. Following Morning Prayer and after breaking their fast on porridge and sweet tea, they took up their weapons and ammunition. Then, departing the camp, they steered their horses north.

The first faint rumble of thunder came a short while later. The men were not dismayed by the sound, nor fearful of being caught out in the open. It was the sign they had been waiting for, the signal which confirmed that the direction they were following and the instructions they'd been given before leaving home were correct. So they remained alert, their weapons primed.

The carnivores that ruled the grasslands were, in the main, night hunters, but that did not mean they wouldn't take down prey during daylight hours. The hyenas that had been so vocal the evening before would, in all likelihood, have retreated to their dens but it would have been unwise to imagine they'd allow an easy meal to pass by unmolested. Though, in this instance, the risk of that happening had been reduced by the men's mode of travel, for while it might have appeared foolish to traverse such potentially dangerous country on horseback, it was the horses that provided Jaafar and his men with security. Collectively, a group of riders presented a substantial and, thus, intimidating outline. Even the larger predators, such as lion and leopard, would think twice before launching a pre-emptive strike against such a strange-looking beast. Not that the men were completely immune from attack. There were other, far more aggressive animals out there capable of exacting harm.

Another low roll of thunder sounded. Jaafar raised his eyes towards the south, to where a band of grey cloud hung low above the horizon. As if on cue, the inside of the cloud layer was lit by pulses of white light. Despite the impressive display, it took a while for the next thunder clap to arrive; an indication that the storm was still a considerable distance away. The pyrotechnics were only visible because there was no significant high ground to obstruct the view, other than a few granite outcrops that showed above the trees. As he watched the lightning flicker once more and then die, Jaafar felt the excitement move through him. Faheem, Suleyman and Irshad, he knew, would have felt it, too.

It meant the rains were on their way.

As the echoes generated by the thunder gods faltered and died, the matriarch paused and lifted her great head. Raising her trunk, she probed the air. She was unaware that her olfactory system contained the largest number of genes dedicated to smell of any mammal on the planet or that the odour filling her senses came from a compound excreted by soil-dwelling bacteria that was carried on the air the second a raindrop hit the ground. She knew only what her instincts were telling her; that the rains were coming and it was time to begin the journey to the northern feeding grounds.

Staring off towards the source of the rever-berations, she emitted a sequence of soft expressive grunts, the sounds resonating deep within her belly. The summons was answered almost immediately.

Repeating the signal, she flapped her ears. Then, with ponderous deliberation, and turning her rear towards the clouded horizon, she set off in a graceful, swaying walk. Her two sisters were the first to fall into line behind her, shepherding her grandchild, a nine-month-old male calf, between them. Her daughter followed next, then her son. There was no hesitation, no dissent. At thirty years of age and standing almost three metres at the shoulder, she was the oldest and the largest female in her family, the one the others looked to for guidance; the one they trusted without question: the leader.

Inevitably, the rate of march was dictated by the calf's walking pace and by the time they reached the edge of the grassland, they had been travelling for some six hours. Water had become the priority.

The odours coming off the river were strong and

pungent as the matriarch led the way through the brush, her trunk twitching. She was leading them to a place she and her sisters knew well. It had become a regular rendezvous for the herd during the annual migration, not only as a place to bathe and quench the thirst but also to gather and to greet friends and family, both old and new.

Approaching the break in the trees that led on to the river bank she hesitated. A new scent was drifting on the air, one that was at once both familiar and yet ... different. She advanced warily. Arriving at the top of the incline, she halted.

The dry season had transformed the Salamat and its tributaries into a string of waterholes connected by dried-out mudflats and low-lying strips of yellow sand bordered by acacia trees and pockets of ragged thorn bush. The majority of the reservoirs were no larger than puddles or else they had been turned into muddy wallows, but a few, like the one before her, were several hundred paces in length, albeit contracted in width, and their depth greatly reduced due to animal disturbance and seasonal evaporation.

From her vantage point, the matriarch took stock. No other herd members were in sight but a variety of animals were competing for drinking room. Zebra, bush pig and waterbuck rubbed haunches with baboon and hartebeest while further down the slope a small group of Kordofan giraffe had arranged themselves into an orderly line, their long legs spread wide as they lowered their heads to the water. Black Crowned cranes, aloof from the crowd, strutted across the higher reaches in search of stranded reed frogs while, on the far side of the clearing, surrounded by a noisy flock of quelea, a dozen buffalo grazed on the last surviving shoots of meadow grass.

The matriarch felt her hind quarters nudged as the calf wandered forward to see for himself. She placed her trunk protectively in the infant's path to prevent him from further exploration as her sisters, anxious at having lost control of their charge, appeared at her shoulder.

All seemed peaceful and the contents of the waterhole beckoned invitingly, but the strange scent still lingered and that made the matriarch exceedingly cautious. Her great bulk and impressive tusks ensured she was unlikely to be targeted by either lion or hyena, had they been lying in wait, but there were other members of her family, most notably the calf, that were far more vulnerable and it was her duty was to protect them, and that she would do until her dying breath.

Observing the scene below, she noted that none of the other visitors to the watering place were showing concern beyond the normal skittishness evident at such gatherings and the tranquillity on display gave her the confidence to proceed. With the next significant body of water more than half a day's march away, it was imperative she and the family made the most of the opportunity set before them. Letting go a rumble of satisfaction, she led them down towards the water's edge.

Ranger Adoum Coelo was buttoning up his flies after taking a much needed piss and was on his way back to the Land Cruiser when he spotted the pile of droppings at the side of the trail. It wasn't as though he'd been scouring the ground for scat but if there was one skill a ranger could count upon when tracking animals for a living it was the ability to memorize the shape, size, consistency, and smell of their bodily excretions, and something about this particular faecal contribution had caught his eye. He wasn't sure what, exactly, until he paused and went back and had a closer look. And then, when he crouched and examined the ground round about, he saw it.

He rose quickly and jogged back to the Land Cruiser where the rest of the team were waiting patiently.

"Boss, there's something you need to see."

Alerted by the urgency in the ranger's voice, Joseph Sekka, lounging in the passenger seat, turned. He was on the point of asking what it was he needed to see, only to find that Adoum was already on his way back to wherever it was he'd come from. Frowning, Sekka climbed out of the vehicle. The other rangers, some of whom had also taken the opportunity to relieve themselves, and who'd been chatting while awaiting their colleague's return, fell silent and, full of curiosity, followed their team leader to where Adoum was waiting.

Sekka squatted and inspected the dung pellets, crumbling the dried matter between his fingers. "Not Zebra?"

Even as he posed the question he could see for himself what had drawn Adoum's attention: the outline of what looked like the curved edge of a metal shoe impressed into one of the dung balls.   Still, it didn't hurt to get a second opinion.

Adoum responded with confirming shake of the head.

"Shit," Sekka swore softly.

"Yes boss." Adoum did not smile. "Horse shit."

Sekka stood and gazed down at the flies that were crawling over the mass and the beetles that were hard at work, trundling balls of the stuff away. For a few of the rollers it looked like an uphill struggle which made Sekka wonder if, in the insect world, shit was like fine wine and that it grew more appetizing and therefore more collectable with age. And then he felt a chill move through him as his thoughts turned to what the presence of riders in this sector of the reserve might mean.

Hoof prints wouldn't have been a worrying factor in themselves. Ranger teams often conducted patrols on horseback. Unlike vehicles, the animals weren't prone to mechanical failure and they could cover territory that would defeat even the most powerful 4x4. But Sekka and the members of Team Jackal hadn't yet made the transition. They'd been set to dispense with the Land Cruiser when their current two-week patrol ended, because motor vehicles didn't like the rainy season. They didn't like the mud or the swollen rivers. Horses tended to cope better in the wet, and they were cheaper to maintain. Plus with six rangers to each team it was a tight squeeze fitting everyone into the back of the pickup, even without the overnight equipment.

There were several African reserves that promoted horseback safaris as part of their visitor experience. They were a popular draw for tourists who wanted to get closer to the wildlife. They also catered to those who viewed vehicle safaris as a threat to the planet. Horses, it was reasoned, were more environmentally friendly than the internal combustion engine, and a lot quieter. But horseback safaris weren't a feature of this reserve. If they had been, it was too late in the year, anyway, as the tourist season had ended.

"How old?" Sekka asked.

Adoum stirred the dung with the toe of his boot. "Not more than one day."

"Can you tell how many?"

In answer, Adoum left the scat and circled the immediate area, studying the ground. "I think four riders, five horses."

Sekka frowned.

"One horse to carry supplies," Adoum explained.

Sekka turned to the rest of his team. They were clad, as he was, in full camo gear: jacket and pants topped either with matching boonies or keffiyehs. Half the men wore their keffiyehs turban-style, while the rest, like Sekka, alternated between wearing them as scarves or else they sported the veiled look.

The latter effect, when offset with dark glasses, could be intimidating but it offered valid protection against the dust and dirt and the muck thrown up by the 4X4's heavy-duty tyres. In any case, they weren't taking part in a beauty contest.

In addition to the military attire, the men were also armed with automatic rifles, Glock pistols, spare magazines, survival gear, and field rations. Their epaulette badges bore the insignia: *Parc National Salma;* the *Garde* tags sewn on to the right hand pocket of their tunics were self-explanatory. A badge adorning the right hand pocket of Sekka's tunic identified him as the *Chef de Groupe,* which was why they were looking to him now, the expressions on their faces telling him that their emotions mirrored his own as they awaited his orders.

Sekka addressed his second-in-command. "Call it in, Matthias. Tell them tracks found, south-east

11

quadrant, and we're investigating. Then I want you, Adoum, and Theo with me. Cesar, I need you and Isadore to follow us in the vehicle, nice and slow, five hundred metres behind. Keep the radio channel open but maintain silence unless you hear from me. If I tell you to hold, you hold. If I call and we need back-up, you have my permission to break the speed limit. The droppings aren't fresh but that doesn't mean the crew that made them aren't active in the area. Don't worry," he added. "If there's contact, you'll get your chance."

Cesar and Isadore nodded, though their disappointment at being told to hang back was plain to see. They watched in silence as their companions checked their weapons and equipment. When that had been done, Sekka eyed them up and down and nodded his satisfaction. "Remember, this is what you've trained for."

The men straightened.

"All right," Sekka said. "Move out. Eyes skinned, ears open. From now on, consider this enemy territory."

It was three hours later when they came upon the camp.

Sekka didn't think they'd be that lucky so soon, given the age of the scat. It was Adoum who found it, partly by chance but mostly because Sekka had assigned him to take point due to him being the team's best tracker. Plus, as it had been his sharp eyesight that had spotted the hoof prints in the first place, it would have been churlish and bad for morale had Sekka given the lead to one of the others.

Telling Cesar via the two-way to hold position, Sekka, Matthias and Theo hunkered down, rising when they saw Adoum trotting back through the long grass towards them.

"How far?" Sekka asked, when Adoum reported what he'd seen.

"Two hundred metres." Adoum spoke quietly. Extending his arm, he made a cutting motion with his bladed hand to indicate the direction.

"Anybody there?"

"I saw no one, boss."

"No horses?"

"No, boss."

Sekka pondered the significance of that admission before radioing Cesar with the information and telling him to maintain his distance. Then, tapping Adoum on the shoulder, he said, "On you. Let's go."

Advancing cautiously in single file, they held their automatic rifles to their chests, forefingers resting alongside the top of the trigger guard. They halted every fifty paces to listen, but the only sounds breaking the stillness were snippets of birdsong coming from the surrounding thickets.

One hundred and fifty metres further on, Adoum raised a fist and brought them to a halt, jerking his chin towards a stand of acacia trees that were blocking a view of the skyline. "There, boss," he said, his voice still pitched low.

Sekka flicked the radio switch and told Cesar and Isadore to stand by, then, with the others at his side, he inched his way forward and studied the scene. .

It looked as if Adoum was correct; the camp did appear to be unoccupied, though from his vantage point, from what he could make out, Sekka suspected the place had not been abandoned, merely vacated. A stash of cooking gear was stowed beneath one of the shelters along with a pair of small jerry cans which, presumably, held water. Coils of rope were suspended from a branch, next to what appeared to be bedding rolls left to air, out of reach of crawling creatures, which indicated that at some point the people who'd set up the camp intended to return. When, or if they did, it was unlikely they'd be expecting a welcome committee.

Despite Adoum's assertion and his own observations, Sekka wasn't prepared to risk a head-on approach. There was always a possibility that a lookout was concealed beneath the trees. Directing Matthias and Adoum to move in from the right, Sekka indicated to Theo to follow him in a flanking movement to the left.

Slowly, they closed in.

In the end, their prudence proved unnecessary. There was no one home. The question was: for how long? Sekka radioed Cesar and told him to maintain his position until they'd searched the camp and surrounding area. If Sekka and his three team members were attacked, it was good to know armed support was waiting in the wings.

They started with the shelters.

There were two, each one spacious enough accommodate two sleepers. Both had been constructed by stringing camouflage netting over a line strung between two trees. They had been pitched low, meaning there was enough headroom for the occupants to crawl inside but not enough to stand up. Standard military bivvies, Sekka noted, and filed that nugget of information away.

Sekka and Adoum's inspection of the first shelter yielded two rolled prayer mats, two backpacks, at least two weeks' supply of powdered and dried food; a spam can of Chinese-manufactured 7.62 x 39 mm ammunition, and a box of ampoules which Adoum recognized from the Arabic labels as being horse vaccine. He held one of them out for Sekka's inspection. "From Sudan, boss."

Theo appeared from the second shelter. "They have a satellite phone."

The phone was an Iridium. It wasn't a top of the line model but it was still a solid piece of kit, as was the foldable Solstar solar charger that had been stored in the same back pack. Neither item came cheap, which told Sekka that whoever these people were, even if you discounted the ammo, they wouldn't get away with posing as itinerant herders.

"Cell phone, too, boss," Theo announced, hoisting the offending item into view. "Battery dead," he added as he passed it over.

Sekka was hefting the phone in his hand when Matthias called out, "Boss?" in an odd tone of voice.

Sekka looked up to see the ranger, who'd been rummaging in one of the backpacks in the second bivvy, holding up what could only have been a pair of military trousers. They weren't dissimilar to the camouflage gear worn by the ranger team, save they were a lighter shade, more suitable as desert wear than the darker colour required for forest terrain. And then Matthias pulled out the tunic and his face turned to stone. "Sudan Army."

"You sure?" Sekka asked.

Matthias turned the tunic over. The badge showing the Sudanese flag was sewn on to the left sleeve. On the right sleeve was another badge: round, with a green crescent containing a stylized image of a

15

secretary bird set above a representation of the globe. Arabic writing ran round the top half of the badge, while, somewhat incongruously, but obligingly, English lettering framed the bottom half: *National Intelligence and Security Service*. It was set above three gold bars: a sergeant's stripes.

"RSF, Boss," Matthias said. "Very bad people."

That, Sekka knew, was something of an understatement.

RSF stood for Rapid Support Forces. Referred to in the singular, despite the 's' at the end, it was administered by the Sudanese security service, hence the badge; while during military operations it came under the command of the Sudanese army. In reality, it was a paramilitary force employed by the Khartoum government, which meant it was a protected organ-ization, with a reputation.

It had come into the world as a child born of war.

The Janjaweed: devils on horseback.

Beginning life as an Arab militia, the Janjaweed had gained its notoriety during the Darfur conflict when the Sudanese president, Omar al-Bashir, had recruited it to help quell an armed insurrection led by the rebel Justice and Equality Movement and the Sudanese Liberation Army, who were protesting against what they considered to be the Bashir government's disregard for the western region and its non-Arab population.

As the conflict expanded, the Janjaweed had grown in stature, visiting its brutality upon an already traumatized civilian population, using rape, torture and pillage as weapons, while preventing international aid organizations from delivering essential food and medical supplies. Not until five years later had the UN been able to deploy troops to the region to calm matters, by which time hundreds of thousands of people were dead and more than two million displaced.

Somehow, despite being branded as a war criminal by the ICC, which issued a warrant for his arrest on charges of genocide and crimes against humanity, Bashir had survived, emerging stronger than ever after a successful election campaign. Acknowledging the aid given to him by the Janjaweed and knowing that his existence depended on its continued support, Bashir had incorporated it into his security organization and given it a brand new name: the Rapid Support Forces.

When, a short time later, the Sudanese parliament amended the country's interim constitution, turning the nation's security apparatus into an official state organization along the lines of the army and the police, the RSF became a legitimate military branch of the Sudanese security service, which gave it free rein to do what it liked.

Rumour had it that the Sudanese general staff had initially refused to accept the Janjaweed into their ranks, because they still considered it to be a chaotic militia following a tribal code rather than the rules of combat. As a result, the RSF, operating on its own terms, was reputed to enjoy advantages over the official Sudanese army. Its equipment was more advanced and salaries were higher. The Sudanese even had a special name for RSF members. They called them 'spoiled children'.

From what Sekka and his men had discovered, it looked as if the kids had snuck out of the nursery and were about to wreak havoc.

Unless they could be found.

At the waterhole, the male buffalo raised his huge head and gazed sullenly at the new arrivals before resuming his foraging. But only for a few seconds. Suddenly, he looked up, his attention fixed on the line of vegetation behind him. As if a silent warning had been passed, other animals also paused in their actions. The air stilled. The zebra and waterbucks stiffened; a sea of heads lifted, and the matriarch froze, smelling the air.

As the queleas exploded from their sandbar in a shimmer of beating wings and the riders broke from the trees.

The peace shattered and with animals scattering in all directions, the matriarch's first instinct was to close ranks. Snorting, ears spread, not quite sure what was happening, and with secretions already beginning to leak copiously from her temporal glands, she turned to confront the threat.

In centuries past, Darfur Arabs had hunted elephants from the saddle, armed only with a single spear. One animal from the herd would be chosen and a lone rider would place himself in front of the terrified beast to distract its attention, allowing his companions - up to two dozen or more - to ride in from behind; their target: the hamstrings, which, when severed, would be enough to bring the animal down. Over time, the surviving herds had learned that the best defence against such an attack was to bunch up so that no individual member could be singled out. It was a strategy still followed; face the enemy head on and form a shield to guard the flanks and protect the weakest members of the herd: the injured, the elderly, and the juveniles.

As Jaafar urged his mount forward, he saw that their targets, led by the big female, had already formed a defensive ring and were attempting to back away from the water's edge and on to firmer ground. Glancing towards the far side of the waterhole, he spotted Irshad and Suleyman emerging from behind a stand of thorn bushes.

As the second pair of riders darted into view, the matriarch roared a warning. The blast echoed around the clearing, sending those birds that had not yet taken flight clattering into the air. Frightened as much by the matriarch's reaction to the appearance of the horsemen as by the actual threat they posed, her sisters bellowed in unison, while the adolescent male and female gave voice to their own new-found terror by trumpeting loudly. The infant, closeted in the centre of the melee, could only bleat impotently as his elders gave vent to their mounting panic, the jostling and shoving almost knocking him off his feet.

Lured by her impressive tusk array, the lead female had become Jaafar's primary target. Hauling back on his reins, he looped them across his saddle horn. Using his thigh muscles to guide his horse forward, he raised the Kalashnikov to his shoulder, only to see the matriarch turn quickly. It was immediately clear that her intention was to lead her family away from the river, towards the trees at the top of the bank. Quickly, retrieving the reins with his left hand, Jaafar raised the Kalashnikov above his head with his right and gestured to his companions to outflank their fleeing quarry, which, by now, had gained flatter and firmer ground. Their stiff-legged gait was propelling them through the underbrush with remarkable speed for animals their size.

But the horsemen were faster.

It was Suleyman who took the lead, racing ahead to cut off the line of retreat, forcing the matriarch to choose either to continue the headlong dash or to stand and fight. Sensing riders to her left and her right, she slowed. By the time she'd brought the family to a halt, there was nowhere left to run. Like a besieged army from a bygone age, the elephants backed into the smallest formation their bulk allowed and, with the infant forced by weight of numbers into the centre of the redoubt, the family prepared to repel the enemy. The matriarch was the first to issue a challenge. Swinging her head from side to side, her roar filled the air as she dared her tormentors to come to her.

Unhurriedly, Jaafar let his reins droop once more. This time he did not bother to raise the Kalashnikov to his shoulder or take aim. He simply levelled the weapon, and with the insouciance born of one who gave no thought to the cruelty he was about to inflict, he flicked the selector to semi-automatic fire and squeezed the trigger.

And the running and the slaughter and the screaming began.

2

Sekka froze. "You hear that?"

The sounds came again: a series of dull, distant thuds, as though someone was driving an axe blade into a tree stump, repeatedly and with great force. Sekka knew it wasn't the thunder they'd heard earlier.

Matthias nodded grimly. "AK."

Sekka did not ask his second-in-command if he was sure as it only confirmed what Sekka had already determined. To anyone who'd survived combat the sound was unmistakable. Plus, the AK-47 was ranger-issue. It was the same weapon carried by Sekka and his team. All Sekka did ask was, "How far?"

Matthias pursed his lips. "Not sure, boss. Two, maybe three miles. Perhaps more," he added almost apologetically.

Despite the flurry of shots - there had to have been twenty or thirty in all - it was hard to tell from where they'd originated. The breeze had shifted and was now blowing from the north, causing the grass to sway gently, and, despite the time of year and the creeping grey clouds, it was a warm day. Sound travelled further in warm weather than in cool and if that was the heading and the sounds had been carried on the wind, there was every possibility the shots had come from even further away.

Sekka flicked on the two-way. "Cesar, on me. Now! Fast as you can."

To the team, he said, "The uniform and electronics come with us. Matthias, we're still in range so call HQ. Camp found. Gunshots heard. We're en route. Damn it, where's the truck?" He hissed the last words to himself.

As if in answer, the Land Cruiser bounced into view, Cesar at the wheel, Isadore braced against the passenger seat, automatic rifle raised. Sekka ran towards it, followed by Adoum and Theo with the backpacks, into which they had stuffed the uniforms and the radio gear, with Matthias close behind, lugging the ammunition boxes. By then, Sekka had purloined the driving seat. He turned to Matthias who, having stowed the ammo, was climbing into the passenger side. "North?"

The ranger clutched his rifle close to his chest and took a moment to think before nodding. Sekka let out the clutch and yelled over his shoulder through the dividing window for everyone to keep their eyes skinned. There was the distinct possibility that what had recently been declared enemy territory might just have become a battleground.

It was an hour before Sekka was forced to admit defeat and bring the Land Cruiser to a lurching halt. Looking for and trying to follow horse tracks would have taken up too much time so they had forged ahead at speed, heading for the general area where they thought the shots might have come from. As a consequence, they had sacrificed accuracy for guesswork and as a result of that they had been driving blind. There had been no more gunfire and confronted by close to twelve hundred square miles of intermittent woodland and savannah, most of which was trackless wilderness, searching for shooters who did not want to be found would have made searching for needles in haystacks child's play. And the day was drawing on. They were going to need help.

While the rest of the team made use of the truck's height above ground to scour the terrain in the vain hope of spotting the source of the gunfire, Sekka held out his hand for the radio.

Giving the call sign, he released the transmit button and waited for a reply. It came through a squawk of static.

"Salma...One. Go."

Sekka pressed the button. "Jackal Team, Sekka. Trail's gone cold. We could do with some help. Can we get someone in the air?"

Another static burst, then, faintly, "What's your position?"

Sekka consulted his GPS screen and relayed the information.

"Standby."

"Roger that." Sekka called up to the men in the back of the pickup. "Anything?"

"No, boss."

The radio crackled. "Salma One...to Sekka. Come in."

"Go," Sekka said.

"Crow...en route. Should...be there...twent-"

Sekka shook his head in frustration. "Did you say here in twenty?

There was another hiss and then, "Affirmative."

"Roger that. Out." Sekka tossed Matthias the radio. "They're sending bird man."

A spark of hope lit up the faces of the team.

"Eyes open," Sekka said.

Crow, seated in the Cessna's left hand seat, flicked off the isolate switch and turned to his female passenger. "Change of plan, Doc. Gotta make a slight detour."

Sabine Bouvier frowned. "Detour?"

"Joseph says we have intruders. HQ wants us to take a look-see."

"Intruders?"

"Gunshots heard."

The woman's face fell.

"Might be nothing," Crow said, though he knew it probably wasn't. Consulting the compass, he banked the Cessna left before levelling off and then nodded towards the passenger door well. "Glasses are in the pocket."

His passenger retrieved the binoculars and brushed a wayward strand of jet black hair from her cheek. "What am I looking for?" The French accent was distinct, but not overt.

"Horsemen."

She turned, her eyes widening, the glasses loose in her hand. "Horse-?"

Crow's eyes were unreadable behind the aviator shades. "Yeah, I know, that's what I thought. And maybe signs of a camp. Or..."

"Or?"

The corner of Crow's mouth turned down in a grimace. "Bodies."

Sabine gazed at him in horror, then her expression hardened and she nodded. Turning, she stared out of the window at the tracts of harsh, sparsely wooded landscape that filled her view as far as the eye could see.

Crow eased the control column forward. "Going down."

The Cessna began to descend; a little too rapidly for his passenger's liking. Pressing herself back into her seat, she sucked in her breath as the ground rose to meet them. Glancing left, she saw Crow's mouth set in a thin line of concentration and, not for the first time, wondered about the man's history. She knew only that he was ex-military, with a lot of hours under his belt, a fair percentage of which, depending on who was telling the story, had involved a variety of shady contracts in a not inconsiderable number of the world's major trouble spots, both in fixed wing and rotary aircraft. Precise details were frustratingly hazy, as was his accent, which, unless she was mistaken, had a faint Antipodean twang. Even his first name was a mystery. He'd never offered it and she'd never heard it uttered. Everyone referred to him simply as Crow, and he seemed content with that. When she'd pressed for more information she'd been advised that it was probably best not to ask too many questions as she might not like the answers. So she'd been resigned to let it go; for now.

She'd flown with Crow a lot over the past few months, in her capacity as the reserve's chief veterinarian. In her mind there was little doubt he was a good pilot. Generally good company, too, it had to be said. Maybe a little too laid back on occasion, with a droll turn of phrase when he put his mind to it, suggesting someone who didn't take life too seriously until it mattered. But, that being said, he'd always treated her with the respect her role demanded and, unlike more than a few fliers she'd met, he hadn't once tried to impress her with war stories or tales of his derring-do, which made her wonder about his age. He wasn't that young, though there was no paunch, no middle-age spread. Rangy was how she would describe him. He still had all his hair, although there were streaks of grey around the sideburns and the tan could not hide the crinkles in the corner of his eyes, which suggested he'd been around for a while. One thing she did know for sure: she'd rarely seen him this focussed.

They were down to four hundred feet when Crow eased back on the column. There was no high ground to bother them, which left bird strike as the greatest risk. If there was evidence of a kill out there, it would have attracted carrion feeders. The last thing they needed was for something big, like a hooded vulture or a martial eagle, to fly into the prop. Not that the size of the bird mattered a jot, and four hundred feet didn't give a pilot much room for manoeuvre anyway, if the shit - or bird - did hit the fan. Whether it was four hundred or even four feet off the ground, you could still end up a heap of twisted metal.

"You see anything," Crow said, "sing out."

As his passenger turned her attention to the world outside the window, Crow checked the radio frequency, flicked the isolate switch back on, and spoke into his mike. "Crow to Sekka. You there, Joseph?"

The reply came through a couple of seconds later.

"Sekka, go ahead."

Crow peered out over the spinning prop. "Approaching your position. You should have me in sight."

"Wait one." The radio went quiet, then: "Okay, I see you. You see me?"

Crow consulted his GPS display. "Stand by."

It took a further thirty seconds before Crow spotted the Land Cruiser and the men alongside it. He jiggled the Cessna's wings. "Gotcha. Where do you want me to start looking?"

"Only advice I can give is to circle and expand your radius from our position."

Made sense, Crow thought, recognizing the pensive note in Sekka's reply. "Okay, we'll give it a go."

Sekka was quick to come back. "Sorry I can't give you more than that. We lost the trail a while back."

Crow pursed his lips then said. "No worries. I've got the doc with me, so we've two sets of eyes. What's *your* status?"

"Thought we'd drive around aimlessly and leave it up to you."

Crow smiled into the mike. "Roger that, I'll keep you posted. Bad news is we've only around twenty minutes of fuel left. Any longer than that and we'll be asking for a lift home."

"Then we're wasting time. Out."

The radio clicked off.

"Was it true?" Sabine asked. "About the fuel?"

"Not exactly."

"What does *that* mean? How much longer *do* we have?"

"More like fifteen tops." Crow jerked his chin towards the starboard window. "Eyes right, Doc. Jump to it."

"You did not fill up before we left?"

Crow wondered if he'd imagined the note of urgency mixed with just a slight hint of rebuke in his

27

passenger's voice, but, then, given the circumstances - the possibility of there being a poaching gang in the area allied to his remark about looking for a fresh carcass – the tone in her query was probably understandable.

Crow kept his reply calm. "There was a problem with the bowser, remember? We siphoned enough for our first job, with a bit left over. That last bit's what we're down to. We'll be able to complete a few passes and then it's home, James, and don't spare the horses. Sorry, bad turn of phrase," he added quickly, though not swiftly enough to prevent his passenger from giving him a look that said, "*Horses? Really?*"

Crow throttled back the engine and felt his passenger tense. "S'okay. Don't panic. Only the slower our ground speed, the better chance we have of spotting something."

She turned. "If we only have fifteen minutes, won't that cut down the area we will be able to search?"

"Calculated risk. Long as we don't stall." Crow smiled at his passenger's expression of mild alarm. "Relax, that ain't going to happen. Why aren't you looking? Keep looking."

Crow didn't wait for a response. Banking the Cessna to port, he removed his sunglasses and scanned the terrain. Even at that height, the odds of spotting men who didn't want to be found, even though they were on horseback, were slim. They'd hardly be sporting racing colours or Hi-Vis jackets. All they needed to do was shelter under a convenient tree to remain out of sight.

It was on their third circuit, by which time they were some three miles north of Sekka's position, with Crow thinking: *this isn't bloody working*, when Sabine

28

came through on his headset.

"I see something." Then, despairingly, a second later. "Oh, no."

The anguish in her voice was enough. Crow levelled off then banked sharply to the right and brought the aircraft round in a tight turn. He looked across Sabine and out of the right hand window to where she was pointing. The most prominent feature was the river, or what remained of it, twisting like a thick brown snake across the landscape, with the last few patches of precious liquid glinting like scales as they were caught by what remained of the afternoon sun as it shone through the gaps in what was slowly becoming an overcast sky.

"There!" Her voice rose in pitch. "By that bend. There's a group of buffalo. Two hundred metres to their left."

The buffalo were clumped tightly together. It was a small herd, if a dozen animals could be called a herd. Spooked by the Cessna's engine noise, they were already in flight mode, heading for cover beneath the trees that bordered the river bank, while a small flock of pink pelicans took off above them, their spread wings casting crooked shadows across the surface of the water.

Then Crow saw it: a large, grey-brown mound lying at the edge of a clearing - the unmistakable shape of a dead elephant.

As Sabine said, leaning into the window, "*Merde.* There is another one."

"Hang on," Crow said quickly, and applied the throttle to haul them round again. The engine note increased, but it still seemed to take an age before the clearing came back into view. "I see them. Shit."

Crow's eyes dropped to the GPS display as he flicked the radio on. "Crow to Sekka, come in."

"Sekka. Go."

"It's not good, Joseph. We have bodies."

There was a silence as Sekka digested the information. Then: "Location?"

Crow relayed his position, adding, "And no sign of any riders. They'll likely have heard us coming and gone to ground. There's thickish tree cover below, us, plenty of place to hide. I've stuff-all line of sight."

"Understood. We're on our way."

"Joseph?" Crow prompted, after a pause.

"Go."

"That puts them over the boundary."

"So?"

Crow considered his reply. Then: "Just saying, is all."

He waited but when no answer came, he flicked a glance at his passenger who was staring forlornly out of the window, and said into the mike, "We're running on fumes up here. Gotta head back. Sorry."

"Understood. Thanks for the help."

"Find the bastards." Crow said, before adding, "But watch your bloody step."

As there didn't seem to be anything more to say, he clicked off. Aware that his passenger was throwing him a look, Crow reverted to the intercom.

"Can we not land?" Sabine's voice carried a desperate note of appeal.

No mention of the killings being outside the park border, Crow noted. Though, the radio chat had been isolated and not relayed through the intercom, and as the Cessna's notoriously excessive engine noise precluded any chance of a headset-free conversation, it was doubtful she'd overheard Crow's side of the exchange. Probably best not to bring the subject up, Crow reasoned.

"Sorry, Doc. Has to be a no. Too risky on that sort of ground, anyway, and the nearest strip is back where we came from. We divert, we'd never make base. Not with what we have left in the tank."

She was close to tears, Crow saw. But there was rage as well as distress in her expression. He saw that she had let go of the field glasses. Her fists were tightly clenched. "Bastards!" she spat, continuing in English. "Bloody murdering bastards."

Crow went back on the radio. "Crow to Salma One. Come in."

The response was immediate. "Salma One. Go ahead."

"It's bad. We have dead elephants. Joseph has the location. Jackal Team are on their way."

The subdued reply took several seconds to arrive. Then: "Roger that."

"The doc and I are heading home," Crow said, before he was asked to give the coordinates. "Out."

As the first drops of rain began to splatter against the outside of the aircraft.

"Shit," Crow swore, staring out at the ribbons of moisture tracking across the wind shield like streams of liquid mercury. "That's all we bloody need."

3

The stench of death was all around them when Sekka and his team arrived at the kill site. The buzzing of flies was relentless.

The rain shower had been brief and had passed over quickly, heading, due to another wind change, towards the north-west, but, in what was probably a foretaste of what was to come when the rains really hit, it had been ferocious enough to turn the churned-up area around the bodies to mud, providing evidence that scavengers had already been hard at work since Sekka and his team heard the first gunshots.

Animal tracks abounded, hyena being the most prominent. They were invariably the first ones to home in on a kill; their eyesight and, critically, their sense of smell was extraordinary and the four-toed indentations with the attached short claw mark that patterned the softened ground around the bodies were unmistakable.

The rangers had spotted the animals slinking into the bush, deterred by the sound of the approaching vehicle. But they had not gone far. Their ungainly shapes and skulking shadows were still visible around the periphery, grunting and chittering away, as if warning their fellow clan members to be patient until the strangers had left and they could return to their meal. They still posed a danger and so Sekka and his men kept their weapons to hand as they left the shelter of the vehicle, From the corner of his eye, Sekka spotted a couple of jackal's trotting away, like guilty pickpockets caught in the act.

The bodies lay on their sides, their wrinkled hides already streaked with bird shit. The surrounding earth was stained with watery blood and viscera. As the team spread out and as Sekka approached the first corpse, a scrum of vultures appeared from between the elephant's thighs, where they had been tearing at the groin and softer inner parts, The birds did not fly off but merely loped a safe distance away, using their half-spread wings for balance, their crops distended, their beaks, necks and talons streaked with gore. It had been the sight of the birds beginning to circle just above the tree line that had guided the ranger team to the exact spot.

Sekka saw by its dugs that the elephant was a female. The wounds in her back legs were instantly visible, as was the line of puncture holes stitched across her hindquarters, a sign that the firing had been indiscriminate. Also prominent was a deep fissure located three-quarters of the way down the cow's back, where an axe had been used to sever the spine, preventing the already severely wounded beast from running away. The area around the hole was black with blood and flies. Sekka moved towards the elephant's forequarters, knowing what he was about to see and dreading the moment.

There was not much head left. In its place was a raw, still bloody, gaping wound. The entire face had been removed. There had been no finesse involved; the cuts made by the axe or panga blade were clearly visible. The true horror, Sekka knew, lay in the probability that the animal had been alive when the deed had been carried out.

Mouth dry, he looked towards the other rangers. Their silence told him they were seeing the same degree of mutilation in the other bodies. A shape under a nearby umbrella thorn caught his attention. At first, he thought it was a fallen log, but it was too big to have fallen from the trees growing around it. Then, as he drew closer, he realized he was looking at the remains of an elephant's trunk. Its proximity suggested it had belonged to the female he'd just been examining. The ragged end showed where it had been hacked off.

He looked up as Adoum walked towards him. Framed by his head scarf, the ranger's face was a dark mask.

"How many?" Sekka kept his voice steady.

"Five so far, boss."

So far.

"They killed an infant." Adoum said.

"Show me."

Adoum led the way.

The bodies were spread out over an area perhaps a hundred yards square. Another adult female had fallen beneath trees, while two younger members of the family - a male and a female - had made it to the edge of the grassland before they were gunned down. As with Sekka's elephant, the faces had been removed to get at the ivory. The tails had also been taken. The infant lay between the two females, who, presumably, had tried to protect it from the poachers' guns.

The body had not been vandalized, Sekka noted with something like relief as he gazed down at the

35

youngster's corpse; at least not by human hands, unless you counted the two bullet holes in the tiny skull. Traces of guano and peck wounds around the eyes and anus showed where birds and what had likely been jackals and hyenas had started to make inroads.

Sekka drew in a long breath. It took at least eighteen months for tusks to appear beyond a calf's lips. This one couldn't have been much older than a year. The killing had not just been a cruel act. It had been a pointless one.

"The tails?" Sekka said.

"To make bracelets from the hair," Adoum explained.

As Sekka was absorbing that titbit, Cesar arrived and said, "There is one more. The tusks have not been taken."

Sekka and Adoum turned.

It was a female, slightly smaller than the one whose severed trunk Sekka had found; the one he presumed had been the leader of the group due to her size. As elephants lived in extended families, led by the oldest and wisest female, there was no doubt in Sekka's mind that the dead animals were all closely related, which made this one probably a sister or a daughter to the matriarch. Young cows between ten and fifteen would start to care for the calves of the other cows in the herd, and could have calves of their own from around fifteen years. So strong were the bonds of family, however, that every member pitched in at some point to help raise the youngsters, with the exception of the males who, when they reached adolescence, would begin to drift away from the herd to forge a solitary life or, in some instances, to form alliances with other bulls.

Sekka wondered how old this one was. Ageing elephants in the field wasn't an exact science as size wasn't always an indication; neither was the length of their tusks. An elephant's growth spurt tended to occur between five and fifteen years of age, so there was always a margin for error. The best indicator was the state of their molars, which were replaced six times during the animal's lifetime, with each set being gradually worn down and replaced by the next set. The replacement could be linked directly to age, so by identifying the molars in use, the life span of the elephant could be gauged.

"I think maybe twenty years," Theo said quietly, as if reading Sekka's mind.

"We must take her tusks," Matthias said. "The poachers may return." The ranger regarded Sekka expectantly. "They will not have gone far, I think."

"Do it," Sekka said. He took the radio as Matthias returned to the Land Cruiser to retrieve one of the pangas stored with the ranger equipment. "Sekka to Salma One, come in."

"Salma One, go."

There was no static this time. Sekka wondered if it was the distant storm that had caused the previous interference.

"We have six bodies. Three medium adults: all female; two juveniles: one male and one female; one calf: male. One of the mediums still has tusks attached. We're removing them now. Over."

"Understood. Any sign of the intruders?"

"Tracks only. We'll take a look around, see if they've left us a trail, but I'm not hopeful."

"Did you find anything at the camp?"

"Supplies, ammunition, sat-phone equipment, and a

uniform."

"Uniform?"

"RSF," Sekka said.

A prolonged silence followed, which made Sekka wonder if the signal had been lost, before a new voice came on. "Joseph."

"Thomas," Sekka said. No identity was required.

"You sure about it being RSF?" The voice was distinct, the accent British.

"Matthias is. That's good enough for me."

There was another pause before the same voice came back on. "You need any help?"

"No. We've got this."

"You don't want Sabine with you? Crow can use the chopper; fly her out there."

"There wouldn't be much point," Sekka said heavily. "It'd be a waste of fuel."

"Understood. We'll set up a briefing soon as you get back."

"Sounds good. We'll pitch camp, leave at first light."

"Roger that. Watch your backs."

"Always," Sekka said.

He shut off the radio and watched as Matthias and Isadore carried the excised tusks to the Land Cruiser. They weren't large but still of a size, each one probably close to eight or nine kilograms in weight.

"Camp tonight," Sekka told them. "Return to HQ tomorrow."

After a fourteen-day patrol, they were heading home.

But no one was smiling.

They set up camp away from the elephant kills and the

risk of animal encroachment, though a fire would always keep the more adventurous beasts at bay. The smell, however, was inescapable, with the air growing more putrid with each passing hour. Occasionally, a change in wind direction would divert the odour of putrefying flesh elsewhere but the respite was usually short-lived as the reek soon returned, as strong as ever, whenever the breeze shifted back again.

For the rangers, all of whom took turns on watch in between periods of fitful sleep, the night sounds were the same. As the hours passed, the squabbles between competing scavengers also grew in number, becoming ever more rancorous as each successive section of carcass was ripped away. A wild chorus of grunts, growls and guttural roars, interspersed with screeches and blood-curdling screams, filled the darkness as the fight for superiority and survival intensified. Periods of uncanny stillness usually followed each frenzied bout but they, too, proved to be temporary, for, within minutes, another deadly tussle would break out and the sounds of combat would recommence, louder and more vicious than before.

When the dawn finally arrived it was something of a relief. Bashas stowed, breakfast over and the fire extinguished, the ranger team loaded the Land Cruiser and, with Sekka in the driving seat, they left the kill zone behind them. There was little point in continuing the search for the perpetrators as the horsemen would have ascertained from Crow's reconnaissance flight and the presence of the ranger team that their activity had been discovered, which meant they would inevitably have gone to ground or had used the night to start their run for the border. Also, as Crow had pointed out, and as Sekka's own GPS had confirmed, the elephants had been killed outside the reserve boundary and, technically, the rangers had no jurisdiction to pursue. All Sekka and his team could do was report back to HQ with the evidence they had found.

But not before they'd paid another visit to the poachers' camp, on the off-chance the occupants might have returned.

In the event, they found the place as they had left it, though there were signs, in the form of multiple animal tracks and deposits of scat, that some of the more inquisitive neighbours had been paying the place a visit. Fresh scratch marks were also noticeable on the bark of the tree below where the bedding rolls had once hung, all of which were now strewn across the ground and looking decidedly the worse for wear.

"Leopard," Cesar informed Sekka gleefully, after placing his nose perilously close to the trunk and sniffing enthusiastically. "Fresh piss; marking his territory."

Good to know, Sekka thought, scanning some of the stouter-looking forks and branches in the trees around them, and wondering if the beast was watching them now. He had yet to spy one of the big, spotted cats but had no expectation of seeing one now as they were notorious at being able to keep a low profile and, as he had discovered with lions, if an alpha predator wanted to stay hidden you were unlikely to distinguish the beast against the landscape until you were right on top of it, and even then it could take you by surprise. As Sekka had discovered, a large percentage of the reserve's work-force, albeit small in number, had confessed they'd never seen a leopard in the wild either.

After the team had determined there were no fresh horse tracks, Sekka gave the instruction to dismantle the camp. Any portable items not collected during the rangers' first visit were also to be transported to Park HQ, where they would be processed and retained as additional evidence. When a final check of the site had been completed, the team returned to the vehicle in a subdued silence and settled in for the drive back to base.

They were around a mile and a half from the camp, Sekka driving, when Matthias drew his attention to movement ahead of them: the vague outline of something big heading through the brush towards the track, on an intercept course. Not a rider; an antelope of some kind from the brief glimpses Sekka had of its reddish-brown hide. Maybe a roan or an eland to judge by its size. The rate it was shifting, it looked as if something might be hard on its tail.

Sekka eased his foot off the pedal. They weren't travelling fast but it wouldn't be the first time a startled animal had bounded out in front of a park vehicle and caused mayhem. Reserve policy gave animals the right of way but as wildlife could be unpredictable at the best of times accidents still happened. Only a month before, another patrol had been hit by a hartebeest on the run. The animal hadn't been that large, but the damage it caused had been considerable. The truck - also a Land Cruiser - had required extensive body work. The radiator grill and light array had also been replaced. The hartebeest had suffered two broken legs and had been put out of its misery by a ranger's bullet.

41

When the roan finally broke from the trees, it did so at speed, crossing the trail only a dozen strides from the Land Cruiser's bonnet and, from its attitude, completely oblivious to the vehicle's presence. Within seconds it had vanished into the brush on the other side of the track. Automatically, Sekka glanced over to see what might have caused the antelope's headlong dash, but, even though the trees had started to thin out, nothing else broke cover. One of life's imponderables, he thought. Just another skittish park inhabitant scared of its own shadow.

Until a few yards further on, when they rounded a sharp bend in the brush and Matthias yelled, "Boss!"

The warning was unnecessary.

A horseman, poised in the middle of the track, his facial features concealed by a black keffiyeh, raising the Kalashnikov to his shoulder.

Instinct took over. Ramming the accelerator to the floor, Sekka spun the wheel left as Matthias tried to bring his own weapon to bear through the open side window. Too late. The windscreen starred as bullets ripped into the cab and a red mist bloomed as the first slugs struck Matthias across the chest and throat. Beads of warm moisture flicked across Sekka's right cheek as warning cries erupted from behind him. They were immediately drowned by the deafening k-k-k racket of an AK-47 set to automatic.

A dark, moving shape in the nearside wing mirror drew Sekka's gaze. A second armed rider, anonymous beneath his headgear, leaning forward over his mount's neck, coming in fast. Sekka hauled back on the wheel. As the Land Cruiser veered right, Matthias's body, unencumbered by a seat belt, was thrown hard against the passenger door. The ranger's automatic rifle had already dropped from his lifeless hand and lay part-way under the dash, caught between his legs. Sekka's AK was clipped into the rack between the front seats; Even if he'd been able to extract one of them, the weapon was too unwieldy to be used single-handed in the confines of the cab. Gripping the wheel with his left hand, Sekka clawed for the pistol at his waist as a rapid burst of fire split the air from the truck's rear bed. At least one of the ranger team was shooting back.

Despite the sounds of retaliation, Sekka knew the terrain favoured their attackers. The way the first horseman had sighted his weapon while still controlling his mount, and the speed at which the second one had suddenly appeared, confirmed the ambushers were skilled riders. Given the state of the ground and the weight of the truck, Sekka knew it was unlikely he could out-run or out-manoeuvre them, which left the men in the back sitting targets. The truck's panelled sides were no defence against the riders' ordnance. If they could find a place to vacate the vehicle and use it as cover to make a stand, then, maybe, they could gain the advantage.

But the next two seconds saw that plan fall apart.

This time, Sekka was given no chance to react. The roan barrelled in from nowhere; a big male, well over five feet at the shoulder, the head and horns adding another eighteen inches to its bulk. Its sudden appearance suggested it was the same one that had crossed their path moments before. Spooked and disoriented by the running gun battle, it was travelling at full pelt when it struck the Land Cruiser's off-side wheel. Six hundred plus pounds of panicked herbivore slamming into the truck's right flank was more than enough to knock the 4x4 off its axis. As the antelope rebounded off the panelling and fell away, legs thrashing, Sekka fought for control. For a brief moment, he thought balance had been restored, until the nearside front wheel found the rim of the gully. The 4x4 passed the point of no return with a screech of grinding metal as it slid over the edge and into the ditch, coming to rest with a bang at an angle against the opposite slope. As the engine died, bullets began to pepper the truck's body and the ground around it.

"Out! Out!" Sekka yelled, knowing even as he gave the order, that it was stating the obvious. The rangers in the back would need no second bidding, if they hadn't jumped already. Releasing the door catch, he thrust his shoulder against the metal, only to discover there was no give. Nothing. The door refused to budge. He glanced right to where Matthias's body, having finally succumbed to the law of gravity, was now sprawled across the passenger seat and gear stick, effectively blocking the opposite exit, which left the driver's open side window as the only available means of egress.

With bullets continuing to strike the truck, there was no time to extricate either of the trapped AKs. Instead, as a fresh wave of slugs took out what remained of the windscreen, Sekka made a grab for the radio pouched on Matthias's chest. Pulling the handset free, he then realized his own body equipment was going to hamper his escape through the window space.

Desperation took over. Bracing himself against the dash and the back of his seat, Sekka drew his knees back and then slammed both feet against the door. This time it gave, though the angle at which the vehicle was wedged prevented the door from opening fully.

But it was enough.

Sekka levered his torso over the sill. For what seemed a lifetime he hung half-in, half-out of the cab, until, with a final push, he levered his way free. Dropping to the ground, he rolled in close to the gully's side, radio in hand. Using the Land Cruiser's bulk as a shield, he drew his pistol. It occurred to him as he did so that had the vehicle's airbags deployed, he might not have deflated his fast enough to exit the cab. Ironic, he thought, that the non-activation of the vehicle's main safety feature had actually prolonged his life. Though for just how long was open to question.

"Boss?"

Sekka spun round and let go a breath when he saw Isadore belly-crawling towards him, AK in hand. There was stark fear in the ranger's eyes. He was missing his headscarf and there were smudges of blood across his forehead.

"You hit?" Sekka asked quickly.

"No, boss." The ranger's chest rose and fell. "You?"

Concern in the ranger's voice prompted Sekka to wipe a hand across his cheek. It came away red. Matthias's blood. "No. The others?"

The ranger shook his head. "Cesar and Adoum were hit. They are dead."

"Theo?" Sekka said, hoping against hope.

"I do not know. He was in the truck and then he was not. Matthias?" Isadore's doleful expression told Sekka the ranger had already guessed the answer to his question.

Sekka shook his head. "How many attackers? Did you see?"

"I think maybe two."

Sekka's mind went back to when Adoum had first

spotted the alien hoof prints. Four riders had been the estimation then. That left two possibles unaccounted for. Not good, Sekka thought and ducked as bullets thumped into the bank above his head. Instinctively, he brought the radio to his lips and depressed the transmit button. "Sekka to Salma One. Come in."

No reply. Not even static. Sekka tried again. Same thing. He stared at the radio, and only then did he see the jagged hole in the casing and the blood splashes on the screen, which had to have come from Matthias's chest wounds. Sekka swore under his breath. Tossing the handset aside, he turned to the ranger. "Radio?"

Isadore blinked and said helplessly. "With Cesar, boss."

"Can you get to it?"

A flicker of doubt crossed Isadore's face, replaced a second later by a look of grim determination. "I will try."

Wordlessly, Isadore passed Sekka his AK. Sekka holstered the Glock, checked the rifle's magazine and flicked the selector to automatic. "I'll give covering fire; you go for it. Yes?"

Isadore nodded.

"Wait one," Sekka said.

Using the tilted front end of the truck as additional cover, he peered over the lip of the gully. There were no horsemen in sight, but, immediately, a hail of bullets struck the radiator grill and spanged off the Land Cruiser's bonnet. Sekka ducked back down. He glanced behind him and saw the ranger hesitate then nod.

"On my mark," Sekka said, knowing, as he spoke, that he had no clue as to where all the gunmen were located, only the general location of one of them. But if he could draw fire by bracketing that one, then maybe Isadore could make a grab for the handset. Gathering himself, he took a deep breath, let it out, slowly, threw a quick glance towards Isadore and nodded. "Now."

Holding the rifle above his head, Sekka loosed off a burst, unsighted, before raising himself up. There was a groan of metal and he felt the 4x4 shift as Isadore clambered on to the cargo bed. Immediately, more bullets began to strike the truck, from what were clearly different angles. Sekka ducked, then rose again and fired another wide burst, before dropping down once more. If his fire had not found a target, which seemed more than likely, then at least it may have deterred the horsemen from launching an all-out assault.

Hearing a grunt, he turned. Isadore was on the ground, his back against the gully wall, his right leg bent awkwardly beneath him. The ranger looked up wistfully. There was no sign of the radio, Sekka noticed. Seeing the look of despair on the ranger's face, Sekka's heart sank. As he watched, what looked like two crimson flowers begin to blossom slowly across the ranger's chest.

"I am sorry, boss," Isadore said softly, as his head slumped slowly to one side.

Springing forward, Sekka placed his fingers against the ranger's carotid and kept them there, but there was no pulse.

And then he heard them. Hoof beats, from the other side of the defile. He rose swiftly and brought the AK to bear but as a second rider appeared from the opposite direction, he knew he'd left it far too late. He hadn't been the only one creating a diversion. It was two against one, with two more possibles at his back, probably using the riders' intervention to mask their own approach.

He loosed off a burst at the attacker coming in from the right and saw the horse stumble and then recover and threw himself aside as fire was returned. But the riders had the advantage of height and there was nowhere to hide. He felt a sharp tug and a burn as the first bullet clipped his left arm and then his wrist jarred as a second slug struck the AK's stock, disrupting his grip. All he could hear, then, was the crackle and whine of bullets, culminating in a savage blow to the side of his skull and after that nothing but darkness.

4

Sekka opened his eyes.

It was the sensation of something moving slowly along his forearm that had roused him. Not that it was an unpleasant feeling. In fact, it was quite soothing, not so much a scratch or a tickle, more like a soft caress, causing the short hairs to rise and then subside gently, as if he was being massaged. But the sense that tiny indentations were also being made in his skin didn't feel right at all.

Then he focussed.

The scorpion paused. At around three inches in length it wasn't that big, though it was large enough to cause Sekka to freeze. It was mostly pale yellow in colour save for a series of alternating grey and orange-yellow stripes that ran horizontally across its impressively broad abdomen, a vivid contrast to Sekka's ebony skin. Its pincers, which were spread wide, did not match the thickness of its body, but, like its six limbs, were long and spindly. The only other visible pigment lay in the dark vertical line that ran from its head to the beginning of its segmented tail, which was in the raised position, stinger poised.

If the scorpion was aware that its presence had been detected, it appeared undecided about its next move. Looking into its eyes provided no clues, despite there being three sets of them; one set on the top and two more on the frontal sides of its head. What Sekka did know was that he was being inspected by one of the most poisonous scorpions in the world: a deathstalker.

The name was enough to induce terror but there was a glimmer of good news. Despite the number of eyes, Sekka knew the deathstalker's vision was poor. The bad news was that it relied on vibrations to determine what was taking place in its environment and, from that, what to do next. Uppermost in Sekka's mind, therefore, was the thought of what might happen if the thing on his arm sensed his waking state and decided to take aggressive action. From somewhere in the depths of Sekka's still-fogged brain there came a memory of being told that while a deathstalker's sting was extraordinarily painful and its venom a powerful mixture of neurotoxins, its bite wasn't necessarily fatal to a healthy adult. The words 'necessarily' and 'healthy' being the operative words.

So he remained very, very still.

It was another ten or fifteen seconds before the scorpion finally made its decision. When it did, Sekka found he was holding his breath. He let it out only when the deathstalker stepped from his arm and headed off across the ground as if bent on some important errand. Sekka watched as it finally disappeared beneath a large rock. Then, cautiously, he raised his head.

And wished he hadn't as a fiery bolt of pain shot through the back of his skull. Closing his eyes quickly, he remained motionless as the pain rebounded from one side of his cranium to the other. It took a while for the throbbing to subside. Only when the pain had dropped to just-about-tolerable on the agony scale did he open them once more. Save for the scorpion's absence, the view was the same: earth, rocks and scrub. He was still in the gully, sprawled half-in and half-out of the shadow thrown by the 4x4 canted above him. Apart from the intermittent bird chatter, it was also unnaturally quiet.

He tried lifting his head again. Another stab of pain moved through him, though not so acute as before, perhaps because he'd been expecting it and somehow his brain was telling him that achieving an upright position probably wouldn't kill him, at least not right away.

Emboldened, he took a deep breath. Then, teeth gritted, he raised himself up and on to one knee. So far so good; apart from the ground, which suddenly took on an alarming tilt. Maintaining his balance proved interesting as he fought back nausea, which, in the end, proved unsuccessful. He felt his stomach lurch and was powerless to prevent the explosion of vomit that erupted on to the earth in front of him. It took a while for the tremors to subside. After a succession of increasingly dry heaves he managed to push himself fully upright. Holding on to the 4x4's tilted bonnet for support, it was then that he felt the warm wetness on the right side of his scalp. Tentatively, he reached up and touched the area with his fingertips. The viscosity of it told him it was blood, and he remembered the bullet strike.

And Isadore.

He turned. The ranger's corpse was where it had fallen, though it was no longer propped upright against the bank, having toppled on to its left side, into a foetal position. Flies had collected around the blood stains on the tunic. The AK was nowhere to be seen and Sekka saw that Isadore's Glock was missing, too. Without looking, he dropped a hand to his own hip. His side-arm was gone as well.

Sekka wondered why the raiders hadn't killed him. The only reason that made any sense was that somehow they'd been taken in by all the blood. Head wounds had a tendency to bleed profusely, often out of proportion to the injury sustained and Sekka's head wound had, from the feel of it, bled a great deal. Plus he already had Matthias's blood on him. It must have looked to the attackers as if the head shot had done the job for them and they hadn't noticed he was still breathing, even when they'd taken his weapon. In too much of a hurry to flee the scene with whatever prizes they could carry to bother checking for a pulse. Or maybe they'd left him on purpose, knowing the scent of blood would draw predators to the scene.

His thoughts turned instantly to the other rangers who'd been in the back of the 4x4, and a wave of guilt moved through him for not having checked their status as soon as he'd regained consciousness. As he climbed out of the gully and on to the truck bed he steeled himself for the inevitable.

Cesar and Adoum lay in a tangled embrace, jammed into the well next to the spare tyre, which suggested their bodies had slid there when the front of the truck had nose-dived over the edge of the gully. It was clear they were dead but Sekka knew he had to confirm that for himself. He gently checked each man in turn. Both had taken shots across their upper torsos. There was a bullet hole in Cesar's left temple.

They, too, had been relieved of their weapons, along with the radio that Isadore had attempted to retrieve.

They weren't the only items that were missing. The backpacks were gone, as well, which meant the satellite equipment and the uniform items were also in the wind.

Of Theo, there was no sign. Sekka stared bleakly out over the expanse of rough scrub, hard-baked earth, coarse grass and thorn trees stretching into the distance. The missing ranger had to be somewhere nearby; possibly still alive and, if so, in need of help, which made Sekka wonder how long he'd been out.

The sun hadn't travelled far across the sky since they had set off but when he went to look at his watch, he discovered his wrist was bare and when he glanced back into the gully, he saw they'd even taken the damaged handset. He knew, though, that the horsemen's main prize would have been the ivory the rangers had removed for safe-keeping back at the kill site. It came as no surprise to find the tusks were gone.

Sekka got down from the truck bed. It was then that he noticed the other body. It lay a few yards further along the gully on the passenger side of the 4x4, half-hidden by a patch of thorn bush. It couldn't be Theo, so maybe one of the attackers? Intrigued, as he didn't think he'd scored a hit when he'd returned fire, he moved closer and only then did he realize that the body was that of Matthias.

The raiders had pulled Matthias out of the driving cab and deposited his corpse in the dirt like a piece of discarded sacking. Sekka could guess the reason why. When he checked the cab, his suspicions were confirmed. The poachers had removed the ranger's body to get at the two automatic rifles Sekka had abandoned in order to facilitate his rapid departure from the cab. Cursing his lack of foresight, Sekka felt the anger rise again, aimed as much against his own negligence as against the men who'd launched the attack.

It took several minutes for the rage to subside and for his thoughts to settle. The priority, he knew, was to determine Theo's whereabouts and the practical approach to that was to retrace on foot the Land Cruiser's course through the brush to the place where the killers had sprung their ambush. Sekka doubted the distance was much more than a quarter of a mile.

In the end, he only had to backtrack a little over a hundred paces. Though, due to the ranger's camouflage clothing, he almost missed seeing the crumpled form, which lay face down a few yards from the flattened vegetation created by the truck's erratic passage through the brush. As he had done when he'd climbed on to the 4x4 to check Cesar and Adoum, Sekka prepared himself, and when he drew nearer to the body and saw how the ranger's head was angled he knew Theo was beyond help. It was clear his neck was broken.

Despite knowing in his heart that it would serve no purpose, Sekka still checked for signs of life and felt no sense of satisfaction when his visual diagnosis was confirmed. Fighting to control the resurgence of anger, he turned Theo's body over and looked for additional injuries. At first he could find nothing untoward until his probing fingers encountered stickiness two inches below the ribcage. It was then that he saw the blood, which until that point had been concealed by the darker patches in the ranger's camouflage jacket. Identifying it as an entry wound, he reached around to Theo's lower back and let go a sigh when his fingers encountered the bullet's exit point, a two-finger span

54

above the ranger's belt.

He sat back. A through-and-through wasn't necessarily fatal. It was entirely possible that had Theo survived what appeared to have been a fall from the truck after being shot, he might well have recovered from his wound. It made the ranger's death all the more tragic. Sekka glanced back at the Land Cruiser, knowing what he had to do. Removing his equipment belt, pouches and jacket, he laid them to one side.

It took a combination of drag and carry to transport Theo into the shade of the 4x4's chassis. It took almost as much effort to recover Isadore and Matthias's bodies from the gully and placed them next to Theo's.

When he had done that, despite sensing it was probably a thankless task, Sekka turned his attention to the Land Cruiser's mechanical condition. A formality, as it had been plain from the offset that the vehicle wasn't going anywhere. Despite the four-wheel drive capability, the angle at which the vehicle had landed had left no room for the rear wheels to make purchase. It was well and truly wedged. But then, even if a giant hand were to reach down and lift the truck on to level ground, Sekka saw that it wouldn't have made a difference. On its descent into the gully the underside of the 4x4 had struck a projecting rock and the front axle and the drive shaft had taken the brunt of the impact. Sekka didn't need a mechanic to tell him he was stranded.

Faced with that realization, he transferred Theo, Isadore and Matthias's bodies from the ground on to the truck's cargo bed and placed them alongside Adoum and Cesar. When he'd completed that task, he covered all five bodies with one of the team's waterproof bashas. By the time he'd finished his shoulder muscles were screaming and his head felt as if someone was probing his frontal lobe with a red-hot poker. His t-shirt was wringing wet and his body was running with sweat.

As he stared in silence at the shrouded forms, the tears began to fall. The rangers had not just been members of his team, they had been his friends; all of them good men, dedicated to their job: preserving the sanctity of the park; men you could trust, men you'd want guarding your back. They had not deserved this.

Distracted by a warm trickle along his scalp line, Sekka went to wipe away a bead of perspiration but when he brought his hand back down he saw there was blood on his fingertips. His head wound had re-opened.

He returned to the Land Cruiser's cab. Reaching in, he explored the well behind the front seats. Hoping the raiders had been too preoccupied with retrieving the rifles to have rummaged through the vehicle's every nook and cranny, he felt a surge of relief when his fingers encountered the straps of the medical grab bag. Allowing his gaze to linger briefly on the blood-splattered dash and seats, he dragged the pack out of the vehicle.

Using the driver's wing mirror to guide his hands, he attended to his injuries. He could see that the gash on his scalp wasn't that big, no more than three centimetres in length and that it was the runnel gouged by the bullet that had led to the impressive blood flow. Careful not to aggravate the wound any more than was necessary, he used the pack's antiseptic wipes to clean the cut and the surrounding skin as best he could. Applying the Dermabond strip proved a challenge but he chose it because it was a more effective method of drawing the edges of the wound together than a regular plaster. The end result wouldn't have won any applause at a paramedics' convention, but Sekka was prepared to live with the ignominy. The graze to his left arm wasn't significant. Nevertheless, he swabbed the area and applied a Traumafix pad to prevent infection. Both dressings were no more than temporary aids but they would suffice until a qualified medic could make a proper examination.

Prescribing himself a couple of Co-dydramol tabs, he swallowed them down with a mouthful of water from the bottle kept in the medical kit. By then, the discarded wipes and empty sachets had grown into a small pile of blood-stained medical waste. Collecting the debris, Sekka stored it in the grab bag's outer pocket and returned the bag to the Land Cruiser's cab.

And settled down to wait.

No matter how many times he entered Salma HQ, Thomas Keel always felt as though he was stepping back in time. It wasn't that the building was old; it wasn't. It was just that the architect had clearly taken his inspiration from watching too many re-runs of Beau Geste. The building was a dead ringer for Fort Zinderneuf, right down to the earthen-coloured bricks and the crenelated facade, and could have been lifted, lock stock and flag pole from any Hollywood film featuring the French Foreign Legion.

It could have been that the design was meant to reflect traditional Chadian building construction, which it did up to a point, but in a moment of whimsy, Keel couldn't help but wonder if it meant that plans were afoot for every park employee to swap their fatigues for a blue overcoat, white linen pants and a képi blanc, complete with neck protector; not the most practical uniform for ranger teams who were required to blend in with their surroundings.

Emerging from his reverie, he removed his beret and tucked it under his right epaulette before entering the building and making his way towards the communications room, where the desk was being manned by Rangers Baptiste and Alfred, both dressed in the obligatory fatigues. They looked up as Keel entered.

"Anything?" Keel asked.

Baptiste shook his head. "Still no word, boss."

Keel looked at the clock on the wall and frowned. It had been an hour since he'd last enquired if Sekka and the Jackal team had radioed in. "Okay, let's give them a call. See if they're up."

Baptiste turned back to the desk, leant in close to the mike and flipped the switch. *"Salma   à Chacal. Répondez."*

The call was met with silence and then a faint hiss.

Baptiste gave it ten more seconds and made the call sign again.

When nothing happened, Keel leant over his shoulder and switched from French to English. "Joseph. You there? Come in."

More hiss.

Reverting to French, Keel addressed the rangers. "Nothing since yesterday?"

It was Alfred who answered. "No, boss"

A jovial man by nature, Alfred's subdued response was a measure of the dark mood that had descended among the reserve staff upon hearing the news that poachers were on the loose and that elephant kills had been confirmed. The event had hit everyone hard. From the ranger teams on the front line to the back room personnel, it was as if members of their own family had been attacked and their lives taken.

Keel looked up at the wall above the desk, at the two maps of the reserve – one a representation of the park's eco-system, the other strategic. The latter was speckled with coloured pins showing the locations of the ranger patrols. There were six patrols out at any one time, with a seventh on standby and the eighth on time off. Keel checked for the Jackal team's black pin, which gave the patrol's last known position, the elephants' killing ground, and then, when he found it, ran his eye along the edges of the map, noting the coordinates around the frame and the dotted line that represented the reserve's boundary. The black pin was positioned less than a hair's width inside the border line.

Still a wee bit too obvious, Keel thought to himself.

He'd spoken with Crow when the pilot had returned from marking the kill site. Crow had revealed that when he'd radioed Sekka with the coordinates, he'd also added in the fact that they placed the location outside the reserve.

"What did Joseph say?" Keel had asked.

Crow had responded with a wry look. "What do you think he said?"

"Could be you were mistaken," Keel said.

Crow had given him a look. "Could be."

"Well, then?

The pin had been repositioned on the reserve's side of the line. Because that was where the slaughter had taken place, if anyone were to ask.

Automatically, Keel's gaze shifted further upwards to the space above the maps and the frieze made up of notices, printed white on black, which listed the major incidents that had taken place in the park since the current management group had taken over. The first notice read: INCIDENT: 5/12/19 - 4 ÉLÉPHANTS. The second read: 10 MOIS. The next: INCIDENT: 15/10/20 - 6 ÉLÉPHANTS. The last notice read: 18 MOIS dans le parc; 8 MOIS dans la zone étendue.

A year and half since elephants were last killed in the reserve, and eight months since any were killed in the extended area beyond the park boundary, but which was monitored by the park authorities. Though, that only accounted for animals killed in numbers and not for single deaths, when the remains were unlikely to be found unless stumbled upon by accident.

Due to its size, it was impossible to patrol every square inch of the reserve twenty-four seven, and it didn't take long for a carcass to be stripped clean. A few days were all it took to reduce what had once been a full-grown elephant into a pile of bleached bones.

Eyeing the space where the new notice would soon be posted, Keel considered his options. Finally, he stepped back and laid a hand on Baptiste's shoulder. "Call Crow. I want the chopper fuelled and in the air in fifteen."

He looked again at the board, noting which patrols were in the field. All were covering different quadrants of the reserve. Team Fox was the closest but it was unlikely to beat the helicopter to Sekka's last known position.

Keel studied the duty roster, posted on the wall below the maps. "Buffalo Team's on standby, yes?"

Alfred nodded. "Yes, boss."

"Tell Christoph to pick two men, ready to go in..." Keel threw another glance at the clock. "...ten minutes. And contact Fox. Tell them to meet us at the coordinates."

Baptiste was reaching for the internal phone and Alfred the radio as Keel vacated the office.

Nudging six feet, with a compact frame, Keel moved gracefully for a tall man. Steel-grey hair, cut short, framed a tanned face, off-set by a pair of ice-blue eyes that gave the impression they had probably seen more trouble than they cared to remember, which, after more than a quarter-century of soldiering, was considerable. His body bore the scars to prove it.

"Thomas?"

The voice had come from behind.

Keel turned. "René."

Keel didn't know if the French used the term 'Old Africa Hand', but if they did then René Deschamps probably fitted the description better than most. Stockily-built and bullet-headed, his skin browned from years spent beneath the African sun, his hair cropped even shorter than Keel's; for a man in his early sixties he still looked every inch the military officer he'd once been, which, given Salma HQ's desert fort appearance, had made his appointment to the park singularly appropriate.

A veteran of the 2nd Foreign Parachute Regiment, the only airborne regiment in the French Foreign Legion, Deschamps had earned his spurs leading men into some of the continent's most challenging trouble spots, from Djibouti and the Central African Republic to the Ivory Coast and the DRC. His last posting, prior to his retirement with the rank of *Colonel*, had been as a force commander with Operation Barkhane, a French military operation to oust Islamic militants from Northern Mali.

An Arabic speaker, Deschamps had come to know Chad and the Sahel - the belt lying between the Sahara in the north and the Sudanian savanna in the south - almost as well as he knew his home country, which turned out to be a prime qualification for what was to follow; retirement having no appeal for a warrior with his experience. His mantra had been, and still was on occasion: "What did they expect me to do, grow roses? Open a vineyard?"

His reprieve - Deschamps had referred to it as his salvation - had come out of the blue, when he'd been asked to take over the management of the Salma reserve. It was a position he'd accepted, with something close to alacrity, though with little understanding of what he might have let himself in for, as was illustrated by the strain now showing on his face.

"Have we heard from Joseph?"

Keel shook his head. "No."

Deschamps frowned. "What do you think? Is he in trouble?"

"Not necessarily."

"But?"

"Crow's prepping the chopper. I'm taking a couple of Christoph's lads with me. We'll head for Jackal Team's last known position; take a look-see. Fox Team's meeting us there."

Deschamps pursed his lips, considering Keel's statement. "So you think there *is* a problem?"

"Just covering the bases."

"Hope for the best, prepare for the worst?"

"I can see why you made colonel."

Deschamps allowed himself a small smile. "And you a major. Good news or bad, you'll keep me posted?"

"Of course."

Deschamps nodded as he turned away. "I'll monitor the radio."

Keel headed for the door. Emerging into the sunlight, his eyes were drawn, not for the first time, to a memorial plaque on the outside wall on which was inscribed a list of names. There were fifteen names in all; rangers killed while protecting the reserve; alongside them the dates they had died.

Keel turned on to the path leading to his quarters.

"Got the call," a voice said from behind his shoulder. "What's the plan?"

Crow, dressed in khaki slacks and an olive shirt with the sleeves rolled to the elbow, moved to intercept. A dark-brown baseball cap bearing the Salma insignia - a black silhouette of a buffalo - completed his ensemble. A pair of aviator shades rested on the cap's peak. A battered knapsack was slung over one shoulder,

"Can't raise Joseph. Thought we'd do a recce. Check out his last position."

"Radio might be turned off."

"Could be, but I'd prefer to take a look."

Crow nodded acceptance. "Okay, no worries. We're set to go." The pilot glanced over to where two slim, camouflage-clad figures were emerging from the ranger's bunk house. Both carried backpacks and automatic rifles. "They with us?"

Keel nodded. "Fox Team's in the field. They'll meet us there."

Crow raised a questioning eyebrow.

"Better safe than sorry," Keel said.

63

"My family motto," Crow said. "How's René doing?"

"How do you think?"

Crow did not respond, but merely nodded. If you inform the reserve's manager that six members of his elephant herd had been shot to death, how was he supposed to feel, other than devastated and angry beyond words?

"I'll get my gear," Keel said. "Meet you at the pad."

Crow took the sunglasses from his cap and put them on. "Roger that. I'll go warm her up."

Crow watched as Keel walked away. Although Keel hadn't admitted it in so many words, Crow could tell he was concerned about Sekka not having radioed in. It had nothing to do with Keel's judgement on Sekka's abilities. Their history in accepting contracts around the globe, either singly or as a team, was proof that neither of them needed a babysitter, and on the occasions that their venture had required the services of a pilot, Crow had seen for himself how good each of them was at his job. But, with armed poachers on the loose, Keel's disquiet was understandable, not just over Sekka's lack of communication, but with the entire patrol's whereabouts.

Crow caught up with the two rangers, Solomon and Idjal, at the helipad – a rectangle of beaten earth - where the Airbus H125 was parked. "Mount up, guys. Major Tom's on the way."

Retaining their automatic rifles, the rangers placed their backpacks into the chopper's stowage compartment before climbing into the rear seats. Crow stowed his own bag and, humming the Bowie song beneath his breath, he commenced his check of the Airbus's exterior.

He was ticking the final items on the engine pre-start check list as Keel arrived, backpack over one shoulder and automatic rifle over the other. Placing his bag with the others, Keel secured the hatch, hoisted himself into the left-hand seat and closed the door.

"Everyone comfortable?" Crow asked as Keel strapped himself in and put on the headset. Adding dryly, "I'll take that as a 'yes'," when there was no response.

Slipping on his sunglasses, Crow checked the main rotor was clear and began the start-up sequence: throttle, master fuel switch, hydraulics, fuses, fuel boost pump, battery; his movements calm and precise. Dropping his eyes to the panel in front of him, he pressed the starter button and watched as the oil pressure and gas producer gauges kicked in. When the N1 gauge hit the required percentage point, he released the throttle button, waited for the temperature to stabilize and then, keeping one eye on the torque reading, brought the throttle up slowly to increase the RPM. With the needle resting on one hundred percent and the turbine whining like an inebriated banshee, he muttered under his breath, "So far, so good," and lifted the chopper off the ground.

5

Sekka, seated in the Land Cruiser's cab, sipped water and, wondered, not for the first time, if he'd made a severe miscalculation in not leaving the vehicle to go for help. The decision was starting to weigh heavily on his mind.

Pockets of human habitation were few and far between. Most were tiny, insignificant, sometimes temporary, settlements; perhaps a couple of dozen inhabitants in all, generally comprising four or five families who, as subsistence farmers, just about managed to support themselves by means of a few hectares of land set aside for the cultivation of basic crops - millet or sorghum - while others, those with nomadic blood running through their veins, were able to eke out a living as goat or cattle herders.

Sekka had consulted the patrol's map – the poachers had left him that, at least - when considering his options. The closest settlement, Hamé, lay some ten miles to the south. It was a place with which he was familiar, though he'd only been there on two occasions. The first had been shortly after his arrival in the reserve when, as part of their induction tour, he and Keel been introduced to an assortment of elders in villages located on or just outside the park's border, Hamé being one of them. The second time had been when he'd accompanied Sabine, who'd been asked to check the settlement's meagre cattle stock for trypanosomiasis, a disease passed on by tsetse fly.

Recalling the place in his mind's eye had conjured up a collection of circular mud huts topped with conical grass roofs, their dark, stifling interiors separated from the outside by a gaily coloured blanket strung across the doorway to keep the flies and other winged insects at bay; each property protected from its immediate neighbour by a woven grass boma.

There had been around thirty inhabitants in all. The meet-and-greet had been conducted in the shade of large tamarisk tree, predominantly a male preserve, while a few yards away, beneath a crude, grass-roofed shelter, the women had laboured over flat rocks and hand-held round stones, grinding millet into flour, wiping the dust from their hands and clothes when they'd finished, so as not to waste a single grain. At their feet, children in cast-me-down clothes played jacks in the dirt while scrawny livestock roamed at will. The air had been heavy with the smell of baking bread, sun-baked earth, and cow shit, the latter being a product of the dozen or so cattle grazing peacefully along the village's outer edge.

Hamé, a name on a map above a dot that could have been mistaken for a partially rubbed out pencil mark, save for one important feature. Next to the name was a small, hand-drawn representation of a radio handset.

It had been part of René Deschamps' strategy for improving the park's defences. As well as installing new communication tools - more efficient radios and a new antenna with an increased range - Deschamps, in an initiative that had extended beyond the park boundary, had reached out to the settlements dotted around the edges of the reserve. In exchange for a firm promise to heighten security in the region, elders in the surrounding district had agreed to contact the park authorities in the event they came across activities they considered to be suspicious. To aid the intelligence gathering, strategically-located villages had been gifted with basic, pre-programmed battery phones and solar chargers.

The thought that he would be able to take advantage of the reserve's early warning system - though that clearly hadn't worked on this occasion - and alert Salma HQ to his situation had been a tempting one and Sekka had been very close to setting off, but in the end he'd abandoned the idea. Not only would it have meant a ten mile trek across harsh, open country, with only a limited water supply and no firearm, but it also went against the first law of survival in the event of a mechanical break down, which was: remain with the vehicle. The truck offered shade and shelter and, more importantly, it would be easier to spot than a solitary figure travelling on foot, dressed in combat fatigues who would have been indistinguishable when set against the similarly coloured landscape. Crucially, it would also have meant leaving the rangers' bodies unattended, and that was something Sekka had been loathe to do.

Besides, he knew Keel would come looking.

Except...

For the past few minutes, he'd become uncomfortably aware of the brutal noises issuing from the bushes less than a stone's throw from the vehicle; the unmistakable sounds of an animal being ripped apart.

Scavengers had found the roan's body.

Sekka had lost sight of the antelope after the collision but the grunts and snarls away to his right told him that the animal had not rebounded far and if it hadn't already died from its injuries, it was suffering, or about to suffer, an agonizing death. To judge from the high-pitched whoops and bouts of giggling, the hyenas were among those taking advantage of the free buffet, while the vultures spiralling down in lazy, ever-decreasing circles indicated that a variety of other meat-eaters were also homing in.

So it might have been his awareness of the feeding or a sixth sense that caused him to glance towards the truck's right-hand wing mirror. Ordinarily, given the angle at which the 4x4 had ended up, the mirror would have reflected nothing more than sky and maybe a few low clouds, but during the attack a bullet strike had knocked it out of alignment. As a result, cracked and distorted by the slug's impact, it now revealed a fractured image of the view directly beyond the truck's rear end, where a coarse-furred, slope-backed shape was padding silently into view, neck extended, head held low and muzzle twitching.

Sekka felt his insides contract.

As if sensing that it was being observed, the hyena paused. Then, as Sekka watched, two more appeared out of the spiked grass behind it. It was as if the first one had been waiting for back-up; a sign that the more rapacious carrion-eaters had been diverted from their main meal by the distracting scent of recently-spilled human blood, and had decided to investigate. Sekka thought about the consequences had the clan picked up the smell when he'd been lying unconscious in the gully. His skin prickled.

Bolstered by the reinforcements, the lead hyena

took a wary pace forward and lifted its snout to sniff the air. Despite their resemblance to dogs, Sekka knew the animals were more closely related to felines, their nearest relatives being genets and civets. Singly, they had a reputation for being cowardly, but, in fact, they were keystone predators, highly intelligent, and, when working in unison, extremely dangerous. Spotted hyenas didn't need to rely solely on carrion as a food source. They were formidable hunters in their own right and had been known to track their prey for miles before making their kill. Save for male lions, they had no other significant rivals.

Sekka's thought about a weapon. With his eyes glued to the mirror, he knew that in the absence of a gun, his choice was severely limited. The raiders had taken the pangas, and the scissors in the medical bag weren't much of a substitute. But maybe...

Opening the driver's door, Sekka exited the cab. Climbing cautiously on to the 4x4's cargo bed, he worked his way around the wrapped bodies of the dead ranger team, and pulled himself up to the Land Cruiser's tailgate.

As he came into view, the hyenas froze.

Their number, Sekka noted with concern, had increased. There were four of them now and they were closer than before, no more than thirty paces away, near enough for Sekka to note their gore-matted cheeks and jowls. Contrary to their demeanour when they'd been disturbed at the elephant kill site, the animals made no attempt to retreat, but held their ground, their alert black eyes following Sekka's every move.

Sekka's target was the panel that had been added to cover the recesses in the tailgate in order to create storage compartments for tools and other equipment. The panel was affixed by means of plastic plugs which popped free from their holdings when the edge of the panel was peeled back. With the panel removed, Sekka looked for a weapon. His eyes alighted on the extendable ratchet. At its full length of eighteen inches, in the absence of a gun, it was the nearest thing to a heavy weapon. Having made his choice, he replaced the panel and took stock, and was unnerved to find that the hyenas, in their curiosity, had grown considerably bolder.

Crouching less than ten paces from the tailboard, the lead animal was larger than its cohorts, with a thicker neck and broader head. As female hyenas were bigger than the males, this suggested it was probably the alpha bitch; a mature animal to judge from her colouring, as the spots which gave the species its name tended to fade with age, leaving the yellow-brown fur almost unblemished, save for a slight, uneven shading, which extended to the ridge of bristled mane that extended from the crown of the head and across the top of the shoulders.

Heads bobbing as they sifted the air, the hyenas seemed content to maintain their distance, until the bitch, emboldened by Sekka's apparent lack of aggression, took another cautious step forward. Following her lead, her acolytes fell into step behind her. So far, none of them had uttered a sound, which made their proximity all the more unnerving.

Until, with a wild yell, Sekka slammed the ratchet down against the side of the truck.

The hyenas stopped dead. Uncertain, they began to chatter among themselves, issuing shrill yips and grunts. Sekka brought the ratchet down again and then commenced hammering the metal tool against the edge of the tailgate in rapid succession, while continuing to roar at the top of his lungs. It was on the third or fourth clout that the hyenas finally retreated, though only by some twenty paces. The big female stared hard at the truck. Raising her muzzle, she drew back her lips as if searching for Sekka's scent. Such was the intensity of her gaze that Sekka felt the short hairs rise across the back of his neck. Then, as he watched, she turned and loped away into the bush. Only when the others had followed suit did Sekka allow himself to breathe evenly.

Until, seconds later, a savage snarl erupted from the 4x4's offside front end.

Sekka pivoted, almost losing his footing, in time to see a set of front paws appear on the rim of the truck's side panel. A wide head and a blunt, blood-stained muzzle rose between them.

Without thinking, Sekka threw himself forward and scythed the ratchet towards the hyena's skull. The blow missed but it was enough to make the animal drop back down to all-fours.

Fighting to regain his balance, Sekka saw that the attacking hyena wasn't alone. There were two of them, neither of which, to judge by their size, was the alpha. Sekka's inner voice shouted a warning just as a sound not unlike the lowing of a cow came from the opposite side of the truck. Sekka knew, then, that he'd been played. The female hadn't retreated; she'd been plotting. The strange ululation had been her way of issuing orders, directing her auxiliaries to attack.

Clever girl, Sekka thought, half in admiration and half in dread, and whirled as the first hyena launched another offensive against the truck's side panelling, bared claws scrambling for purchase on the smooth metal surface. The truck shuddered.

The spotted hyena was the most aggressive of the species, but attacks against humans were considered rare, though anecdotal reports concerning the animals' fondness for human flesh, had surfaced during the war in the Sudan, when corpses had become readily available. There had also been rumours following a WWF news alert, in which it was purported that more than thirty people had been killed by spotted hyenas along the Tanzanian border with Mozambique. There had been no evidence to confirm the story but that hadn't prevented the tale becoming yet another strand in the creature's mythology.

The current attack, though, was no myth. It was real, and Sekka knew his situation had just turned critical. Whatever advantage the vehicle might have given him had evaporated in that moment. He should have stayed in the cab, he knew, but that would have left the rangers' remains at the mercy of the clan. He'd had no choice but to try and defend his position.

A brief disturbance in the sky out beyond the curve of the 4x4's roof caught Sekka's eye; a dark speck against the blue-grey; another raptor of some kind, coming to join the feast, but there was no time to focus as, with a gale of manic laughter, the hyenas launched their combined assault.

Sekka felt the truck shift beneath him and then all his attention was concentrated on the lower front end of the 4x4 which, because of the way the vehicle was slanted had formed a stepping stone low enough to provide access to the truck's cargo bed. The speed with which the female leapt from the ground to the back of the vehicle was impressive, as was the rank odour she carried before her.

Head low, all four paws braced against the angle of the truck, the hyena's jaws hung open. The smell of her reached deep into Sekka's throat. It was the fetid reek of the bush, and of blood and of death, and it was coming off her in waves.

Whether it was a combination of the heat and the hyena's foul stench, Sekka did not know, but as the taste of bile rose sharply on to the back of his tongue, the wound in his skull began to pound in earnest. The ratchet felt suddenly heavy in his hand and as the sweat burst from him, a keening sound broke from the hyena's lips. Lowering her gaze, and as if to dismiss Sekka's presence as a mere inconvenience, she began to nose at the basha, uttering cat-like mews as she probed beneath the edges of the canvas shroud. Sekka realized it was a summons when the second hyena jumped up to join her.

At which point, the thudding in his brain reached a crescendo.

And the scream erupted from Sekka's throat.

It was an explosion born of rage and fear, and as the torrent of invective burst forth he raised the ratchet once more and began to smash at the metal around him; against the tailgate, the sides of the 4x4, the base of the cargo bed, pummelling anything that would produce noise. There was no rational thought involved. It was as if the primal spirit of his Hausa ancestors had been unleashed. Somewhere inside him, a dam had given way and as the vibrations in his ears increased to a pitch that was almost manic in its intensity, Sekka felt himself slipping towards the edge of consciousness.

As his legs buckled and then gave way, through eyes

blurred with pain, Sekka saw the outline of a dark shape rise and spring towards him. Instinctively, he raised the spanner aloft and tried to yell, but all that emerged was a dry croak. Frantically, he began whipping the ratchet back and forth to fend off the attack, but with each swing his movements grew more feeble, and when he felt his arm gripped, he knew then that he'd lost the fight.,

Until a voice he knew said, "It's all right, Joseph. It's Thomas. Cavalry's here. I've got you."

PARK NATIONAL DE SALMA
Gloire à nos martyrs. Paix à leur Âme.

Sekka's gaze dropped from the inscription at the top of the wall plaque to the copper name plates arranged beneath it. Team Jackal's names had yet to be added.

"Joseph," Keel said softly from behind him.

Sekka did not turn.

"It could have been any one of us," Keel said. "Me, Christoph, Zakaria, any of the team leaders, just as it could have been any one of the other teams."

"But it wasn't."

"No," Keel said. "It wasn't. But there's nothing you, or I, or anyone else, can do about it."

"We can grieve," Sekka said.

Keel nodded. "That, we can do."

It had been five days since the attack.

Team Fox, led by their *Chef de Groupe*, Zakaria, had arrived at the ambush site forty minutes after the chopper's touchdown, Crow having redirected them from Jackal Team's last recorded position - the elephants' kill zone - to the crashed 4x4, where the full horror of the attack had been laid bare.

Fox Team and the two rangers who'd accompanied Keel and Crow in the Airbus had been all for setting off in pursuit, but Keel had vetoed that idea, though not without regret. The priority had been to transfer Sekka and his ranger team back to headquarters - Sekka via the helicopter and the rangers by ground vehicle - and, as Crow had also reminded Keel, the park authorities had no powers outside the reserve, certainly not to pursue the killers, which meant handing the case over to Chadian law enforcement. Given that it was more than a hundred miles to the Sudanese border, the quicker the Chadians were given the information the quicker they could begin their investigation and launch a search for the raiders.

Fox Team's 4x4 had been put to use hauling the damaged truck of the gully, which, while not drivable, was still towable. It had been a slow and ungainly journey back, but the alternative would have been to leave the truck where it was and drive or fly a mechanic out, which could still have resulted in a tow being required so the decision had been taken to make the most of a bad situation and get everyone and everything back to HQ with the minimum delay.

While the damaged Land Cruiser was being dragged out of the gully, Keel had relented and directed those rangers not involved in the retrieval to scout the surrounding area to see if they could pick up any of the killers' tracks. What they'd found was a dead horse, with a bullet wound in its side and blood around its nostrils, stripped of any supplies it might have been carrying; indicating that during the ambush Sekka's shot had found its target. The animal had provided no clue as to its owner's identity or its point of origin, beyond the fact that the raiders who'd abandoned it were heading east. From the number and depth of the tracks had come confirmation that there were four horsemen still on the loose.

Despite Sekka's protestations, René Deschamps had insisted that Crow then ferry Sekka from Salma HQ to the clinic at Am Timan, which, being the provincial capital and thirty minutes flying time, was the nearest population centre with a functioning, albeit basic, medical facility.

There, an over-stretched but attentive French MSF doctor on attachment to the Chadian Ministry of Health had taken time out from his rounds in the pediatric ward to attend to Sekka's wounds. The expression on his face as he'd peeled away the Dermabond dressing had made it clear that he recognized the injury for what it was.

"You know I am required to report gunshot wounds?" he'd told Sekka, as he closed the gash with three neat sutures before applying a fresh plaster.

"Do what you have to do," had been Sekka's terse response.

Struck by the expression on his patient's face, the doctor had eyed the camouflage tunic and the Salma Park insignia and handed his patient a strip of antibiotic pills. "I was here during the student protests. I've seen how the police operate. Also my attachment ends in two weeks and I don't need any trouble. Take two of these before you go to sleep and please *don't* call me in the morning. You can remove the plaster in a couple of days. Your sutures will dissolve in ten. Safe journey home."

Sekka had been back at Salma by late afternoon, by which time, Deschamps had contacted the Chadian authorities and African Parks' Joburg office to inform them of the cross border raid and the killings. It had been early evening when Team Fox arrived with the rangers' bodies, which were placed in the cold storage room adjoining the headquarter's main kitchens.

Two Sureté officers, dispatched by the Chadian Ministry of the Interior along with a representative from the Environment Ministry, had flown in from N'Djamena the next day.

The Sureté captain, short and officious, with crooked teeth and bad breath, had led the questioning. The lieutenant, rake thin and clearly intimidated by his superior, had transcribed the interview, presenting Sekka with a hard copy to sign when it was over. Reliving the events had been hard, relaying them a second time to the Environment Ministry's rep had been harder, though unlike the Sureté men, the government man had at least offered a degree of sympathy, both over the deaths of the rangers and for Sekka's own wounding.

"Rest assured, the president will leave no stone unturned in bringing the criminals to justice," he'd told Sekka. "He has great respect and admiration for the work you are all doing here."

The police captain had demanded, somewhat curtly, to view the bodies, so Sekka and Deschamps had accompanied the two officers to the cold room. The captain had regarded the dead rangers and their wounds without a change of expression, as if such a sight was an everyday occurrence.

"What about autopsies?" Deschamps had asked.

"That is yet to be determined," had been the captain's cryptic reply as he made his way out of the room, the lieutenant hurrying in his wake. "The bodies

79

are to be taken to Am Timan for examination. You will be informed after we have made our report."

"The families would like to know when the bodies are to be released," Deschamps had pressed.

"You will be informed," had been the repeated reply, stated as if the phrase had been learned by rote. Deschamps had bitten his tongue. It didn't do to antagonize the Sureté. As part of the Police Nationale, the Sureté's responsibilities extended beyond those of a regular police force. It was the same with the other branches of Chadian law enforcement: the paramilitary Gendarmerie Nationale, the National and Nomadic Guard and the ANS, the Chad Intelligence Service, all of which had the power of arrest. Chad was, effectively, a military state. When dealing with any of the various agencies, it paid not to rock the boat. One big dysfunctional family was the way Deschamps had described it when he'd initiated Sekka, Keel and Crow into the ways the country operated.

Am Timan did boast a police station but, as with all the regional centres in rural areas it had a reputation for being undermanned and underfunded and thus susceptible to bribery, and, therefore, in no fit state to lead an investigation into the slaughter of a small elephant herd, let alone the murder of five park rangers.   Had Deschamps reported the crimes to the Am Timan force, the case would inevitably have been passed up the line to Police headquarters in N'Djamena. Deschamps had circumvented that process by going directly to the men at the top, though he'd confessed to Keel and Sekka that it had most likely been African Parks exerting pressure on the Chadian authorities that had led to investigators arriving so promptly.

80

Whether that would result in fast and immediate action, Deschamps also admitted he had his doubts, a concern he repeated when the military helicopter arrived later that same day, to collect the ranger's bodies and transport them to Am Timan where they were to be examined, and the circumstances of their death determined, by both a medical examiner and coroner assigned and despatched by the Ministry in N'Djamena.

Deschamps had suspected that the Am Timan facilities would leave a lot to be desired, but, as keeping them at Salma was impractical, the only other option would have been to fly the bodies to N'Djamena, four hundred miles distant, where it was more than likely they'd have entered a backlog of cadavers awaiting autopsy. So while Deschamps' misgivings were probably justified, Am Timan had been the least worse option, not that reserve personnel had any choice in the matter.

Keel and Sekka were answering a summons to attend Deschamps in his office; for an update, they presumed.

"Have a seat," Deschamps said, as he showed Keel and Sekka into the room and closed the door behind them. His expression was solemn.

Don't think I'm going to like this, was Keel's first thought, sensing, at the same time, Sekka's unease.

"How's the head?" Deschamps asked.

"Fine," Sekka said.

In the absence of a dressing, the wound showed no evidence of inflammation and the sutures were hardly noticeable against Sekka's dark skin.

Deschamps nodded and returned to his desk.

"So?" Keel said. "What's the news?"

81

Deschamps, his lips set in a thin line, didn't waste any time. "Not good."

"Meaning?" Sekka said.

"Meaning as far as the Sureté's concerned, the investigation is being wound down."

A taut silence followed, broken when Keel said, "*Excuse* me?"

Knowing he was about to impart more bad news, Deschamps took his time before answering then said. "I had a call from the Ministry. The Police have been unable to locate the poachers. It's estimated that by now they will have re-crossed back into Darfur, so further reconnaissance along the border region is considered no longer viable. The search has been called off."

There came another heavy silence.

"You have got to be kidding me," Keel said eventually.

"They killed five men," Sekka said. "My men. *Our* men!"

"What the hell, René?" Keel swore. "I mean; what the *hell*?"

Deschamps shook his head. "I am sorry, Thomas. I don't know what to say."

"Didn't the police send out trackers? Christ, *we* had no trouble finding their bloody hoof prints."

Deschamps took a breath, before glancing at Sekka. "The police did not take Joseph's statement until the day after the attack. If you recall, it rained heavily that same evening. By the time they reported back and sent out an alert, whatever tracks there may have been had been severely compromised."

"But police did visit the villages to see if there'd been any strangers passing through, yes? Asked them if they'd seen a group of horsemen?"

Deschamps hesitated, gathering his thoughts before replying. "There are fourteen hundred kilometres of border between Chad and Sudan. Searching for four men who do not want to be found would be extremely difficult, and if they had split up and were making their way separately, one man on his own would be almost impossible to detect. Also, from what you described of their camp and equipment, they were not without funds. It's possible they bribed villagers to look the other way."

It was a valid point Keel was prepared to accept, but that didn't make the hearing of it any more palatable.

"And Chadian police resources are severely limited," Deschamps added. "They do not have enough personnel to patrol every part of the border.

"I thought Chad and Sudan had some sort of agreement to monitor border traffic; a combined outfit," Keel said.

"They do. The Joint Border Force. Unfortunately, given the current situation in Sudan since Bashir was ousted, Khartoum's priorities have changed. Their emphasis is on trying to maintain internal order. The Chadian contingent can't continue on their own. Cross-border crime has taken a back seat."

"Even when there's murder involved?"

"When there is little chance of bringing those responsible to justice, yes."

"Isn't there *anything* you can do?" Sekka cut in. "Someone in the Chadian Ministry you can talk to? Someone with a direct line to the president?"

Deschamps shook his head. "I tried. Sadly, there was no one."

"So let me get this straight," Keel said, making to attempt to hide his contempt. "When the guy from the Ministry - Saed, was it? - turned up and told Joseph the president would leave no stone unturned he was talking through his arse?"

Deschamps' chin came up quickly. About to say something, he hesitated.

"What?" Sekka said.

Deschamps sat back. "How much did you know about President Déby before he was killed and his son, Mahamat, took over?"

That had been back in '21, Keel remembered, when Déby had gone to visit government troops who were battling insurgents on the country's northern border. Injured during a clash with rebel forces, the president had later died of his wounds.

"Rose to power back in the nineties," Keel said. "Led a rebellion against the previous guy - Habré. Rumour was he had Sudanese and Libyan help. He was one of Gaddafi's pals, so the rumours were probably true."

Deschamps remained silent.

"There were a few hiccups along the way," Keel continued. "Attempts to knock him off his perch but he managed to hang on. Got himself involved in some of his neighbours' petty squabbles: C.A.R and Darfur; sent troops to help you guys out in Mali. Had a lot of fingers in a lot of unsavoury pies."

Deschamps said nothing.

"Don't forget the human rights abuses and the corruption charges," Sekka put in.

"As if," Keel said.

Deschamps threw Keel a look.

"What?" Keel said. "You think we wouldn't do at least a *bit* of research when you offered us the job?"

84

"And yet you still took it."

"You asked, we came. Seemed like a good idea at the time."

Deschamps ignored the sarcasm. "And his personal life?"

Keel frowned. "What about it? What he got up to when he went home for the day was his affair."

"Ordinarily, I would agree with you," Deschamps said. "Except..."

"Except what?" Keel said. "He cheat on his wife?"

"More than likely, seeing as he was on his third."

Keel frowned. "What's your point?"

Deschamps' gaze shifted back. "Call it a conflict of interest."

"You've lost me. Yours or his?"

"His." Deschamps leaned forward and rested his elbows on the desk. "His widow is Amani Hilal. Déby married her back in 2012. A grand occasion, according to the press. It stopped all the traffic...in Khartoum." He let the last word hang in the air.

"Khartoum?" Sekka's head came up.

"Her father is Musa Hilal. Leader of the Janjaweed militia: forerunner of the RSF."

The room fell silent.

Until Keel said softly, "Ah, shit."

"It's said the dowry was twenty-six million dollars; twenty-five million to Musa, the rest to Amani, in gold and jewellery." Deschamp paused, then said, "Not that his wealth prevented Musa from ending up in jail. He was arrested a couple of years ago."

"That sounds like good news," Keel said. "Why am I sensing a 'but'?"

"He is still considered to have influence."

"Within the RSF?" Sekka said.

"It is believed so, but there is now General Mohamed Dagalo. Most people call him Hemeti. "

"Name rings a bell," Keel said.

"He is the RSF's current commander. "

"Right, and he's *not* in jail."

"Correct."

"He was Janjaweed, too?"

Deschamps nodded. "Also one of the leading members; a very powerful warlord. He and Musa started off as allies, but they had a falling out when Musa decided to break away from Bashir and form his own organization: The Revolutionary Awakening Council."

"Catchy," Keel said.

Deschamps allowed himself a small smile. "Hemeti remained loyal to Khartoum. When Bashir was overthrown and General Burhan became President of the Transition Council, he appointed Hemeti as his deputy and made *him* head of the RSF. It is said that it was Hemeti who betrayed Musa to the authorities. There was rivalry over the granting of gold mining rights."

"He was getting rid of the competition."

Deschamps nodded. "General Burhan and he are very close, but with thirty thousand men under his command, Hemeti is said to wield the power."

"And *he* has links to Déby's family?" Sekka posed the question.

"He is a Chadian Arab by birth. His cousin, Bichara Issa Jadallah, was once Chad's Defence Minister."

"Wonderful," Keel muttered. "This just keeps getting better and better."

"Jadallah is no longer in the post but he remains one of Mahamat's closest advisors."

86

"We get the picture," Keel said.. "Not hard to see why the Ministry didn't want you bothering the guy."

"Indeed, and word has it that Mahamat is as worried as his father was about the Hemeti family connection."

"How so?"

"There are those who say that Hemeti is using the vacuum created by Bashir's arrest to consolidate his position and gather allies in order to further his own political ambitions and that he has the backing of the Darfuri Arabs who created the Janjaweed. If they do take over the government then they would seize the revolution from the Sudanese people and transform the country into a militia state."

"And we all know what'll happen then," Sekka muttered tersely.

"I don't get it," Keel cut in. "So why is Mahamat worried?"

"It is thought that Hemeti would support an Arab takeover in Chad."

"Because the Déby family is not Arab," Sekka said.

"Correct. Idriss Déby was of the Zaghawa tribe. Although they have embraced Islam, the Sudanese Arabs still refer to them as 'Africans'."

"There are Arab politicians in the Chad parliament," Sekka pointed out.

"There are, but they are in the minority and Déby was always worried they would not refuse Hemeti's offer of armed support if there was a revolution."

"So it paid Déby to stay on Hemeti's good side," Keel murmured.

"Very much so," Deschamps said.

"Which is why his son's not too anxious to hunt down RSF raiders. He doesn't want to create waves

87

either. Christ, talk about wheels within wheels."

No one spoke for several seconds, until Deschamps said. "At least there is one good thing."

"There is?" Keel said icily.

"The authorities have released the bodies for burial."

"Well, that's all right, then. That's just bloody terrific."

The vehemence in Keel's retort caused Deschamps' face to harden.

"Sorry, René," Keel said immediately. "That was uncalled for."

Of the five rangers killed, four had been from the south and were of the Catholic faith. The fifth, Adoum, was Muslim. Islamic religious law called for burial of the body as soon as possible after death, preferably within twenty four hours, to protect the living from any insanitary issues. The exception being in the case of someone who'd fallen in battle or been the victim of foul play. Keel knew that Adoum's family had not been happy with the delay caused by the police investigation. Now, at least, they could proceed with the funeral arrangements and attain some sort of closure, a word Keel despised.

Even as he expressed regret for his outburst, Keel couldn't stop himself wondering if Adoum's family might have put pressure on someone to close down the investigation in order to expedite release of the body, but then he dismissed the thought. It was unlikely, he reasoned, He knew Adoum's family was from poor rural stock. It didn't have that kind of clout.

Deschamps nodded, accepting Keel's apology. Sekka, however, was in no mood to retract his anger. "So that's it? We're supposed to carry on as if nothing happened?" He fixed Deschamps with a look of disbelief. "And you *agreed* to this?"

Deschamps spread his hands. "I had no choice. Salma is under African Parks' management but we are here at the whim of the Ministry and, ultimately, the president."

"Who has ties with the boss of the men that killed our friends," Keel muttered.

"It's complicated," Deschamps said.

"No shit," Keel shot back.

"The Ministry did tell me that if they do happen to receive additional information regarding the raiders they will will keep us informed," Deschamps said.

"Of course they will," Keel said. "And pig shit smells of violets."

The room fell silent again for several long seconds. Then, when Keel shook his head in frustration, Deschamps pushed his chair back. "Adoum is being buried this afternoon. You will be there?"

Taking the hint, Keel and Sekka rose.

"We'll be there," Keel said and headed for the door.

Sekka followed him out of the room, leaving Deschamps gazing after them in silence.

Keel and Sekka emerged from the building to find Crow waiting outside.

"Well?" Crow said. "The police have any news? Any joy tracking the bastards? Ah, shit. Go on, tell me." The pilot's voice dropped as he took in Sekka and Keel's expressions.

"They've abandoned the search," Sekka said.

Crow's face darkened. "They've *what*? Why?"

"It's *complicated*," Keel said.

89

Crow's eyebrows rose. "What the hell does that mean?"

"It means..," Keel began and then looked at Sekka and shook his head. "Go on, you tell him."

Sekka did so and he and Keel watched as disgust moved across the pilot's face.

"Chris'sakes," Crow said. He stared hard at the ground and then looked up. "So, what happens now?"

"We've a funeral to go to," Keel said. "We pay our respects."

There was a moment's silence, then Crow nodded and let out a sigh. "I'll go get my jacket."

6

Circular in shape, constructed from white-washed mud bricks topped by a conical thatched roof, the safari lodge overlooked the river. With the undersurface of the roof radiating out from a central hub and with the circumference supported by sturdy wooden pillars, the building provided an open-sided viewing platform where the reserve's guests could swap stories about the sights they'd seen during their early morning and late afternoon game drives, and gaze down upon the animals that came to the river to bathe and to drink.

The hub housed a small bar and kitchen along with rest rooms, while the remainder of the floor space contained two cloth-covered dining tables and a lounge area with easy chairs and a couple of well-worn but comfortable sofas. The wall along the back of the bar was decorated with expertly crafted animal sculptures and other native artifacts. Brightly coloured rugs lay across the terracotta floor, their ethnic theme reflected in the patterns etched into the pillars supporting the roof. When evening fell and with the room lit warmly by lantern glow, it was the perfect place to end the day. In the closed season, the reserve's senior staff took advantage of the tourists' absence and so had the place to themselves.

It was mid-afternoon. Keel and Sekka, having helped themselves to soft drinks from behind the bar, had found chairs and were enjoying the breeze drifting up from the water. For several minutes, neither spoke, until their thoughts were interrupted by the sound of footsteps on the tiles.

Keel turned to look over his shoulder. "Sabine get away all right?"

Crow nodded tiredly. "No problem. I made sure her flight left before I headed back."

The park's vet was on her way to attend a summit in Dubai, being held as part of the World Veterinary Association's annual round of conferences. Crow had flown Sabine to the airport at Sahr, in order for her to catch the N'Djamena flight and her onward connection to the UAE via the Ethiopian capital, Addis. He was due to pick her up from Sahr upon her return.

As Sahr was a round trip of some four hundred miles, even with a meal break, Crow's air of fatigue was understandable, despite having used the Cessna to ferry Sabine rather than the chopper, as it was a faster and more comfortable ride.

Sabine's attendance at the conference had been arranged months before. Several of the lectures covered the practice of veterinary medicine in Sub Saharan Africa and were, therefore, pertinent to Salma's remit. Following the killings, however, and having attended Adoum's funeral, Sabine had been reluctant to leave. It had taken considerable effort on Deschamps' part to persuade her that it was in the park's best interest if she did still participate as, despite the appalling tragedy, it would show the other delegates that Salma was fully operational and that its reputation as a wildlife sanctuary had not been compromised. It would prove the park's resilience in the face of terrible adversity and reassure both the Chadian government and African Parks, who were part funders of the event, that their faith in Salma was justified. It would also, Deschamps had ventured to tell her, provide a welcome distraction from the sorrow and helplessness that had continued to gnaw at her in the wake of the killings.

"How about you guys?" Crow asked, as he reached for a can of Sprite. "You doing okay? How was it?"

"Hard," Keel said.

In contrast to Adoum's funeral the previous day, today's interment for Matthias, Cesar, Isadore and Theo had been a combined affair. The four were from neighbouring villages and so the burials had been well attended by relatives and friends of the departed, including their fellow rangers. All had been family men and the outpouring of grief as the shroud-wrapped bundles were laid in the ground beneath the shade of sheets held by the white-dressed mourners had been profound. So it had been with something approaching relief that Keel, Sekka and René Deschamps had eventually made their farewells. The sounds of weeping had followed them as they'd left the cemetery.

Crow nodded and settled into an empty chair. A heavy, contemplative silence descended, broken when another set of footsteps sounded and René Deschamps said from behind them, "I thought we could all use something stronger."

He was clasping a bottle of Laphroaig in his right hand and four tumblers in his left. He placed the tumblers on the table in front of them and uncapped the bottle. "That includes you, Crow. As of now, you are off duty." Pouring two fingers of the single malt into each tumbler, Deschamps divided the drinks and raised his glass. "*À nos frères*. To our brothers."

Crow set down his Sprite, picked up his glass and followed Keel and Sekka as they stood and raised their tumblers to echo the salute. The ritual concluded, Deschamps pulled up an empty chair and the four men sat in respectful silence, taking occasional sips of whisky.

"I had a call from AP," Deschamps said after a further couple of minutes had passed.

"And?" Keel said, sensing Deschamps' disquiet.

"SANparks are concerned about the rhino delivery."

The others waited. Then Sekka said, "They're worried about their safety?"

Deschamps nodded. "It's taken two years for AP and SANparks to agree the purchase. We're almost there. They've been keeping the animals at a holding facility in the Eastern Cape ready for transport but with this thing hanging over our heads...if we can't protect our elephants or ourselves then what hope do we have of protecting rhino? Along with the ellie, it's one of the most iconic animals on the planet. SANparks could end up cancelling the deal, which would be catastrophic. Not that I'd blame them," Deschamps finished.

"Can they do that?" Keel asked.

"We were waiting on final signature, so yes, they can still back out." Deschamps took a sip from his glass. "Their delivery was meant to bolster the park's reputation as a beacon of conservation. If it goes ahead, they'll be the first black rhino in the country for nearly fifty years."

"But if SANparks thinks we can't protect them..." Sekka left the sentence unfinished.

Deschamps pursed his lips.

"It's not only about the rhinos, though, is it?" Keel said. "It's Salmas's reputation that'll suffer. Chad's already listed with most countries' foreign departments as a destination best avoided due to the crime rate, and that's without the risk of more terrorist attacks along the western border. Britain doesn't have any consular representation, neither does the US."

"Correct," Deschamps said. "Salma and the government are anxious to see that attitude reversed, of course, but it won't be easy. We don't get a lot of tourists. We're not the easiest place to get to and because of that we're not a cheap destination. Which means we cater for a certain type of clientele. Plus, visas and vaccination requirements also tend to weed out the not-so-adventurous. But word gets around. There's a cachet attached to visiting Salma. We're a world away from the Masai Mara and the Serengheti. The adventurers come here *because* we're hard to reach. And their reward is some of the best game viewing in Africa."

Deschamps paused, then said, "Cooperation between nations is critical if we're to give these animals a future. The collaboration between AP and SANparks gives us the opportunity to encourage population growth and expand their range. It won't do our attempts to restore biodiversity in Chad any harm, either. If we're successful in reintroducing the rhinos here then there's hope the species will survive across the whole of Africa."

Deschamps fell silent. He looked slightly embarrassed. "My apologies, but this is so important I have a tendency to get carried away."

"And right now," Crow said, "we'll be seen as an easy target. SANparks won't want to send us their rhino, and tourists, even the plucky ones, won't want to risk making the trip."

"And the park needs the funding," Sekka said.

Deschamps swirled his glass. "Every tourist dollar is vital. AP is generous and supportive but we have to prove we're doing our fair share...more than our fair share."

"And if they find the gang that hit us and word spreads that we can and *will* protect the park, that'll deter the poachers and the place stands a chance of surviving."

Deschamps nodded. "God willing."

"How likely is it that the authorities *will* pull their finger out?" Crow asked.

Deschamps sighed. "I am not hopeful."

Crow glanced at Keel. "If this were back in the day..."

Keel acknowledged the comment by exhaling into his glass and then looking up. "Times change. Any case, we've nothing to go on."

"Even if we had," Deschamps said, "we've been ordered not to pursue."

Crow's head swivelled. "Come again?"

"We've been warned off," Keel said.

Deschamps nodded. "It was considered too dangerous."

"By whom?" Sekka asked.

"The Ministry and the police."

"Hang on," Crow cut in. "Does that mean you *did* consider the possibility of us forming our own posse?"

"Posse?" Deschamps frowned.

Crow explained and Deschamps shook his head. "I was not given that option. The minute I notified the authorities about the raid I received implicit instructions that we were not to take the law into our own hands. I was told in no uncertain terms that our jurisdiction covers the park area, and nothing else."

"Too late anyway," Crow said despondently. "We know the trail's gone cold."

"So we pick ourselves up and we get back to the training," Deschamps said firmly. "I know that sounds insensitive, given what's happened and how we are feeling, but we *will* need replacements. We have a list of applications on file. I will take a look at their résumés and whittle them down. Then Joseph and Thomas can make the final choice. It's possible, some of the prospective candidates will have had a change of heart in light of events, but we'll see. In the meantime, we take one man from each of the other teams to create a replacement crew. That way we can keep to the patrol schedules. Are you good with that?"

Keel nodded.

"Joseph?" Deschamps said.

"I'm good," Sekka said, though there was a slight pause before the words came out.

"Then it's settled. If we are to maintain momentum we must prove to AP and the Ministry that we're coping. Plus others will be watching; people who will have it in their heads that because we're five rangers down we're unable to maintain security. I intend to prove them wrong. I don't want to lose any more elephants, and I certainly don't want to lose any more men."

A nerve flickered along Sekka's jawline.

"Joseph," Deschamps said.

Sekka looked at him.

Deschamps held his gaze. "You are not responsible

for what happened to your team. When I asked you and Thomas to come in as trainers I knew I was getting the very best. I have not altered my opinion. We mourn our friends, we pick ourselves up and we do our jobs. Agreed?"

"Agreed," Keel said, throwing Sekka a look.

Crow nodded. Sekka, tight-lipped, followed suit a second later.

"Good," Deschamps said. "Then what say we finish the bottle?"

Deschamps held out the Laphroaig and topped up Crow and Keel's glasses. Sekka shook his head. "I want to check on the truck, see if it's been fixed."

"Are you sure?" Deschamps said. "It can wait until morning."

"Won't take long," Sekka said. "Hold my seat. I'll be back."

The other three watched as he walked away. Not for the first time, it struck Crow that when Sekka moved, whether it was walking or even running, he never seemed to expend energy the way other men did. He also seemed to have acquired the ability to walk in almost total silence. Crow was reminded of the way a cheetah stalked the savanna. "He all right?"

"He will be," Keel said.

"He's taken it hard."

Keel nodded. "His team. His responsibility." Keel looked at Deschamps. "No matter how many times you tell him it wasn't his fault, he *will* take it personally."

"You know that from experience," Deschamps said.

"We've had our moments," Keel said.

"And then some," Crow murmured.

"You've worked a lot together." Deschamps said.

Keel nodded.

Deschamps raised a questioning eyebrow.

Crow said quietly, "Uh, oh."

"When he served under you in the Legion," Keel said, "did he tell you about his background?"

Crow let go a frown. "I thought that was part of being a legionnaire. Your background doesn't matter."

"It doesn't," Deschamps said. "But in answer to your question, I knew very little of Joseph's history until I recruited him for Salma. I learned more about him then than I did for the five years he served as a legionnaire, except for the fact he was one of the best soldiers I ever fought with, which was why I offered him the job training my rangers."

"He tell you then why he joined the Legion?" Keel asked carefully.

"He did."

"And that it involved the two of us?"

"Yes. He told me it was a rescue mission in East Africa that was successful, but which had repercussions."

"If repercussions means there was a price put on our heads," Keel said, "then yes, I'd say that covered it."

"And you were shot," Crow said amiably.

"That, too." Keel took a swig from his glass.

Deschamps looked towards Crow. Crow returned his gaze calmly.

Keel said. "We decided it'd be safer if we went our separate ways, and kept a low profile for a while. In Joseph's case, he headed for the Legion's recruitment centre at Quartier Vienot. I took on contract work in a bunch of God-awful, out-of-the-way shitholes. All things considered, I'd say Joseph got the better end of the deal."

"The sanction is no longer in force?"

"Far as I know, it's been lifted."

"Because?"

"The contractors were made to see the error of their ways."

Crow stifled a smile.

"Joseph insisted I offer you a training position, too," Deschamps said. "He told me it was either both of you or neither. He was very persuasive."

"One of his more noble character traits," Keel said.

Crow hummed *'The boys are back in town,'* under his breath.

"And for some reason," Deschamps said, turning to Crow, "when I told them I could also use a good pilot they recommended you."

Crow grinned. "Based on my winning personality?"

"Something like that," Deschamps said.

"Or he was desperate," Keel said.

Sekka made his way to the park's vehicle workshop. The place was well equipped but major spare parts still had to be ordered off-site and that often meant a wait of several days if not a week or more for a mechanical failure to be fixed. There were auto shops in Am Timan but that necessitated a lengthy round trip by road, unless either the Cessna or the Airbus was available, in which case Crow was assigned the delivery runs. If Am Timan didn't have the necessary spares they were air-freighted from the capital and as commercial flights between N'Djamena and Salma were routed via Sahr, it wasn't unheard of for equipment to go missing while en route. It paid to be both pragmatic as well as patient.

Fortunately, the Land Cruiser was the 4x4 of choice

in Chad, as it was over much of the continent and so spare parts - those that weren't immediately available from local autoshops - were often cannibalized from other vehicles. Sekka had learnt never to underestimate the Chadian ability to get a motor back on the road when most western garages would have consigned whatever it was to the local junkyard without so much as a second glance.

"How is it?" Sekka asked, though he knew what the answer would be.

Antoine, the park's only and, therefore, chief motor mechanic, wiped his hands on an oil-stained rag. "All fixed, boss."

'All fixed boss' was Antoine's stock response when announcing that a vehicle was up for collection. Usually, the mechanic was all smiles, but on this occasion, with knowledge of how the truck had sustained damage still weighing heavily on everyone's mind, he announced the news that repairs had been made with none of his customary enthusiasm but with an expression that spoke of sadness and ongoing concern for Sekka's own wellbeing.

"Good," Sekka said. "We'll be taking her out tomorrow."

"No problem, boss. She is ready."

Sekka was walking away when Antoine called after him. "Boss? I am sorry. I meant to give you this."

Sekka turned as the mechanic reached into the pocket of his overalls.

"You must have dropped it," Antoine said, "when you..." Struck by the expression on Sekka's face, the mechanic's voice faltered.

Sekka gazed down at the object in Antoine's hand and his mouth went dry.

It was a mobile phone.

"Eyes right," Crow said, as Sekka reappeared.

"All good?" Keel asked.

When Sekka did not reply Keel frowned and repeated the question, by which time Sekka was standing by the table.

"What?" Keel said.

Sekka held up the mobile. "Does anyone have a charger?"

"Where was it?" Keel asked, when Sekka told them about the phone's significance.

"Beneath the mat on the driver's side. It must have slipped out of my pocket when I was exiting the cab. My equipment got snagged on the door frame. I forget I had the thing."

"You found it in the poachers' camp?" Deschamps said, gazing at the mobile as if it was some kind of holy relic.

"In one of the backpacks. The battery's dead. Either it's faulty or they planned to recharge it when they got back from the hunt."

"Only one way to find out," Keel said.

"By rights we should hand it over to the police," Deschamps said, gravely.

The other three looked at him, but said nothing.

Deschamps showed his palms in surrender.

"If it's password protected," Crow said, "we're stuffed."

They used the computer in Deschamps' office. Sekka, Keel and Crow crowded around as Deschamps took a USB cable from his desk drawer and connected the phone to his pc.

"Fingers crossed," Crow murmured softly.

No password or thumb print was required, but it took a while before Deschamps had the phone's file contents up on the computer screen.

"What've we got?" Keel asked as the icons appeared.

"Contact numbers," Deschamps said, his eyes flicking across the screen, "and texts."

"Photos?" Sekka said.

Deschamps let out a grunt as folders continued to appear on the pc's screen, "Those too."

"Numbers tell us anything about the locations," Keel asked. "Who they were calling?"

Deschamps clicked his tongue as he scanned the details. "Not who, where. They used the country codes for some numbers: 249, and city code 1. That's Sudan, Khartoum."

"Means they were our side of the border when they made the calls."

Deschamps nodded. "They also used 211. That's South Sudan. I'm not familiar with the city codes over there, though there are not that many."

"These have to be mobile numbers," Sekka said.

"I agree. Landlines aren't widely used. They're too unreliable. Mobile coverage isn't that much better. Half of Chad's population doesn't even have access." The park manager's eyes moved up and down the lists. "I'd say the other calls are internal, Sudan most likely."

"The texts tell us anything?" Keel asked.

Deschamps began to scroll. "They're in Arabic."

"What do they say?"

Deschamps frowned. "They do not look like

conversations. If I were to guess I would say they're verses from the Quran. *'Oh, you who have believed, persevere and endure and remain stationed and fear Allah that you may be successful.'* Here's another: *'Death will find you even if ye hide in fortresses built up strong and high.'"*

"Cheeful sod," Crow grunted.

"Psyching themselves up," Keel said.

"Anything else?" Sekka enquired. "Names? Places? Chats?"

"Not that I can see."

"Probably knew enough to erase the personal stuff," Keel said. "How about the photos? Maybe we'll have better luck."

"Long as they're not porn," Crow said, half under his breath.

Deschamps moved his fingers across the keyboard.

There were around a dozen photographs in all.

"Looks like a family snapshot," Keel said in response to an image showing four people standing to the side of a spindly green shrub in what appeared to be a small, dusty courtyard. Part of an outside wall of a house could be seen behind them. The group consisted of a man and a woman and two bare-footed children, a pre-teen boy and a little girl. The man, dressed in a long-sleeved white shirt and grey trousers appeared slight and wiry. The woman, equally slender, wore a dark blue, ankle-length dress. Her hair was covered by a pale green scarf. The boy was wearing a red football jersey and floppy shorts that came down to his thin calves; the girl, a loose dress, the same colour as the woman's. Despite the shy smiles on the youngsters' faces, all of them, adults included, looked decidedly undernourished.

104

"Mum, dad and the kids," Crow said, "Sweet."

There was nothing in the image to indicate where it had been taken. Two more photographs showed the children on their own in the same location, the snapshots presumably taken at the same time as the family grouping, the little girl clutching a stuffed rabbit to her chest, the boy cradling a toy gun.

Deschamps clicked on the next photo.

"Well, hello, chaps," Crow murmured softly.

Four men, two dressed in sand-coloured army fatigues, leaning out of the back of an open-top truck, brandishing automatic rifles, grins on their faces. The two not in fatigues were bare-headed. The other pair sported bright red berets. One of the beret wearers was clearly the father from the family photo. More troops, similarly attired, hovered in the background. It looked like a couple of mobile units about to head off on patrol.

Sekka let out a hiss. "RSF."

Another photo showed three of the same four men, none of them in uniform, squatting around a camp fire, two with Kalashnikovs resting across their thighs. Part of a bivvy and the corner of what might have been a prayer mat could be seen off to one side. The next photo was a similar shot, again showing three out of the four, but with a change of face for one of them, presumably the photographer who'd taken the previous shot and then swapped places with his companion.

"Got to be them," Crow said. "What you you think?"

Sekka nodded. "It's them."

"You didn't see them close up," Deschamps said.

"It's them," Sekka repeated.

Crow and Keel exchanged glances. There was a

fixed expression on Sekka's face: the look of a hunter when the prey breaks cover.

"Bring up the rest," Keel said.

More photos of the same men; in one, the Sudanese flag was fluttering behind them. In another, they were holding on to the bridles of five thin horses and had AK47s slung across their shoulders.

"There's your clincher," Crow said.

They gazed at the last image for several long seconds. Sekka felt his insides turn over as his eyes took in the now familiar features of the man from the family photograph, who appeared to be wearing the same get-up as the horseman who'd led the attack on the ranger team.

"Question is," Keel said into the uneasy silence, "what do we do with this? René?"

"If we pass the information to the Sureté," Sekka said, before Deschamps could answer, "we'll be sacrificing the only lead we have."

Deschamps said nothing but continued to study the computer screen.

"Joseph's right," Keel said. "They told you they've all but shut down the investigation. Given Mahamat's allegiance, we hand over the phone it'll likely end up in a bloody land fill."

"We could call the numbers," Crow said. "See who picks up."

Keel shook his head. "It'd just be a voice at the other end. We ask who it is and we'd be giving the game away. They'd likely guess the phone has turned up, which'll put them on the alert. We keep schtum and the guy whose phone it is will think it's lost, which has to work to our advantage. They won't know what we know."

Crow let go an expletive. "You're right. Dumb question. Sorry."

Keel continued to gaze at the screen.

"What are you thinking?" Sekka asked.

Keel turned. "That we distribute the photos, send them out to the villages along the boundary. See if the faces jog anyone's memory."

"You're suggesting we by-pass the authorities," Deschamps said.

"I am."

"And if someone's memory is...jogged?"

"We'll cross that bridge when we come to it, *if* we come to it."

"A little incentive probably wouldn't hurt," Crow put in.

"A reward for information?" Deschamps said.

"Why not?"

"Could work," Keel said. He looked towards Sekka. "What do you say?"

"I say we're wasting time," Sekka said. "How many villages were given phones? Nine?"

"Ten," Deschamps said.

"Then we'll start with them."

"Er, question, chaps," Crow said. "What do we do if the police discover we've sent out mugshots or someone tells the bad guys we know what they look like and we're gunning for them?"

Deschamps raised his head. "*Gunning*?"

"Slip of the tongue," Crow said, unabashed.

"It's a plan," Keel said. "I didn't say it was a great plan."

"But it's the best we've got, right?" Crow said.

Keel looked down at the computer screen, his gaze steady and committed. "You take what you can get."

107

Crow smiled ferally. "I ever tell you that's my other family motto?"

7

"So," Deschamps said. "How are they doing?"

"All right, so far," Keel said, "They're keen and they're quick learners."

"And Joseph?" Deschamps asked, his eyes searching Keel's face. "How's *he* doing?"

"He's getting there. As of now he's taking them through field signals training."

Deschamps' right hand played with a pen on his desk. "I hear he's been pushing them hard."

"No harder than he's pushed anyone else."

Deschamps' hand stilled. He waited.

Keel said, "Okay, maybe a wee bit harder, but they can take it. It's what they're here for."

"You'll keep an eye on him?"

"He doesn't need a chaperone," Keel's voice carried a distinct edge.

"That's not what I meant."

Keel let go a sigh. "I know."

Deschamps gave it a couple of seconds, then said, "Luiza and Essie?"

"Tough as nails." Keel released an inner breath, grateful for the change of subject. "From what Luiza tells me, she joined up to get away from her children. Told me it was for the peace and quiet. Essie scored top marks on the range. It's a good job they're on our side."

Deschamps allowed a smile to transform his features. "Reminds me of the old days: instructions to the GSG9 anti-terrorist squads."

"Shoot the women first?"

Deschamps nodded. "They were always the most dangerous."

"Too right. Still are. Wouldn't like to meet any of ours on a dark night. Hell, *any* night for that matter."

Luiza and Essie were members of the new intake. They weren't the first women rangers on Salma's books. Deschamps had made it reserve policy from the start of his recruitment drive, when the wardens were formed into new ranger teams and given military training, that there was to be no discrimination in either the application process or the final selection: men *and* women could apply. Team Viper was an all-female unit – inspired by Zimbabwe's Phundundu Park's *Akashinga* squad - and no allowances were made for gender, not during the training period and especially not on the job. As a result, the women inevitably pushed themselves harder than the men and the men respected them for it.

"Good." Deschamps pushed his chair back. As he did so there was a knock against the side of the open office door.

"Boss?"

Deschamps looked up. Keel turned. A young Chadian male in civilian clothes was standing on the threshold.

"Mo?" Deschamps frowned. "I thought Mongoose Team was off duty? Shouldn't you be home, with your family?"

The aftermath of the shootings had made

110

Deschamps even more mindful that the time the rangers spent with their loved ones was as important; if not more so than the periods they spent on duty guarding the reserve. Mo - shortened from Mohammed at his own request - was the sole provider for his widowed mother and two younger sisters, both of school age. His circumstances were not unusual in a region torn apart by war and revolution and, because of that, Keel knew that Deschamps concern for every member of his staff was genuine.

It was a legacy of his time with the Legion. As a colonel in one of the toughest armies in the world, Deschamps' priority had always been the welfare of his troops. He'd ridden them hard but because they knew of his respect for them, they had followed him into battle without a moment's hesitation. During his time on the reserve Keel had come to see that the ranger teams paid Deschamps the same degree of loyalty.

Deschamps had spoken little of his own family circumstances but Keel had learned, through Sekka, that Deschamps' wife had died after a long battle with leukemia and that he had a daughter - Lucia, a lawyer, who lived with her husband and young son in Lucerne. There was a picture of them in a frame on the desk, happy and smiling, dressed in skiing gear, a range of snow-capped Alpine peaks rising behind them.

"Yes, boss, but I needed to see you." There was an anxious expression on the ranger's face.

"I'll be on my way," Keel said, rising and aiming for the door.

"No, boss," Mo said quickly. "Better if you stay. You will want to hear this."

Keel paused. "What's up?"

"My cousin, Hassan, is here."

"Okay," Keel said again, more cautiously.

"He would speak with you."

"No problem." Keel threw Deschamps a sideways glance as Mo turned and beckoned.

In contrast to Mo's t-shirt and cargo pants, the man who followed the ranger into the room was dressed in an ankle-length jalabiya and turban; the white robe and headwear offset by a grey waistcoat and a pair of brown, plastic sandals. In stark contrast to his costume, his skin was very dark, the colour of molasses. He looked older than Mo though only by a few years, with a sense of gravitas enhanced by a narrow, neatly-trimmed goatee beard that was flecked with thin streaks of grey.

Mo stepped to one side. "Hassan is the son of my father's eldest brother."

Deschamps stepped forward. '*As-salamu alaikum.*"

The reply was voiced with calm dignity, an inclination of the head and a palm flat to the chest. "*Wa alaikum assalaam.*"

"Welcome, sir," Deschamps said, extending his hand. "How are you?"

Deschamps had offered the greeting in French. French and Arabic were the country's two official languages, with French being spoken by the larger percentage of the population, a legacy of Chad's colonial past; though Arabic tended to be the primary language in the north, where it was used in daily communication and by radio broadcasts. Throughout the country, where Arabic was used, regional dialects also came into play; notably in the south, where, in addition to French, Chadian Arabic was accepted as the lingua franca.

As his cousin shook Deschamps' hand and then Keel's, Mo said, "Hassan is a trader. He is respected by many village elders in Chad; in Sudan, also."

Cousin Hassan, Mo explained, conducted his business among the villages and nomadic settlements that straddled the border, as well as in larger townships further afield, in his quest for trade goods, which included everything from tools and tyres to assorted trinkets and farming produce; essentially anything that could command a price. He also made a living as a middle man, acting as broker between locals seeking to exchange one sets of goods for another, charging a small commission for his services.

Which was all very fascinating, Keel thought, until the moment Mo said, almost casually, "Hassan says he has seen one of the men in the photographs."

The office went quiet.

"Which man?" Keel asked eventually, breaking the silence, before realizing that he'd spoken in English. He corrected himself and automatically repeated the question in French.

In answer, Hassan reached into the pocket of his jalabiya and extracted a folded piece of paper. When he opened it out Keel saw it was a crumpled print-out of one of the snapshots retrieved from the raiders' mobile phone. From its condition it had obviously been consulted a great many times.   Handing it to his cousin, he murmured quietly in words Keel didn't quite catch.

Mo nodded and laid the image on the desk. "That one," he said, pointing.

Deschamps and Keel stared down at the photo. It was the shot of the four men with their horses. Unbidden, Hassan prodded the image with the end of his finger, directly at the face of the man on the extreme right of the group. *"Oui, celui-là."*

Keel felt a chill move across the back of his neck. "Where was this?"

Hassan looked to his cousin and when Mo nodded encouragingly said, "Um Dukhun."

At least that's what it sounded like to Keel's ears. Or it could just have been Hassan clearing his throat. Keel look at Mo for an interpretation.

Mo nodded. "Um Dukhun. It is a town across the border."

"Sudan," Deschamps said flatly.

"Yes, boss." Mo said.

"When?" Keel asked.

Mo frowned. "When?"

"When was this? When did he see this man?"

"One week ago."

Keel felt the fluttering of excitement in his chest.

Hassan, according to Mo, had been travelling through the Western Darfur provinces, among some of the more remote villages and thus had no knowledge of the attack in the reserve. It was only after he'd returned to the border that he learned of the killings. When he'd arrived home and been shown copies of the circulated photographs, a face in one of the images rang a distant bell. Mo's time off duty had coincided with Hassan's return and when Hassan had shared his suspicions, Mo had persuaded his cousin to deliver the information in person.

Keel turned to the wall behind Deschamps' desk. Taking up a large proportion of space alongside a map of the reserve was a second map depicting Chad's south-eastern region, encompassing the provinces of Quadaï and Salamat, in which Salma was located. A

114

dotted line at the bottom of the map represented the Chad/CAR border which followed a diagonal path from the south-west to the north-east to the point where it intersected the north-south line separating Chad and a section of Central Darfur.

"Show us," Keel said.

Hassan moved to the wall. He stared at the map for what seemed an inordinately long time, his forefinger tracing the path of his inspection. Keel suspected it might be a fruitless excercise. Mo's cousin would know the borderlands like the back of his hand, no doubt having criss-crossed them hundreds of times, and would have no need for maps, in the same way that migrating swallows navigated their way from Finland to the African veldt and back without getting lost because the route had been implanted in their brains as it had been implanted in the brains of their ancestors over countless millenia. But then, Hassan's finger steadied and hovered above the Chad/Darfur border, and there less than half an inch on the Sudan side of the line was the name: Um Dukhun.

Keel returned to the desk and picked up the photo. "What can you tell me about this man? Do you know his name?"

Hassan hesitated before shaking his head to indicate he didn't know for certain. He looked to his cousin.

"He thinks it might be Faheem," Mo said.

Deschamps let go a derisive grunt.

Keel had recognized the word, too and understood the reason for Deschamps' response. In Arabic, Faheem translated as either 'wise' or 'judicious'.

Keel turned back. "Does he live in Um Dukhun?"

As before, Hassan pondered the question before

115

stating that he didn't know.

"Hassan remembers seeing this man in a coffee house," Mo interjected. "It is possible he is injured."

"Injured how?" Keel said.

Another muttered exchange took place. Clearly Mo's cousin preferred to place his trust in his blood kin to relay the information rather than in his own ability to communicate with what he probably perceived to be a couple of strangers demanding information he wasn't privy to.

Mo turned. "He walks with a stick."

Keel's mind went back to Sekka's account of the ambush. Maybe a ranger's bullet had found another mark as well as the horse, though it was just as likely that this Faheem character had twisted his ankle getting out of bed. "What makes him certain this is the man he saw?"

After another consultation with his cousin, Mo said, "Hassan visits many villages, many towns. It is important that he remembers names and faces. He remembers this man because there was a disagreement with the waiter about payment for the coffee. The owner of the coffee house was called. Hassan was close by when it happened."

Keel turned to Deschamps and indicated the office pc. "We still have Google Earth on that thing. yes?"

Deschamps frowned. "We do."

Keel moved to the desk. Taking up the mouse, he scrolled down to the taskbar and clicked on the tiny blue and white ball.

Mobile coverage in the country might have been sporadic but Salma had internet access thanks to AP funding and Belgium's GlobalTT's VSat satellite service, which provided a conduit to the web via the

116

company's private teleport. It had continued to provide access during the internet block imposed by the Chadian government in the aftermath of the reforms made to the country's constitution by which President Idriss Déby had been given authority to extend his tenure for another decade and a half. Fearing a backlash on social media, access to internet services had been curtailed for close on a year. As a result, for those who could afford it, satellite and VPN subscriptions had become the order of the day. Judiciously, Salma had made use of both. The downside was that even then connection speed wasn't always reliable, particularly during the wet season, as weather could still affect the signal.

Luck, though, was with them. Keel brought up the Google Earth home page, typed Um Dukhun in the search box, and, after several seconds, struck paydirt. As the world revolved, Africa and then Sudan took form until the red pin was hovering above the name. Strategically positioned, the town's hub, if it could be called that, matched its location on the wall map, a smidgin to the right of the yellow line depicting the Chad/Sudan border.

Keel zoomed in closer. The town covered a surprisingly wide area and was clearly the biggest population centre in the region and did appear, on closer inspection, to actually straddle the border. It was split into two main districts separated by what looked like fields under cultivation. The eastern half formed a crescent that hugged the base of large escarpment, the outline of which resembled a fat toad, its back legs splayed. The eastern side of the outcrop was taken up with more cultivation. There were no tarmac roads in sight, just dusty tracks that didn't look wide enough to be called streets, set out in a rough grid formation, until they reached the town's outer limits where they lost all cohesion and expanded into a web of interconnecting trails that wove their way to and fro across the landscape with reckless abandon.

There being no ability to drag the little orange pedestrian down to street level, Keel could only hover above the town to assess its relationship to the land in which it was situated and where there appeared to be no discernable tree coverage and very little vegetation, which made it typical of every other isolated town: a long way from the capital, underfunded by an impoverished government and with no notable infrastructure. It could just as easily have been any run-down, rural township in Chad, the CAR or any one of the other countries that made up the Central African belt of nations.

Keel switched from satellite to the map view and was instantly rewarded with the same image save for a small blue ball containing the outline of a crescent moon and star. Next to it the description: *Um Dukhun Mosque*. No other buildings were highlighted.

Keel switched back to the satellite view and drew Hassan's attention to the screen. "You know this town well?"

It took a few seconds for Mo's cousin to get his bearings before he nodded. *"Na'am."* A pause, then, in French: "Yes."

"It is where he crosses the border to do his trading," Mo explained.

Keel zoomed out, reducing the town's outline until it merged into the terrain, which from the higher elevation showed only more dry scrubland, low hills and winding river beds. "What do we have on this

118

place? Anything?"

Deschamps placed a hand on Keel's shoulder. "We can try ReliefWeb."

"Which is what?" Keel said.

"It comes under OCHA, the Office for the Coordination of Humanitarian Affairs. It's an on-line source for information on global crises. It operates 24/7 and is very reliable. Aid organizations use its resources in order to make decisions and plan their response. I was on attachment with OCHA when I was with the Legion, helping to escort relief supplies into the DRC. The site carries information on disaster areas, which include the Darfur provinces. It's possible there's information on Um Dukhun."

"Go for it," Keel said, conceding the chair.

It took Deschamps a couple of clicks to bring up the ReliefWeb site. Searching for specific information took a while longer, until, eventually, he found the link to a map of Central Darfur showing the location of UN IDP camps. Um Dukhun was highlighted as a centre where humanitarian resources had been made available in the form of emergency shelters, food and health services, notably: water, sanitation and hygiene.

"Looks like the place has seen a lot of refugee movement," Deschamps said.

Mo, who'd been watching Deschamps' study of the screen, nodded. "You are right, boss. It is a small town when compared to Nyala and the other capitals but there are now many people there because of the wars. They still travel to the camps for help."

Keel stared at the screen. As if it had been pre-ordained, Sekka chose that exact moment to enter the room. Like Keel, he was in full ranger uniform.

Keel looked up. "How the hell do you *do* that?"

Sekka looked nonplussed. "Do what?"

Keel shook his head. "Never mind. While you've been off playing tag, we've been slaving over a hot computer."

"Doing what?"

"Hunting down a lead. Joseph, meet Hassan. He's Mo's cousin and he came bearing gifts."

Sekka and Hassan shook hands. Sekka said, "Gifts?"

"Name and possible location of one of our gunmen."

Sekka's head came up quickly. "Who and where?"

"We think his name's Faheem. Last seen by Hassan a week ago; in a coffee house, place called Um Dukhun."

Sekka's gaze flicked towards the pc.

"Sudan," Keel said. "Bang on the border."

"Is he still there?"

"We don't know. Hassan said he was nursing a gammy leg, so he might not be too mobile. It's been seven days, mind, so he could have made a miraculous recovery and hightailed it."

Sekka studied the screen without speaking.

Keel turned to Deschamps. "Seems to me we've a decision to make."

Deschamps remained still for several seconds, then pushed his chair away from the desk and stood. "Mo, would you and Hassan be kind enough to step out of the office for a moment?"

Mo hesitated, then said, "Sure, boss. No problem." He tugged at his cousin's sleeve and the two men left the room.

"Thank you," Deschamps said as he closed the door after them. He turned to Keel. "You're asking what do we do with the information?"

"I am. Way I look at it, we have two choices. We

120

pass the info to the Chad authorities or we go and get the guy ourselves. Either way, the quicker we move the better."

"The prudent way would be to let the authorities know."

"Doesn't mean it's the right way," Keel said. "Given all we know and what they've told us, if you trust the Chadian police to do the right thing then we'll give them the heads up and pass the buck. But do we really believe they'll cooperate with the Sudanese to have the guy arrested? Don't know about you, but I'm not sure Mahamat and the new Sovereign Council in Khartoum, or whatever the hell they're calling themselves these days, see eye to eye. I'd also say the Sudanese have bigger fish to fry, given the way things are going over there; keeping the population in check for one thing. Also, you told us the real power in the country lies with Hemeti. Can't see the head of the RSF handing over one of his own men. Can *you*?"

"You're suggesting we extract him ourselves?"

"I've more faith in *our* abilities than in the Chad police."

"It's not as though we haven't carried out that kind of job before," Sekka said.

"As I recall," Deschamps said, "Your last extraction attempt resulted in Thomas getting shot and a price being put on your heads."

"Oh, come on," Keel said. "Now you're just being picky."

Deschamps gnawed pensively at the inside of his cheek.

"Clock's ticking, René," Sekka murmured.

Deschamps sighed. "All, right, say I go along with your proposal. Do you actually have a plan?"

121

"Been thinking about that," Keel said. "It'll depend on our friend, Hassan."

"Hassan?" Deschamps said dubiously.

"I'm assuming he'll be heading back over the border to resume his trading. I was thinking he could give one of us a lift."

"By one of us, he means me," Sekka said. "Right? Unless you want to draw straws."

"Won't make any difference," Keel said. "We went for rock, paper, scissors it'd still have to be you."

"On account of my dusky hue?"

"Pretty much. Don't worry, I'll go next time."

Sekka feigned a weary sigh. "That's what you said the last time, which makes this the next time, and it's still me."

Keel grinned.

"So Joseph locates Faheem," Deschamps cut in. "Then what?"

"I drag him back here," Sekka said.

"*Drag*?" Descamps said warily.

"All right," Sekka said. "I'll ask him to accompany me."

" And if he doesn't want to come?"

"That will be where the dragging comes in."

While Deschamps wrestled with that scenario, Keel said, "We can have Crow waiting at the border with the chopper. Soon as Joseph and Faheem are across he can fly them back here."

"And we hand Faheem over to the police?"

"After we've asked him a few questions and got the info we want, sure."

"And what information would that be, exactly?"

"The location of his three pals plus the name of the person who gave them their orders."

122

"You don't believe they were acting on their own?" Deschamps said.

"Not with the equipment they had with them. They were funded by someone further up the chain: the ones who took delivery of the ivory."

"And if he gives us that information?" Deschamps said.

"*Then* we hand him over the Chadians. But we can cross that bridge when we come to it."

"We seem to be negotiating a lot of bridges," Deschamps said heavily.

"And this is number one. What's it to be?"

Deschamps took a deep breath and let it out slowly. He faced Sekka. "You understand, the moment you step over that border we're committed. Not just you; all of us, and by us I mean every member of Salma's staff. If you're picked up and detained on the other side, the repercussions will be catastrophic. African Parks cannot be seen to condone your actions, *our* actions. They will cease their support and access to funding. Are you willing to risk Salma's entire future?"

"They killed five of our men," Sekka said. "We let them get away with this and they'll be back, and in greater numbers. More elephants will be slaughtered and more rangers will die trying to protect them. We just sit on our hands and *that's* Salma's future."

"We're not new to this, René," Keel said. "It's what we do."

Deschamps turned. His eyes were focussed not on the computer screen but on the photograph of his daughter and her family. He took another deep breath, held it, and then said to Keel, "Your old regimental motto was 'Who Dares Wins', yes? With the Legion it was 'Honour and Fidelity'. It's something I've always

123

tried to live up to." Pivoting, he walked across the room and opened the door. "My apologies, Mo; please come in."

When Mo and his cousin re-entered, Deschamps turned to Keel. "You have the floor, Major."

Keel addressed the trader: "Hassan, you'll be returning to the Sudan, yes?"

Hassan nodded. "But of course." He looked vaguely surprised by the question.

"Do you know when?"

Hassan looked first to his cousin and then back at Keel. "I go tomorrow."

Keel saw no reason to beat about the bush. "Can you take Joseph with you?"

Hassan blinked. "To Sudan?"

"To Um Dukhun."

Hassan did not reply, but ran a hand thoughtfully across his beard.

Mo turned to Sekka. There was understanding in his gaze. "You go to look for this man, this Faheem?"

"If Hassan will take me, yes."

A shrewd look materialized on the ranger's face. "And if you find him?"

"I'll ask him to to return here with me," Sekka said.

"To Salma?" Mo said, as if he hadn't quite heard correctly.

"We want to ask him some questions, about the men he was working with."

"Why would he agree to that?" the ranger asked doubtfully.

"I'll advise him him it would be in his best interest to do so."

Mo frowned. "And if he says no?"

"Then I'll persuade him," Sekka said, throwing

Deschamps a sideways glance.

"How will you do that?" Mo looked mystified.

"Better you don't ask," Sekka said.

Mo's eyebrows rose. Hassan, who'd been following the exchange let out a low hiss. Even Deschamps looked discomforted. Then, Mo, his face solemn, nodded. "I think this is a very good plan."

He fixed his cousin with what appeared to be an even gaze, though the meaning could not have been made clearer. It took all of two seconds before Hassan inclined his head.

"It is agreed," Mo said. "Hassan will take you to Sudan."

8

"You're sure about this?" René Deschamps asked.

He and Keel were alone in the office, Mo and Hassan having departed to wait for Sekka, who'd gone to collect his go-bag.

"It's down to us, René. Not Déby's lot; not the Sudanese; us."

"You're happy sending Joseph in alone?"

"I'm not *sending* him anywhere. He's going of his own accord."

"Do not play semantics with me, Thomas," Deschamps said curtly. "You know full well what I mean."

"I do," Keel conceded, "but it'd take a braver man than me to try and talk him out of it. You saw that look in his eye."

"I did, and it's one I've seen many times before, when he was in the Legion. It's what made - *makes* - him a good soldier. It's why you and he are here, training my rangers. But this is different. He'll be entering hostile territory, by himself, to look for a murderer."

"He knows what he's doing. He'll have Hassan to guide him."

"Who is now a co-conspirator, as is Mo. We are skating on very thin ice, my friend."

"Something tells me we won't have to worry about either of them. You saw Hassan's reaction to the reward money. He turned us down flat. Way I see it, he and Mo consider it's their civic duty to help out."

"A matter of honour."

"In their eyes," Keel said.

Deschamps smiled laconically. "Blame it on Dumas."

"Dumas?" For a second, Keel had no idea what Deschamps was talking about and then it came to him. "You mean all for one and one for all? Sounds like one of Crow's family mottos."

Deschamps nodded. "A man with a great deal to answer for."

"Crow?"

"Dumas."

It was Keel's turn to smile. "You, me, Joseph and Crow; the only things missing are our rapiers and feathered hats."

"Ah," Deschamps said, "but *we* have satellite phones."

"Heavy ordnance wouldn't come amiss."

"Joseph is not going in armed," Deschamps said sharply.

Keel shook his head. "Hell, no. The Sudanese catch him crossing their border tooled up to the nines and African Parks pulling the plug'll be the least of our worries. He'll go in light, grab the guy and get out."

"*Grab*? You think it will be that easy? Have you consulted Crow?"

"I'm about to. Remind me again, when does Sabine return from her conference?"

"Not for another three days. She's fitting in a side trip to stay with a veterinary colleague working for Dubai's Desert Conservation Reserve before she heads home."

"In that case, we've a bit of leeway. It frees up Crow until she's gets back."

Deschamps nodded. "You said you had yet to consult Crow. Is he with us?" There was more than note of doubt in Deschamps' voice.

"Are you kidding? It'll be like old times."

Deschamps regarded Keel with his head canted, not sure if Keel was being serious. "One day we must all sit down and the three of you can tell me about your adventures together."

"Says the man who ran away to join the French Foreign Legion."

Deschamps stiffened. His chin rose. "I'll have you know I did not run. I walked in a determined fashion."

"Which'll be how Joseph vacates Sudan...fingers crossed."

"From your lips to God's ear. Another of your sayings, yes?"

"My favourite." Keel turned for the door. "I'll go brief the birdman."

"Seriously?" Crow stared back at him. "*That's* your plan?"

"I'm working on short notice," Keel responded.

"Jesus," Crow said, "you ain't kidding.

"No, but are you up for it?"

Crow threw Keel a dry look. "I'll say it again: seriously?"

"Just checking," Keel said. "For all I know you might have lost your edge."

"Hell, we do this, the problem won't be my lack of edge, it'll be my lack of sanity. If there's a more harebrained scheme out there, I'd like to hear it."

"Never stopped us before," Keel said.

"Yeah, well that was when we were young and foolish and before you went grey round the edges." Crow gave a lop-sided grin, then his face turned serious. "You realize the potential for this to go seriously pear-shaped is pretty bloody high, right?"

"Sure, but what's the worst that could happen?"

"Some of us could *die*?"

"Hell of a way to go, though."

A silence fell between them, broken when Keel said,. "Out of interest..."

Crow looked at him. "Uh, oh, here it comes."

"Let's say we need to edge slightly over the borderline..."

"Slightly?" Crow said.

"Wouldn't be hard to do, given the terrain. Anyone can make a mistake, right?"

"You say so."

"They likely to spot us?"

"We talking about the Sudanese?"

"Yes."

"Not at the height we'd be going in. Folks on the ground'll probably hear us but by the time they look up, we'll be a smudge in their rear view mirror.

"No eyes in the sky?"

"You mean satellite surveillance?"

"Daft question?"

"Not at all. They bought their first system a year or so back. Chinese made. No idea if it's any good, mind."

"Could be we'll get to find out. What about actual birds in the air? Anything?

"Depends."

Keel looked at him. "On what?"

"Their main bases are Khartoum and Omdurman. If they do get an alert and they've nothing airborne, by the time they scramble we'll be long gone. If they've got something closer, say patrolling out of El Geneima, then we may have a problem, but that's still a hundred and sixty odd miles away, so unless they have something cruising directly overhead we should make it back in one piece."

"*Should?*"

Crow shrugged.

"How many aircraft *do* they have?"

"Enough, but I heard they're not all fully functional and spares are hard to come by, so they're not operating at full strength. If we're talking numbers we're probably looking at Chinese-made A-5s and F-7s, but their main combat aircraft are MiG-29s and SU-35s."

"Russian."

"Yep, same as their attack helicopters, the Mi-24s. Hinds; flying tanks. Now, they do scare the shit out of me. Been up against them before. It didn't end well."

Keel raised a questioning eyebrow.

"Blew my bird to bits. Bastards."

"Right, I remember. Not that you hold a grudge, though."

"Well, not *every* day."

Crow's attention moved away, then, to a spot behind Keel's right shoulder. Keel turned and saw Sekka with a bag slung over his arm.

"And you agreed to this?" Crow said to Sekka as he drew near.

"You're on board, then," Sekka said drily.

"Oh, absolutely, Wouldn't miss it."

"Now you're just being sarcastic," Sekka said.

131

"Well, no shit, Sherlock." Crow looked towards Keel. "So what's the time frame?"

"Hassan tells me he'll be leaving for Sudan at first light. All being well, that'll see them in Um Dukhun by the afternoon. From there on in, it'll be up to Joseph."

"So we're playing it by ear."

"Pretty much."

"Wonderful. And *you'll* radio us if and when you find the guy?"

Sekka nodded.

"And what? *We* head for the border, find somewhere to park and you tell us when you'll be bringing his nibs across?"

"That's the plan," Keel said. "Any idea of flight time?"

Crow thought about it. "To the border? Top of my head, sixty minutes, give or take. We go in NOE it'll likely be a wee bit longer, but not by much."

NOE was the acronym for nap-of-the-earth. It meant going in at a very low altitude, following ground contours in order to avoid detection, in what was referred to in military parlance as a high threat environment, which was a polite way of saying people would be trying their hardest to kill you. It was a while since Crow had employed the tactic in a war zone, but as a former crop duster, military flier, and now a bush pilot who tracked assorted wildlife at tree-top level for a living, it could be said that it remained an integral part of his skill set. Had he been asked, Crow would have said it was like riding a bike: once mastered, never forgotten. On this occasion, though, no one asked. They knew Crow. They'd flown with him before so they didn't have to.

"So it's doable."

"Well, yeah, but..."

There was a pause. Keel said. "But?"

"I know I'm going to regret asking this," Crow said, "*but* given this is all a bit iffy, *is* there a Plan B? And don't say we're gonna cross *that* bridge when we come to it. You do and I'm going to launch my boot towards your gonads."

"Call it a work in progress."

"Wonderful," Crow said. "And has René given it his blessing?"

"Not exactly."

"Better to beg forgiveness than ask permission, right?"

"Right, and if you tell me that's another one of your family mottos, it'll be *my* boot heading for *your* family jewels."

Crow showed his palms in mock surrender and then looked up as a battered-looking, four-door Nissan pick-up appeared round the corner of the headquarters building, Hassan at the wheel, Mo seated in the front passenger seat. It was hard to tell the colour of the paintwork as most of the vehicle was covered with dried mud. "Ah, well, too late to back out now. Got everything? Sat phone? Toothbrush? Clean jocks?"

Sekka shook his head wearily. "I'll stay in touch."

"You'd better," Keel said. He and Crow watched as Sekka opened the rear door, tossed his bag in front of him and climbed into the truck. No one on board waved as the vehicle moved off.

"Well, I wouldn't worry about Plan A *or* B," Crow said.

Keel turned. "How's that?"

Crow jutted his chin towards the departing vehicle.

133

"State of that thing, they make it as far as the park gates, it'll be a bloody miracle."

The journey to Mo's home village took a little over two hours. There were no breakdowns, which would have amazed Crow, though, it did strike Sekka that any vehicle other than a 4x4, or possibly a light tank, would probably have run into severe difficulties negotiating the winding, uneven dirt tracks that for long stretches appeared to consist mainly of potholes and ruts, many of which were already brimming with rain water from the intermittent showers that spoke of worse conditions to come. He'd tried not to think what the going would be like when the rainy season arrived in full force.

As if the state of the track wasn't bad enough, with Hassan preferring to drive with the windows down, the mud and dust kicked up by the front tyres when the vehicle approached anything close to a decent speed had only added to the discomfort. By the time their destination hove into view, Sekka would have paid good money for the services of a chiropractor and a tube of throat lozenges.

Ma'mun turned out to be a larger settlement than Sekka had anticipated, suggesting that it was a permanent fixture rather than a transient encampment dependent either on seasonal weather fluctuations or livestock grazing requirements, though, more often than not, that amounted to the same thing.

The architecture was a mix of grass rondavels and clay-built huts, with several of the latter supporting roofs made from corrugated tin instead of the usual thatch. Sekka presumed they were either communal store houses or the dwellings of families with a degree of affluence and he was instantly reminded of his father's boyhood home in Bekura, a dot on the map fifty miles east of Zaria, the capital of Kaduna, one of the Hausa city states in Northern Nigeria. Sekka's father had been the first of his family to leave his village to attend university, eventually qualifying as a medical doctor. He'd never forgotten his roots, however, and had often travelled back to visit his family home with his young wife and son in tow.

Mo's salary as a ranger, while not generous by any means, was evidently sufficient to have provided him with one of the clay-built houses, though it was clear that extra walls were still being added as and when funding became available. With four people residing permanently under its tin roof and with Sekka's temporary presence - Hassan having made his own accommodation arrangements - there wasn't a great deal of space.

A curtain strung across the centre of the room provided Mo's sisters and mother with a degree of privacy, but as a legionnaire and as a tracker hunting insurgents through the Nigerian hinterland and the DRC, Sekka had bedded down in less comfortable surroundings.

Awakened by cock crow, to the familiar smell of breakfast fires mixed with the sweet-sour odour of human waste and animal manure wafting in from the nearby fields, Sekka joined the family as they prepared for the day. The first priority was to oversee Mo's sisters as they readied themselves for the two-mile walk to the next village where there was a small school room serving children from the surrounding settlements.

Their departure reawakened more of Sekka's childhood memories. His father had attended a similar place of learning but it wasn't until Sekka had been shown his father's old wooden desk on one of his visits home that he'd begun to understand the obstacles faced by his grandparents in their determination to see *their* only male child achieve the education they never had for themselves.

Sekka's father had demanded the same level of dedication from his own son, and Sekka, not wishing to let his father down, had applied himself to the task with steely determination. A fast learner and diligent to a fault, Sekka had been a keen student, and on leaving school had been awarded a grant to attend a British university. A law degree had been the result, but a career at the bar had been cut short with the death of his father, who'd been murdered by rebels; a life-altering event that had resulted in Sekka taking up arms and pursuing those responsible. It was during those years that he'd met Keel, then employed as a military contractor engaged in seek and destroy missions for the government forces, and a friendship was born.

It was as Mo was waving the girls off that the ranger turned to Sekka and, without warning, said, "If you do not allow me to go with you then Hassan will not take you to Um Dukhun."

There was a pause as Sekka considered his reply. "That wasn't the agreement."

"There was no agreement between you and me," Mo countered amiably. "The agreement was between you and Hassan."

Which was technically true, Sekka thought, but that didn't mean he was prepared to give way. Neither, it seemed was Mo, who, in a measured tone, said, "I am sorry, boss, but I do not think your Arabic is good enough."

Sekka opened his mouth to reply and then thought better of it, knowing Mo's point had him on the ropes. It wasn't that his Arabic was deficient, his time in the Legion having provided him with a good grounding, which meant he could hold up his end of a conversation; but he was still a fair way from being fluent. Chadian Arabic was spoken throughout most of the Darfur region but there were still as many variations as there were winged insects and there were an awful lot of those.

A common root ran through all of them but that didn't mean there weren't anomalies. So while the colour of Sekka's skin would aid his passage across the border, if anything were to hamper his mission it was going to be his means of communicating with the locals, and given that he was heading into what was, effectively, bandit country, he was savvy enough to know he was going to need all the help he could get, and at least Mo was volunteering; he wasn't being coerced.

"Also," Mo added doggedly, "are not another set of eyes helpful when you are looking for a man who does not want to be found?"

Another valid point, Sekka was forced to admit, albeit silently. Mo, he saw, was regarding him with a fresh intent; a gun dog waiting to be loosed after a downed partridge. The seconds ticked by.

"All right," Sekka said eventually, knowing that he had no real choice in the matter. "Where I go, you go;

137

but you follow orders, understood?"

The ranger nodded sagely before showing his teeth in what could only be described as a cheery grin. "I will not let you down."

"I know," Sekka said.

The reply had been automatic, but in voicing it, like a film playing in his head, he was transported back to the ambush and a vision of Isadore rose into view. The look of determination on the ranger's face when he'd told Sekka he would try to get hold of the radio in the back of the Land Cruiser was as clear to Sekka as if Isadore was standing before him at that moment.

There must have been something in his tone, he realized, or maybe a show in the eyes because, as if he'd picked up on Sekka's thoughts, Mo frowned and said, "Then we will leave as soon as Hassan is ready. It will not be long."

The ranger cast a discerning eye over Sekka's wardrobe. Sekka had forsaken his shirt and slacks for a white-and-grey-striped jalabiya and white keffiyeh scarf which was wound about his head, turban-style, leaving his face free. The scarf concealed the bullet scar, which had scabbed over and was healing well. Sekka had decided to hold off shaving and the stubble coating his jawline, while only a couple of days old and therefore still short, nevertheless, would allow him to blend in anonymously with the rest of the male population. He waited as Mo, who'd elected to wear similar traditional garments, nodded his approval.

A coarse engine note sounded.

"Hassan," Mo said, unnecessarily, as the trader's vehicle bounced into sight, still caked in mud and dust.

"We go now," Hassan announced from the open window, as the truck drew to a halt.

Sekka accompanied Mo back into the hut to retrieve their packs and for the ranger to bid goodbye to his mother. When Mo stepped out of her embrace she took Sekka by the hand. The gesture was made in silence but Sekka could read the message in her eyes just as he felt the pressure in her grip.

I have lost one man. I do not want to lose another.

In families such as Mo's, the man was the traditional breadwinner, the decision maker; the females were the house makers and the child bearers. The women were also the ones who grew the crops and performed the domestic chores, while the men socialised and looked after the family's animals. In the aftermath of conflict, however, many of the women had been left widowed and their roles had been broadened, leaving them to take on the tasks traditionally associated with men. With no income of her own, if anything happened to Mo, she would be left with two young children to feed. Her concern for his welfare was, therefore, well-founded.

Sekka indicated that he understood, wondering if she'd overheard the conversation he'd had with her son. Then, turning abruptly, he hoisted his own bag and followed Mo out of the hut.

Two minutes later, they were on the road, though 'road' was still something of a misnomer due to tarmac surfaces being non-existent anywhere in south-eastern Chad.

Also, counter-intuitively, they were heading north. As Mo explained, there were no viable roads of any kind leading directly east to the border, at least none that were able to support sustained and heavy

139

motorized traffic. Any that did exist mirrored the ones they'd already driven along; being little more than rough herders' trails, dry and dust blown in summer and water-logged during the wet season. It was better, therefore, to stick to the more established routes in case of breakdown, and, to a lesser extent, ambush, even if a substantial detour was involved.

The past two decades had seen the region torn apart by military and civil conflict. Tribal resentment still festered. Communities devastated by the fighting continued to suffer, and along the length of the border the majority of people were just trying to survive, which left individuals with larcenous intent free to seek out the weakest and exploit their vulnerability with ease, usually through the barrel of a gun. Armed raiders operated on both sides of the divide and, as Sekka had discovered for himself, they were not averse to committing robbery and murder if an easy target presented itself. So sensible travellers stuck to the main routes, where there tended to be safety in numbers.

It wasn't until they reached the settlement of Dourdoura that they were finally able to turn on to an eastbound trail, but before long they were forced to change direction once more, again on a northern trajectory. It was on this heading as they drew closer to a small town referred to by Hassan as Sakalmoudjou that Sekka began to notice the increasing numbers of battered, ten-wheeler buses with faded blue and white UNHCR banners attached to their bonnets. While some travelled in tandem, others had formed convoys of four to six vehicles, trailing plumes of dust and diesel fumes behind them.

"Refugees from Sudan," Mo explained. "They are

140

being taken back to their homeland."

Hassan pulled out to overtake three of the vehicles travelling in close formation and Sekka braced himself as the Nissan slewed along the edge of the track with inches to spare. Glancing up at the bus windows as they scraped past he saw that most had their curtains drawn. Occasionally, a face would peer out, which made Sekka wonder about the mood of the people behind the glass. Were they happy to be going home or were they apprehensive about what they'd find when they got there?

Many would have been in the UN refugee centres for years; survivors of families torn apart by successive uprisings. It was more than likely that those most in need of assistance - the elderly and the infirm - had probably died on a grimy mattress in some anonymous aid tent and children would have been born not knowing they were exiles from their own country. With the whole of Sudan in limbo following years of conflict and Bashir's removal, and with memories of the Darfur atrocities still fresh in the mind and a civil war still raging in the south, what future did any of them have to look forward to?

During the drive, signposts were in short supply so both Sekka and Mo were reliant on Hassan to keep them updated as to their progress, though the names when disclosed - Gabassour, Birkéli, Koukou - meant little, as did the view from the truck, due to every place they drove past looking not unlike every other patch of human habitation that had slid by before it.

Until Hassan jutted his chin towards a far-off cluster of low, thatched roof tops that materialized out of the landscape ahead of them and Mo, after a consultation with his cousin, announced that they were closing in on the border.

"Next stop Nzili, boss, and then Um Dukhun."

Which explained why the track had become so busy, Sekka reasoned, the number of pedestrians and every mode of transport from trucks and buses to mopeds and donkey carts having increased during the past few miles. They'd passed one extended family group, grandparents through to toddlers, seated not on donkeys or mules but on horned cattle, their belongings piled high around them, while a small goat herd trotted alongside, neck bells tinkling like Christmas ornaments.

Two miles beyond Nzili a rusting metal sign appeared at the side of the track bearing a scrawled Arabic inscription and the French translation: *Poste Frontalier*, at which point Hassan turned off on to an even narrower trail that seemed to lead nowhere except across open scrubland. Sekka was about to query their objective when the track entered a low-sided wadi. After following the course of the dry river bed for several minutes, they emerged on to yet another narrow track and Sekka saw they were approaching the outskirts of fair-sized town, bigger than anything they'd encountered before.

"Um Dukhun," Hassan said.

Sekka stared off through the windscreen. "No border post?"

Hassan waved a hand airily.

So much for passport requirements. Sekka looked to Mo.

The ranger shrugged. "Too many roads in and out, boss. Not enough soldiers to guard them."

If there was trouble in Darfur, Mo revealed, people crossed the border into Chad. If there was fighting in

142

Chad, people escaped the other way. The town's population had settled at around thirty thousand, but there were more than double that number of refugees residing in and around the displacement camps, having made the journey to Um Dukhun because they viewed it as a safe haven. As a result, the number of routes in and out of the region had multiplied almost beyond counting.

Mo's face softened. "There has been a lot of fighting, boss, on both sides of the border."

Um Dukhun itself wasn't immune to the violence. The main culprits, Hassan explained, were members of the Misseriya and the Salamat tribes. Pitched battles had even taken place in the middle of the town, with a high number of people killed and wounded, leaving the streets littered with bodies. Shops had been plundered, with some places set alight. Calm had been restored eventually but it remained an uneasy truce and there was no telling if or, perhaps more precisely, when the violence would erupt again. In the meantime, the citizens had been left to get on with their lives as best they could while the authorities did their best to keep the peace, which meant that border restrictions were periodically eased to allow ease of access in both directions, with the main surveillance being centred on the passenger lists and contents of the larger commercial vehicles passing back and forth between the two countries.

"And that works?" Sekka asked, knowing as he asked the question that if security was half as lax along the rest of the border as it appeared to be in this town, then it was small wonder the poaching gang had been able to wreak havoc in the park and cross back into Darfur without being detected. "What about the

143

Border Force?"

In answer, Hassan rubbed the ends of his forefinger and thumb together in the universal sign for graft and gave a vulpine grin. "*Rashua...baksheesh*."

Which didn't mean there weren't still occasional clampdowns on cross-border traffic, but at the moment things were relatively quiet. Which made Sekka wonder why they were using what was, effectively, the tradesmen's entrance and if his driver had his own reasons for by-passing the town's primary access points.

Hassan's turn-off took them around the town's northern boundary. On all sides, it was the usual crop of grass huts and clay-brick houses, all enclosed within small compounds, protected by shoulder-high grass fences, laid out in a tidy grid pattern. Along the skyline, beyond the houses, a range of low, green-clad hills dotted with trees rose unevenly into the distance.

The number of people on the streets increased the further into the town they drove. Sekka saw the reason why when the alley they were on suddenly opened out and he saw the silhouette of the mosque over to his left and from his memory of the Google Earth image, he realized they'd arrived at the town's market place, which was heaving.

The stalls were packed too closely together and there were too many people present to allow vehicles to enter safely but as they drove past, it wasn't hard to see that this was Um Dukhun's main hub and that the rest of the town radiated outwards from it.

Two streets further on, Hassan finally made the turn and drove the Nissan up to a row of lock-up garages, though it occurred to Sekka as they exited the vehicle that they might also be shuttered shop fronts.

Approaching one of the doors, Hassan undid a large padlock and rolled the shutter up into the garage roof. Driving the truck into the building, he gestured for his passengers to follow and when they were inside, brought the shutter down behind them. A second later, a trio of fluorescent strips flickered on and in their feeble glow Sekka found himself not in a garage, or a shop, but a mini warehouse.

It was immediately apparent that several of the garages had been knocked into one, creating an interior space at least four times the width of the entry door and with a depth twice the length of the truck. Any space that wasn't occupied by the Nissan and its three passengers was taken up by a bewildering array of goods, either stacked on shelves or along the walls. Bales of cloth vied for room with assorted hardware, ranging from car batteries to transistor radios and mobile phones; all heaped in with jumbo tins of cooking oil, sacks of rice and dried herbs, canned fruit and drinks, washing powders, childrens toys, native carvings, racks of assorted clothing, including what looked like army surplus wear...the list went on. Even Mo looked impressed, which made Sekka wonder just how much the ranger knew about the extent of his cousin's trading empire.

"Come," Hassan said as he led the way through the stock to a rear door. The three rooms that lay beyond were simply furnished with the bare necessities that enabled an occupier to sleep, cook, and wash. A second outer door led into a tiny enclosed courtyard containing a small wooden table and four plastic chairs shaded by a green sail-cloth awning, In one corner was an upright, rickety wooden structure which Sekka presumed was the privy. Behind the privy was a door which, from what Sekka could see, opened on to the lower slope of a scrub-covered hill. Late afternoon shadows were already lengthening and the yard was dappled in shadow.

Hassan spread his arms wide. "Welcome to Sudan."

Sekka stared down at the contents of the crate and spoke over his shoulder. "Did you know about this?"

Mo shook his head. "No, boss."

Sekka lifted out the assault rifle and ran his hands over the instantly familiar wooden grip and the banana-shaped magazine. The AK, although clearly not new, had been well maintained. Sekka dropped his eyes to the other four that occupied the crate. The smell of gun oil was heavy in the confined space.

"I have pistols, also!" Hassan said eagerly. "Brownings. Very good guns." He indicated a smaller crate. "I show you."

They were in the warehouse. Hassan had taken them to a section of shelving, cleared the floor around it and slid the unit away from the wall to reveal a shallow alcove. The removal of several large boxes of Daz soap powder had brought the crates to light.

The pistols were 13-shot Browning Hi-Powers or, to be more accurate, a variant thereof. Sekka lifted one out of the crate and flipped the gun over to reveal the *Newark-Ohio Tisas Turkey* engraved along the barrel, identifying the weapon's country of origin. Like the AKs, the hand guns weren't new but they looked well cared for. Nestling at the bottom of the crate were a dozen boxes of 9mm ammunition.

Sekka checked the pistol's clip which was empty and drew back the slide to make sure there was no round in the chamber. "Where did you get these?"

Hassan smiled and shrugged. "I buy, I sell."

Sekka released the slide and engaged the safety catch as Hassan launched into his explanation.

The weapons had been part of a consignment destined for the *Ḥarakat al-ʿAdl wal-musāwāh*, the Sudanese opposition group, known in the west as JEM – the Justice and Equality Movement; a faction of the Sudan Revolutionary Front. They'd been en route from Chad to Sudan, paid for by supporters of the late President Déby, who, as a member of the Zaghawa tribe, was of the same lineage as most of the JEM members, including its leader. Hassan had been one of a number of traders tasked to deliver the weapons. Never one to miss an opportunity, instead of negotiating a fee for his participation and possibly with a long-term strategy in mind, the wily middleman had accepted payment in kind.

Sekka wasn't entirely sure whether to believe Hassan's story. Considering the numerous conflicts that had blighted the region for decades, it was no surprise that caches of small arms turned up in unexpected places. There was always a profit to be made in times of war and as Hassan had been introduced as a man known to village elders both in Chad and Sudan, and given his occupation, it would have been more of a surprise if he *hadn't* been able to lay his hands on a stack of smuggled ordnance. The more likely scenario, Sekka decided, his suspicion swayed by the grin on Hassan's face, was that unbeknownst to the end user, Mo's cousin had simply siphoned off a proportion of the delivery for himself and blamed the discrepancy on a hitch in transit.

"Do you want rifle or pistol?" Hassan asked.

Sekka stared at him, realizing this was why Hassan had shown them the haul.

"In case there is trouble when we find Faheem," Hassan said.

Sekka was conscious of Mo's eyes upon him as he gazed down at the gun in his hand. The danger associated with carrying a weapon had been discussed at length back at Salma. Deschamps had laid out the reasons in no uncertain terms why it wasn't a good idea to travel armed. Top of the list had been the risk of discovery by a border patrol. Better to go in light rather than take a chance and possibly blow the mission before it had even started. God forbid that were to happen. They'd be dead in the water and four killers would be in the wind, with no chance of capture and interrogation..

"I'll take the pistol," Sekka said.

9

Sekka sipped coffee and watched the crowd.

He and Mo were parked in rickety plastic chairs outside a coffee house in a corner of the market place. It wasn't the most salubrious establishment Sekka had ever visited and wouldn't have given Starbucks any sleepless nights, but the coffee, made from fresh-roasted beans, crushed by hand in a pestle and mortar and then simmered in a clay container together with cinnamon and a dash of pepper, tasted like coffee was supposed to taste, despite the fact that it looked a lot like molten tar. The aromas rising from the hot plate behind the counter also helped to mask the more unsavoury odours wafting in off the street.

Mo refilled his cup from from the small clay pot sitting on the tin tray by his elbow. He did so using a high-sweeping motion of his pouring hand, an affectation which, traditionally, was supposed to enhance the bouquet, the sound of the pouring, and the froth.

"Now you're just showing off," Sekka said as Mo took a noisy sip of his coffee, taking the air into his mouth to help spread the scent and flavour across his palate.

Mo lowered his cup, grinned, and watched as Sekka, keeping the flamboyance to a minimum, topped up his own brew,

"Do you think Hassan will find Faheem?" Mo said, his boyish face turning serious. His voice was cautious and pitched low.

It was mid-morning and the outside tables were all taken. On a neighbouring one, two customers were engaged in a game of backgammon while the rest of the clientele were either chatting among themselves, perusing newspapers, or just watching the world go by.

A couple of men were conversing over shisha pipes. Sekka's attention had been drawn to them after Mo whispered that they were contravening the law, the Khartoum goverment having revoked the licenses of shisha cafes at the behest of radical preachers who viewed the practice not only as being detrimental to health but because it provided unmarried men and women an opportunity to mix.

It was possible, Sekka supposed, that the smokers were under the false impression that the law didn't apply to Um Dukhun as it was too far removed from the capital. Frontier town, frontier law, he mused and wondered briefly if this was a good spot to be in if any outraged mullahs decided to raid the place. Not that anyone appeared to be taking any interest in his and Mo's conversation.

"He'll have a better chance than you or me," Sekka said.

Which had been Hassan's main argument when he'd laid out his plan, which was to show the snapshot of Faheem to some of his trading contacts and to the staff and customers in the town's eateries, to see if the poacher's face rang any bells.

"They know me here," Hassan told Sekka. "They do

150

not know you. You ask: 'have you seen this man?' and they will think you are an informer for the police or the RSF. Much better if I ask the questions."

Sekka hadn't been able to fault Hassan's logic. The trader knew his way around the town and the guns concealed in the warehouse suggested he wasn't averse to mixing with characters who operated on the fringes of what probably passed for Um Dukhun's murky underworld.

Sekka, along with Keel, had worked enough contracts - military and civilian - over the years to know that every border town they'd ever visited was frequented by every type of disreputable individual known to man. It was a penny to a Sudanese pound that this place was no different. It was hard to believe that word of the Salma killings had not leaked out and, if the gang had crossed back into Sudan via Um Dukhun, as Faheem's presence would suggest, it was just possible someone on the street had information that would reveal his whereabouts and that of the other men they were seeking.

A few yards from Sekka's table, beneath the shade of a stumpy acacia tree, an elderly Sudanese gentleman sat at a wooden bench, hunched over an equally ancient Singer sewing machine, his sandaled feet pumping the pedal beneath the bench with all the dexterity of a base drummer in a rock band. Rolls of multi-coloured cloth littered the ground around him and he appeared oblivious to the surrounding melee and to the song blaring out from a nearby transistor radio; a folk tune from the sound of it, or maybe the Sudanese equivalent of a country and western lament. The singer's voice rose and fell in volume, as if the signal was being distorted due to atmospheric disturbance.

Across the market, the goods on display were as varied as the contents of Hassan's warehouse, with vendors operating from counters laid out beneath awnings as well as from rush mats and ground sheets strewn across the bare soil. A donkey cart creaked past, piled high with bright orange pumpkins. Dogs fought over scraps of offal tossed from a butcher's stall swarming with flies, while at an adjacent booth, men queued patiently for a haircut and a shave.

From what Sekka could make out, a fair amount of bargaining was taking place, and not just over the more expensive wares. With inflation gathering momentum, even staple items such as bread, flour and salt were becoming more costly by the day; a direct result of the endless civil wars that had played havoc with production and supply routes.

"Another, boss?" Mo asked, pointing to Sekka's empty cup.

Sekka shook his head. "I'm good."

Mo nodded but appeared on the verge of posing another question.

"What?" Sekka said, sensing the hesitation.

Mo said, cautiously, "You were with Boss René in the Legion, yes?"

"I was," Sekka said.

"Boss Thomas, too?"

"No."

"But you and he were soldiers together?"

"We were."

Mo nodded thoughtfully. "Boss Thomas was in the British Army?"

"Yes."

"He was a very good soldier, I think." Mo said.

"He still is," Sekka said, wondering where this was heading.

Mo nodded gravely.

Sekka made no attempt to expand on his statement. He did not consider it his role to provide the ranger with a comprehensive account of Keel's army career. It was up to Keel to release that information, if he so chose. Not that it would amount to much. That was the thing about soldiers either operating or who had operated under the Special Forces banner; they tended not to advertise the fact. Indeed, there were intriguing gaps in Keel's military record that were off limits even to Sekka.

Sekka knew Keel had begun his soldiering in the Paras before joining 22 SAS, at which point, up until the time Keel left the army to pursue greater rewards in the private sector, details were more than a trifle hazy. Over the years, Sekka had come to learn that part of Keel's service had involved attachment to E Squadron, the small cell of operatives assigned to carry out clandestine operations on behalf of Britain's Secret Intelligence Service, but as to when and where Keel had been deployed, Sekka was none the wiser, though Kosovo, Kuwait and Sierra Leone had cropped up in a number of their conversations over the years. All Sekka knew was that there was no one else he'd rather have guarding his back.

Sekka saw that Mo was still regarding him expectantly. "Something else?"

"Boss Crow?" Mo said.

"*Boss?*" Sekka resisted the urge to laugh. "You call *him* Boss?"

Mo smiled and shook his head. "He tells everyone to call him Crow. We do not know if he has a first name."

"Would it matter?" Sekka said.

Mo blinked.

"There you go, then," Sekka said.

"He is a good pilot?" Mo said after a pause.

"He's a very good pilot."

"The three of you have worked together before?"

"Off and on. Why all the questions, Mo?"

The ranger hesitated once more then said, "I am interested to know what sort of men you are."

Sekka put down his coffee cup and wondered why Mo had waited this long when he'd had the length of their journey to Um Dukhun in which to raise the subject.

Mo leaned forward. "You and Boss Thomas and Crow are not from my country, yet you want justice for Adoum and the others. You are willing to put yourselves at risk, for us."

Sekka was genuinely surprised by the question. "Why wouldn't we?"

"Because Boss René was told by the police not to go after the men we are looking for. You do not have to do this"

"We think we do," Sekka said.

Mo frowned. Sekka regarded him levelly. "You said we're not from your country, yes?

Mo nodded.

"Which is why it *has* to be us," Sekka said. "Crow, Thomas and me."

"Why do you say that?"

"We're expendable," Sekka said.

Mo's eyebrows rose.

Sekka said, "If we find ourselves in trouble with the authorities we can say we were doing this on our own, without Boss René's permission. That way, you and the other rangers are protected."

Mo looked sceptical. "Do you think anyone would believe that?"

"I'm hoping we won't have to put it to the test."

"But *I* am here with you, now."

"Yes you are, and as I said to you before we left I did not think that was a good idea."

Mo's head came up quickly. "If it was not for me, you would not be here."

"That's true," Sekka said, "and that's my dilemma. Being here has probably placed you in danger. I've already lost five good men. I do not want to lose another."

Mo's head dipped as he leaned forward, his jaw set. "You do not have to worry about me. I can look after myself. Have you forgotten that it was you who taught me how to track and how to shoot?"

"I haven't forgotten, but that was practice; training exercises to test you. I taught Adoum and the others to track and shoot and *they* died."

"That was not your fault. You were not expecting an attack. You could not have known what would happen."

"Maybe not, but I should have anticipated it and that was my mistake."

And one I have to live with.

Sekka fixed the ranger with a hard gaze. "Have you ever shot at a man, Mo? Has anyone ever tried to kill you...deliberately?"

Mo sat back. "No, but-"

"There is no *but*," Sekka interjected, more sharply than he'd intended. "There never can be. You can take part in weapons drill and field exercises and you can

155

practice on the range at paper cut-outs until you drop, but that can never prepare you for the real thing: coming under fire and shooting back, knowing that if you don't find your target, you become one. It changes a man, Mo. When he trains his weapon on another human being with the sole intention of taking a life, it changes him for ever. It's not like killing an antelope for meat or putting down a sick elephant. Besides, it's not just you I'm worried about."

Mo frowned. "Then who? Hassan?"

Sekka shook his head. "Your family."

"My family?" Mo said, puzzled. "But Hassan is-"

"Your mother is a widow and you have two young sisters," Sekka cut in. "If something happens to you, who's going to look after *them*?"

Mo's gaze dropped.

"Did you even think about that?" Sekka asked, his tone softening.

Several seconds went by before Mo raised his head. "I have to do this, boss."

Sekka looked back at him and finally let go a resigned sigh. "I know."

There followed a long silence, broken when Mo said quietly, "You have hunted men before."

Sekka nodded. "Yes."

"And killed them?"

"Yes."

"With Boss Thomas"

"Yes."

"That is why Boss René asked you to train his rangers."

Sekka did not reply.

"And Crow?" Mo said. "He has killed men, too?"

"You'd have to ask him that."

Mo nodded. Raising his coffee cup to his lips he sipped quietly. When he put the cup back on the table he said softly. "I do not think that is necessary. I think you have given me the answer."

Sekka saw Mo's attention shift suddenly to a point along the street. He followed the ranger's gaze, to where Hassan was approaching through the crowd. Purloining a chair from the neighbouring table, the trader indicated to the pot boy to bring him coffee, and sat down.

He leaned in close, his eyes alight. "I have found Faheem."

10

The first thing Sekka noticed as the worshippers began to emerge, was that there were more than a few men who were reliant on walking aids; crutches as well as canes. Three or four were missing either one or both lower limbs, with one double amputee using a wheeled buggy to propel himself along by means of cleverly-adapted, hand-cranked bicycle pedals. The second notable feature was that not all of the infirm were elderly, which made Sekka wonder how many of them had received their injuries in the wars. Faheem, if he was there and about to exit, might not be that easy to spot.

Um Dukhun's mosque was situated on a dusty corner plot, adjacent to the market's northern edge. Squat and square, its unremarkable architecture matched that of the permanent buildings in the rest of the town, in that it had clearly seen better days and was, therefore, in serious need of renovation and a fresh coat of paint.

Sekka was watching from the opposite side of the street, squatting beneath the shade of a small baobab, a convenient location which gave him a direct view on to the mosque's main entrance. Mo and Hassan, armed with the photographs taken from the poachers' mobile phone, were still somewhere inside the building, having answered the muezzin's call to the Dhuhr prayer meeting a little after midday.

As a Hausa, Sekka had been raised a Muslim, but it had been many years - decades if anyone had bothered to keep score - since he'd attended mosque, or even performed salah on his own, his belief in Allah's all-seeing benevolence having been severely dented by the violent death of his father. In the years since he'd tracked down and dealt with his father's killers, there had been no desire to return to the fold, for while the imams might proclaim that the one true God was merciful in His great wisdom, Sekka's experience in war and the cruelty he'd seen inflicted upon his fellow men told a different story.

In Sekka's view, if Allah did exist, then He was just as merciless and unforgiving as every other deity prayed to by the human race. Sekka had often asked himself if his association with Keel might have helped colour his attitude in that regard.

With few exceptions, Keel tended to view priests in the same way he viewed the majority of politicians: with utter contempt, reasoning that over the centuries, between them, both factions had probably visited more death and misery upon the world that the malaria-carrying mosquito.

It had been Hassan's contacts who'd provided the information that Faheem had been seen attending prayers on several recent occasions.

Could be the man had a guilty conscience, Sekka mused, and he was trying to atone for his sins. If so, it wouldn't work. He could attend mosque and run his mas'baha through his fingers, counting off the beads until his palms bled, but that still wouldn't absolve him. Not in Sekka's eyes, and from their willingness to attend prayers to see if Faheem put in an appearance before Sekka had even delegated the task to them, he suspected that Hassan and Mo were probably of the same opinion.

Sekka had made no public declaration with regards to his lapse of faith so it could have been that Mo and Hassan had somehow sensed his reluctance to enter the mosque when he had no affinity for a belief shared by the rest of the congregation. That didn't preclude the likelihood, of course, that, as followers of the Prophet, Mo and his cousin would have answered the muezzin's call anyway, though neither had attended the earlier, Fajr, service, which made Sekka ponder upon the strength of his companions' own spiritual conviction.

Whichever the reason, inwardly, he was grateful that the decision to surveil the attendees had been made for him, leaving him to man his own observation post outside. With a copy of the relevant snapshot concealed discreetly in his hand in case their quarry put in an appearance without Hassan or Mo having spotted him, Sekka had been content to settle down to wait, albeit it with a rising sense of anticipation that his journey from Salma was, hopefully, about to pay dividends.

The leavers were thinning out. Constant referral to the photo, however, had failed to isolate the suspect and Sekka had begun to worry that Hassan's information was unsound and they were on a wild goose chase, or that the intelligence was accurate but Faheem had decided to miss the prayer meeting or had departed the town. In either case it would mean they were back to square one.

Until Sekka spotted Mo. The ranger was hurrying,

not quite running, but there was purpose in his stride and a look of determination on his face. Sekka, pulse quickening, rose to his feet and dusted himself off.

"He is here, boss!" Mo hissed as he drew level, unable to keep the excitement out of his voice.

Sekka looked off towards the mosque, to where the tail-enders were emerging into the hazy afternoon sunlight.

"There," Mo said softly, jutting his chin towards a slim, unobtrusive figure, dressed in loose-fitting shirt and baggy trousers, his head covered by an off-white skull cap, who was making his way in their direction on the far side of the street. A whispy beard covered his lower face. Even if the man hadn't been using a cane, Sekka would have known his identity. Constant referral to the photographs obtained from the mobile phone had seared all four poachers' features into his memory.

"What do we do?" Mo whispered.

"Turn away, now."

"Boss?"

"Do it."

Sekka had given the ranger and his cousin strict instructions when he'd set them on their surveillance mission. If they located Faheem, they were only to observe his movements, nothing else. On no account were they to give the man any indication that he was being watched.

Mo turned so that it appeared he was in conversation with Sekka. Sekka continued to monitor their quarry over Mo's shoulder, noting how the man used his cane. The limp wasn't extreme, Sekka noted, which made him wonder if the stick had become something of an affectation rather than an aid; an emotional crutch as opposed to a real one. Though Sekka knew that in the right hands it would also function as an effective weapon.

Sekka and Mo spotted Hassan at the same time. Mo's cousin was making his way towards their position, walking purposefully, yet maintaining a strategic distance behind their objective. He arrived just as the target turned away from the market place and started to make his way along what appeared to be a road leading towards the edge of town.

"It *is* the man you seek, yes?" Hassan asked, sounding slightly breathless.

Sekka nodded. "It's him."

"So we follow?"

"We do, but not too close; and split up. I don't want him to know he's being tracked, but I want to see where he's going."

Hassan and Mo nodded to show they'd understood and peeled away, Hassan keeping to the nearside while Mo crossed to the opposite side of the road. Sekka waited for a count of ten, then set off in Hassan's wake.

It wasn't long before the buildings began to thin out. The road, however, remained busy and to judge by the amount of traffic, both pedestrian and vehicular, it was obviously one of the town's main thoroughfares. Donkey-drawn carts, laden with passengers and/or produce, were in the majority, while spluttering mopeds and ancient bicycles competed for right of way with a variety of battered trucks and cars which jolted past with no thought for the people on foot, who were forced to hop nimbly aside and turn their heads to avoid the dust and stones thrown up by the erratically driven vehicles.

They'd covered perhaps a quarter of a mile when

Hassan and Mo slowed to a halt on their respective sides of the road. Ahead of them, Sekka saw that their target was making his way towards a gate set into a head-high, dry-grass fence. As he opened the gate, the man looked back over his shoulder. It was a casual movement and instinct told Sekka not to react and turn his head away but to continue walking. He had no qualms about being recognized. Clad in the ankle-length jalabiya, his head covered by his keffiyeh scarf, there was no chance that Faheem would associate him with the man he and his gang had left for dead, sprawled in a dry gully, his face covered in blood.

As Sekka drew level with Hassan, Mo re-crossed the road, narrowly avoiding being run over by a jolting Datsun pick-up. The two men in the back of the truck shook their fists good-naturedly as Mo dodged out of the way, by which time Faheem had disappeared from view. Sekka eyed the now-closed gate, beyond which could be seen the top of a slanted, corrugated roof and the upper branches of a straggly acacia tree.

"What are you thinking, boss?" Mo asked.

Sekka was thinking about their options. Looking up and down both sides of the road, he saw that each dwelling, whether brick-built like Faheem's or of the circular, thatched roof variety, was separated from its immediate neighbour by a shared fence with access gained by the one gateway. Many compounds looked to contain a single tree, presumably used for shade, while outside it was mostly flat, open ground, which wasn't helpful. The motor traffic had not decreased by any meaningful amount and a significant number of pedestrians were going about their business. On a wide patch of dirt to Sekka's right, a dozen or so children were playing football, using sticks and stones for goalposts, their laughter ringing out as they ran after the ball.

Sekka considered the prospect of approaching Faheem openly and asking him to accompany them back across the border. It was a choice he and Keel had considered but, in truth, neither of them had ever viewed it as a serious option. Now that he'd seen the neighbourhood, Sekka knew there was almost zero chance of entering the home by force, grabbing the man, and making off with him; not without causing a major disturbance, at least in daylight. There would be too many witnesses.

Sunset fell around 7 pm, with sunrise occurring a little after 6 am. If they were to make their move it would need to be under cover of darkness, when there were fewer people on the street. The optimum time would be between three and four o'clock in the morning, the witching hour, when targets were generally at their most vulnerable, in bed and sleeping. The problem with that was the likelihood of there being other people in the home, increasing the chances of the alarm being raised. A comprehensive stakeout of the area would reveal more but that would take time, which they didn't have. What they needed was a quieter, more subtle approach, and sooner rather than later.

"Boss?" Mo prompted.

Sekka turned to find the ranger gazing at him expectantly.

"Still thinking," Sekka said.

"There are men at the gate," Amina said.

Faheem opened his eyes at the sound of his sister's

165

voice and the touch of her hand on his shoulder. "Men? What men?"

"I do not know," Amina replied nervously. "They are wearing uniforms."

Faheem frowned and sat up, realizing he must have dozed off. He'd not intended to fall sleep, only to stretch out in an effort to ease the discomfort in his leg which had developed a dull ache across the top of his thigh, the result of kneeling during prayers, followed by the walk home along uneven ground. The paracetamol tabs he'd obtained from the clinic had gone some way to alleviate the symptoms but he didn't have many left and the pills were exorbitantly expensive and the pharmacist couldn't guarantee when there'd be another delivery. Bed rest had seemed the logical remedy.

Despite the constant ache and the occasional stab of pain, the leg was healing well, but it was taking its time. The bullet had struck Faheem two inches above and behind his right knee, passing through flesh but missing major tendons before boring into his mount's left flank, where it had glanced off a rib, propelling a shard of bone into the animal's left ventricle. The poor beast had continued gamely onwards but its breathing had become more ragged with every stride until it collapsed in an ungainly, lathered heap. Faheem had been lucky not to become trapped beneath its shuddering corpse.

Having determined that his own wound, while inconvenient, was not fatal, Faheem had transferred his saddle to the packhorse and, after re-distributing their supplies and the ivory between them, the four poachers had made their run for the border. The journey to Um Dukhun had taken five days and had

166

been a relatively easy ride, the men having stuck to the same back trails they'd used on the inbound journey. By travelling at night they'd avoided the joint Border Force's lacklustre search patterns and crossed into Sudan without incident and with the merchandise intact, by which time, somewhat inevitably, Faheem's leg had become infected.

Finding someone to treat the wound had not been that difficult. Staff attached to the town's clinics and the main pharmacy were on strike due to not having received their government salaries for two months, and in a town close to so many displacement camps, where medical supplies were at a premium, the black market trade in pharmaceuticals had become a flourishing business, which had guaranteed there'd be at least one disgruntled health employee willing to provide antibiotics for the right price.

As Amina explained that she'd noticed the truck through the gaps in the gate and seen men exit the vehicle when she was collecting the washing from the line, Faheem rose quickly from the bed. Bare-footed and dressed in a thin cotton shirt and pants, he followed his sister out of the room. It was still light outside and the heat was stifling. The shirt clung to him like a second skin. Passing the discarded washing piled high on the table, Faheem arrived at the door at the same time as the visitors. At the sound of a hammering fist, Amina drew her hijab over her hair and took a step back to allow Faheem to open the door.

"Faheem Rihan?"

Two men stood on the threshold: one stocky with a short beard; his companion taller, slimmer, also unshaven but with less facial hair, and wearing sunglasses; both of them dressed in desert-camouflage fatigues and red berets. RSF. Faheem felt the first faint flicker of concern.

"Faheem Rihan?" The question came again, more brusquely this time.

Faheem blinked as he took in the automatic rifles held loosely in the soldiers' hands. "Yes."

The stocky one spoke. "Papers." An order, not a statement.

Faheem hesitated. Then, turning quickly, he went back into the bedroom. Retrieving his wallet, he retraced his steps to find that the soldiers had entered the house. The one in sunglasses held out a hand. Faheem fumbled for his identity card and passed it over.

The soldier turned and without removing his sunglasses studied the card in the light of the open doorway. The examination complete, he shifted his gaze and stared hard into Faheem's face before nodding to his companion, who said curtly, "You are to come with us."

Faheem swallowed. He found his voice. "Why? What have I done?"

"Faheem?" Amina queried hesitantly.

The sunglasses worn by the taller one made it difficult for Faheem to read the thoughts that might have been going on behind the shaded lenses. The look was meant to intimidate and it was having the desired affect. The soldier's companion, meanwhile, was gazing at Faheem as if challenging him to query their right to enter the house without permission. Faheem glanced down at the holstered pistols strapped to the visitors' thighs and the AK-47s. The rifles were not being brandished in a threatening manner, but held loosely, muzzles pointed at the ground. Despite the apparent nonchalance in the RSF men's stance, however, Faheem was not prepared to drop his own guard, at which point he realized, uncomfortably, that they were still in possession of his ID card.

"What do you want with him?" It was Amina who spoke.

The card holder's head swivelled. The muzzle of the gun lifted. "Who are you?"

Her chin rose. "I am his sister. Amina Rihan."

The second one spoke. "Then you are not our concern."

Amina blanched. Instinctively, Faheem laid a warning hand on his sister's arm. Since their parents had passed away, Amina had always been protective of her younger brother but the way the RSF man was studying her told Faheem this was not the time for her to come to his defence. He was thankful that her hair and figure were appropriately covered and thus her modesty protected. It didn't do to antagonize members of the militia, who could be touchy when it came to a woman's appearance and what might be deemed inappropriate attire.

Sunglasses man turned back. It was, Faheem thought, like looking into the eye sockets of a decapitated skull.

"We are wasting time," the first soldier said. "You will come with us. Now."

Without taking his eyes from Faheem's face, the soldier continued in a tone that might otherwise have sounded solicitous, but which, at this juncture, seemed to contain menace in every syllable, "It is for your protection."

Faheem stared at them. "Protection? I don't understand."

"We have been given word that there are men looking for you. They are in the town. They have been asking questions. We think they mean you harm."

"Men?" Faheem said, even more confused. "What men?"

"We do not know their identity. Only that they are from across the border."

A small chill moved across the back of Faheem's neck.

"There have been reports of killings in Salamat," the second soldier added. "They say a unit of game rangers was ambushed." He stared hard into Faheem's face. "Perhaps they think you are involved."

Faheem felt a sharp jolt in the pit of his stomach. "Killings? I know nothing of such killings."

"Faheem?" Amina said. "What are they talking about?"

Faheem shook his head. "I do not know."

The first RSF man shrugged. "Whether you do or do not, our orders are to take you to a safe place."

"Whose orders?" Faheem was struck by a sudden hopeful thought and made a grab for the proffered straw. "Was it Jaafar?"

"Jaafar?" It was the one in sunglasses who spoke.

"Sergeant Jaafar Toubia. He is a friend. He is with the militia. He knows me."

The soldier glanced at his companion, who said dismissively. "We do not know this Sergeant Toubia. We received the order over the radio. We do know that we are wasting time with these questions and that you must come with us. If the men searching for you have discovered your location they could be close by."

Faheem, flustered by the increasing speed of events, stared back at them. "What about Amina?"

"What about her?"

"This is her home!" Faheem protested. "If men are coming for me, she should not be left alone. She must come with us!"

The RSF man shook his head. "We received no instructions concerning your sister. Our orders are to take *you* and no one else. Besides, women are not permitted in the barracks. That is the law."

Defiantly, Faheem took Amina's hand. "I will not go without her."

The soldier opened his mouth to reply but was beaten to it.

"Lamya," Amina said. "I can stay with Lamya." She turned to the soldiers. "She is my neighbour, a friend. She lives in the next house. I can go to her."

"There," the soldier responded coldly, before Faheem could react. "You see? The matter is settled." Adding, in an unexpected and more conciliatory tone, "A patrol will be watching the street. If the men from across the border try to enter the house they will be arrested. Then your sister can return. Now, come. We must hurry."

The barracks, Faheem presumed, had to be the RSF compound situated on the outskirts of the town. It was one of many military camps that had been set up across the Darfur region. It was from such bases that militia patrols were dispatched to monitor anti-government activity. The soldier was right. Even if the law had not prescribed it, they were no place for a woman.

While the RSF men waited by the door, rifles cradled across their chests, Amina hurriedly gathered some belongings into a plastic bag, leaving Faheem to retrieve some of his own effects. Having done so,

171

watched by the two soldiers, he and Amina embraced. As soon as Amina had left the house and yard, the first soldier took Faheem's arm. "This way, quickly."

Exiting the yard, the RSF men directed Faheem towards a 4 x 4 truck parked opposite the gate, driver at the wheel, its motor running. As sunglasses man took the front passenger seat, his companion opened the rear door and thrust Faheem into the vehicle. Faheem barely had time to take his seat before the truck pulled away, fast. As they turned the first corner, he looked back over his shoulder and caught a last glimpse of Amina, framed in the opening to the neighbour's yard, staring mutely after them, an anxious look on her face.

Faheem remained silent as the truck picked up speed, though his brain was still spinning wildly. Who were the men who'd been asking questions? Agents of the Chadian authorities? The Border Force, perhaps? Were either of them the source of the RSF's information? Had Jaafar been alerted by his contacts across the border to warn him that he and his fellow poachers were under suspicion and being tracked? If that was the case, why hadn't Jaafar got in touch himself? None of it seemed to make any sense. Faheem was on the point of asking again if it had been Jaafar who'd arranged for the RSF men to call at his home when sunglasses man took off his beret, reached beneath his seat, withdrew a satellite phone and raised it to his mouth.

"On our way."

Faheem frowned. He'd not understood the words that had been spoken, but he knew they weren't

172

Arabic. A sudden sense of unease moved through him.

He thought back to the moment the RSF had entered the house and replayed the scene in his mind. Something about their presence, he realized, should have set off a warning bell, but what? It took a few more seconds before his thoughts finally coalesced.

Sunglasses man; he was the odd one out. It was the accent. There had been something about it that hadn't sounded quite right. Arabic wasn't the man's native language, Faheem decided. Which meant what? Lingering doubt turned to rising trepidation. Faheem braced himself to look out of the window. If they were heading for the RSF compound they should have been driving northwards. They weren't. The buildings they were passing told Faheem they were travelling west.

In a startling moment of clarity, the realization of just what might be happening made him gasp out loud. Instinctively, he looked for the door handle.

"That would be foolish," a voice said beside him in Arabic.

Faheem turned. "You are not the militia."

"No." The bearded man said, as he, too, removed his beret. "We are not militia."

"Twenty minutes out." The words were spoken tersely and uttered by sunglasses man who still had the satellite phone pressed to his ear.

It took only the span of a single heart beat for the full significance of what he'd just heard to penetrate Faheem's partially befuddled brain. When it did, it was like receiving a hammer blow between the eyes.

English! The man had spoken in English! Faheem stared at the back of the soldier's head and, when he had found his voice, enquired haltingly, in Arabic, "Who *are* you people?"

There was a significant pause before the reply finally came.

"We are vengeance," Hassan said, as he laid the Kalashnikov across his legs with the muzzle pointed at Faheem's belly.

And grinned.

When Sekka had asked Mo's cousin about the army surplus gear in his lock-up, the trader had been reticent in his initial reply, revealing only that the camouflage tunics and pants had come into his possession in part-exchange for some agricultural tools he'd supplied to a village headman near the border with Bahr el Ghazal province down in the south. A statement which Sekka had been prepared to believe until Mo discovered a batch of scarlet berets half-concealed beneath a second pile of fatigues a couple of shelves further along.

Under additional questioning, and upon further examination of the uniforms, Hassan had admitted that they were indeed RSF issue and when Sekka pointed out what looked suspiciously like mended bullet holes in the breast area of two of the tunics and a patched rent in the upper thigh of one pair of trousers the trader had come clean.

The uniforms were all that remained of an RSF patrol, wiped out during a fire fight ten months before with a group of Sudanese rebels who'd been supplementing their meagre incomes by smuggling Eritrean and Somali refugees across Sudan's southern border, a consequence of the Khartoum Process, a deal struck between the African Union Commission and the EU in an effort to deter migrants from making the long trek up from the Horn of Africa and on into Southern Europe.

Had Hassan bothered to create an inventory for his over-stocked lock-up, Sekka suspected the canny trader would probably have filed the uniforms under the category: 'Items which might prove useful at some later date', hoping but probably not expecting that they would, eventually, prove to be a worthwhile investment. The AK-47s and the Browning handguns, had added to the deception, deflecting the eye from the repaired bullet holes. The instantly recognizable red berets had served to cement the disguise.

"How are we doing, Mo?" Sekka asked.

As he posed the question, he pulled the scarlet headwear from the young ranger's head and stowed it under the seat. The beret, more than the fatigues, carried the risk of drawing attention to all the vehicle's occupants and none of them, with the probable exception of their captive, wanted that.

"Good, I think," Mo said, changing down as he brought them up behind a slow-moving donkey cart. Not that Mo was pounding the accelerator. Aside from the berets, an erratically driven vehicle was also likely to attract interest, so they were keeping pace with the local traffic, which wasn't doing anything for Sekka's own heart rate.

Sekka turned to look over his shoulder. "Tell him that if he behaves himself, he might get to see his sister again."

As Hassan relayed the message, Sekka tilted the rear view mirror so that he could witness their passenger's response, which emerged as a desultory nod.

As Mo pulled out to overtake the donkey cart and

said, "I think we are being followed."

Sekka's gaze switched to his near-side wing mirror. Hassan, sensing the sudden shift of mood, sat up. Jamming the muzzle of the AK into Faheem's belly, he glanced back through the truck's small rear window and out over the tailgate. Curious, despite not understanding the exchange, Faheem tried to follow Hassan's gaze.

And failed. Without warning, Hassan, in anticipation of a possible threat, turned quickly, laid his right arm around Faheem's shoulders and pressed the AK's snout harder against Faheem's ribcage. Fearing the shot, Faheem cringed but when he heard Hassan's hissed command to keep quiet unless he wanted to die, he allowed himself to surrender.

"I think maybe it is RSF," Mo said.

Sekka's eyes were glued to the mirror. "I see them."

The Land Cruiser was three vehicles back. Sand-coloured, with what appeared to be dark-olive leaves stencilled haphazardly across the bodywork to create a camouflage pattern, it was maintaining its distance. Due to Sekka's angle of view, the driver's features were unclear behind the truck's windscreen, but Sekka could see two figures wearing red berets and dressed in fatigues similar to his own standing in the back of the truck, braced against the top of the cab. What looked suspiciously like the barrel of a machine gun could be seen poking out between them, identifying the 4x4 as what was euphemistically termed a 'Technical': an improvised fighting vehicle.

Could be nothing, Sekka thought, as he felt down by his side for the AK. Could be just a random patrol, going about their business, whatever that might be.

Mo said, "We are coming to the turn-off, boss."

Sekka looked ahead. They were approaching the edge of the town. Traffic was thinning. After another glance in the wing mirror, he said softly, "Do it. Nice and gentle. Don't rush."

The turning was on the right. As Mo spun the wheel, Sekka lost sight momentarily of the traffic behind them. It wasn't until they'd straightened out that he was able to use the mirror to look back again, to see that the Land Cruiser was still there, and that there were no longer any vehicles between it and the Nissan.

Sekka thought about the ordnance mounted on the back of the Toyota. A DshK machine gun, most likely, to judge by the brief glimpse he'd had of the gun's muzzle. Russian-made, nicknamed the 'Dushka' - 'beloved person' - and almost as common as the Kalashnikov, a single round would make mincemeat of the Nissan's panelling, though whoever was manning the weapon was unlikely to open fire until they knew who they were shooting at, or so Sekka was hoping. Though it could have been worse, he supposed. It could have been an anti-tank gun.

"They are coming," Mo said.

"Keep going," Sekka said. "Keep to your speed. If we don't run, then maybe they won't chase us.

Despite not looking too convinced by that argument, Mo did as Sekka directed.

By now, the outskirts of the town were well behind them and the countryside had flattened out, save to the north where the land rose sharply towards the crest of an escarpment dotted with thin scrub. The rest of the terrain was made up of the usual sand, rocks and thorn trees. Not much cover, Sekka thought bleakly. He took another look in the mirror. The Land

177

Cruiser had picked up the pace and was growing larger by the second.

"Boss?" Mo said, having checked the rear view mirror for himself and seen the Toyota accelerate.

"Maintain speed," Sekka said.

Sekka heard Hassan mumble something in the back seat; uncomplimentary, from the sound of it.

"Keep him quiet," Sekka responded. "Tell him if he tries to attract their attention we'll kill him and go down fighting."

By the time Hassan had relayed the message the Toyota had drawn even closer. When it was less than two truck lengths from the Nissan's rear bumper, Sekka, keeping the AK low, flicked off the weapon's safety catch.

"Tell them they can pass us," Sekka instructed.

"Boss?" Mo said. A look of alarm crossed his face.

"Do it. Stick your arm out and wave them on. We're all friends, remember?"

The Toyota had reduced the gap to a single truck length as Mo made the signal, wafting his left hand in the universal paddling motion that told the driver of any vehicle following another that they could overtake at their leisure.

Sekka willed himself not to look round as Mo drew back his arm and said, "They are coming."

Quickly, Sekka took off his sunglasses and held them out. "Put these on. Act cool."

Feeling anything but, Mo took the glasses and slipped them over his nose.

Sekka wondered about the men in the back of the Land Cruiser and about their elevated position and how much they'd be able to see of the Nissan's interior. Fortunately, Hassan had made no attempt to remove the grime from the vehicle, no doubt reasoning that it wouldn't take long for the truck to get dirty again, so why bother? It meant the rear windows were still caked with the muck thrown up during the previous day's drive. That, plus their direction of travel, which allowed the late-afternoon sun to reflect back off the glass thus creating more shadows, meant, hopefully, that the RSF men wouldn't be able to see that the individual in the Nissan's rear off-side passenger seat was being held hostage by the man hunched next to him who was armed with an automatic weapon. In Sekka's mind, that added up to a lot of what ifs and maybes, but in a situation like this you hoped for the best while preparing for the worst.

The track wasn't that wide and with two vehicles travelling hard abreast there wasn't a lot of room, so when the Land Cruiser pulled out and drew level, its bulk seemed to fill the view out of the Nissan's left-hand windows. Just as well Mo had pulled his arm inside, Sekka thought; otherwise there was every chance it would have been sheered off at the elbow.

Turning his head casually to the left, Sekka saw that the Toyota's cab held only one occupant: the driver, dressed in fatigues, who returned Sekka's perusal with a stone-like gaze. Adopting a neutral expression, Sekka nodded before returning his attention to the road in front, at the same time trying to ignore the thunderous beating deep inside his chest wall. From the corner of his eye, he was aware of Mo giving the patrol vehicle a cursory glance as it kept pace and held his breath as the two vehicles continued to run side by side. But then, with Sekka's nerves stretched near to breaking point, the Toyota began to inch ahead.

Bracing himself, Sekka tightened his grip on the AK,

fully expecting the Land Cruiser to swerve in front of them to force a stop, but to his intense relief the RSF vehicle did nothing of the sort. Instead, it picked up speed, and kept going, gradually drawing ahead of the Nissan. Sekka, ever watchful, kept his eyes glued to the two men in the back of the Toyota as the gap between the trucks widened, but they no longer appeared interested in the vehicle that was now behind them. As his pulse returned to somewhere near normal, noting at the same time that his suspicions about the mounted gun's provenance had been proved accurate, he released his breath. His hand, he realized, was still clamped tightly around the AK's stock. Slowly, he relinquished his grip.

Mo let out his own audible sigh of relief as they watched the Land Cruiser recede.

Sekka took back his sunglasses ignoring the slight tremor in Mo's hand as he did so. "How long before we make the rendezvous?

Mo clicked his tongue. "Ten minutes?"

Sekka said, "Then let's try and make it in nine."

The track, he saw, was entering a shallow defile, a river bed; dry save for a few pools of brackish water and a chain of muddy wallows. When the rains arrived it would become a watercourse and unnavigable for any vehicle not fitted with a snorkel. To confirm that likelihood, it wasn't long before the width of the defile began to increase, while at the same time the walls rose higher, until they were almost on a level with the Nissan's roof. Ridges in the mud ahead of them drew Sekka's eye. Fresh tyre tracks, presumably left by the Land Cruiser which had now disappeared, which made Sekka wonder about the RSF patrol's remit.

The border was, on paper, very close, but Sekka

knew, from their inbound journey and from the periodic squabbles that had sprung up over the years between Sudan and its neighbour, that the frontier had always been something of a fluid concept, due to the nature of the terrain and the nomadic tendencies of the population, so any calculation regarding the border's exact location was often deceptive. Added to that was the fact that Chad and Sudan were ranked among the poorest countries in the world and thus the cost of building a permanent structure nine hundred miles in length wasn't economically viable for either party. Hence the cheaper option: the Border Force, backed up by Army units, like the RSF, representatives of which, were, even now, in dangerously close proximity to Sekka's extraction point.

"Eyes open," Sekka said. "We don't want any nasty surprises this close to home." He raised the sat phone to his lips.

Just as Mo yelled, "Boss!"

And it was Salma all over again.

11

It had likely been a flash flood during the previous rainy season that had torn away the river bank, loosening the roots of the tree, which had then been carried downstream, probably at the speed of a torpedo, to a point where the sheer power of the water had driven it up against the outer rim of the defile, where it had remained lodged ever since, forming an impressive barrier across a good two thirds of the river bed.

The remaining third was blocked by the RSF Land Cruiser.

Taken by surprise, Mo slammed on the brakes, bringing the Nissan to a jolting halt. There was a muttered curse from Hassan who was propelled forward against the back of Sekka's seat by the sudden stop, and a grunt from their captive as the barrel of Hassan's dislodged AK raked across his stomach. Had Faheem acted more swiftly, he might have turned the unexpected halt to his advantage by trying to exit the vehicle, but before he could make a move, Hassan had regained his balance and forced Faheem back into his seat with a warning snarl.

As he took in the view before him: with the Nissan stationary and the Toyota parked eighty yards or so ahead, square on, with one man in the back of the truck, manning the gun, Sekka had to admit that the RSF men had played their part well, knowing that they stood a better chance of halting the Nissan's progress by hemming it in rather than to try and broadside it in open country. With the way forward blocked and the walls of the defile forming a natural barrier on either side, Sekka and his team had nowhere to go unless they reversed back the way they'd come. But even as that option presented itself, Sekka knew instinctively that it wasn't really an option at all, because had he been in the RSF patrol leader's shoes, he'd have made sure of one thing: that their rear exit was cut off, too. The third man had to be behind them, most likely on the crest of one of the adjacent river banks.

Sekka flicked the switch on the satellite phone. "There might be a problem. Stand by." Without waiting for a reply, he addressed Mo. "Keep the engine running. If you hear me yell, steer for the left bank. Do it fast but leave enough room to exit your side. That way our backs are protected and we can use the truck as a shield. Keep a look out for the man behind us."

Mo looked back at him. "What are you going to do?"

"That depends," Sekka said.

"On what?"

"On what *they* do next. So get ready."

Sekka eyed the machine gun in the back of the truck and wondered if this might not just be an RSF patrol asserting its authority by conducting a random stop-and-search, though in his heart he knew it wouldn't be. Why would they lay a road block for men wearing the same uniform? It made him wonder how the patrol had latched on to them so quickly, and, more pertinently, why no one had started shooting. The obvious answer was that they were there for Faheem and curious about the men who'd taken him.

That made him think about the sister, Amina and how she and Faheem had embraced before they'd left the house. It would have been a prime opportunity for Faheem to pass her a whispered message. The question was: for whom?

Sekka considered the number of RSF men confronting them and the mobile recon patrols he'd carried out over the years. It was rare to see less than four men in a crew. A unit invariably consisted of a driver and oppo up front, the latter to ride shotgun and perform navigation duties, with at least two more operatives to man any heavy-duty ordnance that might be mounted in the rear. So why only three men on this occasion? A tiny worm of speculation began to wriggle its way into Sekka's thoughts.

And then Mo said, "I see the other man, boss, in the mirror. He is on the left bank, a little behind us, at seven o'clock."

Sekka did not look but watched the two men in the Land Cruiser who, so far, had not moved, while the gun, he noted, was trained directly on the Nissan's radiator grill. Ideally, he would have preferred to be behind the Nissan's wheel, but to swap places with Mo at this juncture was out of the question. Without turning his head he addressed Hassan. "Keep your gun on our friend. No matter what happens, you stay down. And we need Faheem alive. Do. Not. Kill. Him. Understood?"

"I understand," Hassan growled. "But only if you do not die. If you die then I will shoot him."

Which, Sekka decided, all things considered, was probably the best offer he was going to get under the circumstances. Gripping the stock of the AK with his

185

left hand, so that the gun was hidden from the men in the Land Cruiser by the bulk of the Nissan's door, he stepped out of the truck. As he did so, the Dushka's barrel edged sideways to follow him. The movement was subtle, but Sekka had been expecting it.

What he hadn't expected was the third RSF man's lack of self-discipline, or perhaps he'd misread his orders or he'd caught a glimpse of Sekka's weapon and thought Sekka was about to open fire, and had decided to act on his own initiative. Either way, the AK's chattering reports shattered the stillness. The detonations even took the man's companion in the back of the Land Cruiser by surprise for, without thinking, he swivelled the machine gun's muzzle towards the source of the cacophony, rather than towards the more immediate threat, Sekka's AK.

Fortunately for Sekka, the shooter had fired too soon. As a consequence, and due to the Kalashnikov's notorious recoil, the first bullets missed their target and slammed into the bed of the Nissan and the ground around it, which gave Sekka his only chance. Bringing his own AK up fast, he pivoted and loosed off a volley of shots towards the figure now exposed atop the high ground. The Nissan was already in motion as the body fell away, but by then the machine gunner had re-adjusted his sights.

As had Sekka. Switching his aim, all deception having evaporated, he fired and saw the RSF gunner tuck his head into his shoulders as he tried to make himself invisible behind the Dushka's tubular mounting, as the Nissan headed for the wall of the defile, tyres gouging sand as they found traction.

Sekka saw that the Land Cruiser's driver was also in motion. Having exited his vehicle, and using his own door as a shield, he brought his weapon up, only to duck back down as Sekka fired on the run. But, then, the machine gunner, his confidence regained, or perhaps goaded into action by his companion, opened fire once more. Grabbing the phone, Sekka threw himself towards shelter at the rear of the truck as the heavy rounds slammed into the Nissan's front wing, shredding the nearside tyre and creating a colander out of the open passenger door.

The satellite phone began to squawk.

The Nissan was still ten feet from the bank and taking a severe mauling when Hassan, realizing they were never going to make it all the way, kicked open the rear passenger door and pushed Faheem out in front of him and down on to his knees. Whereupon, after striking the Sudanese hard across the shoulders with the butt of this AK, he grabbed a handful of Faheem's hair and hauled him against the side of the now-stranded Nissan. Once there, head down, he reversed the gun and pressed the barrel against Faheem's cheek.

As Sekka crabbed his way around the Nissan's tailgate towards Hassan's position, with the phone still emitting gobbledegook, Mo made his own exit from the driver's seat. There was no finesse in the way he vacated the vehicle. The driver's door sprang open and the ranger fell on to the ground, chin tucked into his chest as the Dushka's withering hail of fire turned the Nissan's windscreen into pea-sized pellets and interior of the vehicle into chaff.

Protected, at least for the time being, by the engine block, Sekka assessed their position. "Anyone hit?"

His voice was almost eclipsed by the sound from the gun and the slugs striking the other side of the

187

truck.

"No, boss," Mo gasped. "I'm good."

"Hassan?" Sekka ducked as the RSF gunner pumped another round of shots into the Nissan's already perforated bodywork.

Sekka's enquiry was met with a grunt and a string of muttered curses, barely audible beneath the barrage, which Sekka took to be an indication that Mo's cousin had survived the initial onslaught.

The Dushka's rate of fire was upwards of six hundred rounds a minute. Sekka knew there was no way the truck could withstand that sort of punishment for long without their position being even more compromised than it was already. They were closer to the wall of the defile than they had been but not near enough for the truck to have formed a good defensive barrier.

He brought the phone up to his lips and clicked the transmit button. "Thomas? You there?"

Nothing.

Sekka tried again as another flurry of shots kicked up dust and bracketed the Nissan's front section. A wing mirror blew apart and Sekka heard Mo cry out as a sliver of glass sliced through his cheek. "Thomas, come in! Crow? Anyone?"

As a truck engine started up.

"They are coming!" Mo yelled.

The RSF driver was obviously back behind the wheel. Sekka thrust the phone into Mo's hand. "Keep trying."

Inching backwards, Sekka raised the AK to shoulder height, then, gauging his position in relation to the back of the cab so that it hid him from the on-coming vehicle, he rose cautiously to his feet in time to see that the Land Cruiser was less than sixty yards off and homing in fast, the RSF crew secure in the knowledge, despite Sekka's retaliation and their own inferior number, that they were still in possession of the greater fire power.

Sekka knew his movement had betrayed him the moment the RSF gunner let rip once more. Ducking fast, he felt the wind from the slugs sear past his shoulder as they punched through what remained of the Nissan's windscreen and emerged white-hot from the rear wall of the cab.

A rapid burst of fire came from the Nissan's front end. Taking advantage of the RSF gunner's sudden distraction, Mo had forsaken the phone and was shooting back, the AK's stuttering reports instantly recognizable, even above the Dushka's din.

And then, as Sekka hit the dirt, another, more impressive noise came out of nowhere.

Like an avenging angel, the Airbus swept into view above the river bank, flooding the defile with a wave of sound as Crow brought her in low, behind the advancing Land Cruiser.

The chopper was less than twenty feet above the ground and directly above the RSF vehicle, when Keel, held by his safety belt and leaning out of the open door, fired directly down on to the RSF gunner's position. At point blank range, with Crow keeping the chopper steady, Keel rained fire at the RSF man's jerking body.

Sekka, seizing his chance, rose in one fluid movement and launched his remaining rounds towards the driver's side of the Land Cruiser's cab. He saw the glass splinter and the driver jerk violently and then slide away as the vehicle came to a canted stop thirty feet from what was left of the Nissan's front bumper.

Sekka's gun fell silent, the magazine empty.

The throbbing of the Airbus's rotors filled the air as Crow maintained his hover, the down draft from the blades whipping the ground dirt into a mini-dust storm, before easing the chopper to port and bringing her down carefully in the centre of the defile. He remained in his seat and watched as Keel jumped out and made his way to Sekka's position, crouching low and only straightening when he'd cleared the arc of the spinning blades.

"You good?" Keel's eyes took in the camouflaged fatigues and the armament Sekka was carrying.

Sekka nodded wearily and turned as Mo and Hassan, the latter still with his gun pressed against Faheem's belly, emerged cautiously from behind the wrecked truck.

"We are very pleased to see you, boss," Mo said. He dabbed at the blood on his cheek.

"And I you. You're wounded?"

Mo shook his head. "It is only a scratch. I am fine."

"And lucky," Sekka said. "We all are."

Keel nodded to Mo's cousin, who was gazing at the helicopter as if he couldn't quite believe his own eyes. "Hassan."

The trader came out of his trance and responded to Keel's greeting with a tentative smile before turning to Sekka. "You see? I did not kill him."

Faheem looked like a man whose world had collapsed around him, without quite knowing how or why. He looked towards the stalled Land Cruiser.

"Friends of yours?" Sekka said.

Faheem did not reply, but turned back and gazed

190

blankly at Sekka and at the empty AK.

Sekka looked at Mo. "Is my Arabic that bad?"

Mo shook his head. "No boss, he understands you very well."

"Why the question?" Keel asked.

Sekka drew the captured mobile phone from his pocket. "I need to check something." To Mo, Sekka said, in Arabic. "You and Hassan watch Faheem. If he tries to run, shoot him."

Faheem's eyes widened in alarm.

"You were right," Sekka said.

Something in the way Mo responded with what was almost a sly grin made Sekka suddenly wonder if he'd been the victim of an artful ruse all along, and that Mo had expressed doubts about his ability with the language for no other reason than to persuade Sekka to include him in the cross-border abduction.

Sekka, making a mental note to have words with the young ranger later, turned to Keel. "A second opinion would be good."

Keel frowned. "We've made enough noise to wake the dead. We need to get out of here."

"It won't take long," Sekka said.

Before Keel could object, Sekka headed off towards the Land Cruiser, leaving Keel with little option but to follow.

Crow, Keel thought, would be watching and wondering where the hell they were going.

They reached the RSF truck. Sekka pulled open the driver's door. The body, unencumbered by a seat belt, lay slumped to one side. The bullets from Sekka's AK had struck the driver in the neck and shoulders. The arterial spray from the neck wound had darkened the back of the seat around the body and speckled the roof

191

of the cab, which also contained bullet holes, suggesting that some of Keel's slugs had also found their mark. The confined space stank.

"Hold that." Sekka handed Keel his AK, reached inside the cab and tilted the driver's head towards him. With his other hand he held up the mobile phone alongside the dead man's face. "What do you think? He look familiar?"

Keel studied the slack features, compared them to the snapshot on the phone, and sucked in a breath. "If you ignore the blood and the fact that he's deader than Kelsey's nuts." He drew back. "Lucky guess?"

Sekka let the head flop and wiped a smear of blood from his hand on the dead man's sleeve. "A hunch. There were only three of them in the crew. I thought it was a bit odd."

"There's a name tag." Keel indicated a badge sewn above the front pocket of the dean man's blood-stained fatigues.

Sekka smoothed out the material. "Toubia. Faheem asked if he was the one who sent us to the house."

"It's beginning to add up. Let's check the one up top."

They climbed on to the Land Cruiser's bed, where the dead man lay face down. There was a lot of blood. Keel turned the body over and Sekka brought up the shots of the four suspected poachers. They studied the likeness.

Keel nodded. "Tag says his name's Achol. Makes two down, one to go. I'm assuming the body on top of the bank is the other one? Want to try for the hat trick?"

Sekka nodded. "Might as well, seeing as we're here."

They left the truck and made their way to the bank.

Keel held up a hand towards the helicopter, fingers and thumb spread, to tell Crow they wouldn't be long. He knew the pilot would be growing impatient. If he'd been in a car he'd either have beeped the horn or revved the engine to tell them to get a bloody move on.

A section of bank had crumbled away, forming a narrow cleft which provided convenient foot holds, enabling them to clamber on to the higher ground. A few seconds later, they were standing over the body which lay on its back, arms outstretched. A Kalashnikov lay a couple of yards away. There was a small round hole surrounded by a bloodstain in the centre of the dead man's forehead. The back of the skull was a mess.

"Good shot," Keel said.

"Lucky shot," Sekka said. "The rest missed. There wasn't time to aim."

"There rarely is," Keel said. "Let's see who we've got."

Sekka held out the phone and they compared the bloodied features with the photographs.

"Tag says Mursal," Keel said. "Three out of three. Job done."

"Not yet," Sekka said softly.

Keel turned and followed Sekka's gaze to where Mo and Hassan were guarding Faheem, who was kneeling on the ground, hands clasped behind his bowed head. "No, you're right. Not yet." Keel laid a hand on Sekka's arm. "Mo, is he okay? How'd he do?"

"He did well, considering it was his first engagement. Made shots where it counted. I'd have him on my team any time."

"Something to consider come re-assignment."

Sekka nodded.

193

"Hell of a first outing, though."

"Had to happen some time."

"We've all been there, Keel said.

They made their way back down to the river bed. Keel studied the two vehicles, lips pursed, the AK held loosely in his right hand.

"What are you thinking?" Sekka asked.

"That we're leaving a shit load of evidence."

Mo said, "Boss?"

Keel turned.

The ranger looked at his cousin and then at Keel, taking in Sekka at the same time. "Hassan and I have been talking."

"About?" Keel said.

"About what must be done." Mo looked towards his cousin. "Hassan said do not worry. He will take the truck."

"It's a wreck," Keel said, gazing at the Nissan and then at Hassan. "The thing's been shot to hell. It's not going anywhere."

"No, boss," Mo said. "Not *that* truck." The ranger jutted his chin to indicate the Land Cruiser. "*That* one."

Keel exchanged looks with Sekka. "Sorry, Mo. You want to run that by me again?"

A movement over Mo's shoulder caught Sekka's eye. Crow, visible through the chopper's wind shield, was looking back at him, left wrist raised and tapping his watch impatiently with his other hand.

Sekka held up a forefinger. *Stand by.*

"Mo?" Keel prompted, as Crow spread his hands and made a gesture that said, 'What the fuck?'

"It is Hassan's idea," Mo said.

"Right now, I'm open to all suggestions," Keel said. "But make it quick."

194

"Hassan says, he will leave his truck here and take the Toyota. He says it is a fair exchange."

There was pause. "Okay," Keel said. "And then what?"

"He will paint it a different colour," Mo said, as if the answer was patently obvious.

Ask a stupid question, Keel thought. "It'll probably need more than a paint job. But I meant what will he do with it?"

"He says he will either sell it or use it himself."

Keel's eyebrows rose. "An RSF truck?"

"It is a very good truck, boss. Hassan said it would be a pity to waste it. And it will not look like an RSF truck after it has been painted," Mo concluded,

Fair point, Keel thought.

"It *is* drivable," Sekka said.

Keel threw Sekka a look, before turning to Mo. "And the Nissan? Does he have a plan for that, too?"

"He will burn it," Mo said. "First, he will remove the registration numbers."

"Good to know." Keel addressed Hassan directly. "What about its crew?"

Mo hesitated. He looked towards his cousin, who held his gaze without speaking. Mo turned back. "He will remove their uniforms and all their identification and he will take their weapons and their equipment, and then he will burn the bodies with the truck."

Keel stared back at the ranger, inhaled and exhaled slowly. "And you're good with this?"

"Boss?" Mo said.

"This is a big step, Mo. This is serious. This is not reversible. You do this, you cannot go back."

"They killed our friends, boss. They tried to kill us." The ranger stared Keel down. "What would *you* do?"

195

Keel did not reply immediately. He looked towards Sekka as if to say: well, you were right about him.

"Hassan has a lock up," Sekka said. "It probably is doable." He held up the AK. "It's how we got these and the uniforms."

"I did wonder," Keel said.

"So," Sekka prompted.

Keel fell silent. He looked over to the chopper where Crow was now spreading his arms in a mute gesture, then turned back and nodded.

"Let's get to work."

"Everybody in? Okay, seats to upright. Let's get the hell out of here."

Opening the throttle, Crow pulled up the collective to increase the pitch of the blades, while bearing down carefully on the left pedal. Maintaining foot pressure, he continued to increase collective pitch, feeling for the moment when the lift produced by the blades exceeded the helicopter's weight. As soon as he felt the shift to weightlessness through the controls and the aircraft start to rise, Crow adjusted his grip on the cyclic, waited until they were clear of the defile and nudged the chopper forward.

Below them, the Nissan was being consumed by flames at a ferocious rate. As Keel watched, Crow's voice came through the headset. "Your idea?"

Keel spoke into his mike. "Hassan's."

"And the bodies?"

"Still Hassan."

"Tough cookie."

"He probably has form. Joseph says he has a stack of RSF uniforms and small arms back in town. Said it

196

wouldn't surprise him if there was an armoured personnel carrier parked some place, too."

Below them, a plume of oily black smoke rose from the ground.

"That's going to attract attention," Crow said.

"Maybe." Keel followed the course of the smoke column. "With luck, it'll burn fast."

"What about the fire fight? Someone had to have heard the shooting."

"This neck of the woods, people hear gunshots, they tend to run in the opposite direction."

"Unless the guys on fire down there called it in earlier. Uniforms could be converging even as we speak."

"I've a feeling this was a private party. Not something they'd want to pass up the line."

"Unless High Command was in on it."

"Let's hope that's not the case."

"Amen to that. So, what? Hassan's simply gonna drive the Toyota to his chop shop?"

"Be dark in a couple of hours. He's still in uniform. If he waits, no one's likely to flag down an RSF vehicle, especially one that looks as if it's been in a smash."

"Good point."

Keel scanned the horizon. There was nothing moving, though the elevation gave him a view of low buildings in the distance behind them: Um Dukhun's outlying suburbs. "How are *we* doing? We okay for fuel?"

"Jesus," Crow said. "*Now* you ask? Why the hell do you think I was waving at you back there? If I'd known you were gonna hold a town meeting, I'd have switched the bloody engine off."

"We've enough to get us home, though?"

197

"Sure, if we all breathe in."

Keel look sideways at him.

Crow grinned. "It's okay, we're fine. Another five minutes, mind, and I'd have left without you."

"I'd like us to make a stop en route," Keel said.

It was Crow's turn with the quizzical look. "And where would that be?"

Keel told him.

There was a pause before Crow said, "Sure, no worries." Jerking his head to indicate Faheem, who was in the rear seat, bracketed by Sekka and Mo, he said, "You think matey back there will talk?"

"He's seen the rest of his crew taken out and torched. I were him, I would."

Crow's eyes dropped to the altimeter and then the fuel gauge and the out across the upcoming terrain. "I guess we'll find out soon enough."

"Be my guess, too," Keel said.

12

"René thought about having some sort of marker," Keel said. "Maybe an engraved stone. Nothing fancy."

The gully floor carried no trace of the chaos that had followed the ranger patrol's ambush. There were no blood stains to be seen, only rocks and dirt; the latter indented by a web of fresh animal tracks and scattered droppings.

Sekka's attention moved to the lip of the gully to where the side had crumbled under the Land Cruiser's front wheels. A few tiny specks of oil were all that remained, having been missed during the attempt to clean the area of residue deposited by the damaged vehicle following its removal back to headquarters.

"A marker would be good," Sekka said.

Subdued, he turned and gazed out across the scrubland, to where the bones of the roan antelope still littered the ground. Low bushes and a couple of thorn trees blocked Sekka's direct view but the remains had been visible from the helicopter when Crow brought the aircraft down to land.

"We should get started," Keel said. "You ready?"

Sekka looked to where Crow, having switched off the chopper's engine, was painstakingly removing the heavy-duty masking tape which, up until that moment, had been concealing the Airbus's registration letters.

Then, nodding, he and Keel made their way to where Mo was keeping watch over Faheem, who was seated on the ground, once more with his hands behind his head. The Sudanese looked up as Keel and Sekka approached, the apprehension writ large across his face.

Keel squatted down. "Speak English? *Hal tatahadath al'injlizia*?"

Faheem's eyes flickered.

"That a yes or a no? *Na'am 'am la*?"

The response was a shake of the head. "*La*."

No.

Keel nodded thoughtfully, suspecting, despite the denial, that the man probably understood a few words. Standing, he turned to Sekka. "Over to you."

Sekka looked down and spoke, as Keel had done, in Arabic. "Do you know where you are?"

Seeming confused by the question, Faheem shook his head again. He was on the point of lowering his hands, but lifted them quickly when Mo raised the butt of his AK, issuing a warning hiss as he did so.

"You're certain?" Sekka said. "Why don't you stand up; take a look around?"

Faheem hesitated, then, assisted by Mo's persuasive grip on his collar, he rose stiffly to his feet. It was clear that the pain in his leg had returned with some acuteness.

"Think carefully," Sekka said.

More likely it was the tone in Sekka's voice, rather than the directive, that caused movement in Faheem's eyes: the crossing of a dark shadow.

And there it is, Keel thought.

"You're sure this place doesn't look familiar?" Sekka said. "Because it should. It's where you and your friends murdered my men."

There was a faint tremor then, along the length of Faheem's bearded jawline as a nerve pulsed just beneath his skin.

"That was after you killed the elephants and cut out their tusks," Sekka continued, "You and your friends, Sergeant Toubia, Achol, and Mursal."

Sekka took the phone out of his pocket, and held the camera out. "That's the four of you, yes?"

Faheem blinked and stared at the photo of him and his companions holding on to the bridles of their horses, Kalashnikovs slung across their backs. The nerve in his throat began to throb again.

"Whose idea was it to ambush the ranger unit?" Sekka pressed. "Was that you?"

The answer came quickly, too quickly. "I know of no such killings."

"Is that so?" Sekka said, his scepticism at full stretch. "So you didn't cross the border to slaughter elephants and take their ivory, and when you realized a ranger team was on your trail decide to take aggressive action?"

Sekka paused, and then said, "You killed five of my men. You took back the belongings we found in your camp and you helped yourselves to our equipment and our weapons and the tusks we rescued, and then you stole our personal possessions. And you left *me* to die."

The last accusation caused Faheem's eyes to widen. "No, no." He shook his head vigorously. "That is not true! I did not kill anybody. I swear it was not me!"

Sekka's chin lifted. "Not *you*? So you're saying it was your friends; the men with you?"

Sekka waited as a new expression stole across

Faheem's face. It was the look of a man who knew his next utterance was critical, and that his future probably depended on it.

"It was Jaafar." The words came out in a rush. "And Suleyman."

Sekka let out a sigh. "Jaafar Toubia?"

The Sudanese nodded.

"He was the leader?"

Another nod.

"And *he* ordered the ambush and the killings?"

"Yes, yes. It was Jaafar, Jaafar!"

So much for honour among thieves, Keel thought.

"You're lying," Sekka said. "We have the photographs. All four of you are carrying guns."

The Sudanese shook his head vehemently. "No. I only had the gun for protection, against the animals."

"So the elephants attacked you? You were just defending yourselves?"

For a second, hope flared in the poacher's eyes, quickly doused when Sekka said. "You would not have had to kill them. All you had to do was fire into the air. They would have tried to get away. They would have run."

"Which is what they did," Keel said. "But you chased them; rode them down and killed them. Even the baby. That's why you brought the guns. To kill elephants and take their tusks."

"No, you do not understand."

"Make us understand," Sekka said.

"I did not kill the elephants or attack your men."

Sekka waited,

"I was only the cook," Faheem blurted.

Sekka's eyebrows rose. "The *cook*?"

"That's a new one," Keel said, and realized he'd

spoken in English.

"You lie!" Mo raised the butt of the AK.

Faheem flinched. Keel held back Mo's arm.

"Then why weren't you at the camp?" Sekka said.

A pause. "I was hiding. I saw you and I thought bandits were coming to rob me."

"You thought *we* were the bandits?" Sekka said. "You're lying, Faheem, because there is no way you would have seen my advance scout. And even if you had and you hid as you said, where was your horse?"

"My horse?" The response was accompanied by a blank look.

"If you were in camp and hidden nearby, your horse would have been there. It wasn't. Which means you weren't in the camp. You were with your friends. You were part of the hunting party."

"It's written all over your face, Faheem," Keel said. "How many elephants did *you* shoot? Was it the mother? The calf? Was it you who cut the mother's spine with an axe and chopped the tusks from her body? Was that you?"

"No! No!"

"Still lying," Keel said. "And even if you were just the cook, you knew they were coming here to kill elephants for ivory. You wanted to be in on it. You wanted a share of the profit and you didn't care who got in your way."

The Sudanese seemed to slump into himself. When he spoke his voice was a whisper. "I am a poor man. The money was for my family."

"Here we go," Keel said. "The sob story."

Faheem blinked, which made Keel, who'd lapsed momentarily into English, think he'd been right in suspecting that the man might, with the exception of

203

the expression 'sob story', know more of the language than he was letting on, though it was more likely to have been his sarcastic tone, he reflected, when the poacher responded sneeringly, in Arabic. "You people do not know what it is like. In my country there is no work. If there is no work, there is no money. If there is no money there is no food. We know rich foreigners visit the parks across the border. They pay many dollars to see the animals, but the money does not reach those who need it the most."

"It helps the people of Chad," Sekka said. "It goes towards building houses for the villagers. It provides tools for them to dig wells and water their fields, and to build schools for their children and clinics for when they get sick."

"It is not enough."

"No," Sekka said. "You're right. It isn't enough. It never is. But it is a start. If the elephants and the other animals were not there the visitors would not come and there would be no money at all. But you are Sudanese. Why does that give you the right to take the money away from the people of Chad?"

"My mother is sick. How will I buy medicine for her?"

"Ah, now you have a sick mother," Keel said. "I wondered when she was going to turn up."

"You're with the RSF," Sekka said. "Do they not pay you?"

"No! I am not RSF!"

Sekka frowned. "But you were Janjaweed."

"No! I was not Janjaweed. I told you, I was only the cook."

Who carried an automatic rifle and who could ride a horse as well as a Comanche dog soldier, Sekka thought.

"Tell us how they recruited, you," Keel said.

It had not been difficult. A farmer and a herder, whose home was close to the Tagabo Hills, Faheem had been helping a neighbour move some goats between villages when he'd overheard the neighbour talking with a friend who said that some men were planning an ivory hunt across the border. They were looking for a fourth man. Spotting an opportunity to make some money, Faheem had wangled an introduction, via his neighbour, to the gang's leader, Jaafar, and had been taken on as cook and general bottle washer. As job interviews went, it really had been that easy.

And it all sounded perfectly plausible, until Sekka said, "The thing is, Faheem, we found a dead horse. What's left of it is over beyond those trees. It has a bullet hole in its side. I put it there. We also know you have a wound in your left leg. That's why you've been using a cane. You didn't bring it with you, by the way? Did you forget it in the excitement, or is the wound getting better?"

Sekka stared down at Faheem's injured limb. "I think your wound was caused by a bullet; my bullet. Near your knee, yes? The same bullet that killed your horse; the horse we didn't find when we raided your camp; the horse you rode when you killed the elephants and ripped out their tusks; the horse whose bones are lying over there. You're a liar, Faheem. We know you were a willing part of the gang and you took part in the ambush that killed my rangers."

"No! No! I am telling the truth. I was the cook! I did not hunt. I did not shoot at your men! You must believe me!"

205

Sekka waited for the Sudanese to calm down before nodding thoughtfully and fixing the Sudanese with a steady gaze. "You say you did not shoot at anyone."

"That is true!"

"So you do not know me?"

"No! How would I know you?"

"You don't recognize my face?"

A vigorous shake of the head. "No! I told you! Why do you ask these questions?"

"Look at me," Sekka snapped. He stared directly into the other man's eyes.

"I do not know you," Faheem said again, but his voice faltered. Breaking off eye contact, he turned his face away.

"Really?" Sekka said calmly. "That's strange, because you're wearing my watch."

As the significance of Sekka's statement struck home, the furtiveness in Faheem's eyes slid away, to be replaced, first by shock and then by abject fear, as, instinctively, he went to hide the arm bearing the timepieces behind his back. "No, you are mistaken. This is *my* watch. It was a gift."

"So, if I asked you about the words written on to the back of it, you could tell me what they say without looking?" Sekka countered.

Somewhere out of sight a bird screeched. It seemed to jerk Faheem out of his trance. He looked to be on the verge of bolting, while at the same time knowing that he wouldn't make ten feet. As if activated by a switch, his injured left leg began to twitch.

Sekka held out his hand without speaking and waited in silence as the poacher, his eyes downcast, undid the strap and passed him the watch. Still not saying a word, Sekka attached the timepiece to his own wrist.

"It's over, Faheem." Keel said evenly. "We know who you are and what you did. What we need now is information."

Faheem's head lifted slowly. "Information?"

"Well, yes," Keel said, evenly. "You didn't think we brought you all the way out here to talk about old times, did you?"

Faheem's gaze flickered warily between Keel and the still silent Sekka.

"So let's start with who gave Jaafar his orders," Keel said.

The Sudanese frowned. "I do not know. Jaafar was our leader. *He* gave the orders."

"How did you know where the elephants would be?" Sekka asked.

Faheem looked puzzled by the question. "Jaafar knew."

"Did somebody tell him, somebody on this side of the border?"

More confusion, then: "Jaafar said everyone knows where the elephants go when the rains come. It is why they are easy to track."

Even as he'd posed the question, Sekka had suspected what the answer might be. Elephants, indeed virtually every other species of animal that walked, flew, swam or crawled, had been following seasonal migration routes for generations; from elephants and wildebeest to salmon and Arctic terns. Knowing where they were likely to be at any given time of the year was, if not an exact science, as near to one as made no difference. In the right hands, a calendar and a map were almost as reliable as a tracking collar when it came to determining how far along a particular path a migrating herd might be located.

But that didn't mean Jaafar and his crew hadn't been given prior information to help them locate the herd they had targeted.

"What did you do with the ivory?"

Faheem blinked at the change in the line of questioning. "Jaafar kept it after we crossed the border."

"To sell?"

"Yes. He said when the buyer paid him, he would pay me."

"That was trusting of you," Keel said drily. "Did he have a buyer before you left for the hunt?"

Faheem looked puzzled.

Keel tried again, "Who paid for the horses and your supplies, and the satellite phone."

"It was Jaafar. He arranged everything."

"Enterprising son of a bitch," Keel murmured, knowing there had to be more to it. "But he still had to get rid of the ivory. So, I'll ask again. Who was he selling it to?"

Faheem hesitated.

"Well?" Sekka said.

"I do not know."

Frustration must have shown on Sekka's face because the Sudanese hesitated and made as if to speak.

"What?" Sekka said.

"There was a person Jaafar spoke to before we left Sudan."

"Who was this?"

"I do not know."

"But you saw them together?" Sekka pressed.

208

"No, they talked on the special telephone."

"The one we found in your camp?" Sekka said. "The satellite phone?"

Faheem nodded.

"Did you hear the person's name?"

The Sudanese hesitated again. "I know only that it was a man...I heard Jaafar call him *'Aqid'*".

Colonel.

"He was RSF? Was he the buyer, the person who gave Jaafar orders?"

"Perhaps. I do not know. I was only-"

"The cook," Keel said. "Yeah, we got that."

The poacher nodded fiercely. "The cook, yes." His voiced dropped. "May I have some water?"

Neither Keel nor Sekka had a water bottle or canteen with them. Mo didn't have his to hand either. But at that moment, Keel saw Crow, who, as he removed the last strips of masking tape, looked towards them. Raising his hand to his mouth, Keel mimed a drinking motion. Giving a nod, Crow ducked inside the chopper. Emerging with a water bottle, he headed towards them.

"How's it going?" He asked, when Keel indicated that he should give the bottle to the Sudanese.

"Getting there."

Crow watched as Faheem took the bottle and drank greedily. "Thirsty work, confession."

Faheem wiped his mouth and went to hand the bottle back.

"Keep it," Keel said. "You'll need it."

Faheem frowned, and then nodded.

"Get much info?" Crow asked.

"Debatable," Keel said. "He says he wasn't in on the planning. He was only a foot soldier, a last-minute hired help."

"You believe him?"

"Jury's still out. Hard to plead innocence, though, seeing as he was wearing Joseph's watch."

"You're kidding?" Crow said.

"And he has a bullet wound from when Joseph shot him."

"Good. Serve the bastard right."

Sekka had been watching Faheem while Keel and Crow were having their back-and-forth. The poacher's expression suggested that while he might have understood snippets of the exchange, the bulk of it had gone over his head. Either way, he had the look of a man who was still desperately anxious to save his own skin.

"Achol and Mursal," Sekka said. "What do you know of them?"

Not much was the answer, beyond the fact that they were RSF and, as such, associates of Jaafar.

Which made sense, Sekka thought. It confirmed his suspicion about why there had only been a three man patrol.

"You didn't know them before?" Keel asked.

Faheem shook his head vigorously.

Sekka wondered how much of Faheem's account was fact and how much was fiction. It was tempting to believe the man's story, given that he'd seen his comrades gunned down and so was obviously keen to avoid the same fate. Though, even if he was telling the truth, verifying the information with the resources available would be difficult, if not well nigh impossible.

Sekka's thoughts were interrupted when Crow said, "Light's fading guys."

Sekka looked about him and saw that Crow was

right. Dusk was descending rapidly and he hadn't noticed. He addressed Keel. "Anything more you want to ask?"

Keel stared hard at Faheem and sighed resignedly. "I've a feeling we've got all we're going to get."

"Not a hell of a lot, then," Crow said.

"More than we had before. Let's get the chopper warmed up."

Crow nodded. Grim-faced, he headed for the aircraft without a backward glance. Sensing a shift of mood, Faheem straightened.

Keel turned to the poacher. "Something else you want to tell us, Faheem?"

"I have told you all I know."

Keel nodded. "All right, then."

"Are you going to kill me?" Faheem asked suddenly.

Keel looked back at him before turning to Sekka. "Not sure. *Are* we?"

"No." Sekka said, and in a move that was so fast it took Faheem completely by surprise, he drew the knife from the sheath on his belt and slashed the blade across the meat of Faheem's injured left leg. The screech erupted from Faheem's throat as he went down, hands clamped around his thigh, his eyes widening in shock. Stowing the weapon, Sekka jerked his chin towards a point over the poacher's left shoulder. "They are."

Faheem twisted around and looked, in time to see several dark, hump-backed shapes loping silently through the scrub. A soft, chittering sound rose out of the gloom beyond the trees.

Clutching his leg, with the blood now spilling rapidly from between his fingers, Faheem stared up at Sekka in abject horror. "What are you doing?"

211

"Calling in the troops," Sekka said.

It wasn't only the remains of the roan antelope that had caught Sekka's eye during the chopper's descent. His attention had also been drawn to a flattened area of earth and scrub at the base of a low hill around one hundred yards from the gulley, and the dark shapes moving around it, which suggested the hyena clan had chosen the site as their communal den, the place from where they set out to hunt and to scavenge; a base they were prepared to defend by attacking any perceived enemy that strayed too close.

As the implication of Sekka's reply sank in, the poacher's eyes widened in fear. "You will leave me here?"

"That's the general idea," Keel said.

"But you cannot!"

"I think you'll find we can," Keel said. He turned to Sekka. "You fit?"

Sekka nodded.

Mo said, "We should kill him, like he killed our friends."

"We don't have to," Keel said. "The job'll be done for us."

A maniacal giggle sounded over to the right. Faheem let go a frightened whimper.

Keel nodded towards the water bottle lying in the dust. "You might want to hang on to that."

An unearthly scream erupted from beyond the trees, which quickly frittered away into a series of low, snuffling barks.

The Airbus's engine began to turn over.

Now visibly terrified, Faheem tried to push himself to his feet one-handed. "Take me with you!"

"I don't think so," Keel said, and turned away. "Let's

go."

As Keel, Sekka and Mo headed towards the chopper a desperate yell sounded behind them. "Baroud! Baroud!"

Keel halted and turned. "Did you say something?"

"Baroud!" Faheem cried. "It is the name! The name of the man Jaafar was talking to on the telephone!"

Faheem shrank back at Keel's approach. Keel squatted down. "You told us you didn't know the name."

"I was frightened. I could not remember it. Now, my head is clear. I remember! I remember! Baroud. It was Baroud!"

"If you're lying to me, Faheem..," Keel warned.

"No! No! It is the truth. I swear it!"

Keel stared into Faheem's face and saw the panic rooted in the man's eyes. "Colonel Baroud. All right, then."

So much for the High Command not being involved.

Without saying another word, Keel rose, tapped Faheem reassuringly on the shoulder, and rejoined Sekka and Mo. It took Faheem a moment to realize he was still being abandoned. His eyes showed white. "No! Please!"

By the time Keel and the others had reached the Airbus, Faheem had raised himself and had started to stumble after them, dragging his injured leg behind him. "Wait! Wait!"

As Sekka and Mo took up the rear and as Keel climbed into the vacant front seat and put on his headset, Crow nodded through the windshield towards the terrified Sudanese who was still struggling to reach them. "How long do you think he's got?"

"Depends on how hungry *they* are," Keel said and looked off to where half a dozen shadowy shapes were weaving their way through the coarse grass.

Faheem continued to shriek imprecations at them but his voice was drowned out by the chopper's engine. He was still screaming as Crow increased the pitch and took the Airbus skywards. As the aircraft banked left, Sekka watched dispassionately from the rear seat as the poacher appeared to pitch forward on to the ground and the hyena clan padded out from behind the bushes to form a ragged circle around him.

Keel's voice came through the headset. "I didn't know your watch was inscribed. What's it say?"

Sekka turned back from looking down at the ground, his face a dark mask. "Swiss Made - Water Resistant."

13

Deschamps, seated at his desk, stared up at Keel. There was concern and shock in his gaze. "What happened to the plan to hand him over to the police after you'd questioned him?"

"Changed my mind," Keel said coldly. "Too risky. There's no way he wouldn't mention our incursion and the fire fight to the police if we'd delivered him to them, even if it was to try and negotiate some sort of deal for himself. And if you're thinking about possible trace evidence I wouldn't worry. I doubt there'll be any. A few smears in the dust maybe, but that'll be it."

Deschamps said nothing for several long seconds. Then, abruptly, he stood and walked to the window, head cast down. Finally, after taking a series of deep breaths, he gathered himself, turned and said, "So do you think this Baroud exists, or did our friend make up the name to try and save his skin?"

Keel looked back at him. "The sixty-four thousand dollar question. My gut tells me it was the truth. It was likely he was holding out to see what we had planned before he drew his trump card. He played it and still lost. It's his own fault. He shouldn't have sat down at the table if he wasn't prepared to lose his shirt."

"He lost more than his shirt."

"Yes, well, you'll not see me lose any sleep over it."

"So what now?" Deschamps asked tightly.

"And there's your bonus for ten."

Deschamps' quizzical expression suggested he didn't understand the reference. Keel made no attempt to elaborate and, instead, said, "Honest answer? I'm not sure."

Deschamps frowned. "You found your killers and you dealt with them. We looked after our own. Wasn't that the intention?"

"It was," Keel said.

"I sense a 'but'," Deschamps said, and waited.

Keel collected his thoughts, and then nodded. "It was something Joseph said, when he told Faheem that the fees we get from park visitors help fund local communities; that the contributions go into building schools and clinics, projects like that. Faheem complained it wasn't enough. Joseph agreed. He said it's never enough."

"So?" Deschamps frowned.

"So, dealing with Faheem and his crew wasn't enough. I called Faheem a foot soldier. It's what he and the others were. Cannon fodder, as it turned out. Kind of makes me wonder about the general staff, the ones Jaafar reported to."

"The buyers?"

"If they're the ones pulling the strings. The one's further up the line, at any rate. Our Colonel Baroud, for instance."

"If he exists."

Keel nodded. "If he exists. If he does, he's moved to the top of my to-do list."

"Which means what, exactly? You plan to seek him out?"

"Every person needs a hobby."

Keel fell silent.

"What is it?" Deschamps' asked.

"Something just occurred to me. What if Toubia was in contact with Baroud in between the time Joseph interrupted the raid, and the ambush? Maybe Toubia wasn't the instigator. Maybe he reported in and Baroud gave the order to attack Joseph's patrol to retrieve their equipment and the last of the tusks? Maybe we should have pressed Faheem a little more."

Deschamps pursed his lips and stared down at his desk for several long seconds. Then, looking up, he said, "All right, so how are we going to find Baroud?"

"*We*?" Keel said.

"My park; my men; my decision."

Keel shook his head. "Not sure that's a good idea. Right now you can still say you didn't know Joseph and I were operating off-piste and that we did what we did. That's *your* trump card. You might like to hang on to it for a while. Far as we know, we made it in and out without being tracked, but we can't be too sure."

"You're thinking about the sister?"

"Who thought we were RSF."

"Who, we presume, alerted Jaafar and his patrol," Deschamps pointed out.

"Who've since been terminated." Keel paused, then sighed and said, "I agree it's not air tight; no operation is, but that's the risk we took. We take it to the next level and the stakes really will be raised, which means it's probably sensible if you do sit this one out."

"I think we're a long way past sensible," Deschamps said. "Don't you? And what about Mo?"

"I admit Mo's compromised, but that was his choice and as of this moment he doesn't have blood on his hands. That's down to Joseph and me."

"And Hassan?"

"Hassan's a big boy; he can look after himself. I've a feeling he's been doing that for quite a while. Joseph's seen the inside of his knock-off shop. He's probably got more contraband hidden away than the Egyptian customs."

"It's a thin line we're treading," Deschamps said.

"I agree, but we knew that already. It's what you said when we embarked on this thing. But you don't have to cross it. You can stay your side. Let someone else do the heavy lifting."

"And Crow?"

"He'll make his own decision, like he always does."

Deschamps sighed. "Then I repeat my question. How are we - you - going to find this man?"

"Not sure yet, but we won't get a better chance. The park's closed for the season. Joseph and I are due leave. Crow, too. You can get by without him. You've got your own licence; you can fly the chopper *and* the Cessna. Plus your other team leaders know what they're doing. No one'll be surprised if the three of us head off for some R & R. Better yet, tell them we're away attending a security conference somewhere. In the meantime, we'll see what we can dig up on this Colonel Baroud. Him being our only lead means it may not pan out. If it doesn't, we'll just have to live with it."

"We have their phones," Deschamps said.

"Yes, we do, but I'm not entirely certain how we can use the information. We can't hand the things over to the authorities. They'd want to know how we got hold of them. By the same token, if they do hold relevant info we don't want to use it in a way that'll alert the bad guys. At the moment, the colonel will probably be wondering why he hasn't heard from his pal Jaafar. In which case, let him wonder. His remaining in the dark works to our advantage. Let it continue to be one of life's enduring mysteries: the RSF patrol that vanished into thin air."

"And if the sister starts making waves about her brother's disappearance?"

"While in the hands of an RSF patrol? Who's she going to complain to? Amnesty International? From what we know about the RSF, it rules the roost over there. It has connections at the highest level. I can't see any of them mobilizing forces to investigate the disappearance of an elephant poacher. As for Jaafar and his two mates, they've gone up in smoke, literally; while their truck's either been ripped apart for spares, or else it's been pimped to within an inch of its life."

The phones referred to by Deschamps were the ones Keel and Sekka had removed from the bodies of the RSF patrol members before Hassan went to work. So far they had not been examined, so any information they held had yet to be determined.

Deschamps leaned back in his chair, his brow furrowed.

"What?" Keel said.

"I may know someone," Deschamps said.

"Someone?" Keel said.

Deschamps sat up. "Who might be able to give us a lead on our errant colonel."

"I'm listening."

"Let me make a call first. I'll get back to you."

"Care to give me a clue?"

"If I do that," Deschamps said, "I might have to kill you."

Keel went to speak, then, noting the expression on Deschamps' face, nodded, stood up and said, "I'll stand by."

Deschamps waited until Keel had left the room, before he picked up the phone. It had been a while since he'd used the number. He wondered if it was still active.

Time to find out.

"N'Djamena?" Keel said.

Deschamps nodded. "I've set up a meeting with an old colleague, a friend. He's seconded to the embassy."

"Seconded?" Keel said. "You mean he's a spook."

"He is a diplomat on special assignment."

"Right," Keel said. "So he's definitely a spook. DGSE?"

"Ah, jeeze," Crow said. "Not those guys."

"I'm assuming he won't be meeting us at the embassy," Sekka said.

"There'll be a message waiting for you at your hotel," Deschamps said, throwing Crow a cool look. "The Chez Wou. It's close to the airport. Basic but comfortable. I use it whenever I'm in the city."

"Chez *Wou*?" Crow said.

"It a regular layover for Chinese businessmen."

"Well, no shit. Just so long as we don't have to wear a bloody button hole for the meet. Been there, done that."

Deschamps ignored the comment. "I've also been in contact with Sabine. She's on her way back from Dubai." To Crow, Deschamps said, "Instead of you picking her up at Sahr, she'll join the three of you in the capital. You can all ferry back together."

Keel nodded. "Roger that. When do we leave?"

"Your rooms are booked for tomorrow night.

220

Check-in is fifteen hundred. I am not privy to the meeting arrangements, but as it's at least a three hour flight I would plan accordingly."

"Ten-thirty works for me," Crow said. "I'll make sure the Cessna's ready."

"Sounds good," Keel said, and turned to Deschamps. "What's your man's name?"

"Lavasse," Deschamps said, adding, "Probably."

"I wouldn't worry," Crow said. "He'll be easy to spot. It'll be the guy with the stick-on 'tache and a bulge under the armpit."

When Deschamps gave him the eye, Crow said, "Ah, come on, in our business we've all been there."

"How much does he know?" Sekka asked.

"Enough to suit our purposes."

"You trust him?" Sekka asked.

"With my life. I'll leave you to make your own judgement."

Keel nodded in acceptance. "Fair enough."

Which gained him a wry look from Crow.

As they left the office, Keel said, "Stick-on 'tache.? That's the best you could come up with?"

"Hell, "Crow said. "That's just the men. Don't get me started on the women."

The Chez Wou was located south of the airport. Two-storied and built around a central garden, with its own pool, it looked, Keel, thought, with its shabby blue and white facade, like a jaded fifty-room version of an American motel; while Deschamps' description of it being close to the airport was something of an understatement, as it couldn't have been more than eight hundred yards from the end of the main runway,

221

and, therefore, in comfortable walking distance.

As Keel, Sekka and Crow signed in, the receptionist held out an envelope and addressed Keel in English. "For you, Mr. Keel."

Keel took the envelope and while Sekka and Crow received their keys he scanned the enclosed note.

CÔTÉ JARDIN, 4 PM.

Crow checked the clock above the reception desk. "Gives us forty minutes."

"Drop our bags off," Keel said. "Back here in ten."

Late afternoon, and despite the taxi's air conditioning being set to max, the heat was still oppressive; not surprising given that N'Djamena was known to be one of the hottest cities on earth. Turning off the airport road on to the capital's main artery, the Avenue General de Gaulle, the traffic began to slow. There were a fair number of troops about, Keel noticed, along with strategically positioned military vehicles, most notably around the ministry buildings adjacent to the Rond Point Etoile roundabout; evidence that threats of attack by Boko Haram and a possible resurgence of anti-government activity by opponents of the regime were still being taken seriously. Further proof, Keel reflected, that in dictatorships paranoia tended to be a common disease.

The *Côté Jardin* was situated a couple of blocks east of the roundabout, on a leafy side street lined with a variety of eateries and vending stalls selling cheap trinkets and African wood carvings. Keel and Crow made their way through the entrance and found themselves in an attractive, tree-shaded courtyard, dotted with dining areas arranged under thatched-roof gazebos.

"Looks like Robinson Crusoe beat us to it," Crow murmured as they took their seats at an empty table.

A waiter appeared and took Keel's order for two Gala beers, while Crow surveyed the surrounding tables, which were occupied by a mixture of nationalities. There were a few women present, all of them with male company. Neither Crow nor Keel paid any attention as Sekka entered the restaurant with a folded newspaper under his arm and made his way to the bar. As Sekka took his seat, a shape appeared over Crow's left shoulder.

Male, mid-forties or thereabouts; slim built and casually dressed, in an unbuttoned, long-sleeved denim shirt over a grey t-shirt, accompanied by stone-coloured cargo trousers and desert boots. No moustache, but there was a distinct three-day shadow across the lower half of a tanned face, offset by a pair of intense dark eyes and matching dark hair cut just scruffily enough so as to appear fashionably unkempt. A small waxed-canvas knapsack was slung casually over his left shoulder, under which there was no sign of a bulge, a fact upon which Crow declined to comment.

"Major Keel?"

English with a Gallic accent.

"That would be me," Keel said.

"Paul Lavasse. May I join you?"

Keel took the proffered hand. "Please do."

"Crow," Crow said, as the new arrival went to sit down.

"*Enchanté*," Lavasse said as he shook hands once more.

"Drink?" Keel caught the waiter's eye.

"Thank you; a Diablo."

As the waiter retreated with the order, Lavasse placed the knapsack at his feet and settled into his chair. Extending his left leg, he winced slightly as he did so, a move that did not go unnoticed by Crow. Seeing Crow's reaction, Lavasse smiled thinly, reached down, and rapped a knuckle against the side of his lower knee, producing a sound similar to tapping a pencil against a table top, indicating that everything below the joint was a prosthetic attachment. "It doesn't like the heat."

"Who does?" Crow said. "How'd it happen?" Adding drily, "Or is that classified?"

The Frenchman rewarded Crow with a calculating look, and then stared down at the offending limb. "Mali; a disagreement with a Tuareg patrol."

"*Opération Serval?*" Keel said, thinking that Lavasse's English was extremely fluent.

Lavasse looked up and nodded, leaning back as the waiter returned and set his drink on the table.

"That where you met René?"

Lavasse took a sip from his glass and set it down by his elbow. "He said you were direct."

"I like to know who I'm talking to." Keel indicated Crow. "We both do."

The Frenchman lifted his glass once more. "As do I."

Keel waited. Crow took a couple of swallows from his beer.

"*Division,* Sahel Desk."

The Frenchman paused to let the information sink in. As a means of establishing his credentials it had been a succinct declaration, spelling out clearly, and confirming Keel's suspicion that Deschamps' contact was indeed a member of the French security

224

apparatus; in this case, no less a department than *Division Action,* the branch responsible for carrying out the DGSE's clandestine operations; in other words, black ops; the dirty jobs no one else would touch.

When he saw that Keel and Crow had accepted his provenance, he continued: "We received word the MNLA had taken some oil workers hostage. I was directed to negotiate their release. We were close to making the deal when we learnt there was a rival Islamist group in the field - the Ansar al-Din - and that they were taking over MNLA territory. My government was worried that the hostages would end up in Ansar al-Din's hands due to its association with Daesh. We received intelligence that the prisoners were being held in a village on the outskirts of Léré, so there was change of plan. Instead of bargaining for their release I was ordered to get them out before they were handed on. Because I had gained the trust of local sources, my job was to accompany the rescue team."

Lavasse paused, as if to gather himself. "There was an ambush. I was wounded. We were pinned down in the village so we called for support. René Deschamps was in command of the unit that was sent to rescue my team and the hostages."

"Did you get everybody out?" Crow asked.

"We lost one hostage and five men from the rescue squads." The Frenchman rapped his leg again. "I was one of the lucky ones."

Lavasse picked up his Diablo. Keel and Crow said nothing.

"You wanted information," Lavasse said into the silence. He set his drink down and ran a fingertip up the side of the glass, creating a line in the condensation. "Colonel Baroud?"

"Anything you have would be useful," Keel said.

Lavasse nodded, his face suddenly serious.

"I take it he's a bit of a shithead," Crow said.

Lavasse shook his head. "No, he is a big shithead. *Un grand trou du cul.*"

"Let's hear it," Crow said.

The Frenchman waited a moment, then said, "His full name is Fidèle Khalil Baroud. He is forty-two years of age and Chadian by birth, but there is a connection by marriage on his mother's side: to the family of the RSF commander."

"Hemeti?" Keel said.

Lavasse nodded and then shrugged. "It is not that unusual. If you include everyone from immediate relatives to associates, we calculate that the family and its *confrères* make up approximately ten percent of RSF personnel.

"Jesus," Crow said. "That's gotta be, what, nearly three thousand people?"

Lavasse nodded. "Naturally, that includes most of the senior officers."

"Naturally," Keel said drily.

"Sounds like the Mafia," Crow said.

Lavasse smiled thinly. "A good comparison. There is reliable evidence that nearly all the senior ranks are involved in some form of criminal enterprise in addition to their RSF duties. You know how Hemeti came to power, by taking control of the Jebel Amer goldfields from his rival, Musa Hilal?"

Keel nodded. "René gave us a run down."

"It was how he made his fortune. He uses those funds to finance his non-military activities, by means of..." Lavasse paused, then said, "...you would call them 'front' companies, yes?"

226

"Right," Crow said. "So exactly like the Mafia."

Lavasse acknowledged the riposte. "The main one is the Al Gunade Group. It is owned and run by Abdulrahim Dagalo: Hemeti's brother. He is also deputy head of the RSF. You will not be surprised to learn that the company trades chiefly in gold. There are two more: GSK Advance and Tradive General Trading, which is based in the United Arab Emirates. They are controlled by another of Hemeti's brothers: Algoney. They deal in transport, iron and steel, information technology, security, and tourism."

"*Tourism*?" Crow's eyes widened. "Seriously?"

"Yes, seriously," Lavasse said, sounding almost surprised by Crow's scepticism. "That part of the company was set up by Hemeti's cousin, Adel. He was Omar Bashir's Minister of Tourism. It constructs shopping malls as well as hotels and luxury villas, both in Khartoum and the UAE."

"Speculate to accumulate," Keel murmured.

"Jesus wept," Crow said.

"Indeed," Lavasse said.

"And Baroud is heavily involved in the family business." Keel said.

"That is correct."

"What's his background?"

"We believe he arrived in the Sudan around 2010, after being accused of a tribal killing in Am Nabak. He crossed the border to evade arrest."

"In the hope the family connection would come in useful," Keel said. "So, what then? He worked his way up the ranks?"

The Frenchman nodded. "We do not know exactly what he was doing between his arrival in the country and his joining the RSF. We suspect he was part of a

227

smuggling gang."

"Drugs?" Crow said.

"We think cars."

"Cars?" Crow echoed doubtfully.

"Do not be fooled. It is a profitable trade. In Baroud's case, we believe he was part of a group that stole vehicles in North Darfur and delivered them to Khartoum for sale to members of the Dagalo family."

"Serving his apprenticeship," Keel said.

Lavasse nodded. "And very successfully. He was recruited into the RSF when it was formed in 2013. Since then, he has carried out many different duties."

"Now, why," Crow muttered, "do I not like the sound of that?"

"Go on," Keel said.

"He came to our attention when his name appeared in a Human Rights Watch report on an RSF counter-insurgency campaign in 2015: Operation *Decisive Summer*. Its purpose was to spread terror. Villages were attacked and burned, homes looted, women and men beaten and gang-raped and then executed. Baroud was in charge of what you and I would call snatch-squads. As well as taking people off the street, they were known to have entered hospitals to assault and seize patients."

Lavasse's face hardened. "It is alleged he was responsible for the killing of dozens of prisoners from the rebel Justice and Equality Movement, after the RSF's battle with them in Goz Dengu. Several witnesses have placed him at the scene."

"Let me guess," Keel said softly. "But they were too intimidated to take it further."

Lavasse nodded. "One could not blame them. Baroud's superiors, though, were very impressed by his methods. They needed someone to take charge of their detention centres. They were built to house prisoners taken during the government operations. We believe it was Baroud who set up the Fridge."

"Okay," Crow said. "I'll bite. What the hell is the fridge?"

"It is one of the RSF's secret facilities. They call it the Fridge because they use extreme cold as an instrument of torture. It is still in operation today."

"Not that secret, then," Keel said.

Crow glanced at him. "Don't know about you, but I'm *really* beginning to really hate this guy."

"What else," Keel asked.

The Frenchman massaged his left knee. "From there, he was seconded to Brigadier Gedo Hamdan's brigade and given charge of a disciplinary unit. His speciality was sending patrols on to the streets of Khartoum to round up young men. They would have their heads shaved in public."

"Wonderful," Crow murmured. "So now he's Sweeney-bloody-Todd."

Lavasse took a sip from his glass. "When Hamdan took temporary control of the Border Guards, Baroud went with him as his second-in-command. They became part of the Tabin: bandits that specialize in drug trafficking. We think they are also involved in human trafficking."

"Could be where he learned about the profit in ivory," Crow mused. "He probably had some knowledge of it before he did a runner back in '10."

"And from there?" Keel said.

"He was promoted to colonel and given command of the RSF's scouting forces in West Darfur."

"And that would explain how he's linked to our pal

229

Toubia and his mates," Crow said.

Lavasse hadn't finished. "He was re-called to the capital to help quell the street protests in 2019. We think he was the one who gave the order to burn the university's tents and clinics in the June massacre."

Neither Keel nor Crow needed clarification. The killings had made headlines around the world, when, using gunfire and tear gas, the RSF had been sent in to disperse a pro-democracy sit-in demonstration. Hundreds of civilians, many of them targeted health workers, had been injured and more than a hundred killed. Scores of dead bodies had been thrown into the Nile.

"Definitely makes him one of Hemeti's blue-eyed boys," Crow said.

The Frenchman frowned. "I am sorry, I do not-"

"Means he's probably due another promotion," Keel said.

"Lavasse smiled another thin smile. "There *are* rumours he is being considered for the governorship of the Blue Nile State."

Crow frowned. "Remind me where that is."

It was Keel who answered. "Corner of South Sudan and Ethiopia."

A silence settled across the table, broken when Crow said, "Any idea of his whereabouts and what he's doing now?"

Lavasse took a sip from his glass and laid it down carefully on the table. "Our latest intelligence has him in Dubai."

Keel and Crow exchanged glances.

"What?" Lavasse said, sensing an unspoken message.

"Nothing." Crow lifted his glass to his lips. "Small

world is all. What's he doing there?"

"Our sources tell us he has been helping to arrange the purchase and delivery of a supply of fighting vehicles."

"What are we talking? Tanks? Armoured cars?"

Lavasse shook his head. "Toyotas: Hilux and Land Cruisers. The RSF buys them in the UAE and ships them through Jeddah to Sudan. On arrival, they are distributed to service centres and military bases. When they arrive their chassis are strengthened and ordnance is added. It is their favourite attack vehicle."

"You don't say." Crow said, taking a sip of beer, his expression neutral.

"Others are converted into luxury off-road vehicles for Hemeti and his entourage."

Keel frowned. "Toyota has to know what their equipment's being used for. They'll have seen the newsreels. I thought there were trading laws. What about end-user certificates? How come they agreed the deal?"

Lavasse let go a resigned sigh. "Our local sources did contact Toyota. They were told that Toyota complies with all export control and sanctions laws, and that they require dealers and distributors to do the same. They say they have a strict policy not to sell vehicles to buyers who may use or modify them for paramilitary or terrorist activities, which would include military and police operations in Sudan."

"Well, that's obviously a load of guff," Crow said.

Lavasse made a face. "In the dealers' defence, the vehicles are not acquired through a single order. The RSF use separate companies to make the purchases, using the El Nilein Bank in Abu Dhabi as a conduit. All orders, however, are generated through Tradive

General Trading."

"Hemeti's brother's outfit," Keel said.

The Frenchman nodded. "We think there could be at least thirty companies involved in the deal."

"Thirty?" Crow said, with something approaching awe. "How many trucks are we talking about?"

"The last order added up to seven hundred and fifty."

"Shit," Crow muttered. "And here, folk were thinking the next lot couldn't be worse than Bashir. Is there anyone in the upper ranks who isn't on the take?"

Lavasse gave what could only be interpreted as a typical Gallic shrug. "It is too early to say."

"Which is why you're monitoring the situation," Keel said drily.

Lavasse smiled. "As are your people."

"*My* people?"

"The UK; your government agencies."

"Because?"

"The Sahel is an important strategic region. It is in our mutual interest to see it remains stable. There are other actors whose interference is increasing: Israel, Russia, China."

Crow reached for his drink and said casually, "Didn't I read somewhere that it was you guys who gave Déby a leg up in the first place?"

Lavasse shrugged. "I fear both our countries still have much to answer for. However, there are advantages in maintaining a good relationship. In exchange for technical support."

"You mean military support," Crow said.

Irritation flashed briefly in the Frenchman's eyes. "The support covers many fields. France does not deploy troops in Chad. There is only a technical military co-operation agreement. So we provide assistance by other means: munitions, fuel, intelligence, expertise in counter-insurgency tactics. It is the same with all the Sahel states: Mali, Niger, Eritrea, Burkina Fasso and so forth. In exchange, France receives help in dealing with the kidnapping of French citizens and halting the spread of Islamist groups in the Sahel region."

And for that, Keel thought, you're prepared to overlook the human rights abuses. It was ever thus. Sup with the devil and you'd better use a very long spoon.

"I brought you this," Lavasse said. The Frenchman lifted his knapsack, undid the buckle, and reached inside.

The 7x5 photograph was of a broad-faced, arrogant-looking man dressed in camouflage fatigues. The red collar tabs and the shoulder flashes bearing two stars set below the secretary bird emblem identified him as an *'aqid* - the Sudanese equivalent of a colonel. A name tag on his right breast and two rows of medals on the left side of his chest completed the adornment and confirmed his identity.

Keel studied the dark complexion; the unsmiling features set beneath a receding hairline offset by a thin moustache. It was a cruel face, Keel thought; devoid of sentiment.

Crow said nothing as Keel passed the photograph across the table.

Keel addressed Lavasse. "You said he's in Dubai. Do you know where, exactly?"

The corner of Lavasse's mouth twitched in what might have been the beginnings of a smile.

233

Keel leant forward. "All right, so how much *did* René tell you?"

Lavasse gazed into Keel's eyes and took a long breath, which he held for several seconds before exhaling. "Perhaps Mr. Sekka would care to join us first?"

14

"Well, hell." Crow feigned resignation as he pushed the photograph to one side. "Looks like we've been rumbled."

Keel sat back. "Why not? Saves me having to repeat everything." Looking towards the bar, he saw that Sekka, drink in hand, had abandoned the newspaper and was already vacating his stool.

"Swear to God, the bugger's got second sight," Crow muttered as Sekka approached the table. The pilot used his boot to push out the remaining empty chair. "Joseph! Fancy meeting you here. Take a pew. Have you met Paul Lavasse?"

"Only from a distance."

Lavasse smiled wryly as he and Sekka shook hands.

"So?" Sekka said as he sat down.

Keel slid the photograph across the table top. "Meet Colonel Baroud."

Sekka gazed down at the image, his face set. "Location?"

"Last known whereabouts: Dubai."

Sekka raised his head.

"Yeah," Crow said. "That's what we thought."

Crow looked at Keel who looked towards Lavasse and said, "So, where were we?"

The Frenchman paused and then said, "René told

me about the ambush."

"And?"

"And that you believe the killers were not working alone."

"Yes and no," Keel said.

Lavasse blinked.

"We know they reported to a higher authority and we know they had a potential buyer for the ivory. What we don't know is whether those two parties are one and the same. We suspect they are and that it's Baroud. We also can't be certain if he gave the order to ambush Joseph and his ranger team, or if the poachers were acting on their own initiative. Either way, Baroud's the next link in the chain. I think it behoves us to have a talk with him."

"A *talk*?" Lavasse said.

"I use the term loosely."

"Indeed," Lavasse said drily. "From what I know of your record, Major, I would have thought you'd have something a little more *énergique*...forceful...in mind than mere conversation."

"Uh, oh," Crow said.

"You've been doing your homework," Keel said.

Lavasse smiled. "In my position I do have access to certain resources. It would have been remiss of me not to have made use of them."

"And I suppose that would include me and Joseph," Crow said.

Lavasse's smile remained fixed.

Crow grimaced. "Guess that answers that."

"So, is this the part where we sit here and listen to you run through our biographies?" Keel said.

Lavasse shook his head. "Nothing so melodramatic. In any case, what would it prove? Suffice for me to say that I know something of you and your friends' qualifications and reputation in carrying out official and...shall we say...independent assignments. It means I am also aware that in most of those cases, action has tended to speak louder than words."

Crow glanced sideways at Keel and mouthed, "*'louder than words'*?"

Lavasse turned his head. "René spoke very highly of you, too. Mr. Crow."

Before Crow could respond, Lavasse looked around the table and said quietly, "If you *do* confront Baroud and interrogate him and he provides the information you require, what then?"

"That would probably depend on him," Keel said, after a moments pause, thinking: *this is a conversation I've had before.*

Lavasse nodded thoughtfully. "I rather think, Major, that if he gives you the information you require, you may not have a choice. You may have to kill him, too."

"Because?" Crow said.

Lavasse ignored Crow and stared hard into Keel's face. "Because I guarantee Baroud is not the person at the top. He is only the *next* link in the chain. There will be someone above him and someone else above them, and I do not think you will be satisfied until you have reached the one at the end of the chain: the person controlling the winch. The problem you have, therefore, is that if Baroud remains alive, he will undoubtedly warn those above him that you are going after them. It would be better, therefore, if Baroud was not in a position to do that."

"You said *'too'.*"

It was Keel who'd spoken.

"I am sorry?" Lavasse said.

"You said *'too'*, meaning: as well as."

Sekka's head came up. As did Crow's, who said, "Ah, shit."

"So how much did René *really* tell you?" Keel's voice was pitched low.

"Lavasse leant back in his chair and after a couple of seconds let go a sigh. "Most of it. How you tracked down the poachers; how you dealt with them; how you obtained Baroud's name."

"Christ," Crow muttered.

Keel eyes never left the Frenchman's face. "René said he trusted you with his life. Can *we*?"

Lavasse mirrored Keel's stare. "Yes."

"That was bloody quick," Crow said.

"It is the truth. If he asks me for help and if it is within my power, I will do everything I can."

"No questions asked?"

"No questions asked."

"So," Keel said, after everyone had digested Lavasse's response. "Back to Baroud. You don't appear too concerned at the prospect of him not being around any more."

The Frenchman's lips twitched once more. "If he were to die, let us say that we would raise no objections."

Crow frowned. "Because?"

"Because the DGSE has someone in the wings ready to take Baroud's place," Sekka said. "You've an agent in the RSF. That's how you've been getting the information."

Lavasse said nothing.

"You sly boots." Crow wagged an admonishing finger.

"Call me a cynic," Keel said, "but if I didn't know any

better I'd think you had plans to remove Baroud yourselves, until we showed up, and you figured it'd suit the folks back in the *Division* if someone else were to do the job for you."

Lavasse said nothing.

Sekka broke the silence. "Which means you probably do have Baroud's precise location."

Lavasse regarded the three men seated around him, noting the now unsmiling features. After several seconds, he gathered himself and said, "Tradive has offices in Abu Dhabi, but the company maintains residential properties in Dubai. They include two marina apartments as well as a villa on the Palm Jumeirah. One of the apartments and the villa are for use only by the Dagalo family and close associates. The other apartment is for the use of company executives. Our last report indicated Baroud was at the villa. He may or may not be there now."

"Gives us a place to start, though" Keel said. "You have addresses for the company and the accommodation?"

"Of course." Lavasse reached for his knapsack.

Not only company information and addresses, but an aerial view of the Palm with the position of the villa conveniently highlighted, on the north-eastern quadrant of the development, three-quarters of the way along one of the curved fronds.

"Must have cost a pretty dirham," Crow observed.

"Thirteen million dollars U.S.," Lavasse said. "Approximately."

"We're in the wrong bloody job," Crow murmured as he gazed down at the image of one of the world's most spectacular real estate projects.

Designed to represent the shape of a date palm and

239

protected by a circular breakwater, seven million tons of rock and one hundred and twenty million cubic feet of sand had been used in the construction of the archipelago; enough material to form a two-metre-wide wall capable of encircling the globe three times. Financed out of the profits from petroleum sales, its backers had christened it the eighth wonder of the world.

Keel shook his head. "Careful what you wish for."

"Why's that?"

"Did a job for an oil exec a few years back. Told me he'd taken a look at one of the villas. Thought it'd be a nice holiday home for the family. Not quite in the same price bracket as Baroud's, mind. Turns out it wasn't quite what they were hoping for. The developers over-reached themselves; realized that if they wanted to recoup their money they'd have to build more houses, which they did, but it meant they had to cram them closer together. Client said it'd be like living on a council estate, and that if you wanted air con, which you would, it'd set you back another small fortune. You're probably better off with a time-share in the Lake District."

"In that case," Crow said, "my heart bleeds."

"Plus," Keel added, "a lot of the places were bought as an investment. Means some have never been used. So it's not exactly a going concern. If, after all that, you still want to move in, beware the neighbours. You could end up next to Ashraf Ghani or one of Putin's mobster pals...or David Beckham..."

"Yeah, but on the bright side, security wouldn't be a problem."

"Talking of which," Sekka said, pointedly.

Lavasse indicated the aerial photo. "The Jumeirah

development has gate houses with barrier poles at the entrance to each frond and all the properties are linked to the Palm's Command and Control Centre which is located on the main causeway. There were issues with the personnel manning the barriers. Residents complained that procedure was lax and that only single male visitors in cheap cars and taxis and commercial vehicles are screened before they were allowed entry. Things have improved. Police and Security units are meant to be on twenty-four hour call. A similar arrangement is in place at the marina."

"Those prices, I should bloody think so," Crow said.

"Does he travel alone or with family?" Sekka asked. "Does he *have* a family?"

"He has a wife and two children. On this occasion they did not travel with him."

"Who did?" Keel said. "Anyone?"

"A driver who is also his bodyguard."

"What about domestic staff: maids and such like?"

"There are none who live on the premises. They attend during the day. He is a man who enjoys his privacy."

Sekka turned to Keel. "What are you thinking?"

"That we have a lot to think *about*," Keel said, and looked up to find that Lavasse was studying him with what could only be described as a speculative expression on his tanned face.

"Something on *your* mind?" Keel said.

Lavasse pursed his lips, as if arriving at a decision and stuck a hand inside his knapsack once more. Removing a slim envelope, he slid it across the table towards Keel. "If you do manage to confront Baroud you may find these to be of use. It may save you the bother of killing him."

241

Keel opened the envelope and drew forth half a dozen photographs. After glancing at them, he slid the images across the table.

Crow picked up the first photo. "What've we got?"

"Leverage," Keel said. "Maybe."

Crow looked down at the photo. His eyes widened. "Whoa, wasn't expecting that." He passed the image to Sekka. "I can see why he likes to keep things private."

"You haven't acted on these yourself?" Sekka said, as Keel passed the rest of the photographs across the table.

Lavasse shrugged. "The opportunity has not presented itself."

Until now, Keel thought.

Sekka handed the photographs back to Keel, who replaced them in the envelope.

"I also have these," Lavasse said.

Keel found himself gazing down at a set of floor plans.

"They are from the website of the firm that constructed Baroud's villa," Lavasse continued. "They are for customers who intend to purchase one of their homes."

"You're kidding," Crow said, as Lavasse then laid down two 3-D renditions of the same property, showing the layout of the villa's ground and upper floor, complete with computer generated walls and doorways. It was like having a bird's eye view of a film set interior. Each room was identified, from the kitchen to the master bedroom.

"I'm assuming your bosses don't know you're giving us this stuff?" Keel said.

"You assume correctly."

"If we don't...dispose of him, it could be a while

before your man gets a chance to take over."

Lavasse shrugged. "Our time will come." The Frenchman hesitated, and then said, "There is one other thing. If Baroud *is* behind the men who killed your elephants and murdered your rangers, it's possible his presence in Dubai is connected to something else beyond the purchase of army vehicles."

Keel's head lifted.

Lavasse pursed his lips. "You understand that wildlife trafficking is not part of the DGSE's remit? That is the responsibility of other agencies

Keel nodded. "Okay, so?"

"That does not mean we ignore activities that overlap with our own intelligence findings, or that we pay no heed if we see certain patterns emerging."

"Patterns?" Crow said.

"In the activities of targeted personnel; government and border officials, for example, intelligence information and criminal activity often follow the same routes. Traffickers are always looking for new methods of concealment and delivery. Anything that we do come across that we consider significant but which does not directly involve the *Division* we pass on to the relevant authorities."

"And Dubai fits in, how?" Sekka said.

"Wildlife crime is the biggest illegal transnational industry after drugs, weapons and the exploitation of humans. Some say it is worth as much as twenty-five billion dollars a year. When it comes to the transportation of illegal items such as rhino horn, animal skins, bones, and ivory, as well as live animals, Dubai is known to be a major entrepôt for the trafficking gangs."

"Because of its links to the Far East," Keel said.

"Correct. Up until now, most contraband goods have been ferried by air but transportation by sea is increasing. It takes longer but it's cheaper."

"Well, we know Baroud has connections to shipping companies," Crow mused.

"So he could be there to supervise distribution," Sekka said.

"Seems a lot of hassle for ten tusks," Crow said.

"You are assuming Salma's ivory to be the only haul." Lavasse smiled thinly. "What if the tusks from *your* elephants are part of a larger consignment? We've had reports of recent cross-border ivory raids into the CAR and even as far as Cameroon, Uganda and the DRC. Not just for ivory but also rhino horn and lion bones. It is possible the incidents were coordinated."

Lavasse addressed Keel. "I can tell from your expression that you are wondering what you might be getting yourselves into. If you'll allow me to offer a word of advice, I would suggest that if you do intend to pursue this, you should consult with someone who is far more familiar with the trade." Lavasse paused, and then said, "Starting with your veterinarian, Doctor Bouvier, perhaps?"

Crow's head came up. "In your files, too, is she?"

If he was put out by Crow's accusatory tone, Lavasse gave no indication. Instead, he seemed mildly surprised by the question. "But of course. It is a requirement. The records of all former military personnel remain active."

A hush descended upon the table until Crow said carefully, "*Excuse* me?" He looked from Keel to Sekka. "Either of you guys know?"

"Not me," Keel said, while Sekka shook his head.

Keel considered Crow's barbed response to

Lavasse's revelation and wondered what might have sparked the pilot's confrontational attitude. But then a memory surfaced.

There'd been another Frenchwoman in Crow's life, Keel recalled; a medical doctor, working with *Médecins Sans Frontières*. It had been several years ago and Crow rarely, if ever, talked about her; but Keel remembered the pilot revealing that she'd been killed, shot during a mercy mission to airlift a pro-Western Afghan tribal leader to a medical centre across the Pakistan border. The incident and the loss he'd experienced went a long way to explain Crow's reaction and his attempt to protect the reputation of Salma's veterinarian doctor.

Lavasse frowned. "Forgive me. I assumed you were cognisant with Doctor Bouvier's background."

"*Cognisant?*" Crow said, his voice beginning to vibrate.

"Perhaps you'd care to elaborate?" Sekka said quickly, sensing Crow might be about to let rip.

Lavasse shook his head. "Clearly, I have spoken out of turn. Again, my apologies. It would be best, I think, if you spoke either with René or Miss Bouvier herself."

Abruptly, before anyone could offer a reply and, as if sensing that he had probably outstayed his welcome, Lavasse drained his glass and rose to his feet. "Now, if you will forgive me, I really must take my leave. I hope the information has been of use." Gathering up his knapsack, he addressed Sekka with a quizzical half-smile. "Was it your intention to follow me when I left?"

"That was the plan."

The Frenchman's smile remained in place. "Then I have saved you the bother. You know, you are taller than you look in your file."

245

"Oh, that's funny," Crow said. "That's hilarious."

"And you, Mr. Crow..," Lavasse said, arching an eyebrow, "... look a lot older."

"If we require more information?" Keel cut in, before Crow had a chance to respond.

"René knows how to contact me."

The Frenchman shouldered his bag. "A pleasure, gentlemen. Whatever your endeavours, I wish you good fortune. Stay safe."

"You, too," Keel said.

But Lavasse was already on his way. Crow watched, his expression tight, as the Frenchman headed towards the exit and disappeared. Then, turning, he let go a long breath. "Well...shit. So what now, boss man?"

Keel picked up the photograph showing Baroud in uniform and stared down at it. His expression neutral.

"We consider our options."

"How was Dubai," Crow asked.

"Hot," Sabine said.

"And here isn't?"

A taxi had delivered Sabine from the airport to the Chez Wou. After confirming that Keel and the others had checked in but were away from the hotel, she had left a message that she'd meet them upon their return in the hotel's bar. An hour later, showered and changed, she'd found that Keel and the others had arrived first, and were waiting for her, along with a welcoming cold beer.

The bar was situated under a fabric awning, adjacent to the hotel's swimming pool, an unprepossessing rectangle flanked by shaded sun loungers and a few ornamental trees.

Taking the proffered chair, Sabine laid her bag by her feet and reached for her glass. "*Santé.*"

She did not wait for the others to follow, but took a long swallow before putting her glass back down and regarding them all with a wry smile. "*Vétérinaires des Armées.* French Army Veterinary Corps."

They looked at her.

"Uh, oh," Crow said, after a pause. "Looks like our spook pal called René. And, what, René called you?"

"He thought I deserved a...heads up...yes? *I* thought it would save you asking."

"Sneaky bugger," Crow said, adding quickly. "René, not you."

Sabine smiled, and ran a hand through her hair, tucking a stray wisp behind her left ear. "I was still at vet school when they asked if I would consider becoming an Army Veterinarian. It is an offer they make to some students in their third or fourth year. I suspect my father might have had something to do with my selection, though he always denied it. He was a career army officer - a *commandant.* I signed up for two reasons. One, because I thought it would please my father, which it did, and two, that I would get to see some of the world, which I did."

"But..?" Keel said.

She shrugged. "It took me two years to realize I was not happy. The veterinary division is part of the Army's Health Service and so my responsibilities included human food quality and safety, which did not interest me at all. We also undertook research into biological sciences and human and animal disease control, which included developing protection against chemical and nuclear agents. That was slightly more interesting, but only for a while. In the end, I knew there had to be something more. I became a vet to look after animals, not humans." Another quick smile crossed her face. "Also, I was not very good at taking orders."

Crow grinned and raised his glass. "Welcome to the club."

Sabine acknowledged the toast. "So I completed my five years service and then went back to general veterinary medicine. I started out working for small animal clinics, improving my knowledge. I was helping out at a wildlife sanctuary when I heard there was an opening for a vet at La Palmyre, one of the best zoos in France. I knew they did a lot of conservation work so I applied for the post and was accepted."

Sabine's face lit up. "I loved it: working with wild animals, not those that are domesticated. While I was there I met Romain Pizzi. He's the world's foremost specialist in zoo and wildlife medicine. I attended one of his lectures and introduced myself. I told him that if the opportunity ever arose I would like to work with him. Six months later I was in Vietnam helping him in the keyhole surgical removal of diseased gallbladders in bears rescued from illegal bile farming. I never looked back."

"How'd you end up at Salma?" Keel asked.

"I have a friend who works at Matusadona National Park, in Zimbabwe, which also comes under African Parks. She heard that Salma was looking for a vet. I saw an opportunity to put my experiences working with Romain to the test, so I did some research and then contacted AP. I told them what I'd been doing, and here we are."

"You didn't want to try for one of the better known reserves?" Sekka said.

248

Sabine shook her head. "I chose Salma *because* it was off the tourist trail. I knew it would be more challenging than Shamwari or the Kruger." Her voice dropped and sadness touched her face. "That turned out to be true, but not in the way I imagined."

Crow waited a while then said, "How come none of us knew this?"

Sabine took a sip from her glass. "You did not ask."

Game, set and match, Keel thought.

Sabine lowered her drink, her expression instantly serious. "I wish I had been with you."

Keel frowned. "With us, when?"

"With Joseph, when he went after Faheem."

Crow sucked air through his teeth.

"I know what you did, Joseph. I know what you *all* did, how dangerous it must have been."

"Well, hell," Crow said, sitting back. "Why don't I take the Cessna for a spin over Khartoum and trail a fucking banner behind me? Maybe with Salma's phone number on it. Jesus Christ!"

Sabine laid a restraining hand on Crow's arm. "Do not blame René. When he told me I would be meeting the three of you here, I thought that was unusual. When I pressed him on it, he told me you were following a lead on the killings. I asked him what lead and how you came by it."

"And, what, he just caved in?" Crow said skeptically.

"I spoke with him as a former soldier, not as Salma's veterinary doctor."

"And that made a difference, how?" Sekka asked.

Sabine fixed Sekka with an uncompromising gaze. "He knew he could trust me."

Sekka said nothing. Sabine shifted her glance to include all three men. "During my military service I did

249

tours in Libya with the French contingent attached to the NATO Coalition forces, and in Côte d'Ivoire as part of Operation Licorne. I did not take part in front-line combat, but I did come under fire when I was travelling with a UN convoy and we were attacked by Gbagbo loyalists. So I knew people, close friends, who died and whose loss I still feel deeply; the same sadness and anger I felt when our rangers were murdered. I understand the reasons you did what you did, why it was necessary to take action yourselves and not leave it to the Chadian or Sudanese authorities."

Sekka eyed Keel. "So much for our 'need to know' strategy."

"You do realize this makes you an accessory?" Keel said.

Sabine nodded. "I am aware of that." She paused, as if contemplating the wisdom of her admission, then said, "So, *has* your trip here been of use? Have you found out anything?"

Keel did not reply immediately, he looked questioningly across the table at Sekka and then at Crow. Sekka's expression said: 'Why not? It's out of the bag now.' and Crow simply shrugged, as if to say, 'I'm with him.'.

Keel regarded her coolly, considering how to respond.

"Might as well tell her," Crow said, cutting into his thoughts. "What have we got to lose?"

Keel thought about it for a few more seconds, then said, "Yes, the lead paid off. We have confirmation of a name."

"That would be Baroud?"

Keel nodded. "It would."

"So where can we find him?"

We? Keel knew Sekka and Crow would have picked up on that, too.

Sekka said, "We believe he's in Dubai."

Sabine's chin lifted.

"Yeah," Crow said. "Who'd've thought?"

Sabine listened as Keel outlined the information they'd received from Paul Lavasse, then regarded all three of them in turn. "So, is it your intention to pursue him to Dubai?"

"Still working on that," Keel said. "Lavasse suggested we should first speak with someone who knows the illegal wildlife trade."

Sabine's hand stilled around her glass when she realized all three men were gazing back at her expectantly. She did not respond immediately but regarded them thoughtfully. Finally, she nodded. "Buy me dinner and I will tell you what I know."

"About bloody time," Crow said, before Keel could respond. "I'm starving. Anyone for Chinese?"

"How much did Lavasse, tell you?" Sabine asked.

"About the trade? Not a lot. He said it wasn't his department." Keel took a look around the room. It was mid-evening and Chez Wou's restaurant was half full. There were a few Europeans present but most of the diners appeared to be Chinese. Hotel guests, Keel assumed. The menu on offer reflected the clientele, in that it was composed mainly of Oriental dishes, with a selection of American fast food favourites tossed in to cater for those with a less adventurous palate: hamburgers and omelettes and the inevitable club sandwich, all served with a portion of thin-cut French

251

fries.

Their main meal over and with plates and cutlery cleared away, Keel stirred his coffee, which had been served black and unsweetened. "We know Dubai's a major hub but that's about it."

Sabine nodded. "You understand I'm not an expert."

"Anything you can give us will help," Keel said.

Sabine sighed, gathering her thought. When she spoke, her voice was subdued. "The coveting of ivory is nothing new. It dates back millennia. In Europe, they have found ivory jewellery and tools that are at least twenty-five thousand years old. It is thought that by around 3000 BC, the Egyptians may have exterminated all the herds from their part of the Sahara region. From there, the demand for ivory can be traced forward through Roman times, when the North African herds were wiped out. By the end of the seventh century the herds in Asia Minor had disappeared. A thousand years later, the Islamic states ruled the East African trade, while West African ivory – it is how the Côte d'Ivoire got its name – was being transported north, across the Sahara to the Mediterranean.

"There were two major periods when the trade expanded after that: following the industrial revolutions in Europe and the United States, It is estimated that in the 1500s there could have been as many as twenty-five million elephants. Four hundred years later that figure had dropped to around ten million. A century after that, which would be during the 1970s, the Asian demand for ivory led to the depletion of the East African herds. Fifty thousand elephants were being slaughtered every year."

"Jesus," Crow said.

Sabine's features clouded. "It gets worse. By the

252

end of the '80s, if you take the continent as a whole, more than half of the entire elephant population had been killed; around half a million animals. You've heard of CITES?"

"The animal protection organization," Keel said.

Sabine nodded. "The Convention on International Trade in Endangered Species. In '89, CITES was so alarmed by the amount of poaching that was going on it banned all international trade in ivory from African elephants."

"But that's not what happened," Sekka said.

"No, it is not..." Sabine paused, then said, "Look, it is not me you should be talking to. You need to speak to someone who is closer to the problem."

Keel leaned forward. "And who would that be, exactly?"

"Someone from CITES or one of the other protection agencies." Sabine paused once more, then said, "Believe it or not, there is another conference being held in Dubai. It is to discuss the rise in wildlife crime. It is hosted by TRAFFIC, that's the NGO that monitors the trade in animals and plants. Their mission is to ensure that it does not threaten the conservation of nature."

Keel ran a hand across the table cloth. "I'd say they have their work cut out."

"Now more than ever. There will be representatives from other organizations there. They are the people who'll have the information you seek. If you were considering travelling to Dubai, that is." She threw Keel a speculative glance. "A number of attendees are there already. I met a few of them before I left."

Keel took a sip of coffee and returned his cup to its saucer, before looking up. "Got any names?"

253

"On one condition," Sabine said, looking Keel squarely in the face.

"I've a feeling I'm not going to like this," Keel said warily.

"Probably not," Sabine said, and smiled

15

Keel, Sekka and Sabine were in Deschamps' office. Deschamps was standing by his desk. An angry flush showed beneath his sun-browned face. "You cannot be serious!"

Sabine fixed him with the same expression she'd bestowed on Keel the previous evening. When she spoke her voice was calm. "I am perfectly serious. Your friend Lavasse advised Thomas to speak to someone who knows about the ivory trade. He suggested me, but there are other people more qualified so I told Thomas about the TRAFFIC conference. I have met some of the delegates. If I go with them, I can make the introductions."

Deschamps shook his head fiercely. "This is not a good idea. Tell her, Thomas. Please."

"Oh, I tried," Keel said, and indicated Sekka. "Believe me, we both did. But what Sabine says makes sense. We need an intro and this is the best way. Better than Joseph and me going in cold. We do that and by the time we've sussed out who's who, the bloody conference will be over and we'll be left with our thumbs stuck up our arses with nowhere to go."

"You're my senior vet," Deschamps protested, swinging round. "I need you here."

Sabine shook her head. "I am your *only* vet, but you

can spare me for a few more days. My last call-outs were not to attend to any of our animals, they were to advise local villages on how to keep their stocks free of disease, and if you remember, Crow and I were flying back from seeing the village headman at Koro about his goat herd when we got the call to help Joseph look for the poachers." Sabine's features softened momentarily, then grew hard again. "Even if I had been here in camp, there was nothing I could have done to prevent the killings."

"What about the collars," Deschamps countered, making a desperate grab for the nearest straw. "Have you forgotten those?"

"No, but they are not due to arrive for at least week."

The collars were tracking collars, six of them. African Parks had provided part of the finance and had arranged shipment through Smart Parks, a Dutch company specialising in environmental protection technology. Each collar housed a GPS sensor capable of sending real-time location updates to the ranger teams, allowing them to monitor the movements of the senior herd members selected as wearers: three matriarchs and three bulls, all of them with notable tusk arrays. Although the collar was an extremely robust piece of kit and maximized the park's ability to detect the wearer's location, it had minimum impact on the animal's natural behaviour, allowing it to roam at will.

Deschamps took a deep breath and walked over to the window. After staring at the outside world for what seemed a lifetime, with the late afternoon sunlight playing across his face, he turned, his frustration still clearly visible. "And who is going to pay for this...excursion?"

"I'd prefer to call it a reconnaissance," Keel said.

"Don't play games, Thomas," Deschamps snapped, his forefinger vibrating as he jabbed it towards Keel's face. "It's beneath you. And the question is still relevant. Salma does not have unlimited funds. I would have a hard time justifying the expense of supplying three of my senior staff with airline tickets and accommodation in one of the world's most expensive cities; especially now, given the cost of those collars. They were not cheap. And if you say that Sabine's charges in attending her seminar were covered, I would point out that her participation was arranged and funded by AP more than six months ago. I'm certain they would not extend the same courtesy on this occasion. Their first question would be to ask the purpose for your visit. I'm not sure I could come up with a good enough reason; not for all three of you. Their second question, if I did manage to think of something, would be: why now, when our first priority is to safeguard the park? Which, after all, is why we are being sent this new equipment." Deschamps stared at Keel as if expecting an argument, but Keel was just looking back at him with an even expression on his face. "What are you not telling me?"

"That you don't have to worry about the expense."

Deschamps, clearly flustered and possibly feeling more than a little self-conscious following his outburst, lowered his hand. "What does that mean?"

"It means we'll pay our own way. Joseph and I will cover the cost."

Deschamps blinked. Then, while absorbing the offer, he turned to Sekka and said accusingly. "You're very quiet, Joseph. Have you nothing to say?"

Sekka shrugged. "Only that I have nothing constructive to add, and that I'm with Thomas on this."

Seeking support, Deschamps fixed Sabine with a mute look of appeal but when she remained silent he re-addressed Keel. "So, when did you intend to leave?"

"The sooner the better. Tomorrow."

Deschamps tipped his head to one side, a light of understanding in his eyes. "You've already made the travel arrangements, haven't you?"

Keel nodded. "While we were in N'Djamena. We bought the last three seats. Ethiopian Airlines."

"Accommodation?"

"Taken care of."

"So, why didn't you just depart from N'Djamena rather than come back here," Deschamps enquired testily.

"Professional courtesy?"

Deschamps's eyes flashed once more. "You have the devil's own nerve, my friend. Has anyone ever told you that?"

"Once or twice."

Deschamps massaged his forehead. "Why do I feel as though I have been backed into a corner?"

Keel looked back at him without sympathy. "Five rangers, René. I know I'm repeating the mantra but five rangers were gunned down and six elephants slaughtered, and the authorities have done bugger-all to hunt down the men responsible. So it's left to us. And now we think we have the name of the guy who recruited them, and a location. We've come this far, we can't back off now."

Deschamps threw Sabine another imploring look.

"I am sorry, René," Sabine said. "That goes for me, too."

For the first time, Deschamps offered a reluctant smile. "Is that the veterinary doctor talking or the former soldier?"

Sabine offered a faint smile back. "Both."

"I see." Deschamps said, though his still-clipped tone suggested he didn't. He headed back to his desk.

"And I need a favour," Keel said.

Taking his seat, Deschamps let go a sigh as the fire left his eyes. "I am afraid to ask."

"Any chance Crow can ferry us to Sahr so that we can make the connecting flights? And before you ask, we'll pay for the Cessna's fuel as well."

Deschamps stared at Keel. "If I say no, will Crow fly you there anyway?"

Keel said nothing and waited.

"So, when you get to Dubai," Deschamps said heavily, "what happens then?"

"With Sabine's help, we'll talk with some people," Keel said. "Guaranteed, they'll know about the shootings. Could be they'll be keen to help us."

"To do what?"

"For a start, we can toss them Baroud's name. See if it means anything."

"And if it doesn't?"

"If that is the case, and he's still there, depending what other info we can glean, it's probably worth us having a wee chat."

"You would seek him out?"

"It'd make sense. It's another reason why we need to act fast. We don't know his agenda; how long he's going to be in town. For all we know, he might have left already, but he *is* the next link. Either way, if we can, it'd be interesting to try and and find out what sort of operation he's running."

259

"You think if he *is* there and you confront him he's going to *tell* you?"

"Anything's possible."

"That," Deschamps said, "is what worries me."

Sucking in his cheeks, he held his breath and then released it slowly. "Very well, if this is how it is to be, starting tomorrow, you may consider yourselves to be officially on leave. I'll cover for you as long as I can." He fixed Keel with a penetrating stare. "Be careful this does not consume you, my friend."

"I'll do my best."

Deschamps nodded, as if satisfied, then said, "There is one other thing."

"What's that?"

"Come home safe."

Crow, dressed in a set of well-worn, grease-stained khaki overalls and an equally grubby, backwards facing baseball cap, had removed the Cessna's cowling and was halfway through draining the aircaft's oil when Keel gave him the news. The Cessna's prop was set at the twelve to six o'clock position to prevent unwary spectators from spearing themselves on the blades, while a new filter, the size of a small camping gaz canister, rested on a nearby trestle table, alongside an impressive array of tools, a box of spark plugs, various lengths of rubber tubing, and a prominent supply of greasy rags; hands for the wiping of.

"How'd it go?" Crow reached for one of the less tatty bits of cloth and used it to remove oil and dirt from between his fingers, though from what Keel could see, there didn't appear to be much improvement after he tossed the rag aside. "I'm guessing he wasn't too chuffed."

"No, but he agreed to let you fly us to Sahr."

"He had a choice?" Crow let his eyes drift towards the stream of molasses-coloured gloop streaming into the jerry can he'd positioned beneath the engine block. "How'd he take Sabine's involvement?"

"He wasn't happy about that either."

"I'll bet. He does know she's old enought to make her own decisions, though, right?" Crow said.

"He knows."

"Good." Crow watched as the oil flow began to diminish. When it eventually ceased dribbling he turned back and found that Keel was regarding him with an amused look on his face. "What?"

Keel shook his head wordlessly.

Crow sighed. "Look, I like Sabine, okay? And René wouldn't have employed her if he didn't think she knew her stuff. Which means he also knew she was in the bloody army and that she could probably look after herself. Hell, I've seen her fire a tranquillizing dart. She can probably shoot the balls off a fire ant at two hundred paces."

Keel raised his palms in surrender. "I didn't say a word."

"No, but you were bloody thinking it. Ah, bollocks." Crow picked up another piece of rag and began to clean his hands again.

"She's the same age as his daughter," Keel said. "He feels protective."

"You'll keep an eye on her, though, right? You and Joseph?"

"Absolutely."

"Because if you don't..." Crow tossed the rag to one side and left the sentence hanging.

"Right, well, gotta go," Keel said. "Things to do, people to see."

"Good idea," Crow said. "Need to get this done if you wanna catch your flight. What was departure time again?"

"Ten forty-five."

Crow nodded. "No sweat. I'll get you there. Catch you later."

Keel turned and headed away. Crow watched him go, shook his head and let go a muttered curse. "'*You'll keep and eye on her?*' Jesus, Crow. Seriously?"

"Call for you," Deschamps said.

Keel frowned, took the phone and held it to his ear. "This is Keel."

There was a pause before a voice with a distinct British accent said evenly; "Hello, Thomas. H here. It's been a while."

Keel stared at Deschamps but the Frenchman's face held no readable expression.

Finding his own voice, Keel said cautiously, "Yes, sir, that it has."

There was a chuckle. "I told you, don't call me 'sir'. Our line of work, major still outranks captain."

"I'm a civilian now," Keel said. "Didn't you get the memo?"

There came another soft laugh. "Makes two of us, then. So, Chad. How's that compare with Helmand?"

"Rainy season's a bitch, but the food's a lot better."

"Oh, I don't know; hard to beat a dash of Hot Diggidy Dog and a Jammy Dodger when the mortars are raining in."

"Or a three-year pizza," Keel said.

262

"Now you're talking." There came a pause, then, in a sombre tone: "I hear you've been having some trouble."

"I'd question the word 'some'," Keel said. "How much do you know?"

"That 'trouble' was the wrong word to use as well. I read René's report. I'm desperately sorry. I've sent personal messages to the families. We've also arranged for the dependants to receive financial support. I know several patrol members had children, and we're making provisions for them, too. It's a bad situation, Thomas. I can imagine how you must be feeling with regards to the Chadians calling off the search."

"*They* might have called it off," Keel said. "Doesn't mean we have."

Keel saw Deschamps' eyes glitter. The line went quiet for several seconds and for a moment Keel thought they'd been cut off, before the voice at the other end said, "Indeed, I understand you've been doing some digging of your own, gathering intel. How's that going?"

"Drawn a couple of leads."

"And?"

"The first one panned out. That led us to the second."

"And?"

"Could be tricky...trick*ier*."

"How so?"

"It'll be an away game."

"Ah, right, and are their supporters likely to be hostile?"

"If it all goes south," Keel said. "Very."

"Nothing you haven't handled before."

"No. Difference is they would have been sanctioned

263

ops. Most of them, at any rate."

"And someone else was footing the bill. No worries about overheads."

"Plus we were the ones taking orders, not handing them out."

"You weren't keen on that as I recall: taking orders. Got you in deep water a few times."

"Sez he."

"Ouch."

"You've matured now, though, right?"

"I wouldn't believe all you hear in the press."

"That'll be the day," Keel said, and waited.

"So we're talking about a private op."

"We are."

"Which won't come cheap."

"Possibly not," Keel admitted. "It's manageable so far, but that might change."

"A sponsor would be useful, then." There was a pause, then: "How about I make a few calls?"

"Whoa," Keel shot back quickly. "I appreciate the offer but I can't let you do that. Word gets out, you'll be crucified."

"So what's new?

"You say that, but this is different. A shit storm won't begin to describe it. If you think wearing a dodgy armband was a dumb move, or hunting buffalo in Argentina..."

"That was when I was young and foolish, and before I married a vegan. You heard she persuaded me to sell my guns? Made sense, mind. They didn't really go with my AP role and the conservation work. You do *know* I've left the family firm and gone self-employed, right?"

"I might have heard something," Keel said, "How's

that working out?"

The soft chuckle came again. "Borderline lucrative, as it happens. We were able to pay back what we owed the Excheque, which means we pissed off *GB News* and *The Guardian* big time, so a sound result all round. We carry on that this rate and the buggers'll be running out of things to moan about." There was slight pause then, "This could be my only chance of repaying the debt, Thomas."

"Excuse me?" Keel said.

"Don't give me that. You know what I mean."

"And I told you at the time, there *is* no debt to pay. You don't owe me a damned thing."

"You say that but you're wrong. I owe you everything. Even more so now I have other... responsibilities. Though, it does mean I've more freedom to call in favours. Plus, the other half has a very full address book. I'm sure there'll be a few willing donors in there somewhere, as long as it's on the down-low"

"See you've picked up the local lingo, then," Keel said.

A laugh sounded at the other end of the line. "When in Rome, right? Look, you have to let me try. This is important. So no argument. Okay?"

Keel lowered the phone to his chest, looked at Deschamps with something like resignation and then lifted the phone back to his ear. "Okay."

"Good, then we're on the same page. If I do come up with anything I'll be in touch. Or rather *I* won't, not directly. This little chat was a one-off; old friends catching up. If someone does contact you, with good news or bad, they'll make it clear they're speaking for me."

Keel took a long breath.

"Thomas...you still there?"

"Thank you," Keel said. Even as he uttered them, the words sounded profoundly inadequate.

"It's what friends do." The line went quiet again, then: "It's been good talking with you."

"You, too," Keel said.

"Take care of yourself. Watch your back."

"Will do," Keel said and then hesitated. "H?"

"Yes?"

Keel took a breath. "When I said it was an away game, You didn't ask me where."

"Does it matter?"

"This time it might. It's the UAE, The big D. Your family has ties with the sheikh."

"*Had.* Ties were cut after the Shamsa and Latifa incident. So don't sweat it."

"You sure?" Keel.

"Positive. Besides, you're talking distant family now, so you're cleared for take off. Someone will be in touch."

"All right, then," Keel said. "You want progress reports?"

"That won't be necessary. If I don't hear anything I'll assume it's gone according to plan. It's if anything hits the headline that I'll know it's been a clusterfuck."

"Understood," Keel said. "In that case, I do have one question."

"Which is?"

"Please tell me I'm not in your memoir."

A splutter of laughter was still sounding as the phone was put down.

Keel replaced the receiver. Looked up at Deschamps. "He told me he'd read your report."

266

"He's AP's president," Deschamps said, sounding vaguely surprised. "Of course he has."

"How'd you know he and I have history?"

Deschamps responded with a raised eyebrow. "You think I wouldn't do at least a *bit* of research when I offered you the job?"

"Touché. So how much did he tell you?"

"Only that you and he had met. Not the full details."

Which were still classified. Which was just as well. If word ever leaked out, the press would have had another field day; still could, in fact. At the time, the media blackout had helped. Until an Australian glossy had let the cat out of the bag. Even then, there were still things that had gone unreported due to their sensitivity. The fact that they had never seen the light of day was proof that loyalty among men who served together could be as strong as steel.

Keel made a decision and hoped he wasn't going to regret it, but the phone call alone proved that Deschamps could be trusted. That, and the former legionnaire's own service history.

"There was a convoy," Keel said. "Helmand Province. Ground troops and a Scimitar recon vehicle operating out of a British FOB - JTAC Hill; Operation Herrick. I was part of a contracted detail working close protection for a TV crew filming inside a Ghurka unit and we'd tagged along for the extra padding. We were about two miles out when the Scimitar drove over an IED. Blew the tracks to smithereens.

"Scimitar was a right-off; ended up half-in, half-out of an irrigation ditch. When the Taliban activated their second device at the back end of the convoy, they had us hemmed in. Everyone hit the deck. We laid down covering fire so that the Scimitar crew could egress.

267

The first two guys made it, the third didn't. He went down and one of the first guys went back for him. So happened I was in the nearest vehicle and I did something monumentally stupid. I left my protection buddies to look after the news crew and I went to help drag the first injured guy clear. As we were doing that the guy who'd gone back for him was hit. I dragged him into cover as well and we hunkered down. They had us pinned for a round thirty minutes until reinforcements arrived and the Taliban backed off. Turned out the second guy was H. Could have been anyone who pulled him clear, just happened it was me."

"He was *shot*?" Deschamps said, aghast.

"He was hit. His vest saved him. All he had to show for it was a bloody great bruise. They shipped him back home a couple of weeks later after the Aussie rag released details about his deployment on the front line. I spoke to him before he lifted off. He'd only been out there ten weeks. To say he was pissed is an understatement. Want to know what's funny, though?"

"Funny?"

"All right, spooky. The Scimitars were employed as extra protection for the off-road patrol vehicles. Code name for those was 'Jackal'."

Deschamps stared at him. "There are those who would call that an omen."

"Some would. Normal folk'd just call it coincidence."

"And I'm sure Joseph would agree with you," Deschamps said, leaning back against the corner of his desk.

"How much of the conversation did you get," Keel asked after a silence.

Deschamps pushed himself off the desk. "Enough."

"It gets out, there'll be hell to pay. And then some."

"No one knows he took a bullet so they've managed to keep *that* quiet. What's it been? Twelve, thirteen years?"

"And the rest, but this is different. This is way beyond that. Plus he's not as protected as he once was."

"His decision," Deschamps said.

"His bloody neck," Keel shot back.

"I spoke with him before you arrived. He's very determined. He wants to help."

"I know."

"So let him," Deschamps said.

"He wants to *what*?" Sekka said.

"You heard," Keel said.

"What did *you* say?"

"I told him I'd wait to hear."

"He's taking a big risk," Sekka said doubtfully.

"Not big," Keel said. "Bloody massive."

"But if he comes through..,"

Keel did not reply.

Sekka gave it a few seconds, then nodded. "Okay, so what's next?"

"Head for Dubai. Take it from there."

"Sounds easy."

"Doesn't mean it will be."

"Never is," Sekka said. "I'll go pack."

Three hours later, Keel received another summons.

"Phone call," Deschamps said. He gave Keel a

pointed look.

Keel took the receiver. "This is Keel."

"Good afternoon, Major. My name is Flint."

Keel hadn't expected to hear a woman's voice. "What can I do for you Ms Flint?"

"Mrs.; I'm calling on behalf of a mutual friend."

"Prove it," Keel said.

What might have been an intake of breath sounded at the other end of the phone. Then: "Would Hot Diggidy Dog suffice?"

"That'll do nicely," Keel said.

"Yes, he did mention your sense of humour."

"Pot, kettle, black," Keel said. "What can I do for you, Mrs. Flint?"

"I've been appointed as your intermediary."

"Appointed? There was more than one candidate?"

"If there were, I doubt the others have my experience."

"Ouch," Keel said.

"Do you have something to write with?"

Keel ran his eye across the top of the desk and spotted a note pad and a pen. He pulled them towards him. "I do. Go ahead."

"I have a name and a number."

"All right," Keel said. "Go."

"HSBC," the voice at the other end of the phone said. "Dubai Customer Service Centre in the Dubai Mall. Do you know it?"

"Yes." Keel wrote as the number was dictated.

"A Global Money account has been activated. A bank card will be provided and funds made available upon the production of appropriate identification and a password. The same one I used at the beginning of this conversation will suffice."

270

"Understood."

"Should you require further assistance you may reach me on this number and I will relay all messages. Do you have any questions?"

"I do have one," Keel said.

"Which is?"

"What colour are your eyes?"

The line went dead.

16

Sekka, dressed in a grey t-shirt and tan slacks, gazed out over the small lozenge-shaped plunge pool to where turquoise wavelets lapped gently against the villa's private stretch of sandy beach. "Remind me what the rental is on this."

"Ten grand a week U.S., give or take."

Sekka shook his head wearily and turned. "Just as well you got us a discount, I'm all out of small change."

Keel smiled. "It's who you know."

Sekka descended the steps on to the sand and looked back, taking in the villa's pale yellow exterior with its white shutters and white-painted balcony set against a cloudless blue sky, while at the same time gauging the distance between the villa and the homes on either side, before staring off along the line of properties that extended in both directions along the full length of the gently curving shoreline. A few feet from the bottom of the steps, a trio of empty sun loungers sat next to a furled sun umbrella. "Thought you said your man was put off by the overcrowding? This doesn't look so bad."

"It's not his original choice. He upgraded."

"Had to spend his bonus on something I guess," Sekka mused. "And..?"

"He said if I ever needed a favour I should give him

a call."

Sekka waited.

"So I gave him a call."

"And?"

"He said we could have the place as long as we wanted."

"Gratis."

Keel smiled. "Gratis."

"Definitely a tax write-off," Sekka murmured.

"I didn't ask." Keel paused. "Neither did he."

"He must have liked your work."

"I guess so."

Sekka waited for Keel to expand on his less than effusive response.

Keel sighed. "Short version: it was a kidnapping. His wife was on a week's break in Croatia; company for a girlfriend who was going through a messy divorce and looking for some R & R. They'd hired a car and were there a couple of days when they were hi-jacked on the way back from a shopping trip in Dubrovnik. Wife was taken; the girlfriend was left to contact hubby. Usual demand: money in exchange for her release. No police or they'd send her back in pieces."

"Nice. How much?"

"Five million euros."

"Lordy."

"Right. Anyway, I was recommended by a mutual associate so he called me in to assist with the cash drop-off and recovery."

"You told him that paying was no guarantee he'd see his wife again."

"I did."

"And he didn't attempt to bargain or negotiate the price?"

"No. He loves his wife, and as you can tell..," Keel spread his hand to encompass the villa, "...he's not short of a bob or two. While he was making the arrangements with his bank, I recruited a couple of pals, and we flew out."

"Pals?" Sekka said.

"Mike Logan, Harry Donovan."

Sekka's eyebrows went up. "Those guys are still around? Thought they'd called it a day a few years ago."

"They're around, plus they knew the area and were close.

"Good choice," Sekka said.

Keel smiled. "I thought so,"

Sekka frowned. "How come you didn't give *me* a call?"

"You weren't available. You were still running around playing *Luck of the Legion*."

Sekka nodded sagely. "That case, you're forgiven. Obviously, the client got his wife back safely."

"He did."

Something in Keel's expression made Sekka pause. "Why am I sensing a 'but'?"

"The kidnapping wasn't a random snatch. It was sanctioned One of my guy's senior executives had a gambling problem and was in debt to some very dicky characters. He knew about the wife's trip; saw an opportunity to pay off his creditors. He passed them the info on his boss's domestic arrangement and the wife's travel plans. They sub-contracted the snatch to some of their more unsavoury continental associates. It was a very smooth operation, apparently; military precision."

"They must have done something wrong," Sekka

275

said. "We wouldn't be here, otherwise."

"Right. Turned out the gambler was the soon-to-be divorcée's imminent ex-husband. She got to thinking that he'd been asking a few too many pertinent questions prior to her trip and she passed her suspicions on to my guy, who called in his firm's head of security. Pressure was applied on the QT. The guy wilted under questioning and revealed all. The security guy worked his way along the line, managed to get word to us with identities of the kidnap crew and where they were holding the missus. We went in and got her. Solid result all round."

"Were they locals?"

"Lead bad guy was former KLA, the rest had ties with the Croatian Mafia."

"Strange bedfellows. Any of them make it out?"

"They all did. Not saying they were in perfect condition, mind. A couple are probably still in traction."

"How about the shifty exec? He get his just desserts?"

"Depends what you mean by 'just'. His employment was terminated and word passed around that he was persona non grata. I heard he ended up working as a gopher for some rinky-dink Indonesian oil and gas outfit. That was before he was found floating in the surf off the Samui Chaweng Beach Resort."

Sekka raised an enquiring eyebrow.

"Ko Samui, Thailand. Most likely, his creditors were tidying up loose ends. There was no way they were going to recoup their losses, plus it was a warning to others not to upset the apple cart."

As Sekka pondered on that, Keel brought a pair of field glasses out from behind his back and joined

Sekka on the sand. Raising the binoculars to his face, he aimed them towards the line of homes occupying the shoreline on the adjacent frond.

The view, Keel mused, would mirror, without much deviation, the one belonging to someone on the opposite frond looking in Keel's direction, in that it would comprise a line of expensive waterfront properties, cast in various pastel shades and separated from their neighbours either by a low courtesy wall or ornamental shrubbery, or sometimes both, complete with steps and wide terrace, invariably supporting some sort of pergola on one side and a compact pool at the other.

While, architecturally, there were several features that were common to the majority of the homes, the developers had made a half-hearted attempt to ensure that villas of the exact same design had not been set side by side. The resulting illusion did lend the development a certain degree of exclusivity but in Keel's mind, even when taking the often eye-watering prices into consideration, this was, when all was said and done, still little more than an upmarket housing estate, one street long and two blocks wide, with only the names to differentiate one frond from another, Keel's donated villa being on the south-east facing, inner curve of Frond E - *Buma'an* - with Baroud's larger property situated on the outer, north-westerly curve of Frond D - *Al Barhi.*

"What do you think?" Sekka asked.

Keel gazed out across the water. "Frond to frond straight across is about three-fifty yards. Matey's pad's on the diagonal to ours so it's a wee bit further. Call it five hundred, maybe five-fifty max."

Keel passed the binoculars to Sekka who held them

to his eyes. After several seconds of study, he lowered them back down. "Looks quiet. This heat, though, anyone with any sense isn't going to be soaking up the rays. They're going to be in the shade, with a cold drink."

"Sounds like a plan," Keel said.

Footsteps sounded. They turned at the same moment as Sabine, dressed in a cream slacks and a navy linen shirt, sleeves rolled up to the elbow, crossed the terrace towards them, mobile phone in hand. A pair of sunglasses was propped on top of her head.

"How are we doing?" Keel asked.

Sabine held up the phone. "All set, the conference is being held at Le Méridien. He will meet us there; the main lobby."

"When?"

Sabine glanced at her watch. "He said to give him an hour."

"And he's the TRAFFIC guy, right?" Keel said.

"Duncan Bryce, yes. He is one of their wildlife crime monitors. He acts as liaison between TRAFFIC and the other conservation agencies." Sabine nodded towards the binoculars still in Sekka's hand. "What can you see?"

"A tourist boat and a couple of kayakers."

"Baroud?"

Sekka shook his head. "We're at the wrong angle for a sighting. Doesn't mean he's not at home, though."

Sabine looked back along the frond, beyond their own villa. "I will not ask how you managed to get us this place, Thomas, but you must have a very interesting address book." She smiled. "Either that or else somebody owes you a big favour."

"Both," Keel said. "And we struck lucky. I figured

278

just being somewhere on the Palm would be useful. I'd no idea we'd be this close to our target."

"Target?" Sabine said, one eyebrow raised.

"Slip of the tongue. I was going to say that fortune doesn't always smile on the righteous, but when it does, you don't ask too many questions." Keel looked at his watch. "We should get going."

Sabine nodded and the three of them headed back into the villa. The interior was cool - courtesy of the expensive air conditioning units – and spacious, with marble floors and high ceilings. The décor and furnishings were Mediterranean in design rather than in the more traditional Middle Eastern style, which tended towards the ostentatious, usually incorporating an over abundance of gold fixtures and fittings, everything from bath taps to chandeliers. It was a non-too-subtle way of displaying the wealth and status of the property owner, as if the price paid for the place wasn't evidence enough.

The rental was a Suzuki 4x4, picked up at the airport upon their arrival. Keel drove.

"I forgot to ask," Sabine said, as they approached the gatehouse that stood at the entrance to the frond, Keel signalling his thanks as the security guard raised the barrier to let them on to the slip road that led on to the Palm Jumeirah Road, the dual carriageway that ran along the trunk of the palm and which linked the development to the mainland. "How is it you are travelling on a Dutch passport?"

Sekka, who'd taken a rear seat, leaned forward. "Dutch nationals don't need a visa to enter Dubai. If I was travelling as a Nigerian citizen, they'd want to see health insurance certificates, six months worth of bank statements; the whole nine yards. It'd take too long and we don't have the time."

"You have dual citizenship?"

Sekka nodded. "Our line of work, it makes travel a lot easier. Plus, it also made more sense after Thomas and I bought the bar."

"Bar?" Sabine echoed. "What bar? You *own* a bar?"

"We did. *The Pelican*. We had a restaurant as well, for a while, but it was too much like hard work."

"Harder than *la Légion*?" Sabine smiled. "Where was this?"

"Amsterdam."

"So you sold them?"

"Not entirely. We still have a half-interest in both places and we keep apartments there. It's a great city to unwind in between contracts."

Sabine turned to Keel. "I am having a hard time picturing the two of you waiting on tables."

They were approaching the junction leading on to the roundabout that would direct them beneath the monorail and on to the opposite side of the carriageway. Keel flicked a glance towards his wing mirror as he eased the Suzuki into the left-hand lane. "We did our fair share, but we were more the meet-and-greet side of the business."

"Don't tell me; and Crow was your sommelier."

"He doesn't like to talk about it. He's worried it'll ruin his image."

Sabine smiled. "I am not sure I believe you."

"It's true," Sekka said. "He's even got a *tastevin*; wears it under his shirt. Take a look next time you see him."

"Now I know you are joking," Sabine said.

Leaving the Palm behind, their route led them towards what, at first sight, looked to be a cat's cradle of junctions, carriageways and over passes that wouldn't have looked out of place had they been on the outskirts of LA or Chicago.

Keel followed the signs to Sheikh Zayed Road and looked for the north-bound lane. A sliver of green caught his eye as he did so: the hedge bordering the Emirates Golf Club. The flash of vegetation, fleeting as it had been, seemed at odds with the concrete and asphalt landscape that stretched away on all sides.

The lines of traffic began to converge. Keel picked up speed. A phalanx of what might have passed for pale-painted replicas of the Empire State building reared up on the left side of the highway, while to the right, ranks of high-rise commercial blocks loomed like canyon walls against the cloudless blue sky. The only indication that they were not cruising along an American freeway were the speed-limiting signs and the vast billboards promoting the Dubai Mall's fast food outlets; though the listings for luxury apartments, mobile phones and fast cars bore English as well as Arabic script.

The conference centre lay a block south of the airport, which necessitated an approach via the Al Garhoud Bridge. As they drove over the Creek, Keel glanced to his right and out across the parapet. A generation ago, the view would have been of wooden dhows berthed against ancient jetties fronting rustic warehouses. Today, the scene bore no relation to what had gone before; consisting as it did of a wide expanse of dredged waterway dominated by the Marsa Plaza on one side, looming above the surrounding reclamation like a glass-fronted fortress; while on the opposite bank, the two hundred and eighty metre high D1 Tower soared skywards above the Jaddaf

Waterfront; the cost of an apartment in either structure easily matching the price of a villa out on the Palm.

Arriving at the centre, Keel steered the Suzuki into an empty parking bay. The heat hit them the moment they exited the air-conditioned vehicle and headed for the hotel's main entrance.

Entering *Le Méridien's* blissfully cool lobby. Keel saw that substantial renovation work had taken place since his last visit; though the vast room still looked as if might have served as a prototype for the USS Enterprise's mess-deck, albeit it with a lot more gold leaf on display. Keel presumed it was leaf as opposed to the real thing. In Dubai, it was often hard to gauge the difference.

"There's Duncan," Sabine said, as a figure with a tangle of dark hair and a shaggy beard rose from a nearby chair and ambled, towards them, smiling broadly.

Mid to late thirties, dressed casually in black cargo pants and a gaudy Hawaiian-print shirt, unbuttoned over a black sweat-shirt bearing an image of Bruce Springsteen's head and shoulders and the motif *'THE ONLY BOSS I LISTEN TO'* imprinted beneath it, he looked, Keel thought, with his wire-framed spectacles, like everyone's idea of a cool, younger-than-expected university lecturer as he greeted Sabine with an easy-going grin.

"*Bonjour, Mam'selle Bouvier!*"

"You have been practising," Sabine said in English, returning the smile and accepting a triple kiss on her cheeks. "Doctor Duncan Bryce, these are my friends Thomas Keel and Joseph Sekka."

"Hi, guys," Bryce said, as he shook hands firmly,

before offering three credit card-sized tags with long ribbons attached. "Visitor passes. You're now official conference attendees." The accent was English, with a hint of Tynesider thrown in for good measure.

As Sekka slipped the ribbon over his head he glanced around the lobby. "Conservation work must pay better than I thought."

Bryce smiled crookedly. "I wish. Fact is, we get preferential rates. The Sheikh picks up the slack. Likes to portray himself as a philanthropist and a supporter of worthy causes."

"When he's not writing poetry and abducting his kids," Keel said. "Though, I'm surprised he has any money left after that divorce settlement."

The corner of Bryce's mouth twitched again, to form an ironic slant. "You may say that. I couldn't possibly comment. Any case, what management loses on the room rate, they make up for in the price of the beer, so you've been warned. Talking of which, you guys up for a cold one? We might as well chat in comfort."

Receiving no vocal dissent, Bryce led the way across the lobby.

"I think I'm dreaming," Sekka said as they entered the bar.

"Welcome to the Dubliners," Bryce announced breezily.

It was as if they'd been transported back through time to old Kilkenny, or maybe a John Ford version of what an Irish pub might look like. From the peat-brown flooring to the faux tobacco-stained walls with Guinness signs and sepia prints of Dublin's fair city artfully arranged alongside a selection of navvy tools, kettles, whiskey jars, a fiddle case and, in one corner a collection of pipes and cylinders that looked suspiciously like someone's ides of a poteen still, it appeared that no expense had been spared in creating a small corner of the Emerald Isle, or at least a nostalgic version of it.

If there'd been a wax effigy of a twinkly-eyed Barry Fitzgerald or a dentally-challenged Shane Macgowan seated in one corner, hugging a glass of Porter, Sekka wouldn't have been at all surprised. It was hard to square the image with the near forty degrees of desert heat they'd just left behind them. Music emanated softly from wall-mounted speakers; something folksy with a vague Irish lilt, thankfully of a low enough volume so as not to rise above the sounds of tinkling glasses coming from what appeared to be quite a healthy crowd. A mix of hotel and conference guests, Sekka assumed, along with what was probably a smattering of ex-pats.

"Yeah, I know," Bryce said as he led the way to a corner booth. "Corny as hell, but they serve a decent pint and the food's not bad, considering. No Newcastle Brown, mind. I'm working on that."

As everyone found their seat, Bryce caught the eye of a waiter. "My shout, what'll it be?"

The drinks ordered, Bryce's face turned serious. "Sabine told us about the raid on Salma. They have any leads on the bastards?"

"Still an ongoing investigation," Keel said.

Bryce acknowledged Keel's response with an understanding nod, though, behind the spectacle lenses, his eyes narrowed slightly. "Hell of a thing. I was you, I know what *I'd* like to do to them."

The drinks arrived and were distributed. Bryce took hold of his glass but did not raise it to his lips.

"Sabine said you were after information on the trade. You following a lead?"

"We need to know what we're dealing with. That way maybe we can stop it happening again. Sabine gave us the short version, so there are a few gaps. She figured us coming here would help fill some of them in. Anything you can tell us would be appreciated."

"I'll do my best."

"Sabine said the trade's worth billions," Sekka cut in.

Bryce nodded. "And likely to get bigger."

"Despite the bans."

Bryce shook his head. "The bans weren't supported by countries that had or have effective elephant conservation programmes; they reckoned a total ban on ivory sales'd hamper their capacity to fund conservation. Oh, sure, every so often, a few countries would see an increase in its herds; the Congo for instance; but then numbers would slide again, usually wherever there was conflict - the CAR and Angola are examples of that. But, then, numbers crept up towards the end of the nineties, so CITES allowed certain countries to down-list their elephants to Appendix Two..."

"Back up," Keel said. "Appendix?"

"It is a list," Sabine said. She glanced at Bryce who nodded for her to continue but, instead, Sabine shook her head. "Sorry, Duncan, I did not mean to interrupt. Go ahead."

"It's like Sabine said." Bryce shifted in his seat. "There are actually three lists; three categories. Appendix One is for species threatened with extinction; the highest priority. Appendix Two covers species that are not necessarily threatened with extinction but may become so unless the trade's closely controlled. In other words, trade *is* permitted under certain conditions, in order to avoid utilization incompatible with their survival."

"And three?" Keel said.

"Ah, now, three's is a little more open to interpretation." Bryce jiggled his hand, fingers spread. "It's a list of species that are included at the request of a member country that already regulates trade in the species, when that member needs the cooperation of other countries to prevent unsustainable or illegal exploitation."

"Sounds like a direct quote." Keel said.

Bryce smiled softly.

"But animals can move between lists if their survival rate changes," Sekka said. "Yes?"

Bryce nodded. "Depending on the circumstances. With Appendices One and Two, they can only move between the two or be removed from them if all parties to the Convention are in agreement. With Appendix Three, species can be added or removed at any time, unilaterally, by any party, though consultation generally takes place beforehand, usually whenever there's a CITES conference. There's also the fact that certain animals within species can appear on different appendices. Wolves native to Bhutan and India are listed under Appendix One, whereas the European wolf comes under Apendix Two, that sort of thing."

"And all elephants are Appendix One," Keel said.

"Yep, Asian as well as the two African sub-species, savannah and forest. Except for the ones in Botswana, Namibia, South Africa and Zimbabwe. Their numbers are considered sustainable, at this time. Forest ivory, by the way, is worth more on the black market than savannah ivory. It makes for more enhanced carving."

"Good to know," Keel said caustically. "How effective are these appendices?"

"Not very, it would seem to me," Sekka said, "unless everybody's signed up."

"Which they haven't," Keel said.

Bryce shook his head. "No."

"So, basically, the system has more holes than a bloody sieve," Keel said.

Bryce spread his hands in a fatalistic gesture. "That's the trouble when you've got so many parties involved. There's always going to be a certain amount of manipulation."

"Manipulation?" Sekka said.

Bryce made a face. "Sounds better than bribery and corruption."

"By?"

"The usual suspects. The Chinese have a proven - by that, I mean bad - track record when it comes to applying pressure."

"How's that work?"

Bryce gave a small shrug. "Comes under the heading: *quid pro quo*. A Chinese business conglomerate might bankroll the Indonesian delegation's attendance at a conference in exchange for them voting a certain way. Not to upgrade pangolins on to the critically endangered list, say. When it just so happens that China maintains pangolin farms. That sort of thing."

"Pangolins," Keel said.

"Armoured anteaters, pine cones on legs, wandering artichokes; pick a name. Though, they're closer to cats and dogs than they are to actual anteaters."

"I know what they are," Keel said.

"Right, sorry. Fact is, what's really sticks in the craw is that despite the farms, they're virtually impossible to breed in captivity. They're lucky if they survive six months. One of the reasons they're the most trafficked animal in the world."

"Let me guess," Keel said wearily. "For medicinal purposes."

"You got it. It's the scales that folk are interested in. The Chinese figure them a cure for a shed load of ailments; rheumatism, palsy, poor blood circulation, you name it. Plus they also like to snack on the little buggers. Which is mad when you think about it. Do you know what a zoonotic virus is?"

Keel frowned. "A diseases that can pass from animals to humans, yes?"

Bryce nodded. "There've been rumours for years that pangolins carry viral diseases. Remember that SARS outbreak back in '03? They discovered the virus was transmitted from bats to civets, Himalayan Palm Civets, to be precise, which is, wait for it, another Chinese delicacy. You ever been to a Chinese wet market? They're petri dishes on steroids. All it needs is a transference from a bat to a pangolin to a customer and we're in a world of trouble, and I do mean *world*." Bryce shook his head, then said, "Where was I? Oh, yeah, well, the Indians grind them into a paste to cure boils. In Sierra Leone, they use them to ward against impotence. Go figure."

"And Nigerians believe they can bestow the power of invisibility," Sekka said.

Bryce stared at him.

Sekka shrugged. "I'm Hausa."

288

"So whichever way you look at it," Keel said, seizing the opportunity to bring them back on track while Bryce was still struggling to come up with a response, "elephants are up shit creek."

Recovering, Bryce nodded tiredly. "We're still losing around forty thousand a year. Population's dropped from around one point three million forty years ago to around four hundred and twenty thousand now. More are being killed by poachers than are being born. Oh, and talking of which, did you know that because of years of heavy poaching, there are places, like Mozambique's Gorongosa Park, where elephants are being born without tusks? Darwin'd bloody love that."

Bryce paused then shook his head angrily. "But y'know what really pisses me off? It's that every elephant that dies is another nail in the planet's coffin. You take forest elephants, right? Most people who live outside Africa have no idea there is such a thing and yet they're actually helping to keep us alive.

"Forest elephants fight climate change. They do that because they like to eat. When they forage they go for the younger trees and to get to them they step on other smaller, younger trees, which reduces the density of the vegetation. The trees they leave behind, the bigger ones, are left with better access to water and light, which means they grow taller and bigger than the other trees. And because they're bigger and taller, they absorb more carbon dioxide than the smaller trees that would have grown in their place. Which is a good thing, because forests sequester carbon from all that CO_2 and transform it into biomass through photosynthesis.

"CO_2 has a market value. Not long back, a group of biologists worked out that the carbon capture service

289

provided by forest elephants in the current climate - no pun intended - is worth around one hundred and fifty billion dollars. Divide that by the forest elephant population and you end up with around one point seven five million per elephant. Cost of the ivory poached from a single elephant? Around forty thousand. Do the maths. Even an idiot can see that it pays to keep elephants alive. Here endeth the bloody lesson."

There was silence around the booth's interior, until Bryce said sheepishly, "Sorry guys, force of habit."

There was another pause, broken when Sekka said, "It's the Far East that's fuelling the bulk of the trade, yes?"

Looking thankful to have been asked a pertinent question, Bryce nodded. "China and Vietnam, mostly."

Keel frowned. "I thought China pulled out of the ivory business a while back?"

"Officially, yes; they shut down their domestic ivory trade back in 2017, but the buggers've discovered ways around that."

"How so?"

"Easy. They use their neighbours as intermediaries: Vietnam, Thailand, Indonesia, hell, even Japan. Ivory's always fetched a high price there. They use it to make jewellery and samisen picks. Hanko, too. That's name seals to you and me. You have to remember that ivory obtained before the 1990 international trade ban can still be bought and sold and it's not difficult to hide poached ivory within lawful ivory shipments. A number of African countries did submit resolutions, accusing Japan of contravening the ban and calling on it to cease its domestic ivory transactions. Didn't do 'em any good."

"The Japanese said no?"

Bryce's features darkened. "Same way they keep insisting that the killing of minke whales is purely for scientific purposes. Might as well try pissing against the wind."

"So it could be that Salma's ivory is being shipped from Dubai to Japan?"

"Or Vietnam or Thailand or any of the other transit points. It's impossible to monitor the trade twenty-four seven. Though ROUTES is trying its best." Bryce paused to see if the name meant anything. When Sabine nodded and Keel and Sekka remained silent, he continued. "It stands for Reducing Opportunities for the Unlawful Transportation of Endangered Species.

"It's a partnership, set up under USAID. It's made up of government agencies, development groups, transport companies, conservation organizations and law enforcement, plus donors. Its remit is to disrupt wildlife trafficking by reducing the use of legal transportation supply chains. IATA's one of the partners, along with the WWF." Bryce paused, then said, "I've asked one of their guys to join us."

Sabine let go a frown.

"'S'okay," Bryce countered quickly. "He's cool. Truth is, I'm more your conservation management and strategy guy. Cade is what you might call investigation and containment. I'm thinking that might be more up your street."

"Cade?" Keel said, the slight dip in tone earning him a quizzical look from Sekka, though neither Bryce nor Sabine appeared to have picked up on it.

About to reply, Bryce's eyes latched on to a movement close by and raised a hand as a signal. "Talk of the devil."

291

A shadow appeared at Keel's shoulder.

"Sorry, guys, got held up. Maxwell Cade. Mind if I grab a seat?"

The greeting had been voiced in an easy-going accent that hovered somewhere between James Arness's Matt Dillon and Eastwood's Josey Wales, with the voice-owner's appearance almost matching Eastwood's once-rangy frame. As Bryce made the introductions, a pair of keen brown eyes gazed out from under a Marine Corps Gunny crew cut, which in turn topped a craggy face that might have been carved from a weathered hickory stump.

"Good to meet you," Cade said. Leaning over, he extended a hand to each of them. "How's it going?" Reaching for a chair that had become vacant at a nearby table, the newcomer pulled it towards the edge of the booth and sat down.

The waiter, spying a fresh arrival, swept in and asked Cade if he wanted anything. Cade gave an order for a club soda and the waiter departed.

"Welcome to Dubai," Cade said. "So, Duncan here said you were after some intel. That right?"

"Ivory trafficking," Keel said. "Routes and main players. Been told you're the man we should talk to."

Cade pursed his lips. "Okay. And you want the information because..?"

"They're from Salma, Max," Bryce interjected. "I told you. Remember?"

The waiter arrived bearing Cade's drink. The American took a long, slow swallow before setting his glass down. Whereupon, he fixed Keel with a penetrating stare. "And you're hunting down the bad guys?"

"Something like that," Keel said.

292

Cade nodded thoughtfully as his hand played idly with his glass. "Like old times."

A shadow flitted across Keel's face.

"Oops," Cade said softly.

An uneasy stillness seemed to settle upon the table as Cade and Keel held each other's gaze. Bryce flicked an urgent enquiring glance towards Sabine as if to ask her if she knew what was happening.

Sekka's face remained unreadable.

Sabine's answer was to reach down for her bag and say calmly, "Duncan, why don't we leave these gentlemen to discuss whatever it is they need to discuss in private. You can tell me about your plans for the conference," she added as she rose to her feet and, with a graceful movement, eased herself out of the booth, almost before anyone else realized what she was doing.

Bryce, recognizing the subtle invitation for what it was, hesitated for all of two seconds before pushing himself upright. "Sure, why not?" Adding, as he glanced at his watch, "Got a meeting with Ginny West from Born Free in ten, so I was about to head off anyway. You know her, right?"

"Ginny?" Sabine smiled in genuine pleasure. "Yes. I met her on my last visit. I would love to see her again."

"Excellent. Then, let's you and me skedaddle." Bryce held out his hand. "Thomas, Joseph, really good to meet you." To Cade, he said, "Catch you later, Max? We'll have that drink."

Cade looked up and nodded. "You betcha."

"Nice to have met you, Mr. Cade," Sabine said coolly, while at the same time throwing Keel a pointed look.

Cade, appearing not to have noticed any of the forced interchanges, raised his glass in a salute and

293

watched admiringly as Sabine and Bryce walked away through the bar. "Nice lady," he said as they disappeared. He turned to Keel and, without preamble, said, "Well, shit, of all the gin joints..."

"Hello, Max," Keel said wearily. "Been a while, how are you?"

17

Cade took a leisurely look around the room. When he turned back, a half-smile hovered around his lips. "I'm good. How about you? Been in any decent wars, lately?"

"Not officially," Keel said.

The smile expanded into a fully focussed grin. "Still working freelance, then. How's that working out?"

"It's had its moments."

"Knowing you, I'd say no shit." Cade threw a speculative glance at a still silent Sekka.

"Max and I worked together," Keel said.

"Really?" Sekka said. "I'd never have guessed."

Cade smiled. "Hunting down more bad guys. Good times."

Sekka did not respond.

"Ah, right," Cade said. "So he really doesn't know." He looked at Keel. "Should we tell him?"

Keel thought about it, then shrugged. "Sure, why not?"

"You trust him?" Cade asked with a smile.

"Probably more than I trust you," Keel said.

"Whoa," Cade said, feigning indignation. "That's harsh. So, what's it to be, redacted version or the whole enchilada?"

"Oh, don't hold back now," Keel said.

Cade smiled. "All right, then." Taking a sip of his soda, he placed his glass on the table and faced Sekka full on. "Bosnia, the nineties; you remember that far back?"

Sekka said nothing.

"I'll take that as a 'yes'," Cade said. "So you'll know what the I.C.T.Y. is..."

"International Criminal Tribunal for the former Yugoslavia," Sekka said. "Court of law set up by the UN to deal with war crimes committed during the fighting."

Cade nodded. "Very good. Give the man a ceegar." Taking another leisurely sip from his drink, the American took another, equally slow, survey of the room, as if hunting for potential eavesdroppers.

Satisfied there was no one in close proximity, he turned back. "Okay, so, you want a definition of a nasty little war, Bosnia'd be it. A complete cluster fuck. Violence on all sides, carried out by shitheads with guns carrying grudges against other shitheads with guns, linked to blood feuds that go back decades. They managed to round up a few of the chief shitheads after the war but there were others who ran for the hills, some of them seriously bad guys. Serbs, mostly, though the rest didn't exactly cover themselves in glory. Me and your pal here were part of the operation to hunt them down. I say operation; fact is, there was a lot more than one. There were even a couple or three that made the evening news. The more interesting ones didn't."

"He means they were politically sensitive," Keel said.

Had Cade been looking for a reaction from Sekka then he was destined to remain disappointed, though he took Sekka's continued silence in good grace. "So the main op was called Amber Star. Don't know why. They got drawers full of dumb names; Torn Victor, Little Flower, Buckeye. I guess Amber Star was one they just happened to pull out. Started off as a multi-national team, made up of guys and gals with SF and intelligence backgrounds; the ones at the sharp end; black ops trained. Americans, British, Dutch, French and German, along with reps from their police forces. Joint ops, usually, though every so often a country'd work on an individual target, like Karadzic. He was one of ours. Would have got to him, too, if the Frogs hadn't tipped him off."

Cade's face darkened. "After that, we started to go our own way every time." A pause, then, "Anyways, upshot was, the ICTY came up with a wanted list: a *Who's Who* of shitheads, if you will. Karadzic, Milosevic, Mladic, Tolimir, they were all there, plus a collection of Bosnian-Croat paramilitaries, Bosnian-Muslim camp commanders, KLA guerillas, hell, they even threw in a bunch of rogue medics.

"There are some who reckon it was the most successful manhunt since World War Two, more effective than Nuremberg. A hundred and sixty-one names all told. It was the Brits who made the first collar; his old outfit." Cade indicated Keel. "The boys from Hereford. What was the name of that op?"

"Tango," Keel said.

Cade nodded. "There you go. None of that Operation Dead-Eye Dick shit. What was it? Two targets: one dead, one captured, right?"

Keel nodded.

"That was back in '97. It took the ICTY another fifteen years before number one-six-one was picked up. Goran Hadzic; they cornered him in a Serbian wood, no money, no friends, no boots. A shithead shit out of luck. So job done. Well, kind of. One-six-one was the official tally. Unofficially, there were a few more who weren't on the list and who were still in circulation, but managing to stay down wind, because they knew we'd be looking for them, on account of their crimes being even worse than the ones carried out by the shitheads who'd already been caught. They were the ones *we* went after. The really, really bad guys."

Cade offered one of his trademark smiles. "The powers-that-be thought it'd be a good idea to create a separate tracking unit, a shadow outfit, one which had the same goal as the ICTY but which operated outside the tent. The ICTY's remit was to send out teams to round up the listed perps and deliver them to The Hague for trial. Like the records show, they did a pretty good job. Okay, so some of the bad guys died while in detention, like Milosevic and Kovačević, but most of 'em got jail time. More than a few are in for life. The ones not on the list? Let's just say the plan wasn't to shift them to the Hague, it was to deal with them in-country."

"Kill them," Sekka said.

"Hell, yeah; easier and cheaper than keeping 'em locked up, and because the head honchos didn't want to go down official channels using serving personnel, they went looking for freelancers to work off the books. That meant people they'd worked with before. Folk with proven track records who wouldn't blab and who could be trusted to work independently. Like me and him," Cade nodded towards Keel. "On account of we had what Liam Neeson might call a particular set of

298

skills."

Keel remained silent as Cade continued. "In the end there were six assholes left: two KLA guys and four Serbian warlords. Took us nine months, but we got 'em, disappeared the bastards. It was like they never existed."

Cade sighed. "Soon as the last termination was confirmed the unit was disbanded and we all crept back under our rocks. No promotion; no medals; no mention in despatches. Isn't that what you Brits say?"

"And where was *your* rock located?" Sekka asked.

Cade looked back at him, "Nowhere you'd call specific."

"That sounds like Company speak," Sekka said.

Cade's eyes narrowed. "We liked to think of ourselves as dark matter."

"Say again?"

"The force that orders the universe but can't be seen?" Cade said.

Sekka's eyebrows rose. "You were an agent of S.H.I.E.L.D?"

A small smile creased the corner of Keel's mouth while a bright light flickered momentarily in Cade's eyes before dissipating quickly as he answered softly, "Jaysock."

Cade had had delivered the word if he'd expected Sekka to know what it meant. Which Sekka did.

It was an acronym. It stood for JSOC - Joint Special Operations Command. Based at Fort Bragg, it was the closest thing the Pentagon had to a secret army, incorporating the US Navy's SEAL Team Six and the US Air Force's Tactical Squadron as well as the Army's Delta Force and Special Ops Aviation and Ranger regiments. Its remit was extensive, from carrying out hostage rescue missions to hunting down Al Qaeda, ISIS, and Taliban leaders, operating in countries as varied as Iraq, Afghanistan, Yemen and Somalia, and even Sekka's home turf: Nigeria. It had been SEAL Team Six that had infiltrated Pakistan air space in order to taken out Bin Laden.

But the unit, Sekka recalled, had also had its failures, having been behind the catastrophic attempt to rescue the Iranian hostages in the dying throes of the Carter administration, as well as the operation that had resulted in the downing of a Black Hawk chopper in Somalia. Add in the mission to rescue the British aid worker held by Taliban affiliated insurgents that ended when the hostage was killed by a fragmentation grenade thrown by one of the rescue team, and it was little wonder the outfit preferred its activities to remain hidden.

Probably best not to mention that, Sekka reasoned, so he said nothing and waited.

"Thought I'd seen the last of our pal here," Cade continued, indicating Keel. "Until we ran into each other back in that bar in...Panama City? Jeez, when was it? Hell, I forget. I was tracking a couple of narco kingpins and you were enjoying some down time after guarding that Swiss guy. What was he? Some kinda diplomat? The two of us had beards then. Would've walked past each other, only I couldn't help noticing the hair."

Cade looked at Keel's cropped grey cut and grinned. "Been that way ever since. A couple years'd go by and we'd run into each other again, usually in some third world shithole: Colombia or Mexico or Iraq maybe and we'll grab a few beers and swap war stories and that'll be it until the next time. Like now. Different country, different friggin' bar, but hey..." Cade took a swallow of his soda and sat back. "Now you're a God-damned game ranger. Never would have seen that coming. How'd you end up with that gig?"

"Helping out a friend," Keel said. "I take it you're not with Jaysock any more, unless the job description's changed."

Cade shook his head. "What did Duncan tell you?"

"He said you were, and I quote, investigation and containment, whatever the hell that means."

Cade smiled. "Yeah, well, I'm what you might call the liaison guy. Been working with ROUTES a couple of years. It helps that I got the right contacts in a lot of agencies, domestic and foreign. Interesting work, plus there's not so many assholes shooting back at me." Cade pulled himself upright and fixed Keel with a calm, steady gaze. "So, whaddya need?"

Keel leaned forward across the table. "You'll have known about the Salma killings, I'm guessing before Bryce spoke to you about us?"

Cade nodded. "AP put the word out real quick. Didn't know you were involved though."

"The team that was ambushed; Joseph was the patrol leader."

Cade's eyes widened. "The one they left for dead? Shit, man. I'm sorry." The American's face softened but only for a few seconds before it turned serious once more. "We heard the Chadians called off the search for the guys that did it. That right? That's gotta hurt, them getting away with it."

"Actually," Keel said, "they didn't."

Cade had been about to reach for his drink. His hand stilled. "You found them?" he said quietly.

"We found them."

301

"And?"

"They won't be bothering us again."

"Y'mean like our Bosnian bad guys won't be filling any more mass graves."

Keel did not respond.

"Just you and Joseph?" Cade said.

"We had help."

"Okay."

"We persuaded one of them to talk."

"After he saw his buddies taken out, I'm guessing?"

"That's generally how it works," Keel said.

The corner of Cade's mouth twitched. "So, what did you find out?"

"That they were members of the Sudanese RSF working to order."

"No shit. Any idea whose?"

"We think an RSF colonel, name of Baroud. If it *was* him, he has friends in high places."

Cade pursed his lips. "The guy's a colonel, be surprised if he doesn't."

"His name ring any bells?"

"Not off the top of my head."

"Okay, well, we think he's here in Dubai."

Cade considered Keel's statement. "And how would you know *that*?"

"We have friends in *low* places," Sekka said.

"Supposedly, he's here buying hardware for the RSF," Keel said, "but we think he might also be here to check on his ivory investments and to oversee transportation; most likely to the Far East."

Cade nodded. "Makes sense."

"So," Keel continued, "we'd like you to tell us how that works."

"In your capacity as investigation and containment

liaison supremo," Sekka finished.

"Bear in mind," Keel said, "we're likely to be on the clock, depending on what info you can give us."

"I can see why you two work together," Cade said looking from one to the other. "You oughta be in freakin' vaudeville."

"So?" Keel said.

There followed a short silence, then Cade sighed. "So, you've come to the right place." Taking a drink, he set his glass down. "Okay, so pretty much all illegal wildlife goods moving between Europe, Africa and Asia channel through the Middle East. And it ain't only a hub, it's also a destination, for what they call exotics: that's cheetahs and falcons to you and me; sakar falcons in this case. The locals like to use them for hunting out on the dunes, and by locals, I'm talking the elite: royalty and government officials, the ones with all the dough and all the influence. You can set the kitty cats and the birdies to one side, though. They're small change compared to the cargoes in transit. They're the ones that are causing the most headaches.

"It's the goods that determine the routes. Pangolins are moved through Turkey, rhino horn goes via Qatar and so forth. Ivory comes through here. Knowing which product uses which route helps us enforcement guys target the transportation methods." Cade's face clouded. "But we're still screwed by lack of man power, and not all countries are willing to assist." Pausing, he then said, "Which brings us to the prime reason the bad guys favour the region as a halfway house."

"And that is?" Keel said.

Cade smiled thinly. "There ain't that many seizures."

"Because?"

"Because DXB's the busiest airport in the Middle

303

East and a major transit hub for *legitimate* goods and passengers. Seizures cause delays, delays disrupt transit times and disruptions to air travel cost money. From an enforcement point of view that sucks big time. There's an outfit, C4ADS. It gathers data from around the world and uses it to produce analysis on conflict and transnational security issues. According to their Air Seizure Database, Dubai's one of the two most prominent transit cities for wildlife trafficking by air anywhere in the world. The other's Doha, if you're interested. And, yeah, the biggest portion's made up of stuff heading for the Far East, like your ivory.

"We reckon around sixty percent of all smuggled ivory passes through DXB, less than a mile from where we're sitting. Chances are it's bound for either mainland China or Hong Kong, or maybe KL, either by air freight or hidden in carry-on baggage and clothing."

"Hong Kong and China," Sekka said. "Is the stuff flown there directly? Duncan told us it's shipped through intermediaries."

Cade nodded. "Duncan's right. From Dubai the next stop's usually Thailand or Vietnam. Either way, it's then routed to China through Laos."

"Duncan didn't mention Laos," Keel said.

"Probably because he's not as close to the action as we are. But I'll tell you this: the place is right at the top of our shit list."

"Why's that?"

"Combination of things. You got years of colonial oppression, non-stop border clashes, internal insurrection, not to mention Uncle Sam's bombing campaign back in the day. Still gonna take 'em years to clear all the unexploded ordnance, that's if anyone who cares lives that long or even if they have the

304

funding. Which they don't. The place relies on foreign aid and you've got a quarter of the population living below the poverty line. The country's a basket case, and you know what that leads to."

"Corruption," Sekka said.

"Bingo. Now tie that into location. You've got China and Burma to the north – yeah, I know it's Myanmar, but I'm old school – Vietnam to the east, Cambodia to the south, Thailand to the west. In other words, you got a corrupt state surrounded on all sides by corrupt states, some more corrupt that others. Laos hasn't conformed to any regs prohibiting the export and import of ivory, so it's a friggin' open market. Far as I know, there's only been one seizure since they joined CITES back in '04, which means hardly any arrests or prosecutions. The stuff's traded openly, like flip flops'n rice. Even if that wasn't the case there, Laos has more cross border smuggling routes than the Sinaloa Cartel."

"And the Chinese are the ones doing the trading," Sekka said.

Cade nodded. "Forget the ban, China's still the main market. The last lot of stats showed it was responsible for more than twice as many ivory trafficking instances as the next country down, which happens to be, whaddya know, Thailand. Anything that's decorative is nearly all made to suit Chinese taste, which is intentional because most of the outlets are run by Chinese traders who are selling the stuff to their own people: Chinese tourists from across the border. They buy up around eighty percent, the rest goes to places like South Korea and Malaysia."

"And the Lao government does nothing about it?" Keel said.

"Hell, the damn Lao government's in on it. Country

has the biggest dealers in endangered wildlife in the world. Most of 'em farm the animals themselves and use the farming licences to launder species they've caught illegally. Plus, they got worldwide connections. Means they'll deal in anything, ivory, rhino horn, tiger bones, bear bile, you name it. And that's not counting the live stuff; leopards. snakes, lizards, hornbills; anything that walks, slithers or crawls and that you can either eat or grind down into parts is up for grabs. There's money in them thar hills and the government's more than happy to take a cut of the action, in exchange for providing protection."

"You said the dealers have worldwide connections. Any of them have names?" Keel asked.

"You looking for the boss man?"

"Is there one?"

"Good question. We didn't use to think so. But then, the past coupla years the same name kept cropping up and that made us wonder if we'd got it wrong. You ever hear of SEZs, Special Operation Zones?"

Keel thought about it and nodded. "They're business and trading areas set up in a country that have different economic regulations than the rest of the same country, yes? They're granted tax breaks in order to attract foreign investors."

"Sounds like you've been reading *Forbes Magazine*."

"Heard a friend mention them once. He's a pilot, done a lot of flying around South-East Asia."

"Useful guy to have around."

"You have no idea," Keel said, avoiding Sekka's eye. "Why d'you ask about the zones?"

"Our Mr. Big runs one of them."

"All right," Keel said, "Start talking."

"His name's Zheng Chao; a billionaire. Owns a

company called Jīn Lin Huā - Golden Lotus - registered in Hong Kong. Around ten, twelve years ago the company signed a ninety-nine year lease with the Lao government on a patch of land in Bokeo Province, just across the the Mekong from Thailand. Came in at around four thousand acres. They've used twelve hundred of them to construct a casino resort called Golden Kingdom. According to the Lao government site that promotes the SEZs, it cost around ninety million U.S. dollars to set up. Lotus has an eighty percent stake, the Lao government the other twenty.

"Place opened back in '09. Since then they've built themselves a nice little town to go with it. They got hotels, restaurants, a shopping centre, banqueting halls, gardens, a temple, a zoo, massage parlours, and a banana plantation; yep, you heard right, bananas. Even added on a private boat dock and a thirty kilometre access road from the nearest town, Houayxay. There's an airfield there but GK's building its own strip, next door to a local hamlet, place called Simuang Ngan. It was delayed for a while due to a dispute with local farmers over land rights, but they upped the compensation packages, which means it's backed by Beijing capital. As for the place itself, think smaller Oriental version of Las Vegas, minus the sophistication. Gambling's illegal in the rest of the country, just so you know."

"Sounds just right for a weekend getaway," Keel said.

"'Tis if you're Chinese. You were dumped in the centre of the place and your blindfold was taken off you'd swear you were in downtown Shanghai. It's China in everything but location. The place runs on Beijing time and has Chinese cell phone coverage.

307

They won't even accept local currency. The prices are all in yuan or Thai baht. The workers are mostly Chinese and Mandarin's the official language. Hell, it's even got its own Chinese security guards. Though, get this: Zheng's head of casino security is a guy called Saul Bracken. Born in Malaysia but he's actually an Australian citizen. Got an Aussie contact address - some place called Wagga Wagga? - plus one in Laos, as well as two more, in Thailand and Malaysia."

"Have you been there?" Sekka asked.

"GK?" Cade shook his head. "Got most of my info from a local asset. Not sure I'd get through the door even if I did turn up."

"How do you mean?"

"I'm *Gweilo:* a round eye. Anyone not Chinese or Thai ain't always made that welcome. They've got to thinking that foreigners might want to stir up trouble; like journalists or animal rights activists. There've been a few videos put out, made by people going in under cover to highlight the activities going on there, but they've been hard won.

"Not saying I wouldn't get in, but I'd likely have to take precautions. Pose as a backpacker, maybe, or a citizen of some country that Laos does business with. There was a U.S. journalist who went for a look-see a couple of years back to prep for a book she was writing on the poaching trade. Dolled herself up as a Russian hooker. Not a stretch in case you're wondering. They got a bunch of Ukrainian girls there providing escort services. Anyways, she took her husband and friend along as her jacked-up pimp and john, hired a local translator and got in that way, complete with hidden camera. My guess is the security people were probably too distracted by her trashy outfit to notice she was taking snapshots. What she found was basically a free-for-all illegal wildlife supermarket. That's when ROUTES started to sit up to take notice."

"So," Keel said, while attempting to remove a vision of Cade posing in backpacking togs. "This Zheng, what's his background?"

"Kinda hazy is the flip answer, but we've been able to join up a few dots. Hailed from northern China originally. Made his first fortune trading in lumber before moving into the gambling rackets. Ran casinos in Macao during the late nineties. Made a packet and moved to Mong La, Burma, to set up gaming tables there."

"Odd place to choose," Sekka said, frowning.

Cade smiled thinly. "Yeah, you'd think. It's a rebel stronghold up on the Chinese border, run independently from the rest of the country by two asshole militias; the National Democratic Alliance Army and the United Wa State Army. But turns out they're into all sorts of shit: gambling, nightclubs, prostitution, wildlife sales, you name it. Mostly, though, they make their money from drug production: methamphetamines. They're pretty open about it. Head guy's called Sai Lin. You look up the guy's occupation in Wikipedia and I shit you not, it says 'Warlord'.

"He and Zheng became BFF. Sai Lin initiated Zheng into the drug trade and they used the profits to set up Zheng's casinos. Business fell away, though, when Beijing banned their officials from visiting the place on account of they were gambling away state funds in Zheng's pleasure palaces. That was when the Lao government stepped in and offered Zheng a deal. He used the money from his Mong La profits to bankroll the Laos property. Far as we can tell, he's never looked back."

Sekka cleared his throat and addressed Cade. "You talked about goods and routings earlier. What about the suppliers, the ones who arranges the shipments and deliveries? There a Mr. Big for that, too, or do they rely on mules to smuggle stuff in?"

"There's both. We've had idiots trying to board aeroplanes with live turtles hidden in their jockstraps and found tusks concealed in crates labelled agricultural equipment in the cargo bay. It's the profit margins that rule. Any method that makes money is considered. Goes without saying, the bigger the consignment, the bigger the risk. But it ain't the money men who take the risk, it's the little people, the peons paid to carry the goods in their carry-ons. You take rhino horn; it's more valuable by weight than gold, diamonds or cocaine. Asian market puts it around sixty thousand dollars per pound. Average weight for an African white rhino horn is four kilos, so that's what, nine pounds? Do the maths. You pay some innocent-looking schmuck a thousand bucks to take a horn through customs and they make it, you're looking at making a ton of dough at the other end."

"Ivory?" Sekka said.

"Absolutely, but the ban's affected the value, no doubt about it. Plus, the price tends to be linked to the economy. China's income dips, demand drops and the price goes down. Economy picks up, there's a bigger demand, price goes up. Still being smuggled in, though. It's the buzz they get from owning it that generates the trade as much as the monetary value. It's become a status symbol, stuff to be hauled out at parties and

310

business meeting to impress the guests. Cade fixed Keel with a perceptive look. "But, then, your fight ain't really about the ivory, is it? Not any more. It's about the principle."

"And getting even," Sekka said softly.

"Well, yeah," Cade said, nodding and adding, "I kinda took that for granted."

"So?" Sekka said. "You were saying; the supplier; got a name for him, too?"

Cade took a moment, and then said, "Ain't so much a him as a *they,* as in an entire friggin' network. There's this counter-tracking organization called Freeland, based out of Bangkok. They've taken to calling it *Hydra,* on account of every time they cut off one head another couple takes its place.

"Outcome is, they've narrowed the field to what they think are two main guys: brothers. Names are Bach Mai - his friends call him *Boonchai* - and Bach Van Limh. Vietnamese born, but their base of operations is kinda flexible. As of now, Mai's based in Nakhon Phanom, Thailand. It's on the border with Laos. HQ is a corner shop beneath an apartment block, some sort of beauty salon. His girlfriend fronts the place. She's his main cashier."

"And Van?" Sekka asked.

"Operates the Vietnamese end; he's got this warehouse in Son Tay, coupla hours by road from Hanoi. Between them, they control all the cross-border smuggling routes. They got what you might call affiliates, in South Africa, Mozambique, Thailand, Malaysia, Vietnam and, guess where, China. They're also implicated in primate trading. There's evidence linking them to a Vietnamese company with ties to a Miami based group that imports monkeys from around the world for use in animal research labs."

"They sound like real princes," Keel said.

"Not the word I'd use. Anyways, they got a couple of import export companies they use as fronts: Vinasakhone and Vannaseng. According to Freeland, both of 'em are involved in animal trafficking, using a bunch of smaller suppliers to move the cargoes around. You name it, they'll transport it. A regular friggin' FedEx. They also run farms in Laos; and when I say farm I ain't talking cows and chickens. I'm talking tigers, bears, turtles, birds; a whole fuckin' menagerie. They were granted approval to trade by the Lao government, in exchange for a two percent tax levied on the value of each of their transactions. Everyone's a winner, right?

"'Course they don't actually call 'em farms, they call them safaris, or zoos; on account of they're there to help promote conservation and tourism and aid scientific purposes. Which is a crock of shit, obviously, because most of them have special slaughter areas were the animals are butchered and the skins and bones are prepared for shipment."

Cade sighed. "Not that animal trafficking is their only source of income. The Thais are after them because they're linked to a drug smuggling ring operating out of Myanmar." Cade smiled. "Starting to sound familiar?"

"Wouldn't be Mong la, by any chance?" Keel asked.

"There you go. Zheng's old buddy, the United Wa State Army, is the main producer. They mix methamphetamines with caffeine to make this stuff called *yaba*. The ingredients are shipped in from China. The Wa have got strong connections with the CCP; it's the Chinese who supply them with weapons. And if you're wondering how they get away with making the drugs, there's a pact, signed between the Wa and the *Tatmadaw*, the Burmese Military. The Wa has agreed not to fight against the government forces, in exchange for the freedom to – and I quote: pursue whatever business activities it chooses; end quote. And we are talking mega business. From Mong La, the stuff's transported overland to the Mekong and shipped downriver. Around twenty percent of it gets offloaded at Golden Kingdom for distribution there. The rest finds its way to the main ports and on to western markets. I'm told the Aussies have taken to it big time."

"Nice to know Zheng's keeping his hand in," Keel mused.

"According to Treasury, the drug dealing alone is worth millions to the Wa *and* to Zheng; on account of he's the Wa's main broker."

"And they're in with the Bachs."

"Big time. The brothers are rumoured to be millionaires, too. One big happy family. Wanna hear something funny? Zheng was actually asked about his involvement in the drug trade around ten years ago; an interview with *Al Jazeera*. Denied it, of course; big surprise. The US Treasury Department chose not to believe him, equally big surprise, and went ahead and named him as the head of a transnational criminal organization. Accused him of everything from drug trafficking, down through money laundering and bribery, as well as the animal trafficking, with the Laos property being used as a laundering hub.

"Treasury and the UN Office on Drugs and Crime asked the Lao government to have the guy brought to account but were told to fuck off. Means you're looking at a 'what happens in Laos stays in Laos' scenario. Oh, the Lao police'll stage the odd raid every few years for appearance sake and broadcast that they've found a badly-hidden stash of meth, worth a couple of million bucks – friggin' peanuts in the general scheme of things – or a flagon of tiger bone wine and the stuff'll be confiscated and that'll be it. No knuckles rapped and Zheng stays in business. Like I said, the place is well protected. The Lao president and the PM have both made visits, smiling their asses off for the cameras. They even have government officials chairing SEZ committees, f'r Christ's sake." Cade paused again, then said, "Which was why the US decided to go it alone."

"How so?"

"Well, they can't go in and get Zheng so they had to stump up the next best thing, which was to have the Treasury Department issue sanctions."

"Against Laos?" Sekka said, frowning.

"GK. Meaning the company plus Zheng and his cronies. They include his wife, Qinyang Lei; though rumour is she's not so much a spouse; more like a business partner, seeing as she's also one of the company directors. She keeps a lower profile than he does so we don't have a lot on her. The other sanction targets are the security guy, Bracken, and a Thai national, Ram Chantharat. He's Zheng's main business partner and another co-director. He and Zheng's wife are accused of moving money illegally to fund their various operations. Outcome is: Treasury's frozen their assets and prohibited US individuals from doing business with them. It's the best we could do under the circumstances. Doesn't mean we still wouldn't like to go in and snatch the motherfucker. But do that and we'd have ourselves a major diplomatic incident.

314

People have short memories when it comes to US incursion into South-East Asia.

"But they're not so fussy about China, obviously," Keel said.

"You got it. State reckons it's all part of their *Yi Dai, Yi Lu* - One Belt One Road - policy. You heard of that?"

"Enlighten us," Sekka said.

"Okay, well, officially it's known as the BRI: the Belt Road Initiative. State says its intention is to establish a comprehensive system to shape the globe according to Chinese interests. Their words not mine. Basically, they wanna take over the world. So far, they're making a pretty good fist of it. You only have to look at the money they're throwing at Africa and Latin America, never mind their neighbours. Hell, they're building concrete runways in the South China Sea, a nuclear power station in the UK, and they're probably helping Erdoğan finance his freakin' canal project. While Europe's been taking its eye off the ball wondering what that little shitweasel in the Kremlin's gonna do next, Xi's been consolidating his power. What, with their God-damned Confucius Institutes sprouting up in every friggin' major city, if we ain't careful, in another twenty years we'll *all* be speaking Mandarin."

Cade's face darkened. "Beijing'll try and convince you that it's all in the name of trade and international cooperation, but you take a look at what we've been discussing here. In Myanmar, they're supplying the base drugs to Wa chemists *and* weapons to the Wa army so it can ward off any threats to its territory and its labs. Oh, and by-the-by, if you think that's just a coupla boxes of QBZ assault rifles, think again. We're talking surface-to-air missiles, heavy artillery and armoured fighting vehicles. Meanwhile, over in Laos,

315

they're plowing money into Zheng's casino resort like it's going out of fashion. Main investors are all Chinese companies backed by Beijing. Everything you'd need to build your Golden Triangle paradise; from construction and property conglomerates to agricultural companies and hotel chains. There's even a plan to introduce a cattle breeding base. Last count had the total investment valued at around eight hundred million dollars.

"Zheng's got it made. He's got contacts up the wazoo and there's not much he doesn't deal in, including human trafficking, according to State, which makes you wonder about some of the GK staff. Those massage parlour are kept pretty busy. Interestingly, that's another thing linking him to the Bachs.

"Bach Van runs a prostitution racket alongside his *yaba* dealing. Smuggles cars, too, according to the Thais. Could be he supplies Zheng with women as well as drugs and wildlife products. Wouldn't be difficult. The Mekong flows right through the heart of the place, transportation'd be a breeze. Van does have a couple of legitimate businesses as cover, hotels and a café plus a gold trading company and an outfit that provides immigrant workers, but that ain't fooling anyone."

Keel's chin lifted. "Interesting."

"Which? The migrants or the gold?"

"Both. I told you our Colonel Baroud was RSF..."

"Yeah, so?"

"The head of the RSF is a guy named Hemeti. His brother, Abdulrahim, owns a gold trading company. Plus, Hemeti's other brothers run businesses based here in the UAE; hotels and tourism. They use immigrant labour. And Baroud used to smuggle cars. Could be just a bunch of coincidences, but it pays to keep an open mind. You know if the Bachs have ever visited Dubai?"

"Couldn't tell you."

"But you can check if they have?"

Cade nodded. "Can do." Sitting back, Cade gazed at them both, sighed, and said, "Look, cards on the table, what are your intentions here, guys? Are you only after this Baroud guy or are you planning to move higher up the food chain?"

"Still gathering info," Keel said.

"Right. Not sure that answers my question, though. I'd like to know what I'm dealing with. I got responsibilities."

"Okay, then how about we want to track down as many bad guys as we can and disrupt their operation?"

"And when you say 'track down'..?"

Keel did not reply but as he returned Cade's penetrative stare, his gaze was calm.

A couple of seconds passed.

"All right, then." Cade said. "Seems to me we got a common enemy. Maybe we should join forces."

"Maybe we should," Keel said carefully.

Before Cade could respond, Keel said, "Look, Max, way I see it is you asked me if I'd been in any decent wars recently and I told you not officially?"

"Yeah, so?"

"So this *is* a war. A multi-billion dollar a year war, according to Bryce, and right now Joseph and I are part of it. Unofficially. The reason we're involved is because of what happened to *our* elephants and *our* rangers. With other folk it's about rhinos and pangolins and bears and snow leopards, and the men and women who are trying to protect *them*. Too many animals are being trafficked and too many reserve staff are dying trying to do what's right. René Deschamps, the guy we work for, told me that over the past ten years close to a thousand rangers have been killed trying to protect their animals. Around two thirds of those were taken out by poachers. So I say it's time someone took the fight to the enemy, show them that if they go after *any* animal there are going to be consequences."

Cade said nothing for several seconds. Finally, he nodded. "I hear you." Then, glancing down at his watch, he made a face. "Damn it. Look, guys, this has been fun and all, but I gotta go. I know this has been a lot to take in, for you and me both. What say I send you the CliffsNotes version and you can take a closer look at the main details? Where are you staying?"

"On the Palm." Keel said. "I called in a favour."

"Nice. You've got Web access, right?"

Keel nodded. "Sure."

Cade took his mobile from a side pocket. "What's your number and e-mail? I'll zap you the intel on Zheng and his pals and anything else I can find. There'll be other people here at the conference that can maybe help with that. You decide what you wanna do, and we'll talk again."

"We can do that." Keel took Cade's number and gave the American his own contact details and watched as Cade stored them on his phone.

"Okay." The American stowed his mobile and rose to his feet. Keel and Sekka followed suit. Cade held out his hand. "Good to see you again, Major. I mean it. And good to meet *you*, Joseph. Something tells me we'll be hooking up again, maybe real soon. Until then, you guys take care."

Watching him head for the exit, Keel and Sekka

318

resumed their seats.

"S.H.I.E.L.D?" Keel said. "Really?"

"Seemed appropriate," Sekka said.

"Better than U.N.C.L.E?"

Sekka grinned, then his face turned serious. "Lot to think about."

"And then some."

"So, what now?"

"Rule one-oh-one. Never go into battle on an empty stomach. I say we grab a bite then head back to base and await Max's info."

"*Battle?*" Sekka said.

Keel shrugged. "Prepare for the worst, hope for the best."

"You trust him?" Sekka asked. "Cade?"

"With this?"

Sekka nodded.

"We've watched each other's back in a few places, so yes."

"He's been around a bit then?"

"Long time, far as I can tell. Worked for various US government agencies, first as an employee and then as a freelancer. Mostly in the dark arts. Put it this way, I'd rather have him on our side than have him working for the opposition."

"He'd probably say the same about you." Sekka smiled, then looked up and raised a hand in greeting. "Here's Sabine."

Keel turned as Sabine reached the booth.

"So how was Ginny?" Keel asked, as Sabine slid smoothly back into her seat and placed her bag by her feet.

"Very well, thank you." Sabine fixed Keel with a dry smile. "And *your* meeting?"

"Very productive."

"You and Mr. Cade had met before, then? I wasn't imagining it."

"We might have shared a few foxholes over the years."

Sabine frowned. "Fox-?"

"Tight corners. How's Duncan? He all right? You both left in a hurry."

"He is fine. And you, Major Keel, are trying to change the subject."

When Keel did not reply, Sabine sighed. "Duncan had the feeling that if he stayed he might end up hearing something he should not. He thinks he knows why you were looking for information and that while Max Cade was the best person for you to talk to, he also said the man has a reputation for ignoring protocol. There are rumours that he used to work for American intelligence before he joined ROUTES."

"I shouldn't believe all the rumours," Keel said.

"Just some of them, perhaps," Sabine said, adding, before either Keel or Sekka could respond, "So Duncan decided it might be safer if he was not around while you had your meeting. What he does not know he cannot reveal."

"Probably for the best," Keel said.

"I, on the other hand," Sabbine said archly, "am *very* interested to hear what you and Mr. Cade talked about."

"Not a problem," Keel said. "You hungry?"

"Starving."

"Good." Keel raised a hand to summon the waiter. "Let's see what they've got on the menu. We can fill you in over dinner."

18

Cade's message was waiting for them when they returned to the house. The villa's owner had installed a ground-floor study, complete with a Dell home office system, and had provided Keel with the log-on password. It took but a few seconds to boot everything up and for Keel to access his Gmail account and the single message that was hovering in his inbox. The subject line read simply: "As mentioned – M."

The attachments ran to a couple of dozen pages. Keel printed them off and took them through to the dining room table where Sekka and Sabine were waiting. Keel spread out the documents. The information comprised biographies for Zheng and his main associates: his wife, his head of casino security, and Chantharat, the Thai national named by Cade, plus the two import-export guys. Separate sheets carried information on the Golden Kingdom SEZ.

Keel opened with the biographies and the accompanying photographs.

Zheng's biographical details confirmed what Cade had already revealed. Zheng's photo showed a slender, trim-looking individual with suspiciously dark hair for a man in his mid-sixties. Dressed in a short-sleeved, open-neck maroon shirt, white trousers and startling white slip-on loafers, he was seated, one leg crossed over the other, in a plain, upright chair and gazing directly at the camera with a serene smile on what appeared to be a remarkably unlined face. The lack of ridges across his forehead and the minimal lines around the corner of his eyes and jawline hinted that there might have been a visit to a cosmetic surgeon at some point in his recent past. He looked, Keel thought, not unlike Joseph Wiseman, the actor who played Fleming's Dr. No.

As for his wife; in contrast, there wasn't a great deal of information. Born in Liaoning Province, Southern China, and listed as a Hong Kong resident, Qinyang Lei was, according to the attachment, five years younger than her husband, though in the photo she looked marginally younger than that, suggesting that she, too, might have spent time under the knife. No smile, however, serene or otherwise. Dressed in a short, dark blue dress, handbag clutched to her chest, and standing next to a silver Rolls Royce Ghost; the scowl on her face, accentuated by her hair which was drawn back in a tight bun, implied she wasn't too happy at having been captured for posterity.

"She has nice legs," Sabine observed, drily.

The next photograph showed two very pale-skinned, slightly overweight Asian men, bare-chested and dressed in shorts, seated side by side, clutching drinks. Across the bottom of the image was the inscription: *L to R: Boonchai, Van*. Both men looked more than a little the worse for wear; leaning in to each other. Van's arm was draped languorously over Boonchai's shoulder in the way a drunken pal hangs on to his mate at the end of a boozy night out. A second photo showed Van topping up his glass, while Boonchai was leaning back awkwardly, arms

322

outstretched as if he was about to slide off the bench. The circular edge of an ornate tattoo covered what could be seen of his left arm from shoulder to elbow; some form of mandala motif. It was difficult to make out details. As with Zheng, the men's written biographies matched the information that Cade had relayed earlier,

"Looks like they were enjoying themselves," Sekka murmured, gazing down at the photos.

The information pertaining to Zheng's Australian head of security, Bracken, was more expansive than that of Zheng's wife, but not by much. What could be determined from the grainy snapshot showed him to be a well-set, crop-haired man with Eurasian features dressed in a dark blazer, white open-neck shirt and khaki-coloured chinos. A typewritten paragraph listed an Australian father and Malaysian mother, his birth place as Temerloh, Malaysia and his age as forty-seven. After that, his biography was succinct. Educated at Balwyn High School, Victoria; served for sixteen years in the Australian Armed Forces before joining the overseas division of Crown Casinos as a security consultant, based in Macao. He'd resigned from the company in the wake of the jailing of more than a dozen Crown Resort employees found guilty of illegally promoting gambling in China. There was no date indicating when he'd defected to Zheng's organization. Keel suspected it was probably not that long after the court case.

There was even less information on Chantharat, Zheng's Thai business partner. Other than his nationality being confirmed he was listed as being forty-four years of age and a resident of Mae Fah Luang district, Chiang Rai. There was no accompanying photograph.

Keel laid the biographies to one side and turned to the remaining pages, the first of which contained information on the two front companies used by the Bach brothers. The locations of their farms were given, along with a list of the species they were permitted to handle by the Lao government. The live animals being bred included all the species named by Cade, while the list of traded animal parts covered lion skulls, rhino horn, tiger skins and claws, python skins and pangolin scales; all of which were known to have been supplied by the Vinasakhone company to Zheng Chao's casino resort. The same items were regularly shipped across the border into both Vietnam and China.

The next couple of pages concerned Golden Kingdom. There was a brief history of its founding, a location map as well as a satellite image taken from Google Earth, and a selection of photos showing various areas of the resort, including exterior and interior shots of the casino and hotel, plus street scenes, notably of shops selling animal products; everything from ivory figurines and leopard skins to traditional medicines, along with eating places where it was possible to order such delicacies as tiger bone wine, monitor lizard steaks, pangolin stew and bear paw soup. One of the satellite images showed an aerial shot of what looked like an isolated building set in its own grounds, contained within an outer wall, upon which Cade had scrawled: *Zheng's private compound.*

One of the downloaded pages contained a list of animal protection and conservation websites which detailed the illegal activities allegedly being conducted within the Golden Kingdom resort. Among the agencies named were Freeland, Poaching Facts, the

324

Environmental Protection Agency, Earth League International, and Save the elephants. There were also links to articles in the UK's *Guardian* newspaper, *The Sydney Morning Herald* and the *Asia Sentinel* as well as to several blog entries written by Westerners who'd visited the resort, some of them following tourist trails; others having infiltrated the resort by stealth to conduct undercover investigations, including the female investigative journalist who'd visited GK under the guise of a sex worker.

The last attachment page contained a copy of the press release issued by the US Treasury Department's Office of Foreign Assets Control, headed: *'Action targets criminal network tied to drug trafficking, money laundering, bribery, and human and wildlife trafficking facilitated through Laotian Casino'*.

Keel's eye was drawn to the third paragraph, which did not mince words: *'The Zheng Chao crime network engages in an array of horrendous illicit activities, including human trafficking and child prostitution, drug trafficking, and wildlife trafficking.'*

The Treasury's designated targets were Zheng and the three individuals named by Cade plus his companies operating in Hong Kong, Thailand and Laos. The release concluded with a warning that the penalties for violating the order were possible imprisonment for a period up to twenty years and fines up to one million dollars.

"Cade wasn't kidding, was he," Sekka said, his expression grim.

"Doesn't look like it," Keel agreed.

"And the Lao government lets all of them get away with it," Sabine said hoarsely, her eyes fixed on an image of a dozen ivory bangles laid out across a store counter, behind which could be seen a gallery of tiger skins stretched out and affixed to a nearby wall.

"Money talks," Keel said. "Always has, always will."

A distant ping sounded; the office computer signalling the arrival of another e-mail. Returning to the office, Keel saw that Cade had sent a follow-up message. Keel read the subject line, printed out the message and the attachment, and, after permanently deleting the e-mail and the one that had preceded it from the mail cache and performing a factory reset on the printer, he took them back to the dining room. "Looks like we've got a p.s."

'Freeland has no mention of Baroud but they do have a record of the Bachs visiting Dubai in November last year. They also have a copy of the bill of lading for a consignment of auto parts addressed to Vinasakhone from a Dubai based outfit called Tradive General Trading. Freeland advise they're a company of interest. Copy attached. M'

Keel studied the document. The bill was for a sea-borne cargo of automobile air conditioning units and catalytic converters. The shipper was listed as Tradive General Trading LLC, Emirates Road, Dubai, the consignee was Vinasakhone Trading, with an address in Wireless Road Lumphini, Bangkok. The carrier was given as AG Global, while the load was assigned FCL. Dredging his memory, Keel remembered that FCL stood for 'Full Container Load', which meant the shipper had paid for the use of a container exclusively for their product. It didn't mean the container was full; it meant it could be partially loaded and not shared with another shipper, ensuring privacy with the container sealed prior to export to its destination. It was often the quickest way to transport sea freight.

"When was it shipped?" Sekka asked.

Keel checked the bill. The vessel's name, he noted, was the *Sulawesi Star.* "Three days ago according to this."

"And according to Lavasse, Baroud would've been here then. Any idea of the sailing time Dubai to Thailand?"

Keel shook his head. "Not a clue. Too many factors; type of vessel, stop-off ports, weather conditions, could be anything from five, six days to a couple of weeks."

"So whatever it is they're shipping, even if it really is auto parts, it's still en route."

"I'd say so."

Sabine looked up. Her jaw was clenched and there was a trace of moisture at the corner of each eye. Taking a deep breath, she let it out slowly, then said. "What do we do now, Thomas?"

Keel stepped back from the table and looked towards the floor to ceiling doors that opened out on to the terrace with its view across the lagoon to where lights from the houses on the adjacent frond, twinkled brightly in the darkness. Without speaking he walked across the room and stepped outside. The humidity of the day had begun to wear off but the evening was still very warm, with a faint sea breeze. Exchanging looks, Sekka and Sabine followed.

Sekka was the first to speak. "What are you thinking?"

Keel continued to stare off across the still, dark water. "That it's a nice night for a paddle?"

Baroud's eyes flickered open. For a second or two he

327

remained still, caught in that foggy moment of uncertainty between sleep and wakefulness, aware that his slumber had been disturbed, sensing that something about his surroundings had changed, but unsure as to quite what, or why.

Raising himself on to one elbow, his first thought was that it must have been a noise from outside that had awoken him and his eyes moved automatically to the sliver of moonlight showing through a thin gap in the drapes. But the night appeared quiet and the only sound he could hear was the low, steady hum emanating from the air conditioning vents.

Until...

Movement: a dark figure detaching itself from the gloom, The sudden realization that he was no longer alone jolted Baroud upright. The bedsheet slid away as he fumbled for the light switch.

As the light snapped on, he felt pressure against his right temple, a sharp, prickling sensation, as if made by a needle or a stiletto point.

"*Marhaba, 'Aqid.*"

Baroud froze, his arm still extended.

Only when the object was removed from the side of his skull was he able to retract his arm and half-turn towards the direction of the voice. His brain registered immediate shock as his eyes took in the appearance of the person standing over him.

The intruder's body was encased in a close-fitting, grey-black, camo-patterned, neoprene wet suit. No logos were visible. Cautiously, Baroud's gaze travelled upwards, searching for some sort of identity. His eyes widened further upon seeing that the person who'd invaded his sanctum and addressed him in Arabic had distinct European features, none of which he recognized.

He managed to find his voice. "*Min 'ant?*"

"Doesn't matter who who *I* am," Keel said.

A nerve flickered along the side of Barroud's jaw. His eyes dropped to the weapon in Keel's gloved hands and his breath caught.

Due to the UAE's strict gun control laws, entering Dubai with any kind of firearm had not been an option, while attempting to obtain an illegal handgun on site would also have been too risky. Keel and Sekka had known, therefore, that if they were to confront Baroud, who would, almost certainly, have obtained the permits required when employing an armed bodyguard, they would have to source an alternative means of offence and protection.

Spear fishing with scuba tanks was prohibited in the Emirates but spear fishing while free diving was effectively unregulated and no licence was required. The FREEDIVER store in Dubai's IT Plaza had provided the equipment: wet gear and a brace of Seac Sub Asso 30 pneumatic spearguns. Keel had spear-fished before, in the warm waters off Mombasa. On those occasions he'd used a rubber-powered gun. For the current task in hand, however, the pneumatic version had the advantage. At only a little over 30 centimetres in length, the Seac was small enough to be worn in a waist holster, supplied as part of the package. With compact spears to match, and with fewer attachments to hamper manipulation, the gun was a more convenient option than any of its longer and more unwieldy rubber-powered cousins. It was also a more powerful weapon and, therefore, more accurate.

Baroud dragged his eyes away from the spear point. "How did you get in here? If you are here to steal from me I have nothing of value."

"The only thing I want from you," Keel said, "is information." He watched as a cautious frown crossed the other man's face.

"Information? I do not understand."

"Tradive General Trading has shipped a container to Vinasakhone Trading in Bangkok. I want to know what's in it."

Baroud stared up at him. "What? I don't..."

"Yes," Keel said. "You do. The *Sulawesi Star* sailed from Jebel Ali three days ago. I want to know what it's carrying; and don't tell me it's auto parts."

"Container? What is this? I know nothing of containers, or of this ship. You are insane! You enter my home...!"

Now wide awake, Baroud seemed to have forgotten the weapon Keel was holding and made to push himself upright but was forced to jerk his head away as Keel brought the muzzle of the speargun to bear. Hampered due to his by then semi-prone position, he flinched as Keel laid the tip of the spear against his right cheek.

"Wrong answer, Colonel. I've seen the bill of lading. Tradive's the shipper and AG Global is responsible for the handling. I'll ask you again. What's in the container that's not on the manifest? Is that how you're moving the ivory out of the country?"

Up until that moment it had been all bluster and protest, but at the mention of ivory, what might have been a genuine flicker of alarm appeared in the other man's eyes.

"You ship it to Bangkok and the Bach brothers organize transport from there," Keel said. "That's why you're here: to supervise the cargo, yes?"

330

"No! What? Ivory? I know nothing of ivory! I am here to purchase military vehicles!"

Keel sighed. "I know about the trucks Colonel. They don't interest me. I've told you what does: the ivory. Tell me, does Algoney know you're using his company to move the stuff? How about his brother: your boss, Hemeti? Or are they both in on it? What else are you shipping out? Rhino horn? Lion bones? Pangolin scales..?"

Baroud's jawline pulsed. The tremor had returned. He threw what he must have hoped was a surreptitious sideways glance towards the bedroom door.

"Your man can't help you, Colonel," Keel said. "It's just you and me...and him."

Keel lifted his chin to direct Baroud's gaze towards a corner of the room that still lay in shadow and waited for a reaction. Baroud gave a sharp intake of breath as Sekka stepped forward into the light, his face a dark mask.

To judge by the expression on Baroud's face, Keel guessed the man was wondering if it had been his own bodyguard who'd betrayed him, allowing access to those who would wish him harm.

Keel had no desire to reassure Baroud that that wasn't the case and that his bodyguard had, in fact, acted commendably while attempting to defend him. Nor did he feel the need to explain that the said bodyguard was sprawled at the base of the stairs, still clutching the shaft of the 7mm thin steel spear that had pierced his throat with the ease of a hot knife through butter. In all likelihood, Baroud's man had breathed his last without fully understanding what had killed him.

331

For the Seac wasn't just powerful, it was also relatively silent.

"It was Faheem who gave you up, Colonel," Keel said. "In case you were wondering."

"Faheem?" Throwing a baleful look towards the still silent and immobile Sekka, Baroud turned back. This time, he looked genuinely perplexed. "I know of no such person."

"No?" Keel said. "He was a friend of Jaafar. You remember Jaafar? Sergeant Jaafar Toubia? He was the one who led the raid on Salma. There you go." Keel watched as the nerve across the top of Baroud's cheek began to flicker in earnest. "*Now* you remember."

Baroud blinked. He eyed Sekka again, more cautiously. Sekka still hadn't moved. "Who *are* you people?"

"Your worst nightmare," Keel said, pressing the point of the spear into the fleshy part of Baroud's right cheek. A spot of blood began to seep from beneath the steel tip.

By this time, Baroud's spine was jammed against the headboard. He was wearing some sort of cotton night shirt. The neck was unbuttoned and had fallen open, revealing matted strands of greying chest hair and surprisingly pale skin. A thin sheen of perspiration covered his top lip. It looked as though his moustache was leaking.

Sekka said in Arabic, "Who gave the order to kill the rangers at Salma? You?"

The money shot. Baroud's face suddenly seemed to fold in on itself.

Sekka took a step forward. Instinctively, Baroud pressed himself further back into the headboard, without success.

"Simple question, Colonel," Keel said evenly. "You did send Jaafar and his men across the border to steal ivory, yes?"

The man in the bed watched, mesmerised, as Keel, using his free hand, unzipped the waterproof pocket attached to his thigh and drew out a thin rectangular object: a mobile phone. Opening up the phone's directory, Keel used his gloved thumb to scroll down the screen, paused, and then pressed auto dial.

And waited.

Baroud's gaze flicked back and forth between Keel and Sekka, his chest now rising and falling at a quickening rate.

On the bedside table a second mobile phone emitted a tinny burst of Arabic music.

Baroud started. His face, already sallow in the half light, seemed to leach even more colour.

Keel allowed the ringbone to sound for two more seconds before terminating the call. He indicated the phone in his hand. "This was Jaafar's. One of the numbers in its directory matched one we were given by a French intelligence agent. Your number, Colonel. The one I've just dialled. You'll be pleased to know the French have quite a dossier on you; your background, your career in the RSF, personal details. They don't like you very much. They even gave us these."

Keel's thumb moved across the phone's face. Then, reversing the screen he held it out so that the content could be viewed by the man in the bed. "This is you with a male friend, having sex. We thought your friend's face looked familiar so we compared it to your man downstairs. Azim, yes? Your bodyguard? Explains why you prefer to travel just the two of you. Certainly gives new meaning to the words 'close protection'. Oh, and Jaafar won't be reporting for duty any time soon, either."

Baroud seemed transfixed by the explicit image on the screen, all attempt at bravado having evaporated.

"From what I've heard, Colonel," Keel said. "Sudan takes a dim view of homosexuality. I looked it up. It's punishable by imprisonment and/or death. Even if someone just comes under suspicion it means a beating or a public lashing. Not like dragging someone off the street and giving them a haircut. Makes me wonder how your bosses will react when we send them this and the rest of the reel. Maybe the DGSE can find a way to post them on RSF's Facebook page...unless you give us answers."

Keel waited for a response. He could tell that Baroud was considering his options, which, after being informed that Jaafar was very probably dead, he must have known were severely limited. After several seconds, Baroud said hoarsely, "What do you want to know?"

"Is the container on the *Sulawesi Star* carrying ivory?"

It was a few seconds before Baroud offered a begrudging nod.

"From the elephants killed at Salma?"

Another nod, more subdued.

"And from other places? Uganda? Cameroon?"

"Cameroon," Baroud's voice had dropped several octaves.

"CAR, too, maybe?"

Baroud's head dipped.

"What else is being transported? Rhino horn? Bones?"

No reply

"I can't hear you," Keel said.

Another reluctant nod. "Horns."

"And bones? Lion bones?"

Nod.

"The Bach brothers; did you meet with them when they came to Dubai? Is that when you made your deal? That you would send the ivory and the horn to Vinasakhone and they would sell it on?"

Despite the air con, Baroud was now sweating to such an extent it looked as though he was suffering from some sort of virulent fever. A sour smell was also coming off him in waves. Evidently shocked by the revelation that Keel knew of the brothers' existence, when he answered this time his voice emerged as a dry whisper. "*Naeam.*"

Yes.

Keel straightened. Baroud, free from the pressure of the spear point, exhaled but made no attempt to sit up.

"Did you order the killing of the rangers at Salma?" Sekka asked again as he moved to Keel's side. His wetsuit matched Keel's, as did the equipment belt and the speargun contained in the holster strapped to his thigh. The difference lay in the SIG Sauer semiautomatic he was holding against his right leg, which Baroud recognized as the same model carried by his bodyguard, Azim. The confirmation that his bodyguard was certainly dead, probably as a result of the sound that had awoken him, caused his insides to lurch.

Without warning, Sekka placed the pistol muzzle against Baroud's forehead. Baroud froze. A small mewling sound emerged from between his parted lips.

Passing the phone to Sekka, Keel stepped away from the bed and headed for the door. "I'll leave you to it," he said. "Don't be too long."

Leaving the room, he closed the door behind him and made his way downstairs.

When the shot came, it did so as a sudden, sharp report. There was a finality to the sound that would have been familiar to anyone with a working knowledge of small arms fire, but at that hour, a person not versed in the use of firearms would have had little cause to raise an alarm over a split-second noise from which they were disassociated, either by distance, direction, lack of knowledge or even, possibly, disinterest.

Keel was in the lobby, when Sekka reappeared, the pistol held loosely in his hand.

"He own up?" Keel asked.

"What do *you* think?"

"I think he probably fingered Jaafar," Keel said.

"And you'd be right."

"Didn't make him any less guilty."

"No."

"Of a lot of things."

"Correct."

Sekka walked to where Azim lay crumpled on the tiles. There was a wide pool of blood beneath the corpse. Careful not to step in it, Sekka, handed the pistol to Keel before crouching and easing the bodyguard's fingers from the spear shaft. Such had been the gun's power, with no line attachment fitted, which might have impeded penetration, the spear had driven through Azim's throat to the extent that the head of the shaft, containing the flopper, was protruding from the exit wound. Gripping the shaft and following the weapon's trajectory, Sekka pulled it free of the body and rose to his feet.

"All good?" Keel asked.

Sekka nodded.

Keel dropped the pistol onto the bloody floor, within reach of the corpse's empty hands. "Then let's get the hell out of here."

The kayaks were where they'd left them, in the shadow of the steps linking the adjacent villa's terrace to its own section of the beach. An earlier recon had established that the property was unoccupied and as there was no wall or fence separating the two homes, it had been their chosen landing spot. Keel assumed the omission of a physical boundary - in line with most of the properties - was because the developer had determined, optimistically, that the security gates and speed bumps at the entrance to each frond were a sufficient deterrent. A lapse that had proved helpful when Keel and Sekka made their run an hour after midnight.

The kayaks had come with the oil exec's villa and were for the use of family and guests; two Aquaglide single inflatables. At only nine feet in length, they were also kitted out in a subdued grey/blue colour scheme, which, combined with their low profiles, meant that once on the water they were less likely to be seen by either an inadvertent glance or even by watchful eyes, though their deployment, while eliminating the need for a five-hundred metre swim, was not without risk.

Local ordnances stated that after sunset all waterborne activities along the lines of kayaking, paddle boarding and sailing within the waters of the Palm were strictly prohibited, and Keel and Sekka had been keenly aware that the longer they remained afloat the more danger there was of them still being spotted.

They'd also had to consider the fact that the kayaks, being inflatable, weren't built for speed, a disadvantage not helped by the water being choppier than expected due to the proximity of the gap that had been cut into the eastern breakwater.

The gaps - a second formed part of the breakwater on the western side of the Palm - were designed to counter the risk of stagnant water building up within the lagoon due to the reduced tidal flow, which could have created a pollution problem had the openings not been there. In the end, it had taken a good fifteen minutes, thankfully without incident, to cover the distance between the fronds, though the chop had proved useful as it had also helped to break up their outlines.

Gaining access to the villa had not been difficult. While the place might have had a multi-million dollar price tag, the same couldn't be said for the rear entry points, a factor Keel had been counting on, having gauged the standard of the lock mechanisms at the oil exec's rental villa. The outer garage door at Baroud's had taken eleven seconds to breach while getting through the inner connecting door had taken nine.

The only obstruction had been in the person of Baroud's bodyguard, who, despite Keel's attempt at a silent entry, had evidently caught the sound of the assault on the door locks, and had launched his intervention at the moment Keel, who was working point, exited the corridor en route to the main lobby and the stairs.

But while the bodyguard had acted with commendable speed, what he hadn't allowed for was there being not just the one intruder, but two of them. Emerging from the shadows, pistol raised, he'd presented Sekka with the perfect profile and Sekka, unlike his target, hadn't hesitated. The sound of the pistol hitting the marble floor had caused a unnaturally loud clatter, but, with Azim's life blood draining away rapidly, it had taken Sekka but a second to scoop up the pistol and follow Keel to the first floor and thence into Baroud's bedchamber, in time to surprise its occupant who'd been roused from sleep probably by the smack of Azim's gun hitting the downstairs tiles.

One hundred yards out from the shore, Keel raised his paddle and looked back. No alarms appeared to have been raised and Baroud's villa lay in darkness once more, Sekka having extinguished the bedside light when he'd exited the room. His other parting gift had been to leave Jaafar's mobile phone on the bed, close to Baroud's body, its screen turned off. The image of Baroud and his bodyguard making the beast with two backs would be the first thing anyone saw when the screen was re-activated. Keel having copied the image from the photos provided by Lavasse.

A touch theatrical, perhaps, but with luck, given the rest of the phone's content, it would help muddy the waters for whichever investigative team was assigned to the scene once the alarm was raised. The Sig, from which the fatal shot had been fired, would come up as registered to Azim, who would be identified from the photo as being Baroud's bedmate, whose own corpse would be discovered with an unexplained neck wound and the pistol lying nearby. To confuse matters further, there would be no powder residue found on the bodyguard's hands, though his would be the only prints on the gun. Sekka, like Keel, was wearing Neoprene gloves.

"Tick-tock," Sekka called softly, drawing Keel's attention away from the view.

The night remained still. Despite the hour, there were plenty of homes along both shorelines that were showing lights, and music could be heard drifting distantly across the water. On the surface, however, nothing appeared to be moving. A security patrol boat was supposed to inspect each frond every morning but Keel wasn't sure if the Palm employed boats at night. There were no running lights or engine sounds to indicate that any motor craft were near but it didn't hurt to assume that might not be the case. As a precaution, both men had deployed their hoods to conceal their features and, in Keel's case, his paler skin tone.

At the halfway point they ceased paddling, gathered up the spearguns, spears and holsters into single bundle secured by the holster straps, and dropped them into the water. The holes drilled in the guns' alloy muzzles, designed to allow quick retreat of water in the barrel, would, in this instance, along with the combined weight of the steel shafts, ensure the weapons sank like stones.

The return journey took twenty-two minutes.

As they arrived back at their own beach and dragged the Aquaglides clear of the water, a slender figure seated on the terrace steps rose to greet them. Sabine looked anxious. "Was he there?"

Keel nodded.

"Did he talk?"

"He did."

"And?"

"Later," Keel said, as he knelt to release the air valve on his kayak. "We need to move."

There was a brief hiss as the valve was opened. Sabine closed her eyes, and let out a long breath. "He is dead, isn't he?"

"Yes. How's the flight looking?"

For second, Sabine hesitated, and then said, "On time. Four twenty-five departure."

"Good. Soon as we get these squared away and change into some dry togs, we'll be off. How are you doing, Joseph?"

"Almost there," Sekka was holding his now fully deflated Aquaglide under the fresh water shower at the side of the pool to rinse away the salt. That task completed, he folded the kayak into its storage bag and then, still in his wetsuit, stepped under the shower himself before stripping down to his trunks and repeating the process. Taking one of the two towels Sabine had brought with her, he dried himself off.

Keel followed suit.

The three of them had made the trip utilizing only carry-on baggage. Nevertheless, to facilitate a speedy departure, packing had been completed before Keel and Sekka's night time sortie, so it was only thirty minutes after beaching, with the kayaks stowed in the pool locker along with the donated wet gear, when Keel locked up and dropped the keys into the safe on the villa's outer wall. A minute after that, they were in the 4x4 and heading for the airport.

It wasn't until three hours later, as the Ethiopian Airlines Airbus was lifting off the tarmac, bound for Addis, when Sabine leaned across to Keel in the darkened cabin and finally asked. "So, can you tell me now?"

Keel did so.

At the end of the telling, Sabine went quiet,

341

allowing the hum of aircraft to envelop her before she turned back to Keel. "Does this mean it is over?"

Keel did not reply immediately. He looked out of the window at the view beneath the wings. Dawn had broken but there were still lights twinkling below them. Holding the view, he wondered idly how long it would be before the bodies were discovered. There was no way of knowing, and speculation would serve no purpose. He looked at her. "Honest answer?"

Sabine frowned. "Always."

"I think it's too early to tell," Keel said.

19

It was a little before nine and the terminal at Addis Ababa was already teeming as Keel and his two companions were dropped off at Arrivals by the over-crowded shuttle bus. It was while they were en route to the departure gate for the connecting flight to N'Djamena that Keel took the call.

"What the hell's that ruckus?" Max Cade asked, his voice sounding surprisingly clear. "Where are you?"

"Bole," Keel said. "It's rush hour."

"Jeez, sounds like it. So, you guys left early."

"Didn't want to overstay our welcome," Keel said. "Plus we had a plane to catch." From the corner of his eye, he saw Sekka throwing him a quizzical look. "What can I do for you, Max?"

"Okay, got it; you're on the move so no small talk. No problem. Just thought I'd let you know I got me some fresh intel on our Chinese friend."

"What sort of intel?"

"Word is he's gonna be holding an auction."

"Auctioning what?"

"Well, it ain't likely to be fine art. According to Freeland, the sale's taking place at the GK resort ten days from now. That's forty-eight hours after the *Sulawesi Star* docks in Khlong Toei. So if that container *is* carrying animal parts and Vinasakhone's delivering 'em for the sale, we could be talking some serious contraband."

Keel paused in mid-stride, took a breath, then said, "It does and you are."

It took Cade a couple of seconds to respond. "Say again?"

"The container *is* carrying animal parts: ivory and rhino horn, including Salma's ivory. Lion bones, too, for sure, which probably means a heap of other stuff as well."

Keel was conscious that Sekka and Sabine had both stopped and were looking back at him.

"And you know that, how?" Cade said.

"Got it from the horse's mouth."

"Sorry, pal, you're gonna have to give me a clue."

"Our RSF colonel."

A pause, then: "You paid him a visit."

"We did."

"What, and he just fessed up?"

"After some prodding."

Another pause, then: "That's what you said about the last guy you questioned. Should I even ask?"

"Probably best if you didn't," Keel said. He saw that Sekka and Sabine were about to walk back towards him. He held up his free hand to halt them.

"Okay, but you didn't think to give your old pal a heads up?"

From Cade's reaction, it sounded as if word of Baroud's killing might not have reached the wider world. Or maybe Cade was just feigning ignorance.

"No time. Like I said, we had a plane to catch."

There followed a taut, two second silence.

"Okay, gotcha," Cade said. "My source is gonna try and find out more, maybe download an items list and some of the invite names. I-"

The last part of Cade's sentence was suddenly and loudly interrupted by a two-tone chime from the tannoy above Keel's head. The ADD/NDJ flight was about to commence boarding.

"Shit," Cade swore, before Keel could speak. "I heard. Look, if you're interested, lemme give you a call when you're back at base. Depending on further info, I might might wanna run something by you. You guys got a decent connection down there?"

"Wouldn't call it decent," Keel said, "but we're contactable."

"Okay. In the meantime, like I said, I'll try raising my source. Catch you later."

Cade clicked off.

"What was that about?" Sekka asked. Over his shoulder, the gate staff were calling passengers forward.

Keel stowed his phone away. "Not entirely sure. Cade's heard that Golden Kingdom's going to be hosting an auction."

"He tell you what they were selling?"

"Reckons it could be that container load on the *Sulawesi Star*. He'll try and find out more and make contact when we're back at Salma as he might want to run something by me – end quote."

"He say what?" Sekka asked as they approached the scrum of passengers at the desk.

"No."

"Think it'll be legal?"

"Knowing Cade," Keel said, "I doubt it."

It was close to sunset when Crow brought the Cessna

to a stop at the edge of Salma's dirt runway. "Welcome home, folks."

There were only two flights a week between the capital and Sarh, both early morning departures. Due to the inconvenient lunchtime arrival of flights from ADD, if they'd chosen to fly commercial all the way, their routing would have meant another two night stay at the Chez Wou. As the hotel held no allure, a prior arrangement with René Deschamps, had ensured that Crow was there to meet them at N'Djamena. By the time they arrived back at Salma they'd been travelling for the best part of seventeen hours and awake for a great deal longer, apart from the times they'd been able to nap between take-offs and landings.

When the three of them had showered and changed, Deschamps met them in the lodge overlooking the river, where Crow joined them after he'd checked and tethered the Cessna for the night. Deschamps had briefed the kitchen staff and a selection of simple dishes had been prepared and made available, kept warm by a bank of hotplates arranged along the bar.

"So?" Deschamps enquired. "Was your visit productive? Did you get the information you were seeking?"

Keel waited while Crow helped himself to a beer and a bowl of lamb and potato stew before joining the table, then said, "Mostly, yes."

"You saw Colonel Baroud."

A statement, Keel noted. Not an inquiry.

"We had a conversation, yes."

"And?"

"He admitted to his part in the raid and that Salma's ivory is on its way to Thailand, possibly for auction."

"Anything else?"

The room seemed to go unnaturally quiet.

"Sounds to me like you already know the answer to that," Keel said. "Spit it out."

Deschamps' eyes narrowed. "I know he's dead, Thomas. I've spoken with Paul Lavasse." Deschamps hesitated, then said, "He sends his felicitations..."

"*Felicitations?*" Crow said.

"...and his thanks," Deschamps finished.

"For?" Keel said.

"Paving the way for his man would be my guess," Sekka interposed quietly.

"Excuse me?" Sabine held up a hand. "Would somebody mind telling me what is going on? Or is this a private club, boys only?"

"The DGSE's got an agent inside the RSF," Sekka said. "Remember? Lavasse told us they wouldn't shed any tears if Baroud was taken out, as it would mean their man was in line to take his place."

Sabine sighed. "Sorry, yes, you're right. I'd forgotten. Forgive me. It's just that it's been a long day and I am more than a little tired." She went quiet, then frowned. "Did Lavasse *ask* you to kill Baroud?"

"If he had done," Keel said, "the answer would have been no."

"But Baroud *is* dead," Sabine pressed.

"He is. So the DGSE can slot their agent into position. It's a major coup for them, probably for western intelligence as a whole."

Deschamps cut in. "The Dubai authorities believe Baroud was shot by his bodyguard and they are not looking for any other suspects. It seems compromising photographs were found that showed the two men had a sexual relationship." He fixed Keel with a penetrating

347

look. "The police are of the opinion there was a falling out. In other words, it was a *crime passionnel*; a private matter. Paul subsequently received information that as far as the Emiratis are concerned the case is closed. Baroud's superiors have accepted the findings."

"That seems a tad quick," Keel said. "How come?"

Deschamps continued to regard him shrewdly, then shrugged. "Diplomatically, it was the most convenient conclusion."

"*Convenient?*" Sabine said.

"Means they *wanted* it covered up," Crow said, pushing his empty bowl aside.

Sabine frowned.

"Indeed," Deschamps said. "If you recall, officially, Baroud was in Dubai to finalize the purchase of vehicles for the RSF. Given what the contract is worth, I doubt either party would want the deal compromised by a lengthy police investigation. The UAE would not like it thought that the killer might be an Emirati citizen, and by the same token, I would suggest the RSF general staff would not want attention drawn to the fact that one of their senior officers, a relation by marriage to their leader, had been engaged in an inappropriate liaison with his bodyguard."

"We've probably got the DGSE to thank for the diversion," Keel said. "It was most likely their sleeper who took the photos."

"Indeed, and if they were to be made public, it would bring shame not just upon Baroud's wife and children but his extended family."

"Yeah," Crow growled. "All the way to the top. Not that the lot of them aren't up to their ears in all sorts of illegal shit. Bloody Sudanese version of Zheng and the Bach boys."

348

"Zheng?" Deschamps said, frowning. "Bach boys?" He regarded them all in turn. "Is there something else I should know?"

"Ah, jeez, mate," Crow murmured softly. "How long have you got?

"About that..," Keel said.

"So this Zheng," Deschamps said, when Keel had finished laying out the information provided by Bryce and Max Cade, "he is untouchable?"

Keel nodded. "Pretty much. He's obviously no fool. He knows to stay on his side of the line, and as a Chinese citizen the Laos'll never hand him over, on account of he brings in money and Vientiane is in hock to Beijing for billions. Hell, the Chinese hold damned near half of Laos' public debt. Neither side wants to see that deal scuppered."

"And the Bachs?"

"I'd say they come under the heading 'moving targets'."

Deschamps frowned.

"He means they're harder to hit," Crow said dryly.

"And someone else's responsibility," Deschamps said firmly. "I believe we've done all *we* can do, yes?" He eyed Keel pointedly, "In fact, more than enough. Wouldn't you agree?"

Keel nodded. "It would appear so."

The comment earned him a lengthy, speculative stare from Deschamps, who then returned the nod and said, "Good, then let that be an end to it. We still have a reserve to manage in case you've all forgotten, and there is much to do before the rains hit; which means we don't have much time to attend to our priorities, which should begin with the assessment of our new recruits. I want them fully operational as soon as possible. Secondly, with that objective in mind, we need a new unit to replace the Jackal Team. It occurred to me while you were away that Mo would make a good *Chef de Groupe*. What say you, Joseph?"

"I was thinking the same thing," Sekka said.

"Thomas?"

"I agree," Keel said. "He's earned it."

"Good, then I'll leave you to make your selections. We're also due delivery of those tracking collars, so ideally we'll need to fit them before the rest of the herd heads for the drier feeding grounds. Which brings me to my last point. Don't worry, I know you're all exceedingly tired, but this won't take long. I wanted to let you know that we'll be receiving visitors the day after tomorrow. It's a small group from Manovo Gounda St Floris National Park. As you know, Manovo's a World Heritage site adjacent to our southern border and it's in a bad way. A census has shown that that many of their large mammals have all but disappeared, including elephant, bongo, African wild dog, lion and leopard. Buffalo, waterbuck and Kordofan giraffe *have* been seen but in very small numbers.

"Some of it is down to poachers but they also have problems with pastoralists and fishermen, and even artisanal miners. They've also suffered from armed group incursions. As a result, a plan has been proposed by the CAR's State Party, UNESCO and the Wildlife Conservation Society, with funding from the Norwegian government, to create a trans-border protected area, to be controlled by Manovo *and* Salma. It's hoped to secure additional support from AP. Our

350

own experience would suggest the idea of a joint operation is a sound one, so they're sending a manager and a representative acting for the CAR's Protected Areas Director. Their Anti-Poaching Coordinator will also be with them. That's a recent appointment so they'll be looking for our recommendations. I know it's sudden but the arrangements were made at the last minute to take advantage of the roads before they become totally impassable."

Deschamps turned to Keel. "If AP does step in, Manovo will want to employ more rangers, so they'll want to talk to you and Joseph. You, too, Crow, as the plan will be to include aerial surveillance, finance permitting."

"No problem," Keel said.

"Ditto," Crow said.

"And you, Sabine," Deschamps continued. "They'll be looking for veterinary advice as well."

Sabine nodded and Deschamps pushed back his chair. "Good, then, we are all set. Meeting adjourned." Catching Keel's eye, as everyone rose to their feet, he said, "A word, Thomas, before you go."

Keel nodded. When the others had departed, he said, "What's on your mind, René?"

Indicating that Keel should sit back down, Deschamps walked behind the counter and emerged with the unfinished bottle of Laphroaig. Returning to his seat, he poured them both a drink. When he spoke, his expression was glacial. "So tell me, Thomas; killing Baroud...was that justice or revenge?"

Keel took a slow sip from his glass. "Maybe they're the same thing. For five dead rangers I've no problem with either. What do you want from me, René?"

"The truth. Reassurance that will allow me to sleep

easier in my bed."

"That case, I'd say it was a little of both, though I'm not sure you knowing that is going to cure your insomnia"

"*Little?*"

Keel shrugged. "Turn of phrase. What's done is done."

Deschamps gazed into his glass. "The hunting and punishment of the men who killed our friends, I can justify, because of what they did and because the authorities were not willing to pursue them. The killing of Baroud is a different matter." He looked up. "Was it really necessary?"

"After his bodyguard made the first move, I'd have to say yes. At that point we didn't have a choice. We were committed."

"You *always* had a choice."

"Joseph and I didn't see it that way. Look, I'll shed no tears for the bastard. Faheem and the others were the hired help but Baroud was management. He was the one giving orders. My conscience is clear. Joseph's, too."

Deschamps looked Keel in the eye. "So was it you or was it Joseph who-?"

"Does it matter?" Keel said curtly.

Deschamps considered Keel's answer and sat back. "And Sabine?"

"What about her?"

"She was with you."

"When Baroud died? No, of course not, and if you want to know how she feels about it, you'll have to ask her yourself."

Deschamps fell silent.

"We can't take it back, René," Keel said, "I'll repeat

this until I'm blue in the face but we did what we had to do, because we were the only ones prepared to take action." Keel leaned forward. "And I think I know you well enough to say that if Baroud and Faheem and the rest of them had got away with killing our guys, you'd never have forgiven yourself for not going after them. You were a soldier, damn it. It would have gnawed away at you for the rest of your days. Tell me I'm wrong."

Keel waited.

It took a little time, but eventually, Deschamps shook his head and said in a subdued voice. "No, you are not wrong."

"Well, then."

An uneasy silence fell between them, broken when Keel drained his glass and rose to his feet. "And on that note, I'm away to my pit. We've busy days ahead and we're all going to need our shut-eye."

Deschamps nodded absently but remained seated. Keel patted his shoulder and headed for the door. When he reached it he turned back. "René?"

Deschamps looked up.

"It gets easier," Keel said, and left.

"There's been a change of plan," Deschamps said.

Keel waited.

"The Manovo people are enroute."

"A day early," Keel said. "Okay, we can cope."

Deschamps nodded. "They've had to alter their plans on account of the Bahr Crossing being no longer fordable so they'll be coming in by air instead of by road and the helicopter was only available for charter today."

"Understood. Any idea what time they're due?"

They radioed just before they left. ETA one hour, possibly a bit longer."

"Roger that, though Sabine and Crow might not be back by then."

It was late morning, the day after the return from Dubai. Crow and Sabine had left at first light, in the Cessna, to pick up the tracking collars, which had been flown, along with a box of veterinary medicines, by air from N'Djamena to Am Timan. Deschamps had traced Keel to the main office.

"Joseph?" Deschamps asked.

"With Mo. They're in the field, running the new team though its paces. We can radio them if needed."

"Very good."

The team selection had been made earlier, in conjunction with a decision on the choice of name under which the unit would operate. Deschamps had suggested *Genet* and *Otter* as possible candidates, but he'd been easily persuaded by the entire ranger force to keep the name *Jackal* in memory of the men who had died.

"Just you and me, then," Keel said. "I'll keep my ears open."

Deschamps nodded and left. Keel suspected Deschamps might still be brooding following their conversation the previous evening. Not that Keel was unduly worried. He knew René would get over it.

Ninety minutes later, Keel picked up the whup-whup of approaching rotor blades and made his way to the airstrip. Deschamps arrived around thirty seconds later, as a compact, red-painted Hughes 500 appeared over the tree tops and began its descent. Although prepared, Keel and Deschamps were still forced to duck and turn their heads to avoid the swirl of debris being whipped up by the down draught. By the time they'd turned back, the chopper had landed.

When the blades were still, the rear doors opened and the passengers clambered out. Keel assumed the unsteady-looking African in the ill-fitting suit, who was mopping his brow with a handkerchief, was the government rep; the briefcase being the other giveaway. The second African, tall and shaven-headed in casual slacks and open-necked shirt, was probably Manovo's manager, while the third man, a stocky but fit-looking European sporting a goatee beard and clad in khaki with a matching baseball cap, had to be the anti-poaching coordinator. All as expected, then. But as Deschamps and Keel stepped forward to greet the new arrivals, a fourth man, bareheaded, his eyes hidden behind a pair of dark sunglasses, appeared around the nose of the chopper and let go a roguish grin.

"Hey, bud," Max Cade said, removing the glasses and adjusting the knapsack that drooped from his right shoulder, "How's it hanging?"

"Nice place you got here," Cade said.

They were in the lounge overlooking the river. The tables had been cleared along with the hotplates, cutlery and utensils from the night before. They were alone, the Manovo delegation having accompanied Deschamps to his office. Deschamps had not looked that convinced with Cade's explanation that as a ROUTES agent – Cade had produced his credentials to prove it – he'd hitched a ride in order to renew his acquaintance with Keel following their unexpected reunion at the conference in Dubai, and that he

355

wanted, on behalf of ROUTES, to gain more information about the raid to steal Salma's ivory. The look in Keel's eyes, however, had suggested to Deschamps that discretion was probably the better part of valour under the circumstances and that he should suppress his reservations. And so, with the Manovo trio in tow, Deschamps had headed off to start the introductory tour.

"Hitched?" Keel said. "What, you just happened to be in the area?"

Cade let go a smile. "Well, yeah, but it took some doing. That bit about snagging a lift's true, though. Flew commercial Dubai to Addis, then hopped a ride on an aid flight outta Addis to Bangui. From there an internal to N'Délé, chopper to Gounda, Gounda to here. Wherever the hell 'here' is. Look, I knew about the WCS plan for Manovo, okay? It came across our desk at ROUTES. I did some checking, found out about the guys' visit, asked if I could tag along."

"Tag along?" Keel said.

"They said if I could get to N'Délé in time, then yeah, there'd be a spare seat. Thought they meant a truck but we brought the chopper instead, something about a road being flooded?"

"And so here you are."

"And so here I am."

"So, what do you really want?"

Cade let go another smile. "Ah, you know me so well, brother."

Keel did not respond, causing Cade to hold up his hands in mock surrender. "Okay, okay," Looking towards the bar he made a face. "So, you got anything cold to drink back there. Got a hell of a throat."

"I'll take a look. Beer?"

Cade shook his head. "Club soda'll do fine, if you've got it."

Keel nodded and indicated one of the chairs. "Take a seat."

Heading to the counter, Keel wondered about the true reason for Cade's visit; the man's journey to Salma having been too convoluted for it to be a genuine social call. He presumed it was the promised follow-up to the phone conversation they'd had during the Bole transit and that an explanation would be forthcoming at some point. Sooner rather than later would be good.

Keel opened the bottle of soda, filled two glasses, added ice and returned to where Cade was sitting, gazing out at the river below, where a small herd of gazelle had come to drink.

"This is some spot," Cade said, as he took his glass. "But, jeez, Chad? Really? You couldn't have found anywhere closer to home?"

"You go where the work is," Keel said.

"And decent offers don't grow on trees, right?"

"Something like that," Keel said.

"And I guess this is as good a place as any when it comes to living off grid. Our line of work, we do tend to attract folk of an unsavoury disposition who might want to get even. Helps to be hard to find."

"*You* found me," Keel said.

"Yeah but I don't have an unsavoury disposition. I'm always sunny and bright."

"You say so," Keel said.

Cade grinned, then his face turned serious. "So, anyways, Zheng and GK. Supposedly, this ain't the first time an event like this has been held. They've been holding regular auctions since the place opened; couple of times a year, and it ain't only animal parts.

357

We could be talking narcotics, too, maybe weapons. Advance notices are posted on WeChat or Zalo or sometimes the Dark Web and I hear they can attract some pretty high-rollers. There's bidding in person as well as on-line. I'm still waiting on my asset to give us some more info but she's gone dark."

She? Keel thought, and said, "That doesn't sound good."

"No shit."

"You have any other assets in place?"

"Just the one."

"So you're worried about her safety?"

"Severely."

"And you couldn't have told me all this with a phone call?" Keel said.

Cade made a face, which hinted at some sort of apology.

Keel sighed. "Okay, I'll try again. What's going on, Max? Why *are* you here?"

Cade gazed into his glass and swirled the soda around. The ice made a thin tinkling sound as he did so. He looked up. "Like I said when you were in Addis; I wanted to run something by you. Didn't wanna discuss it on what might be an open line."

"This far off grid, I doubt anyone's listening in," Keel said.

Cade smiled and raised his glass and then took a sip of his drink. "Yeah, but in our world, a little paranoia's a good thing, no? Especially with this Pegasus shit that's doing the rounds. The UAE's one of NSO's main clients. They might have sponsored the conference but you can bet your ass there'll be a slew of delegates on their shit list, given what we know about illegal animal traffic routing through DXB. Means our phones could have been compromised."

Keel waited.

"So," Cade said, "as I was about to say, we got to thinking that this auction might be a way to infiltrate people into GK."

"*We*?" Keel said. "Who's *we*?"

"Me and a collection of interested parties."

"Like?"

"ROUTES, TRAFFIC, Interpol, State."

"By State you mean the Treasury Department."

"That'd be correct."

"Anyone else?" Keel said drily. "FBI? CIA?"

"They haven't replied to the memo."

"Can't say I blame them. So what happens then?"

"Then?"

"Once boots are on the ground."

"We do a look-see."

"There's that *we* again. With what aim?"

"To extract Zheng," Cade said, and waited.

"You mean kidnap," Keel said flatly.

"Tomayto, tomahto. I like to think of it as delivering a master criminal to justice."

"Right," Keel said. "Now, I know I'm going to regret asking this, but did you have any particular infiltrators in mind?"

Cade smiled silkily. "Well, that's kinda why I'm here. Cards on the table; how are you guys fixed for a bit of extra-curricular activity?"

And there it was: the follow up.

"*You* guys?" Keel said.

"You, Joseph, that ex-crop duster you got working with you..."

"His name's Crow, and he's a hell of a lot more than an ex-crop duster."

"Hell, I know that. I've seen his record."

Keel nodded and then sighed. "Max, let me ask you this: why in God's name would you think we'd be even remotely interested in such a bloody lunatic idea?"

"Because it *is* lunatic? And because it's right up your street."

"You mean no one else'll touch it."

Cade nodded. "And no one else will touch it...officially."

"You're out of your tiny mind," Keel said.

"Heard that before and I'm still here. So are you, and you've carried out other contracts like this. Successful ones."

"More by luck than judgement."

"That what you told yourself when you axed Baroud?"

Keel looked at him.

"Seriously?" Cade said. "You think I wouldn't figure it out? Come on, man. This is me talking."

Keel waited a beat then said, "In Baroud's case, it was definitely down to luck, if you factor in the assist we got from *la Piscine.*"

It was Cade's turn to stare. "French Intel? Jeez, you kept *that* quiet."

"DGSE's got an agent embedded in the RSF who's ready to take Baroud's place at the top table. He was in position to persuade the RSF *and* the Dubai authorities that it'd be in their best interests if Baroud's death was treated as a domestic spat and dealt with in-house. Means no one's looking for us."

Cade's eyes widened. "You're shitting me. Damn, the Frogs always were a devious bunch. All right, so maybe this time you were right about the luck part. I guess if you taking out Baroud hadn't fitted in with their master plan, you could've been fending off the roaches in some Dubai lock-up..."

"It'd still be the honeymoon suite, compared to a cell in Vientiane...or Beijing."

Cade looked at him. "You were me, don't tell me you wouldn't be here asking *you* the same question."

"That may be so. Doesn't mean I'd take the bloody job."

"Fair point." Cade took a sip of soda. "Had to try, though, on account of I couldn't think of anyone else who's qualified at this short notice."

"And willing to work off piste."

"Well, yeah. We sure as hell can't dispatch SEAL Team Six. Told you before, there's no way the US'd sanction an official op."

"And so you came all this way? I'm flattered, but what about the Thais?"

"Too close to home, too many local connections, too many loose tongues. Someone'd tip Zheng off, no question."

"Plus using freelancers means everyone can claim plausible deniability when it goes tits up."

"Jeez, at least grant me an 'if' not a 'when'."

"God loves an optimist," Keel said.

"That he does. Though I'm wondering what happened to that 'Who Dares Wins' shit."

"I left it in my other suit."

Cade took a sip of soda and leant back in his chair.

"Look," Keel said, "even if we were insane enough to consider your offer, we'd have a hard time running it past our boss, and not just because it's mad; it's because we used up the last of his good will when we headed off to Dubai."

"He knows about Baroud?"

Keel nodded. "He does and it's fair to say he wasn't happy with the outcome. Figured it was overkill. Literally. I told him we didn't have a choice once the bodyguard made his play."

"He likely to blow the whistle?"

Keel shook his head. "Hell, no. He's still ex-Legion at heart, so he knows the score. Besides, I told you, there's no wreckage that can lead back to us. He's a good man, Max. He covered for us when we went after the poachers and he put us in touch with the *Division*, who gave us the dossier on Baroud. It's true he wasn't keen on us following the lead to Dubai, but he didn't stand in our way. Right now, though, with the poachers slotted and Baroud out of the picture, as far as René's concerned it's mission over; time to pick up the day job."

Cade's eyes narrowed. "He know about Zheng and Golden Kingdom?"

Keel nodded. "He does. "

"The auction?"

"I told him what you told me."

"Think we can we make use of that? Your ivory's likely a part of the sales lot, so there's a personal connection."

"*We* again?" Keel said. "It's getting tedious."

Cade resumed his forward stance, his expression serious. "Well, *can* we or *can't* we?"

"Whoa, back off," Keel shot back. "How the hell would we justify it? We *knew* the poachers and Baroud were directly involved in the the Salma killings. Zheng's a whole new ball game. Plus it's Laos, for Chris'sakes. I don't know a damned thing about the place."

"Yeah, but maybe Crow does."

"Come again?"

"Plus he's got contacts in Thailand. That's only a pitcher's toss across the river from GK."

Keel stared at him

"Told you," Cade said. "I've seen his record. He's that pilot pal you mentioned back in Dubai. The one who has, and I quote: *'done a lot of flying around South-East Asia.'* End quote.

"You're pushing it, Max," Keel said, unable to mask his growing irritation.

"You use what you have." Cade's expression grew more intense. "And don't try and tell me you're not interested just a tiny bit. I've seen that look before."

Keel, aware that Cade's statement was uncomfortably close to the challenge he himself had put to René Deschamps the previous evening, shook his head. "Didn't say I wasn't interested, I'm saying that anyone who took up the offer would need their skull examined."

"Doesn't mean it can't be done."

"Didn't say that either."

Cade sat back and sighed. "Okay, if I can't persuade you, how'd you feel about taking another look at the info I sent you back in Dubai. Treat it like an exercise: if it *was* you going in, maybe see how it *could* be done. I do find someone else, it'd be good to have something they can use as a starting point. Sort of plan we used to make back in our Bosnian days. Most of them worked out pretty well. Like that compound we targeted outside Jajce. 'Course, it'd have to be sooner rather than later, seeing as that auction date's coming up real fast."

"Nice try," Keel said. "Was there anything *else* I can't help you with?"

363

Cade nodded then put his head on one side and pursed his lips. "What if *I* had a word with the boss man?"

"Oh, yeah? To say what, exactly?"

"Shit, I don't know. Pitch the idea to him on behalf of ROUTES? Think he might come around then?"

"You think he'd fall for ROUTES asking for assistance to commit an armed cross-border extraction of a foreign national? Seriously?"

"Who said anything about armed extraction? I'm talking a feasibility study."

"Of course you are, and pigs might sprout wings."

Cade shrugged. "No harm in asking. He knows your background right? He wouldn't have employed you otherwise."

"You're not going to leave this one alone, are you?" Keel said.

Cade spread his arms. "Hell, I've come all this way. Gotta go for it."

Keel sighed inwardly. Cade was like a terrier with a bone. Though the man did have a point. If Faheem and his crew were the hired help and Baroud middle management, then Zheng and his allies - the Bach brothers - were fully paid-up Members of the Board, or, to use Freeland's own analogy, the heads of the Hydra. According to legend, Hercules cut off the Hydra's heads, cauterized the necks and the beast died. It was a tempting image.

"All right," Keel said, in a less than successful attempt to curb his exasperation, "I'll make you a deal. If René okays it, then I'll consider taking a look at the thing. Sorry, no, amend that; the three of us'll consider it."

"Three?"

"Me, Joseph and the ex-crop duster."
Draining his glass, Cade grinned.
"Attaboy!" he said.

20

"Is he serious?" Sekka asked.

"He's in with René now," Keel said.

Sekka chewed the inside of his cheek and gazed out across the stretch of grass-covered, savanna to where Mo was leading the newly-formed Jackal team in the latter stage of their training exercise: the tracking and subduing of a gang of armed poachers, ably represented by members of Kudu team, decked out in a variety of gaudy t-shirts and assorted baseball caps. A few yards away, the two Manovo guys and the government rep were watching the final take down as Mo and his fledgling team, having apprehended the 'poachers' and confiscated their weaponry, were instructing their captives to kneel and place their hands on top of their heads.

Watching the display, it was noticeable to both Keel and Sekka that Mo's contribution to the exercise appeared, at times, to be a little too robust for comfort, suggesting the young ranger was either overly keen to justify his promotion and show he had the stones to command a patrol, or, quite possibly, he was channelling emotions triggered by recent events: the ambush and murder of the original Jackal team, or perhaps a memory of the violent confrontation with the RSF patrol and how that had been resolved with no quarter given by the two men who'd trained him. Struck by Mo's energetic commitment to the exercise, Sekka was prompted to wonder aloud if it might not have been too soon to involve him in such an enactment.

Keel's answer was to shake his head. "Got to give him free rein at some point. Might as well be now. Plus, it's not as though he hasn't been through the real thing." Adding, as Sekka threw him a pensive look, "Best keep an eye on him, anyway."

The exercise over, with the ranger crews congratulating each other on their role playing, and with the visitors looking suitably impressed, a break for lunch was called. As the ranger teams left the field, Keel and Sekka escorted the Manovo trio to the river lounge, where the tables had been reset and two volunteer members of the kitchen crew were on hand to act as waiters.

Keel had been expecting Deschamps and Cade to be there, but both men were absent. Instead, it was Sabine who met them and showed the visitors to their table. The latter didn't seem at all put out, either by René's or Cade's non-appearance. Following her return from Am Timan, Sabine had spent the first part of the morning with the Manovo team, discussing the employment of the tracking collars while sharing her experiences in protecting the welfare of Salma's wildlife, and so they greeted her like a long-lost friend.

As the guests took their seats, she drew Keel aside to tell him that René had requested his presence in the office. Excusing himself and leaving Sabine and Sekka to continue as hosts, Keel made his exit, As he left, he felt two sets of eyes - one male, one female - boring into the back of his neck.

"Come in, Thomas," Deschamps said. "Close the door."

Conscious that there'd been no welcoming smile, Keel did so, avoiding Cade's eye. The American was seated in one of the two chairs positioned in front of Deschamps' desk.

"Mr. Cade - Max - has been telling me more about this man, Zheng," Deschamps said, as Keel sat down. "It would appear you did not exaggerate the significant positions that he and his associates hold with regards to the illegal wildlife trade or the involvement of the Lao and Chinese governments and the assistance they render to him."

Keel remained silent.

Leaning forward, Deschamps placed his elbows on the desk, forming a bridge with his clasped hands, and tapped the ends of his thumbs against each other in front of his pursed lips. After regarding Keel thoughtfully for several seconds, he lowered his arms and sat back. "There's also the matter of the auction. It grieves me to know that Salma's ivory is likely to be among the items being sold. Max has informed me that ROUTES and TRAFFIC are attempting to obtain more information; in particular, details of the items being auctioned and the identity of the buyers they are likely to attract.

"He also tells me, depending on the intelligence gained, that certain other agencies are looking at the possibility of using the event as a means to acccess the site, with a view to apprehending Zheng, so that he may be delivered before an international court of law and tried for his crimes. He told me your assistance would be appreciated in that regard, in an advisory capacity, of course, but that you would not commit unless I gave my approval. Is that correct?"

"We talked about it," Keel said.

Deschamps nodded, noting Keel's noncommittal answer. "So if I voiced no objection, you would be happy to volunteer your services?"

"It wouldn't only be me," Keel said. "I'd want Joseph and Crow involved as well."

Deschamps frowned."Why Crow?"

"If it comes down to surveying the possibility of a snatch job, a chopper'd be the quickest way in and out. Crow has experience with that, plus he's familiar with the region. And I trust him."

"You've spoke to them?"

"I have."

"And?"

"They said they'd leave the decision to me."

"I rather think you mean *me*," Deschamps said, fixing Keel with a meaningful stare.

Keel allowed himself a conciliatory smile, "Of course."

"You would be required to relocate."

"Temporarily."

"For how long?"

"The auction's the trigger point. So that's in...what? Seven days?"

"And what of Salma?"

"We've had this conversation before. Salma can cope. She'll outlive the both of us."

"That's not what I meant."

"I know. Priorities. The main one's fitting the collars. With all hands on deck, it shouldn't be more than a two-day job. Possibly do it in one if we put our minds to it. After that..." Keel turned to Cade, who'd been following the interchange. "Max?"

Cade nodded. It was clear he'd been waiting for an invitation to speak. "That'd work. There's a USAF C130 that's been on loan to the Chadian Air Force - what's left of it - that's routing N'Djamena to Riyadh in two days' time. It's due to make a courtesy supply drop-off at Am Timan before carrying on to the Kingdom for refuelling and a crew change. Then it's Hyderabad and on to Bangkok. If you can get your asses to Am Timan in time there are seats on board. The in-flight entertainment'll be shit, but you've travelled freight before; you know the drill."

"We get the collars fitted, we can do that," Keel said. "René?"

Deschamps hesitated then said, "You'll liaise with Sabine?"

"Of course."

Deschamps pursed his lips, nodded and turned to Cade. "Very well, Mr. Cade. On the understanding that the collaring is completed to my satisfaction, and that of my vet, and nothing untoward arises in the meantime, I have no objection to Thomas and the others giving you the assistance you have requested."

Cade smiled. "That's great to hear, René. On behalf of ROUTES, I really want you to know how much we appreciate your help."

"You're welcome, however I do have one more stipulation."

"Of course," Cade said. "Anything."

He wasn't sure why, but Keel's immediate thought was: *Here it comes.*

Deschamps stood. "It's not for you, Max. It applies to Thomas." Turning to Keel, he said, "You will have ten days. That gives you time until the auction and a further three days in which to return home. Any longer than that, and you, Joseph *and* Crow will be required to seek alternative employment." Deschamps drew himself up, "Is that understood?"

And there it was.

"Perfectly," Keel said. He wasn't sure but he thought he heard Cade emit a soft sigh of relief.

"You'll advise Joseph and Crow?"

"I will."

Deschamps nodded. "Good, then I suggest we re-join our other guests. They'll be wondering where we've got to." Moving out from behind his desk, he spread his arm to direct them to the door. "Shall we?"

"So let me get this straight," Crow said. "The boss man's happy for us to go gallivanting off into the wide blue yonder in order to help bring down Lao's Casino King?"

"I wouldn't call him happy, exactly," Keel said.

"Well, yeah, given his ultimatum, I was using the term loosely. So what's the plan?"

"Plan A is we fit the tracking collars," Keel said. "We've two days if we want to make that USAF flight and Plan B."

"Does Sabine know we're up against the clock?"

"René said he'd brief her."

"He going to tell her why?"

"He told me he would. Be hard to keep her in the dark."

"She's going to be pissed," Crow said, "not to be included."

"Why's that?"

"You have to ask?" Crow said, one eyebrow raised.

"After the week we've just had?"

Keel did not answer but gazed skywards to where the Manovo crew's helicopter was disappearing into the distance, the throb of its engine fading but still audible as the sound drifted back towards them on the late afternoon breeze.

The Manovo crew's visit, although short, had been deemed a positive interaction. They'd seen the communications set-up and watched the ranger teams in action, Sabine had briefed them on veterinary requirements, and Crow had extolled the virtues of using aircraft - specifically helicopters - not only to monitor animal numbers, activity and behaviour, but to aid the mobile patrols by providing aerial surveillance and the ability to move personnel from one part of the reserve to another with maximum speed. They were also a vital means of keeping in touch with the surrounding settlements. More than once, as Crow had explained, his services had been requested in order to deliver medicines to outlying villages and, on occasion, to ferry injured villagers to a medical facility in Am Timan.

Inevitably, the killings and their effect on Salma's ability to function in the aftermath had formed part of the discussions, but Deschamps had done his best to reassure the visitors that the incident, while undoubtedly a tragic event, was less likely to happen again, particularly once the two reserves had joined forces. A united and heavily armed front was the way to defeat the poaching gangs, with comprehensive training being the key, bolstered by an effective management team and access to the right equipment.

If African Parks agreed to arrange financial support for Manovo along with the benefit of their expertise, then the future of both reserves looked assured.

"Your pal Cade's a piece of work," Crow said as he and Keel threw a final glance at the receding aircraft and turned away.

"Because?" Keel said.

"Guy smiles way too much. Got the same vibes from him as I did with Lavasse. You said he'd been some sort of spook. Once a spook, always a spook. You ask me, the bugger's only using ROUTES as his cover story."

"Anyone ever tell you you're a cynical bastard?" Keel said.

"Most days. Doesn't mean it isn't true, though, and don't tell me you haven't had *your* doubts."

"Doubts, no. I took it for granted."

Crow's eyebrows went up. "Now who's the cynical one."

"Not cynical; realistic. I've known the man too long."

"But you're still planning on us helping him out, right?"

"From what we know, I figure Zheng's a legitimate target, so if we can, yes. You still want in?"

Crow grinned.

"Not worried about the ultimatum?" Keel said.

"Ultimatum, schmultimatum. We can't work something out in a week, we should probably try a different line of work. In the meantime, when's wake-up?"

"Sabine wants us moving by first light. René'll be going up in the Cessna. Between them, he and the patrols should've reported the herd locations by then. They'll guide you in by radio. Sabine'll do the darting and the crews on the ground'll secure the site. We fit the collars, wake jumbo up. Job done."

374

Crow nodded. "Easy peasy." He nodded towards where the Airbus was parked on the far side of the strip, next to the Cessna. "I'll give 'em the twice-over, make sure they're fuelled and ready to go."

Keel watched as Crow walked away and thought about the pilot's take on Max Cade. He'd wondered about Cade's true role himself. Duncan Bryce had vouched for the man as being a ROUTES operative and there had been no reason to doubt Bryce's sincerity. But knowing Cade's background as he did and taking in the American's own admittance to having maintained his contacts within the intelligence world, Keel wouldn't have put it past the man to have undertaken assignments for his former bosses while ostensibly being employed by the ROUTES partnership. The fact that he'd been able to arrange transport on the USAF flight proved that he still had clout somewhere along the line. Maybe, Keel thought, it was best not to ask too many questions until such time as they were absolutely necessary. Though, given what could lay ahead over the next week, that opportunity might not be too long in coming.

Crow brought the Airbus round in a tight sweeping turn and lined up on his target, one hundred feet below and two hundred metres ahead, in line with the chopper's right skid. Given its bulk, the elephant - an adult male - was moving at a good clip, ears flapping like sails, trunk whipping frantically from side to side as it sought to escape its pursuer. Churning up dust as it ran, it was likely roaring its head off, too, either in fear or defiance, though whatever sounds the beast was producing were made inaudible by the racket produced by the chopper's turbine.

Team Badger had located the animal, close by a waterhole in the north-east quadrant of the reserve. The water source was a favourite, used by many of the park's larger residents - buffalo, kudu and giraffe, as well as elephant - and a well-known haunt for this particular bull, who'd been identified by the ground team as one of the six adults chosen by René and Sabine to be fitted with a tracking collar.

The bull was on his own, which wasn't an unusual occurrence; though young males, upon leaving the family herd, commonly around their mid teens, often gravitated towards other single males, knowing, through inherited instinct, that safety lay in a number greater than one. Alliances, however, could be fleeting and individuals would often drift away from their group, sometimes for extended periods, in order to follow their own course. This was because bulls were born with one unerring purpose in mind: to find a receptive female. Today, this bull's odyssey had been rudely interrupted and, now, much to his obvious resentment, he was on the run.

Elephants, however, while remarkably nimble for their size, were not built for speed over an extended distance. Therefore the skill required by anyone bent on pursuit lay in knowing when to move in and when to back off. Crow, upon seeing that the elephant had run out of steam, brought the Airbus to a hover, this time one hundred metres from the beast's broad, undulating rump and spoke into his headset. "How we doing, Doc?"

Sabine, strapped into the rear seat, planted her right shoulder against the rim of the open doorway, the Dan-Inject rifle clasped firmly in her hands.

"Ready."

"Roger that," Crow said.

Aiming the helicopter's nose at the now stationary but still clearly agitated bull, Crow re-opened the throttle and nudged the cyclic forward. The Airbus dipped and picked up momentum. Suspecting immediately that the increased engine note signalled a renewed danger, the bull raised its trunk, flapped its ears, and took off once more. Crouched in the rear, Sabine eased herself forward so that her knees were jutting beyond the edge of the door. Raising the rifle, she braced herself as the bull broke into a stiff-legged lope.

Crow took the chopper down to sixty feet. They were flying over what was mostly scrubland, interspersed with clumps of spindly acacia, so while he was concentrating mainly on keeping the elephant in full view and the helicopter on an even keel, he was also acutely mindful that an inadvertent collision with an acacia's top branches would put a serious dent not only in the Airbus but in his and Sabine's prospects of living to tell the tale.

So when the tusker performed a sharp right-angled turn and headed off towards a thickening clump of trees. Crow spat out a curse and swung the Airbus sharply away in an attempt to cut across the animal's course. As he did so, a sharp exclamation of *"Merde!"* erupted from his headset.

"Sorry, Doc," Crow mouthed silently as he levelled off.

Then, with the Airbus fifty feet above the scrub, and the acacias looming ever closer, the bull changed course yet again, this time towards open ground.

Crow let go a sigh of relief, tilted the chopper over,

and began to take up the slack.

To an onlooker it might have looked as if the bull was motoring though in reality the animal's ground speed was little more than fifteen miles an hour. It was, therefore a one-sided race. Manoeuvring the helicopter so that the bull was directly below them and once more slightly to the right of their starboard skid, Crow held the Airbus steady.

Sabine, secured in place by her safety harness, raised the Dan-Inject, took careful aim and fired. There was no loud report, simply a soft, barely audible *phut*. Then, pulling herself back inside the cabin, she secured the rifle against her hip and tapped Crow on his left shoulder. "He is hit."

Crow eased back on the throttle and swung the helicopter away and then back around to give them a full view of the darted animal.

Who was still in motion.

Crow looked off towards the periphery and spotted the Badger patrol vehicle coming in fast.

The danger, now that the elephant had been darted, was to ensure that it didn't go down in an inaccessible area - a fold in the ground or impenetrable shrubland or inside a treeline - which could either result in injury to the animal or, if it had landed in an awkward position, make fitting the collar an impossibility. And they were up against the clock. It took around eight minutes for the 10 mgs of Carfentanil to take effect. After which, they'd have twenty minutes for Sabine to administer the reversal drug and complete the job. Any longer than that and there was a chance the animal wouldn't wake up at all.

The first five collarings had gone without a hitch. Four had been completed on the first day, while the last female had been darted that morning. Females were generally less of a problem to dart as they lived in family units and a herd was easier to find than a lone male. If there was a flaw in that argument it lay in the family bond, for when a member of the herd went down, especially if it was the matriarch, her relatives would often form a protective cluster around her, making it difficult for the ground crew to approach. Which was when the advantages of using a helicopter were made plain. The aircraft was a very effective herding tool and the means by which the elephant's family could be kept at a convenient distance, allowing the ground crew to move in unhindered, while using their patrol vehicle as an additional shield.

The elephant had turned to face the Airbus. The dart had struck him high on his left rump where it remained embedded, flopping in time to his side-to-side movements. Having felt the stab as it pierced his hide, and irritated by the resulting sensation, he wasn't happy. Facing the beast through the chopper's windshield, it struck Crow that a *torero* probably experienced a similar feeling when faced by a huge fighting bull that had just been stabbed with a couple of brightly coloured banderillas.

This bull was showing no sign of fear, only increasing confusion and not a little anger. Conscious that they were still in reach of the acacias, Crow had positioned the chopper between the elephant and the trees, his intention being to use the rotor wash to divert the animal's attention until the drug took effect, which seemed to be taking a while. To do so had meant taking the chopper even lower, so by now the skids were on the same level as the bull's impressive tusks, a fact not lost on their owner who, in his befuddled state, suddenly appeared intent on attacking his tormentor.

But they were mock charges and, due to the sedative, no real threat, though Crow, mindful of the damage that would be sustained by both parties were a collision to take place, wasn't taking any chances. Like a boxer dipping out of the way of a wildly swinging opponent, he maintained the chopper's position, mirroring the bull's movements, until, finally, the elephant's rear legs began to buckle. By the time it had toppled slowly on to its side, Crow had landed and Sabine was exiting the helicopter, her equipment bag in her hand.

With five collars already fitted and lessons learned along the way, the ground crew swung into action, jamming a twig in the end of the trunk to prop the airway open and folding the massive ears forward over the elephant's eyes to protect them and to make room for the collar. The tactic also served to expose the web of veins behind the ears, one of which would receive the antidote.

Within fifteen minutes the collar was secure around the bull's neck, which gave the crew, under Sabine's guidance, extra minutes in which to perform a quick check on the animal's general state of health, which appeared to be good. That done, Sabine directed the ground team to move away to the safety of the patrol vehicle while she administered the wake-up shot.

Having remained with the chopper, Crow watched the proceedings as he had watched the ones before, seeing the care and respect given to the sedated giant by the entire team - vet and rangers - as they fitted the collar and checked the elephant's welfare. He saw, too, the concern on their faces as they waited for the bull to show signs of movement after the antidote had been given, and the broad smiles and shaking of hands as the beast slowly raised his head.

The bull heaved himself up as Sabine arrived back at the chopper. Stowing her bag in the rear, she climbed aboard and attached the headset. Together, she and Crow watched in companionable silence as the animal ambled away, unconcerned by the tracking equipment now fastened around his neck.

As the ground-team vehicle departed, Crow prepared to lift off, only to pause as Sabine placed her hand on his arm.

"Doc?" Crow said.

Sabine had turned to face him. "Can we sit quietly for a while?"

Crow returned her look, saw something in her eyes that he couldn't quite explain and said. "Sure," before powering the chopper down.

The stillness that descended around them, however, was broken by a squawk from the radio.

"Go ahead," Crow said.

"*Patron*, Elias."

Elias was the Badger team leader.

"Go," Crow said.

"We do not hear your engine, boss," Elias said in English. "You okay?"

Crow looked off to where the patrol vehicle had moved out of sight. "Yeah, no problem. Just gonna hang loose for a while. Keep an eye on our patient."

There was a pause, then, "Okay, understood. Elias out."

Crow wondered if it was his imagination or if he had picked up a soft chuckle as Elias hung up. He turned to find Sabine had removed her headset and was gazing out at the scenery around them. In the distance a large grey shape could just be seen plodding slowly out of view behind a belt of thick scrub.

"What's up, Doc?" Crow winced inwardly as he said it.

Without speaking or looking at him. Sabine unclipped her belt and exited the chopper. Frowning, Crow opened his own door, climbed out and made his way around to where she was standing, hands in trouser pockets, looking off to where the bull had disappeared.

"Was it enough?" she said. "Will it make him safe?"

"Safer than he was before," Crow said. "Short of caging him up and shipping him to a zoo."

"That is not why we're here."

"No," Crow agreed. "It's not."

She turned and studied his face. "It will not stop them from being killed, will it?"

"You don't know that. It might. Someone coming in and spotting those collars might think twice. They'll figure on a quicker response from us if they see we've fitted monitoring equipment."

She remained quiet for what seemed like several minutes, then she said, "There are people who say animals do not possess souls. I do not believe them. I have looked into an elephant's eyes. Have you ever looked into an elephant's eyes, Crow?"

"Can't say as I have, no."

"You should. You will learn a lot about yourself. There is an author: Peter Matthiessen, an American. He wrote books about the wilderness, about Africa. He was fascinated by elephants. He wrote that there was a mystery behind an elephant's *visage*. He called it an ancient life force. I saw it in that one today. I saw it in the others, too. It is a precious thing, Crow. We *have* to protect it."

"We're doing our best."

She looked at him for a moment before folding her arms and gazing bleakly towards where the bull had merged back into the landscape. "Then we must learn to do better, or it will be too late; not just for them, for all of us."

"Think René'll come and see us off?" Crow said as he stowed his bag in the back of the truck.

"Probably not," Keel said.

Crow frowned.

"He'd see it as a sign of affection," Sekka said, as he followed Crow's gear with his own.

All three of them were in civilian clothes.

"And he wouldn't like us to think he's stopped being pissed at us," Crow said.

"Maybe that, too," Sekka said.

"Well, at least someone's here," Crow said. "Morning, Doc."

"Gentlemen," Sabine said brightly, as she approached the vehicle, "and Crow."

"Oh, nice," Crow said. "Come to wave us goodbye?"

Sabine fixed him with a straight gaze. "Why would you think that?"

The three men stared back at her. Like the others, she was dressed in civvies: grey cargo pants, olive shirt with rolled up sleeves over a burgundy t-shirt. A grey baseball cap completed her ensemble.

"What?" Sabine said. "You thought you would leave without me?" She looked passed Keel's shoulder to

383

where Mo was sitting in the driving's seat, his elbow resting nonchalantly on the window rim. "You did not tell them, did you?"

Mo smiled. "I thought I would leave that to you, Doctor. It is a beautiful morning and I did not want to get into trouble."

Sabine narrowed her eyes in mock accusation, then nodded. "In that case you are forgiven. My bag is on board, yes?"

"Yes, Doctor. I loaded it myself."

"Excellent, thank you." She turned. "So, we should go if you want to catch that plane, yes?"

No one moved.

Sabine sighed then said, "With the three of you away, I suggested to René that it might be the right time for me to visit to my father. It has been months since I went home. I told him I would travel with you to the airport and take a connection flight from there."

"Airport?" Crow said. "That's a stretch. It's barely an air*field*. And what connection flight? I thought there were only two flights a week Am Timan to N'Djamena."

"That is correct."

"Really? Well, the last one went yesterday. It was the turnaround plane from the one that brought the collars. Means the next one's not for two more days."

"I must have misread the timetable."

Crow shook his head in mock sorrow. "You're a terrible liar, Doc, and I'm bloody sure René didn't believe you either. What the hell's going on?"

Sabine's eyes flashed. "Very well." She turned to Keel. "René told me that your friend Max Cade has asked for your help. You think I do not know you well enough by now? I know you would not send someone else to do a job you could do yourself. You intend to visit Golden Kingdom, yes? *Nĭ shuō Pǔtōnghuà ma?*"

Sabine paused, and when no one replied, then said, "I asked if you spoke Mandarin. Apparently you do not. Did you not think that might help?"

"*Ya nyemnózhka gavaryú pa rúski,*" Sekka said.

Sabine turned and looked at him. "Yes, well, that might prove useful when you're talking with one of the Ukrainian hookers. They will have been taught Russian at school."

"And you just happen speak Mandarin?" Keel said.

"I took a language course when I left the army. I thought it might come in useful."

"Of course you did," Crow said quietly. The grin slipped from his face when Sabine gave him the look.

"Besides," she added, "if it had not been for me, you would not have gone to Dubai and met your friend, Cade, and without him you would not have known about Zheng. Am I right?"

No one spoke. Sabine waited, one hand on her hip. She wasn't tapping her foot, but she might well have been.

"Ah, shit," Crow said.

Keel looked at him and then at Sekka.

"I do not think they will hold the aeroplane for you," Sabine said archly.

Keel remained silent.

"Could give us an edge," Sekka said. "Every little helps."

Keel looked at the ground and closed his eyes. Opening them and lifting his head, he sighed. "One question: are you speaking as a vet or a former soldier?"

Sabine regarded him squarely, her face deadly serious. "What do you think?"

Keel considered her reply without speaking. Then, after what seemed an extraordinary long time, he nodded. "Ah, hell, get in the damned truck. And Mo, take that bloody smile off your face."

"Yes, boss," Mo said, grinning as he started the engine.

As the others climbed aboard and before he took his seat Keel looked towards the office window, to where René Deschamps stood motionless behind the glass with no discernable expression on his face. As the two men locked eyes, Keel nodded. For a moment it looked as though Deschamps was not going to respond, but then, just as Keel was about to sever the link, Deschamps returned the gesture, at the same time raising his hand into a fist, thumb and folded fingers facing outwards, in Keel's direction. By the time Keel had climbed into the truck, Deschamps had turned away, his features once more hidden from view.

21

Having come from the huge skies, wide open spaces and the relative quiet of the African savanna, the sights and sounds of Bangkok's crowded night-time hubbub were something of a culture shock and, although he was familiar with the city, it had taken Crow a while to re-acclimatize and to get his bearings. The cacophony created by the raucous symphony of scooter klaxons, trishaw bells, taxi horns, countless engine exhausts and the shriek of police sirens was loud enough to raise the dead. When tied to the thumping disco beat drifting up from the bars and massage parlours that lined the street, all illuminated by Chinese lanterns dangling from the eaves of the food stalls and eating houses and, from higher up, by an eye-searing kaleidoscope of pulsating neon signs, it was like entering some enormous, adult-rated amusement arcade.

It wasn't just the noise and the lights that battered the senses, though, for as Crow made his way through the night-time crowd, he was assailed on all sides by a bewildering variety of smells; from the inviting aroma of roasting meats and spices to the heavy stench of diesel fumes, densely packed bodies and the fetid whiff of raw sewage arising from the overflowing drainage channels that ran through the city like irrigation ditches. It was enough to make the lungs itch.

Welcome to Patpong.

Sammy's Bar was tucked down an alleyway off the main drag. It obviously wasn't the most salubrious bar on the strip, but neither was it, by any stretch of imagination, the worst; though, in all likelihood, it might have been the darkest and possibly the noisiest.

The music hit Crow with the force of a pneumatic drill as he moved through the entrance and into the stygian interior. He was forced to blink several times before his eyes adjusted to the dim lighting, though he could already see through the haze that the room was packed.

The majority of the customers were Westerners, although there was a smattering of Japanese punters present; more than likely courtesy of ANA's sex charters, the Thai capital being a lot less expensive than Tokyo, where the pursuit of a more adventurous nightlife was concerned.

The main focus of attention was centred on a quartet of bikini-clad go-go dancers who were grinding away atop a raised platform behind the bar. The B-girls moving slinkily between the tables, sometimes pausing to smooch with the eager clientele, were similarly attired.

Crow couldn't see Leece. He elbowed his way through the crush and ordered a beer. When the bottle was placed in front of him he asked the barman for Leece's whereabouts. A jerk of the head pointed the way. Picking up his drink, Crow headed for the door half concealed in the darkness at the back of the room. There was no bouncer on duty and he went through without a challenge. A gloomy, hip-wide passageway ran for some twenty paces before breaking on to a run

388

of half a dozen steps leading down to yet another darkened doorway, beyond which could be heard a babble of excited voices. Preparing himself, Crow opened the door.

The space beyond was large with a very high ceiling. It was crammed with people, most of whom were screaming at each other. The racket was even greater than the bar noise that had followed Crow down the passageway. The occupants – perhaps two hundred in total, all male, from what Crow could see – were seated in closely packed tiers around a roped-off square of sand. Spot lamps set high along the grimy walls cast a pale, sulphureous glow over the ring and the heads of the crowd.

Beyond the ropes the world was grey, inhabited by dancing shadows that played across the animated faces of the spectators as they competed for attention, chattering and hand-signalling to their companions around the room. Fistfuls of paper money were in abundance. A blue-grey pall of smoke hung like a layer of fog above their heads and the air reeked of sweat, stale beer, cheap tobacco, and dope, a lot of dope.

Crow peered around the wall of faces and struck lucky. Leece was in the second row, sitting motionless as if oblivious to the melee around him; an island of calm detachment. A hand-tooled cigarette was perched precariously at the corner of his mouth. It emerged from the fungus of his moustache like a rifle barrel poking through foliage. A half-empty bottle of Singha beer stood between his feet. He glanced up as Crow squeezed onto the wooden bench beside him. "Thought you were dead."

"Good to see you, too," Crow said.

Leece had the appearance of a man trapped in a

time warp, a refugee from Woodstock, or maybe an outcast from a West Coast rock band. He was as thin as a rake and if it hadn't been for the fact that he was the colour of burnt cork, he'd probably have looked borderline cadaverous. He wore his hair long. Fairish, but with a lot of grey strands and bleached by a tropical sun, it was pulled back from his face by a turquoise band at the back of his neck. The moustache was thick and, like his hair, there was a lot of grey in evidence.

His wardrobe consisted of a faded black t-shirt, emblazoned, somewhat inevitably, with a Grateful Dead motif: a bleached skull topped by a crown of roses. A pair of scruffy cargo pants completed the ensemble. Given his looks and apparel, a casual observer might have expected to see a string of beads around his neck. Instead, there was a leather thong from which hung a small leather pouch which, Crow knew, would contain a few shreds of loose tobacco, a pack of Rizla papers and a battered metal Zippo lighter engraved with the insignia of the US Army's 75th Ranger Regiment.

The jabber around them was increasing in volume. Crow looked down to where the combatants were being prepared. To judge by the amount of betting that was taking place, this was to be a keen fight between two well-matched opponents, although in no way could it be compared to the more upmarket *Muay Thai* contests that took place at Lumpini and Rajasamnern, the city's main stadia. Nor could it be called a tourist lure. There was a handful of Europeans in the gallery but the vast majority of spectators were Thai.

Some of the bars along Patpong did cater for the tourist trade in a more blatant way; by holding all-female contests or by arranging challenge matches between local fighters and members of the audience who felt they could impress their pals with a sterling display of pugilistic dexterity. Which usually ended in bruised ribs, several loose teeth, a severely deflated ego and a good deal of heckling from the hapless challenger's corner, who should have known better than to propel their drunken chum into the vicinity of an eight stone weakling who could move like greased lighting without breaking sweat.

"Whaddya want?" Leece did not turn but kept his eye on the fighters who had moved into their respective corners.

Crow doubted the pair were carrying more than one hundred pounds apiece, if that. Dressed in baggy shorts - one in black, the other in red - their gloves looked huge in proportion to their small frames. Their feet were bare. Each one sported a brightly coloured headband. Stripped down, they looked very young and very vulnerable.

Thai boxing was essentially a martial art and possibly a derivation of the Shaolin tradition of Southern China, so preparations for the bout contained a degree of ritual. Dropping to their knees, the two fighters commenced their limbering-up movements while saluting their trainers and offering prayers for victory, at which point a fresh round of betting broke out. A lot of cash looked to be riding on the result.

"That's it?" Crow said. "No hail, fellow, well met; how the hell are you?"

"Been three years," Leece said. "You think I give a shit?"

Crow shrugged. "Hell, no. I'm only amazed you

remember how long it's been, given you were in the same bloody seat last time we spoke. Same outfit, too, from the look of it. This your new digs? You send out for food and booze, or what?"

"Fuck you, too," Leece said, as the fighters removed their headbands, and approached the centre of the ring. Touching hands, they bowed, broke away and began to circle warily.

Muay Thai bouts consisted of five three-minute rounds, with rounds one and two generally being uneventful while the fighters sounded each other out. It also gave the gamblers time to decide who to bet on in earnest.

So by round three, the excitement had built.

The first serious clash occurred at blinding speed. One moment they were dancing on the spot, the next they were trading blows with the ferocity of wildcats. It wasn't hard to see why the alternative name for the sport was the Art of Eight Limbs. Fists, elbows, knees and shins were all employed with equal vigour.

The noise from the spectators was deafening, while the fight action was making Crow's head spin. It didn't help that the humidity was high and ventilation in the room non-existent. It was becoming as hot as a sauna and Crow could feel the dampness seeping down from his armpits. Next to him, though, Leece still looked as mellow as he had when Crow had taken his seat. It was a relief when the bell went at the end of the round.

Which was when Leece turned, removed the cigarette stub from his mouth, and grinned as he threw his left arm around Crow's neck. "Ah, fuck it. Three years ain't that long. Good to see you, man. I mean it."

"Me too," Crow said, making no attempt to pull

away "How've you been?"

The American released his arm and picked up his drink. The two men clinked bottles and took swigs. "Booze is cheap, so's weed. The ladies not so much, but I got no complaints. You?"

"Same old, same old. Long as the beer's cold."

"Amen to that, brother." Leece clinked his bottle against Crow's a second time and then, as the bell rang for the start of the fourth round, he switched his attention back to the ring.

"Who's your money on?" Crow he asked as the red fighter suddenly launched a series of lightning fast blows towards his opponent's head.

The move prompted a chorus of loud chants to break out on one side of the ring. "*Sĭ daeng! Sĭ daeng! Red! Red!*"

"Black" Leece said. "No question." He lifted his bottle and tipped its open top towards the ring below them. "Watch and learn."

By the end of Round Four, Crow was having serious doubts about Leece's powers of reasoning because up until then the red fighter appeared to be in the ascendance, due mostly to his being the taller of the two, which gave him a marginally longer reach, an advantage he was determined to exploit.

Though the black fighter looked to be trying his best. The round had ended with him side-stepping a flying kick to the groin and aiming a devastating retaliatory strike towards his opponent's head. Somehow, the blow had failed to land, the punch being blocked by an upward moving forearm, while a right uppercut had scythed through the black fighter's defence, smashing into his left shoulder. The black fighter recoiled, pain slanting across his face, his teeth bared in a sudden grimace. Crow felt certain the man's collarbone must have snapped under the impact. The red fighter's supporters must have though the same, for they were screaming encouragement as the bell had rung.

During the break, both fighters continued to breathe heavily, their bodies glistening in the lamp light. A cursory examination was made of the black fighter's shoulder. A nod and a pat on the back indicated it was still sound.

From the way the red fighter bounced out from his corner, he knew the fight was his. The last strike had clearly sapped the black fighter's strength and as the round progressed he looked to be fading fast. He was slow to keep his guard up; his stance was growing visibly weaker, and the red fighter was exploiting every opening presented to him, curving punches and kicks into his opponent's ribs with what seemed to be hypnotic regularity. Some of the crowd were beginning to voice their disgust and the red fighter, sensing imminent victory, moved in for the kill, egged on by his supporters who were baying loudly, eager for their man to deliver the coup de grâce.

The black fighter looked to have forgotten any advice he might have been given by his trainer. He was back-pedalling across the sand like a trick cyclist. Crow wondered how the man could have lost the will to win in such a short space of time, unless he was throwing the fight and was a really bad actor. The man looked positively bewildered. An earlier punch, Crow reasoned, must have brought on some sort of delayed concussion.

There couldn't have been more than twenty seconds to go as the red fighter gathered himself. He knew the contest was over and that one swift knockout punch would finish it.

Which was when Crow spotted the subtle shifting of balance and the microscopic ripple of awareness than seemed to run through the black fighter's lithe frame. He felt Leece tense up beside him.

Something of the change must have registered in the red fighter's brain, for even as he drew breath to deliver the final blow his eyes widened. And in that fleeting moment of hesitation, the black fighter made his move. Suddenly transferring his weight onto his back foot, in an act of stunning, artistic savagery, he unleased his front foot - his right - towards his opponent's chin. The sheer speed of the assault was frightening, the result devastating. The edge of the black fighter's right heel slammed into the red fighter's jaw, snapping the head back with such force that Crow could have sworn he heard the snap of bone above the roar from the crowd.

For a second the red fighter's body hung motionless, as if suspended in free fall, before crashing back against the ropes with all the uncoordinated grace of a drunk in a bar room brawl.

There was a moment of stunned silence, followed by an explosion of sound as everyone realized the contest was over. The sound of the bell came as a mocking afterthought.

"Told ya," Leece said casually, taking a swig from his bottle as the red fighter's seconds moved quickly to assist their man. Then, turning to the spectator on his opposite side, he held out his hand. When he drew the hand back it was clutching a wad of banknotes. He turned back to Crow and grinned.

"How much did you win?" Crow asked.

"Two hundred bucks. C'mon. Let's get out of here. Drinks are on me."

"Gotta be a first," Crow said. "Lead on."

Crow didn't know what the new place was called or even if it had a name. He'd simply followed as Leece had led the way out of Sammy's anonymous rear exit. There had been a couple of turns and a recrossing of the main street before Crow followed the American through a low-slung open doorway that looked more like the entrance to Aladdin's cave than the eating establishment it turned out to be, there being no signage to indicate the service provided within.

Which made it a hangout strictly for locals, as was made evident in that Leece and Crow were the only non-Asians in the place, an observation that did not deter the elderly woman, who Crow presumed was the proprietor, from greeting Leece like a long lost son almost as soon as he was through the doorway.

"Meet Yaai Dao," Leece said, when he'd extricated himself. "She owns the place."

It occurred to Crow that Yaai Dao could have been plucked straight from central casting, Hollywood's idea of what an elderly Asian grandmother should look like, right down to the hair in a bun and a face full of wrinkles. Crow's wai was greeted with an inclination of the head, a smile, a stream of Thai, most of which Crow was unable to follow, and a beckoning signal which Crow took to mean they were being led to an empty table. A few customers glanced up as they trailed Yaai Dao towards the rear of the room. but none looked that surprised, while a couple even nodded at Leece as he patted a few shoulders en route.

Even if the lady's greeting hadn't made it clear, Leece was obviously something of a regular.

"Best *Tom Yum Goon* in the city," Leece said, as they took their seats.

No menu was presented and Crow found himself a mute onlooker as Leece reeled off what was presumably an order for food. The request was met with an enthusiastic nod and a wide smile and as Yaai Dao headed away, Leece grinned and said, "Don't worry, it's all good."

Before Crow could respond a waiter arrived bearing two bottles of chilled Chang beer.

"*Chok dee,*" Leece said as they touched bottles. "Eat first, then we can parley."

It might have been three years since Crow had last seen Ray Leece, but he'd known him for a lot longer than that. Even so, he still wasn't entirely certain of the man's origins. They'd met when Crow had been trying to cadge a lift from Bangkok to the Brunei pipelines where he'd heard they were looking for helicopter pilots to fly workers and equipment to and from the rigs. Crow had been given Leece's name by two French pilots from whom he'd hitched a ride from Yangon in a barely airworthy Fokker Friendship.

At the time, Leece's official job, supposedly, had been as a stringer for an international news agency and as such he'd made a lot of contacts, many of them among the freelance operators and contract fliers who made a living arranging and ferrying ad hoc flights around most of South East Asia, a fair few of the drop-off points having been classified at various times as political hotspots. But he'd come through for Crow, arranging for him to deadhead Bangkok to Brunei International via Kuala Lumpur and Kuching in a rickety DC-3, owned and flown by a couple of Kiwis who'd been glad of a little extra company.

But that result aside, there were those who'd sworn, usually in a lowered voice, that Leece plied a different trade entirely, one that had commenced during the mid-'70s, when, during the latter stages of the Vietnam conflict, he'd had been attached to Air America, the airline owned and run by the CIA, and that he'd taken part in missions to insert and extract US personnel, while providing logistical support to the the Royal Lao Army and the Hmong Army under command of Vang Pao.

Rumour also had it that in the dying stages of the war, as part of Operation Frequent Wind, he'd supervised some of the last evacuation flights out of Saigon and was said to have been on board the Air America helicopter that had been photographed for posterity, lifting people off the roof of the apartment building at 22 Gia Long Street, the address used by USAID and CIA employees.

The stories had continued after that, one being that when Air America had been made redundant in the aftermath, it had been Leece who, as a member of the negotiation team, had arranged the sale of surplus AA aircraft to several shady South American republics, and that from there, he'd built a reputation as a middle man, dealing in everything from military hardware and munitions to drilling equipment, aid supplies and just about anything else that might be going spare, for a price.

Crow had no idea if half of the stories were true but even if they weren't then Leece had to be pushing seventy if not close to overtaking it. Not that he'd ever given an indication that he was in danger of losing his edge. Crow had kept in contact with him over the intervening years, sometimes just to touch base, at other times to let Leece know that he was available for hire. A series of odd jobs had been the result.

Crow had flown geology teams on to the Khorat Plateau, medical supplies out to islands in the Andaman Sea, ITN and BBC news crews into Northern Sumatra in the wake of earthquakes and tsunamis, explorer naturalists into the New Guinea Highlands, and UN agency staff into refugee villages along the Myanmar/Thailand border area. Most of the charters had been legal, some of them not so much, but the money had been good, even taking into account Leece's cut.

As far as Crow was aware, Leece was still active among those in the know and well able to arrange introductions and special delivery on a variety of goods, albeit not all of them via legitimate means, a factor reflected in his sometimes eye-watering commission. Though it wasn't unkown for him to offer a friends and family discount when the mood took him. Crow was hoping that his success at the *Muay Thai* bout had put him in a generous mood.

Leece hadn't lied. The food was good, made doubly so by seeing the meals freshly prepared only metres away. Leece's recommendation of *Tom Yum Goon* - spicy shrimp soup - had been followed by a mouth-watering selection of sweet and sour dishes, rounded off with a generous bowl of mango sticky rice, while the beers had been topped up as and when requested. When the last bowl had been collected by the ever smiling Yaai Dao, and glasses of *Oliang* - iced coffee - served, Leece sat back and removed makings from the pouch around his neck. "So, let's get to it."

Crow waited and watched as Leece constructed and set fire to his cigarette, then said, "There's some equipment I need. You still in the business?"

"Might be," Leece said. "What're you looking for?"

"I've got a little list." Crow doubted Leece would get the *Mikado* reference.

Leece inhaled and blew out smoke. "A list? Sounds interesting."

"You haven't seen what's on it," Crow said.

Leece plucked a shred of tobacco from his lower lip. "Sounds like it might be expensive."

"We're good for it," Crow said.

When Keel had visited the Silom branch of HSBC on their arrival in Bangkok to present his credentials, he'd advised the manager that there were likely to be substantial withdrawals made over the coming few days.

"We?" Leece said.

"I'm part of what you might call a joint venture," Crow said.

Leece nodded thoughtfully and held out his hand. "Okay. Let's see it."

Crow reached into an inner pocket and withdrew a folded sheet of A4. He passed it over the table. Leece opened the sheet out and read the contents. He looked up. "*Little*? You serious?"

"Very," Crow said. "Can it be done?"

Leece scanned the list again. "I'll need to make some calls, talk to my suppliers. When do you want it by?"

Crow smiled.

"Ah, jeez," Leece looked up. "Whaddya think this is? Amazon Prime?"

Crow said nothing but remained calm as he

returned the American's incredulous stare.

Leece shook his head in disbelief, then stared down at the list once more as if he hadn't believed it the first or second time. Finally, he took another drag on his cigarette. Then removing it from his mouth, he said, "I'll see what I can do. I come through, it's gonna cost...big time. "

"You said that already."

"Yeah? Well, that don't include the delivery charge, either. I'm making sure you and your joint venturists, or whatever the fuck you're calling yourselves, get the picture. You think this stuff grows on trees? Shit."

"It's why I came to you. I have faith."

"And faith can move mountains and this here is a mountain of stuff. Yeah, yeah, I get it." Folding the list, Leece placed it on the table in front of him. "What the hell have you gotten yourself into?"

"Not sure you'd believe me if I told you."

"In my game, you'd be surprised what you end up believing. You should know that."

"All right," Crow said. "Know anyone in Laos?"

Leece's eyes narrowed. "Depends."

"On?"

Leece tapped out ash. "What you'd want 'em to do."

"Noted. How about Golden Kingdom? Name mean anything?"

"Sure." Leece let go a frown. "Chinese-run casino resort other side of the Mekong."

"Ever been?"

"It's thirty-seventh on my bucket list." Leece threw Crow a pitying look. "Tell me this isn't another *Ocean's 11* remake and you ain't planning on robbing the place?"

"Do I *look* like George Clooney?" Crow said.

Leece waggled his hand. "Maybe a little, around the eyes."

"Funny."

Leece sat back. "You wanna tell me, fine. You don't wanna tell me that's okay, too."

"Probably safer," Crow said. "If I need extra assistance I'll let you know."

Leece took another drag on his cigarette, pondered Crow's response for a couple of seconds and then nodded. "Where're you staying?"

"InterContinental."

"Your own name?"

"For now."

Leece eyed him speculatively, his hands playing idly with the folded piece of paper. "Heard a rumour you were working for some conservation outfit down in the boonies."

"Oh, we're way past the boonies," Crow said.

"Yeah?"

"Place called Salma. Wild life reserve on the Chad-CAR border."

Leece's eyebrows lifted. "Shit, you weren't kidding. That's beyond the back of fucking beyond. How the hell d'you end up there?"

"Couple of ex-military pals were taken on as instructors to train the park's ranger teams. They needed a chopper pilot; asked if I'd like to join them. I said sure, why not? They're good people."

"Interesting work?"

"Keeps me on my toes."

Leece took another draw on his cigarette, exhaled, and gazed at Crow through the smoke that drifted across his face. Finally, he nodded "All that crop dusting must've come in useful."

"You have no idea," Crow said. He looked down at his watch. "Okay, been a long day. Gotta go." Reaching into his pocket, he extracted some notes.

Leece waved them off. "Told you, it's on me. Besides, the rate I'll be charging, you're gonna be needing that."

"My accountant thanks you," Crow said as he rose to his feet. "Good to see you, Ray."

"You, too, bud."

"I'll wait to hear," Crow said as they shook hands.

Leece nodded. "Always a pleasure, my man. I'll be in touch."

Releasing his hand, Crow turned and headed for the door. Catching the eye of the proprietress, he touched his chest and inclined his head as a sign of thanks, receiving a bow and a smile in return.

Leece remained seated. He watched as Crow disappeared then picked up the piece of A4 opened it out and took another look at the contents.

"Jesus," he murmured softly. Then, folding the paper once more, he stowed it in the pouch around his neck, and took another long drag on his cigarette.

22

"How'd we do?" Keel asked.

"He'll get back to me," Crow said. "I can tell you this, though, it's just as well, we've still got a wadge of cash in the kitty."

"Noted," Keel said. "Did he query anything?"

"Other than our sanity, you mean? Not specifically,"

"But he'll be curious."

"Sure," Crow said. "Who wouldn't be? He knows the score, though. His business, it pays not to ask too many questions."

Keel nodded. He'd expected as much. He took a look around the room. It was mid-morning and the Bangkok Intercontinental's Balcony Lounge was generating about as much local ambience as that conjured up by the Dubliners pub back in Dubai. With its mahogany panelled walls, brown leather chairs, sofas and soft cushions, and walls hung with framed monochrome prints, the venue could have been lifted lock, stock and smoking jacket straight from any one of St James's gentleman's clubs.

"Late night?" Sekka asked, gazing at Crow with some amusement.

Crow threw him a look. "Jet lag."

"A pilot who suffers from jet lag?" Sabine said.

"You're not helping," Crow said, and reached for his

coffee cup.

Sekka looked past Crow's shoulder. "Eyes right, here comes your man."

"Hi guys," Cade said as he approached the table. "Welcome to Bangkok."

"Cade," Crow said, offering a brief nod.

"Miss Bouvier," Cade said to Sabine as he sat down.

"Mr. Cade," Sabine said.

Cade acknowledge Crow and Sabine's muted responses with a smile and glanced around the room. "Good to see you aren't slumming it."

"Don't have to if you don't need to," Keel said. "You want a coffee?"

Cade shook his head. "I'll pass, thanks."

"So," Keel said. "What have you got for us?"

"I got news that the *Sulawesi Star* docked yesterday. Cargo's been off-loaded and the container delivered to Vinasakhone. Freeland thinks the contents were transferred to a truck which was last seen heading north. Could be going all the way to GK by road, though they could transfer the cargo to a boat somewhere along the route and ship the stuff up river, direct to GK's front door."

"Got a question," Crow said. "If the authorities suspect the container was carrying ivory and animal parts, which are now travelling by road, why haven't they stopped the truck and opened it up?"

Keel shrugged, with a glance towards Cade. "Vinasakhone's a Lao-owned company. Unless they're given solid grounds to search it, the Thais'll probably allow the goods to transit. Plus we're talking Thailand and Laos, remember? Grease the right palms and most anything'll slide through the net."

"Oh, yeah," Crow said. "Duh..."

406

"Unless," Sekka said, addressing Cade, "you haven't confirmed with anyone that the ship *was* carrying illegal animal parts. We're the only ones who know that for certain because Baroud confessed. Freeland only *suspected* it was. They might not want to sabotage their relationship with the Thais on a hunch, especially if the truck was stopped and found to be empty."

"Or maybe," Crow cut in, "you're closer to the US Treasury than you are to ROUTES and Co, and you told Freeland to stand down. If the consignment's confiscated en route, that could alter Zheng's plans for the auction, which'd put the kybosh on your master plan. Far as you're concerned, Zheng's the main priority, not our ivory and a bunch of lion bones. Yes, no?"

Cade looked to be on the point of replying when he was forestalled by Keel, who said, "Is Freeland tracking the truck, or what?"

Cade's gaze swung back. He nodded. "As best they can, yeah. So, how you gonna play this?"

Keel paused, then said, "Joseph, Sabine and I'll head north, scope out GK, look for any weak spots. Crow's got a few errands to run. He'll join us later."

Cade nodded. "When do you leave?"

"Tomorrow," Keel said. "VietJet to Chiang Rai, and we need a favour."

"Which would be?" Cade said.

"There's a transport issue," Keel said.

"Okay," Cade said, and waited.

"We'd like to look around independently, but we know the regs. The Laos don't permit hire cars to cross the border. The vehicle has to be registered to the driver. Any chance you can help us out?"

Cade pursed his lips, gave Keel a level stare.

407

"Maybe."

"That a maybe yes, or a maybe no?"

"What's your arrival time Chiang Rai?"

"Eleven-ten."

Cade let out a breath, nodded. "Leave it with me."

If the American Treasury Department's suspicions about the man were correct, it wasn't that hard to see why Zheng had chosen the spot as the location for his casino resort, on the threshold of the area designated the world's second largest opium producer after Aghanistan. It had been the CIA that had labelled the confluence of the Ruak and Mekong rivers, the place where Thailand, Laos and Myanmar met, as the Golden Triangle, and from where Keel, Sekka and Sabine were standing, it was possible to view all three sides of it at once; they were that close.

They were in Ban Sop Ruak, a village on the west bank of the Mekong, a popular destination for tourists keen to explore the Triangle for themselves. There wasn't a lot to the place, if you discounted the *Phra Chiang Saen Si Phaendin*, the huge golden statue of the Buddha that was positioned on the river bank and which dwarfed the vessels moored below it, and the House of Opium museum, dedicated to the drug that had given the region its name. Apart from the odd temple, that was pretty much it.

It wasn't the attractions on the Thai side of the river, however, that drew the attention of Keel and his companions, but rather the collection of buildings less than half a mile distant on the opposite bank, in the People's Democratic Republic of Laos.

The Golden Kingdom Casino Resort dominated the

408

skyline, the most notable feature being the large yellow-painted building undergoing construction, that rose above the trees like an enormous crock of cheese. It was destined, according to the brochures, to be a five-star hotel. The casino squatted in its shadow. A huge, ornate crown sat atop its flat roof. Painted gold and as big as two challenger tanks stacked one on top of the other, it was almost as high as it was wide, and appeared to have been built for no other purpose than as a deliberate veneration to Mammon and thus a counterpoint to the giant Buddha on the Thai side of the divide. At the other end of the same roof, to the right of the crown, could also be seen a large gold-painted dome. Beyond the resort, a low range of forested hills ran the length of the horizon.

"Not what you'd call subtle," Sekka murmured, eyeing the regal adornment.

"It's a statement," Keel said. "Zheng wouldn't be the first millionaire casino owner who likes to flaunt it."

"But wealth does not buy you class," Sabine said. "Is not that what you say?"

"Frequently," Sekka said.

Keel's eyes were drawn to the activity on the river below them. Being one of the Mekong's main border crossings, it was a busy stretch of waterway. Noticeable were the low-slung, heavily-laden cargo barges, either heading north to ports in Myanmar and China, where the river ceased being the Mekong and became instead the Lancang, or south to Cambodia and Vietnam and down into the Mekong Delta and, eventually, the South China Sea.

Narrow and faster passenger craft zipped between the slower moving freight vessels with ease, as nimble as barracuda, while fishing boats competed for right of way with riverscape tourist boats and blue-painted passenger ferries, courtesy of the Golden Kingdom Resort, that scuttled back and forth between the two shores like brightly coloured water beetles. The noise from a multitude of engines and outboards created a constant buzz, as loud as an insect swarm and as invasive as tinnitus to anyone within earshot.

"Okay," Keel said. "Let's get to it."

Journey time across the river from Sop Ruak to the *Sam Liam Kham* border post on the Lao side would have been a matter of minutes by boat, but Keel and his companions were taking the long way round, the scenic route. It would add up to more than a three hour drive, but routing by road would give them a better understanding of the area and the landward approach to the GK resort and the terrain that surrounded it.

An advantage made possible by Cade having come through with the transport.

As Keel had previously stated, Laos didn't permit entry by hire car, as all motor vehicles making the transit had to be registered to the driver. One solution would have been to cross the river by boat and hire a vehicle on the Lao side, but as that would have meant engaging the services of a local driver as well, Keel had swiftly vetoed the idea, which had left them with only one viable alternative: to buy their own set of wheels.

Which, was where Cade had stepped in, with a Toyota Fortuner 4x4. Keel, as the new owner, had no idea if the paperwork for the sale was genuine. He assumed it was, as the dealership to which they'd been directed had all the trappings of a legitimate company, complete with a modest supply of saloons and SUVs on its forecourt. As it was also situated on the approach road to Chiang Rai airport, Keel half-suspected the Toyota was probably a spruced-up ex-hire that had had its mileage recalibrated.

Cade has also come through with the additional paperwork, in the form of insurance and a vehicle passport which allowed cross-border travel. As he'd handed over the documents, the salesman had advised them that once across the Lao border they'd be required to buy additional insurance to cover the period they were in the country, a simple procedure as there was an insurance office next to every Lao border checkpoint. Keel was also made aware that while in Thailand they drove on the left; in Laos, they drove on the right.

"Have a nice day," had been the dealer's parting words, in remarkably good English, the avaricious smile on his face due, in no small measure, to the agreement that he would buy back the SUV once it had served its purpose, at a substantially reduced rate, of course. Cade would be laughing at that, Keel reflected, if he wasn't already in on the deal.

"Good job your friend 'H' had a whip round," Sekka murmured as they'd driven away.

"'H'?" Sabine said. "Who is this 'H'?"

Sekka sighed. "You going to tell her, or should I?"

The drive south to the Chiang Khong Friendship Bridge took a little over ninety minutes, along good roads. The shorter route would have been to drive to the Chiang Khong ferry, five miles north of the bridge and cross the river from there. But the salesman had warned Keel that not only was the ferry subject to crowding and therefore delays, the customs and immigration officials in charge of the ferry checkpoint were far more officious than those operating the bridge border post, often when dealing with Europeans, who were advised - some would probably say pressured - to use the bridge anyway.

The tip paid off, though it didn't prevent the three of them from holding their collective breath as the car documents and their passports were forensically examined, first on the Thai side of the bridge, and then, with visas purchased and motor insurance duly obtained, by the customs and immigration officials manning the second border post on the Lao side. Fifty minutes later, though, they were back in the vehicle and continuing on their journey, only releasing their breath once the border post had disappeared from the rear view mirror.

The route took them north towards Huay Xai, Bokeo's provincial capital. Keel figured the well-maintained state of the road was due in part to it serving the airport, which lay to the east of the town, and which, despite its modest facilities, was, along with the river, the main link between Huay Xai and the country's capital, Vientiane.

By-passing the town, Keel continued on the main highway which eventually turned west towards the Mekong where it then veered north to follow the river's contours. Keel realized it had to be the road Cade had told them about: the one constructed by Golden Kingdom as a means by which upmarket guests could travel from the airport to the resort, and even though Keel and his companions wouldn't have regarded themselves as tourists, it was a picturesque drive, running as it did between steep, wooded slopes and past rice paddies, fish ponds and villages with thatched market stalls and white-painted temples that hugged the side of the road. At one point, a small herd of buffalo ambled slowly across their path, seemingly oblivious to the queue of vehicles forced to give way before them.

Gradually, however, the trees thinned and the road and the land around it broadened out, and more modern structures started to spring up, many still under construction. What looked like a row of apartment blocks appeared in the distance. Clearly, a sizable town was emerging from what, only a few years ago, would have been agricultural land and thick forest.

They knew they'd reached their destination when they came upon a large, bright blue sign which proclaimed that they were about to enter the Golden Triangle Special Economic Zone, and it wasn't long before they found themselves on a wide avenue lined with mature trees and shrubs. A short time later, they caught their first glimpse of the golden dome and the jewelled crown mounted on the casino roof.

As Sekka had remarked back in Sop Ruak, it didn't look as if subtlety had been in the developer's - or, more likely, Zheng Chao's - mind when plans for the zone were being hatched. The contrast between the resort's architecture and that of the rustic villages and temples they'd driven past was extraordinary and not a little surreal.

Disney World meets *Ben Hur* was the thought that flashed through Keel's mind as they neared the casino building, due to the impressive columns that framed the entrance and the statues that were set in niches along the outer walls, in the form of the same bearded male figure, displayed in a variety of regal poses.

413

Draped in a robe, the figure was hefting either a long spear or a bladed weapon, and, in one instance, what looked to be a sceptre. Keel assumed the carvings were meant to represent some form of classical deity, though the period effect was somewhat marred by the enormous multi-coloured neon sign set above the portico which spelled out in both Chinese and English: BLUE ORCHID CASINO.

The Lotus Garden Hotel was a stone's throw from the casino and lay behind what was possibly meant to be an homage to the gardens at Versailles, in that the area was laid out in a series of circular lawns and flowered borders divided by wide pathways and banks of low shrubbery. Several ornamental fountains had also been employed in the design, though the effect still looked like a work in progress.

As for the hotel itself, the colonnaded front, rather than complementing the architecture, gave it, instead, the air of an antebellum mansion from America's deep south crossed with N'Djamena's Chez Wou, an effect not helped by another garish neon sign which spanned the width of the roof and spelled out the establishment's name in English, Lao, and Chinese, in the same vivid hues as those employed above the casino.

Despite the inelegant facade, the car park contained several high-end vehicles, including two Phantoms, a dozen expensive-looking Mercs and BMWs and, tucked into one corner, a sand-coloured Humvee, which dwarfed the handful of Toyota Mark II saloons parked in its shadow. The latter were so uniform in colour, Keel guessed they were GK company cars. Two of them, he noted were not carrying number plates, suggesting they might be security vehicles.

414

Parking the SUV alongside one of the Beemers, Keel locked up and the three of them took their bags and headed for the hotel entrance, Sekka walking side-by-side with Sabine, his right arm draped proprietorially over her shoulder, with Keel keeping pace to the side of them in close protection mode.

They kept to the illusion at the reception desk, Sekka and his companion hanging back, while Keel, posing as general factotum, dealt with the paperwork, having booked the rooms in advance: one deluxe double and one matching twin, with a door connecting the two, the implication being that Sekka and Sabine would be occupying the double, while Keel, in his guise of a CPO required to maintain close contact with his principal, would be in the twin. In reality, Keel and Sekka would share the twin leaving Sabine with the double.

It was something of a pleasant surprise to find that the standard of accommodation was better than the outside of the hotel had suggested, the rooms being furnished in a contemporary style and decorated in muted shades of red and grey, presumably to remain in keeping with the classical theme.

Sabine was the first to draw attention to the hotel brochure contained in a rack on the dressing table. "You should see this," she said, her expression mirroring her dismay as she examined the pages, which, this time, supported only Chinese script.

In design, it was no different from any brochure found in any other hotel room in that it contained glossy photos and descriptions of the facilities available for guests to enjoy, from the hotel spa to the nearby Chinatown with its restaurants and giftshops, as well as information on river trips, nearby hiking trails, and excursions to visit local hill tribes. The casino and the zoo were mentioned, as was, bizarrely, a firing range where guests could indulge their fantasies by shooting a variety of automatic weapons, including AK-47s and a selection of hand guns.

What had caught Sabine's attention, however, was the photograph of a complete tiger skeleton submerged in a large tank of amber liquid. It sat alongside a rack of bottles containing, according to the text, tiger bone wine. On a facing page there was an image of a golden cat trapped in a cage and below that a photograph of a pangolin curled foetally at the bottom of a wooden crate. They were arranged next to a snapshot of a menu board from the Opal Moon restaurant, which left little doubt as to their intended fate. As well as cat and pangolin, the board listed, in English and Mandarin, other specialities, including leopard penis wine, gecko, snake and turtle.

Sabine grimaced. "They call it *Yewei*. It means 'wild flavour'. We would say: 'exotic meat'."

Keel laid the brochure back on the desk. "So let's go check it out," he said.

The shopping area was less than a five minute walk from the hotel and easy to find on account of the approach being marked by a towering wooden entrance gate that had to be at least twenty-five metres in height, its ornately-carved surface painted in bright blues, greens and reds. Above the central arch, framed by a pair of gold-painted dragons, was set a panel upon which was written *Chinatown* in the now inevitable Lao, Chinese and English characters.

On the inner side of the gate, a large stone statue occupied pride of place: Confucius, caught in traditional pose, smiling serenely, his clasped hands raised, as if to welcome the visitor into his inner sanctum, which consisted of a broad street lined with pagoda-roofed stores, fronted by red-painted columns and matching red-shuttered doorways.

With Keel maintaining a dutiful distance, Sekka and Sabine took point. Sabine stiffened as she approached the first open doorway. The sign above the door identified the building as the Treasure Hall. When Keel moved closer and looked inside the store he saw what had caught her attention.

At the foot of a stairway were two stuffed tigers. Teeth bared in silent, angry snarls, they stared glassily out towards the street as if looking for an escape route. Through an archway behind them, three adult tiger skins could be seen, splayed out across a far wall.

"Not a word," Keel warned softly.

Bracing herself, Sabine led the way inside, past a cabinet containing an innocuous selection of herbs and teas, towards a low wooden table upon which were laid two more tiger skins, a leopard pelt and, looking somewhat out of place, a three-foot-long stuffed crocodile.

To the left was a glass-topped counter backed by a ceiling-high display case. Both contained a wide selection of carved tusks and figurines as well as a collection of smaller ivory products including amulets, beaded bracelets, pendants, rosaries, and two chess sets, all intricately fashioned.

"*Wǒ kěyǐ bāngzhù nǐ ma?*"

They turned as a dour-looking Asian woman dressed in a crimson tabard emerged from behind a strip curtain in the corner of the store. Sounds of a television wafted from the vacated room behind her.

Keel assumed they were being asked if she could

417

assist them. Sabine made no attempt to reply but continued to peruse the items beneath the counter.

"Nice," Keel said, smiling at the woman and lifting his chin towards the shelves.

The woman nodded and offered a cursory smile, though her eyes appeared wary. Keel wondered if she'd understood what he'd said.

"American?" the woman enquired awkwardly, suggesting Keel's observation had registered.

"*Français,*" Keel said. Then, indicating Sekka: "*Afrika.*"

The woman's gaze flickered slightly as she nodded again and regarded Sabine and then Sekka expectantly. Sabine ignored her while Sekka returned her gaze in haughty silence, before switching his attention to the display behind the counter.

"My friend would like to buy a gift," Keel said, in English, pointing to Sekka and then Sabine and then his wrist. "Jewellery?"

It was clear the woman understood the gist of Keel's enquiry. As if sensing a possible sale, she placed a bit more emphasis into her painted-on smile, inclined her head, and moved her hand to indicate the goods arranged beneath the glass.

Sabine spoke in French, without looking up, her expression disdainful. "Ask her where they are carved."

Keel repeated the question in English, making a whittling motion with his hands.

The woman nodded. "*Fujian.*"

It confirmed the information obtained from Max Cade. Fujian was a province just over the Chinese border. The SEZ's Chinese traders maintained connections there because it was an important entry and exit point for illicit wildlife products and a main processing hub where ivory, rhino horn, helmeted hornbill, and pangolin were turned into finished items. It was also home to several taxidermy companies and the likely supplier of the two exhibits currently on guard inside the Treasury Hall's entrance.

"*Celui là,*" Sabine said, tapping her fingertip on the glass immediately above a chunky ivory bracelet, secured with a gold clasp.

The woman lifted the bracelet from its shelf and placed it on a cloth on top of the counter.

"*Combien?*" Sabine said.

Keel relayed the question. Reaching behind her, the woman brought out a calculator. Tapping the keys she showed Keel the result. The price quoted was five and a half thousand yuan, not far short of nine hundred US dollars, which meant the larger carvings in the display cases had to be worth a great deal more.

Keel kept his expression neutral as he relayed the price to Sabine who turned to Sekka as if seeking his opinion. Sekka took the bracelet and turned it over in his hands, before shrugging dismissively and dropping the item back on the counter. "*Bari mu tafi,*" he said brusquely in Hausa, and jerked his head. Sabine pouted and threw Keel a petulant glance before following a bored-looking Sekka out of the shop.

Keel looked at the woman, shrugged, and shook his head apologetically. Turning away before she could respond, he returned to the street, where Sabine was already moving on to the next store, with Sekka several paces behind, as if content to let her cool off.

"One down," Sekka murmured, as Keel caught up with him.

The second store contained similar items to the first, though this time there were no stuffed tigers.

419

There were, however, two beautiful clouded leopard pelts displayed on one wall. Cabinets occupied the other three walls, with gold jewellery and ivory representations of the Buddha prominent among the rings, bangles, chop sticks and cigarette holders on show. On a lower shelf, two trays contained pendants made from mounted tiger teeth.

Sabine had slipped her sunglasses down over her eyes in an effort to hide her anger, but Keel saw her hands clench the strap of her shoulder bag as she regarded the wares for sale.

A middle-aged man, who was clearly Chinese, and a young woman appeared from behind the counter. The woman's complexion was slighter darker than the man's suggesting she was of Lao extraction, or perhaps from one of the Chinese border regions.

Keel and Sabine reprised the routine they'd established in the first store, with Sekka maintaining his role as an aloof benefactor. Though, as Sabine went through the pantomime of examing the trinkets, he allowed his eyes to stray towards a pair of elephant tusks positioned one either side of an inner doorway.

Unmarked by any decoration, Sekka wondered about the age of the animal from which they'd been harvested. If he were to hazard a guess he'd have said upwards of twenty-five years at least; a life cut short for no other reason than to produce a trophy for an exhibit in a shop doorway.

Keel watched as the female vendor followed Sekka's movements. He could tell by her body language that she was intrigued; one of the likely reasons being the colour of Sekka's skin.

Sekka, aware of the perusal, looked up. *"Nawa?"*

Keel turned to the woman. "How much?"

420

The calculator was brought out. Ten thousand yuan, a little over fifteen thousand dollars.

Had it not been Sekka who'd initiated the enquiry, Keel knew it was unlikely the sales staff would have been so forthcoming. Cade had told them that prices, especially for the most expensive works, were unlikely to be shared with Westerners because the sales people knew such items were too large to be smuggled back home. Also Westerners tended only to enter stores for nefarious purposes: one of them being to conduct secret filming for conservation agencies. In other words, they weren't to be trusted, which explained the woman's demeanour in the Treasure Hall. Sekka's heritage, however, was uncommon enough to have prompted a degree of curiosity and cooperation from both retailers.

Sekka gazed at the price without expression, then, turning, he ran his hands over the tusks once more before gazing at Keel as if to prompt a reaction.

Keel addressed the salesgirl and made an expansion gesture with his hands, indicating he was interested in something bigger.

The girl's eyes widened. Turning, she conferred with her male colleague in Mandarin. Sabine, still browsing, made no sign that she understood what was being said. After a short discussion, the girl turned and waved her hand in the general direction of the street, as if to say that a shop further along might be able to meet Sekka's requirements. Keel glanced at Sekka to check he'd understood. Without a word, Sekka turned on his heel and walked out.

Keel tapped Sabine on the shoulder. *"Allons."*

Sabine looked up, as if surprised to find that Sekka had left, whereupon Keel offered a curt nod of thanks to the sales couple and led the way out of the store.

"Two down," Sekka said. "You saw the cameras."

Keel nodded.

"Cameras?" Sabine said.

Keel nodded again. "Second sales area, corner above the display. Another one on the second shelf down, cabinet behind the counter. Did you catch what they said?"

"They were most interested in Joseph. They marked him as the one with the money."

"So you and I are the hired help?"

"You, yes. They think I am his whore."

"They actually said that?"

"By implication."

"Charming," Keel said.

"The man told the girl to phone the next store to tell them we would be calling in."

"Good. Then let's go pay them a visit."

Staffed this time by an elderly man and a younger male assistant, the third store had an even greater selection of ivory on display; figurines as well as plain tusks, ranging in height and length from twenty centimetres to well over ninety in the case of some figures. To one side of the room a large glass case, as tall as a man, contained an elephant's thigh bone, covered in what looked to be Buddhist iconography.

The store also had something which the previous ones did not and that was rhino horn, fashioned into pendants decorated with images of Confucius and the Buddha, along with small figurines carved in the shape of standing figures meant to represent, Keel guessed, the eight Daoist Immortals. Other pieces had been cut into flower shapes: chrysanthemum, frangipani and jasmine.

422

Rhino horn was recognizable by its colour and by its dark, heart-shaped central core; the darker the horn, the more valuable the item, which when polished, took on a translucence and lustre that increased with age. It was hard to believe it was composed of nothing more spectacular than keratin - a protein found in hair and human fingernails - and yet it was deemed more valuable than ivory, as was illustrated by the tags affixed to some of the objects beneath the counter glass, a number of which, surprisingly, showed the price in US dollars as well as yuan. Though the dollar rate, Keel noticed, was poor compared to the official exchange rate.

As he considered the prices, Keel knew the next move was going to be critical. Because if they were to maintain the charade they were going to have to make a purchase. They had decided earlier that when it came to the moment of choice, it would be Sekka's call.

The figurine was set on a round wooden base and had been fashioned from the top portion of a single elephant tusk. Some twenty centimetres high, it had been carved in the shape of an elderly, bearded figure cradling a bird. Setting the piece on the counter top, Sekka reached into an inside pocket and withdrew two items: a small UV torch and a jeweller's loupe. The action drew a startled look from the younger vendor who turned to his senior colleague. For a moment the older salesman looked equally taken aback, but then his eyes narrowed and, after interpreting the challenging expression on Sekka's face, he nodded in silent acquiescence.

Sekka held the piece up and directed the black light across the figurine's contours, noting the effect the process had on the pristine smooth surface. Genuine

423

ivory tended to fluoresce white, while plastics and resins fluoresced blue or blue/white. The result looked positive but the test wasn't foolproof. Laying the torch aside, Sekka held the loupe to his eye.

Ivory was formed by living tissue. It had a grain structure and the direction and forms of growth were unique to each ivory-bearing species, and impossible to replicate in artificial substances. As a general rule, the grain always ran along the long dimension of a piece of authentic worked ivory.

The key feature in identifying the real article, however, was to note the pattern of crosshatching that could appear in the cross-sections of a tusk. The lines were actually rows of microscopic tubes known as Schreger lines, and where they crossed they formed Schreger angles. Their presence always verified a piece as genuine elephant ivory. They were most prominent around a figure's base or where cuts had been made at right angles to the grain.

Sekka removed the loupe. Returning the figurine to the counter, he nodded at Keel and stepped away.

The price tag listed both Chinese RMB and US currency. Keel could see the man's brain working. The dollar price would be more advantageous. Keel pointed to the dollar sign.

Cade had warned Keel that in Laos ATM services outside the cities were somewhat creaky and that dollars were widely accepted, so Keel, despite having the HSBC card as his main access to funds, had also taken the precaution of stocking up with a substantial supply of greenbacks beforehand, for use in situations such as this, where cash was king, with fewer questions asked.

Keel wasn't surprised when the calculator was

produced. A few deft swipes across the keys followed before the dollar price was shown.

Keel nodded, withdrew the billfold from his pocket, and peeled off thirty one-hundred-dollar bills. A receipt was scrawled while the junior salesman wrapped the carving in bright red tissue paper and placed it in a gift bag.

Which was when Sabine tugged Sekka's sleeve and pointed to a tray of ivory bracelets she'd been studying. Sekka stared down at them and then inclined his head as if giving his begrudging permission for her to take a closer look. Sabine caressed Sekka's arm, flashed her eyes, and indicated to the junior salesman which of the pieces she wanted to view.

Watching her, Keel could only admire her acting skills as she held the bracelet up to the light before slipping it over her wrist, the ivory bright against her tan as she presented it to Sekka for his agreement. Sekka nodded, as if bored by the whole process. Sabine indicated she would wear the bracelet as, this time. Keel unfolded the required amount from his wad of notes.

As junior dealt with the receipt, Keel diverted the senior salesman's attention to a pair of large tusks set against a wall. "How much?"

The price was twenty thousand dollars.

Through broken English and mime, Keel was able to establish that larger items could be shipped to any destination of choice. When Keel smiled and indicated to the shop keeper and his junior that they would return, the shopkeepers' smiles appeared almost genuine.

As they left the store, Sabine, unexpectedly, reached for Sekka's hand. So intense was her grip that her knuckles gleamed pale through her tan and Keel, walking behind, knew instinctively that she was holding on, not for appearance's sake, but for tactile support. It took several steps before she halted, inhaled deeply, and let go.

"You okay?" Keel asked her, as she removed the bracelet from her wrist. He held out the bag and with a look of disgust she deposited the bracelet inside it.

Massaging her wrist as through wiping away dirt, it took a further second or two before she answered. "What have we done, Thomas?"

"What we came here to do," Keel said. "These aren't souvenirs."

"No?" she said, her jaw almost rigid with anger. "Then *what*?"

"Evidence," Keel said, "and maybe an entry ticket."

23

"*Putain!*" Sabine hissed angrily. "*Bâtards!*"

Keel was trying not to let his gaze linger on the cage or its contents: a small bundle of dull black fur which, when it uncurled, revealed itself to be a sun bear cub that couldn't have been more than a couple of months old, if that. The pale 'U' shaped patch on its chest was unmistakable.

There was no floor to the cage which meant the crouching cub's belly was laid across the bottom slats in such away that its paws were resting on the ground beneath. It was poking its blond snout through the front of the cage and snuffling and every time it did so, which was often, it cast a fearful glance upwards, showing the whites of its eyes, which only served to emphasise its obvious distress. Keel didn't think he'd seen anything quite so pitiful, though he noticed that none of the other passers-by appeared in the least affected by the animal's plight.

The bear cub was making faint grizzling noises. Sabine didn't have to curse again for Keel to know what thoughts had to be running through her mind. In the course of her career as a veterinary surgeon, she'd have treated hundreds of distressed and injured animals and put many to sleep in order to end their suffering; all the time while keeping her emotions in

427

check, and yet, despite that, and no matter what culinary habits she might have witnessed while working among cultures alien to her own, the sight of the cub being offered up as part of a restaurant menu would be tearing at her soul.

The cage was on the pavement outside the Opal Moon, the eaterie advertised in the hotel's brochure. It was located down a side lane off the main shopping area and accessed via another carved gate, conveniently bearing the sign: *Food Street.* When Keel glanced through the doorway, beyond the menu board, he could see the large tank complete with its submerged tiger skeleton.

"You up for this?" he asked.

In answer, Sabine held out her hand for the gift-wrapped figurine and bracelet and when Keel gave the gift bag to her, she stowed it away in her own shoulder bag. "It is why we are here, is it not?"

Her voice, Keel noticed, had regained its strength.

"Joseph?"

Sekka nodded.

Stepping around the cage, Keel led the way inside. He did not allow his eyes to linger on the tiger skeleton or the row of bottles next to it which read: *Hǔ gǔ jiǔ,* which, Keel knew from the incriminating photo, was tiger bone wine.

The place couldn't have been described as intimate, though the lighting was relatively subdued. The decor was mainly red and gold with a dragon motif being the dominant feature on everything from the wall paper to the light fittings. The place was three-quarters full, with the majority of the diners appearing to be Chinese. Several eyed Keel and his companions as a waitress showed them to a table, their interest likely generated by Sekka's appearance, though that soon dissipated after he and the others took their seats. When the menu arrived it didn't bear much resemblance to the outside board. Evidently, wild flavour dishes weren't presented as an option to non-Chinese patrons. Keel wasn't sure whether to be relieved or insulted. He threw a glance at Sekka, who paused from looking around the room and smiled, as if to himself.

Sabine caught the look. "What?"

Sekka shook his head. "Nothing, only it occurred to me that where I come from, some of the dishes on that board aren't all *that* special."

Sabine stared at him.

"We have wet markets, too, back home; everything from tortoise to monkeys and rats; you name it, they sell it. A lot of Nigerians eat bush meat, and I don't just mean the poor. The well-off all tuck in."

"'Tuck in'?"

"Indulge themselves."

"So you...?" Sabine said.

"Oh, I'm pretty sure my grandmother would have served it at some time. Probably in one of her stews. And when we were hunting down the rebels, we survived on what we could catch. When you're living rough in the bush and short on supplies, you tend not to be too fussy about what goes in the pot." Sekka threw a look at Keel. "Right, boss?"

Sabine turned. "You, too? You weren't worried about transmission risk?"

It was a reference to Bryce's comment about zoonotic viruses. Keel made a face but nodded. "Wasn't something we thought about at the time. Anyone attached to special forces gets taught how to live off

429

road kill. It wasn't all MREs."

"MR-?" Sabine frowned.

"Meals Ready to Eat: military rations. You had them in France. RCIRs..?"

"Ration de Combat Individuelle Rechauffable," Sekka chuckled. "The Legion's favourite."

"Any good?"

"*Immangeable*," Sekka and Sabine said together.

"There you go then," Keel said. "Hell, Sabine, how long have you been at Salma? I guarantee most of our rangers will have chowed down on bush meat at some time or other, either from choice or necessity; probably still do, and if you're about to accuse me of employing double standards, then, yep, guilty as charged. But there's a hell of a difference between what Joseph and I might have done in a past life and asking some chef to turn out a plate of tiger fritters just so someone can feed their bloody ego - no pun intended - or because they think it'll cure genital warts. Sod it, maybe I'll just have the salad."

"Risky," Sekka said. "You don't know what it's been washed in."

"That case," Keel said, "I'll stick with the pork."

They ordered an assortment of dishes from the regular menu – roast duck, spinach noodles, stir-fried pasta, shredded pork and dumplings - but drew a line at the tiger bone wine which was available if requested, opting instead for the local and more appealing Beerlao.

Observing examples of the food being served to some of the other diners, it was apparent that more than a few had chosen the *Yewei* option, albeit to be consumed behind closed doors. Two waiters passed by, heading for what was, presumably, a private room;

430

the server closest to Keel bearing what might have been mistaken for a thick vegetable stew had it not been for the upturned bear paw in the middle of it. His companion was carrying another meat dish, which, judging from the artistic way the food was arranged, looked to be some sort of fricasseed rodent, cut into thick strips. Bamboo rat, Keel guessed.

"Think we've piqued anyone's interest?" Sekka asked, as they worked their way through what was an acceptable, if a somewhat surprisingly bland meal.

Keel made a face as he skewered a slice of duck liver. "Hard to say. The fact that we bought ivory will probably have registered. Whether the info's been passed up the line, your guess is as good as mine."

"Maybe we need to up the ante," Sekka said.

"You have something in mind?"

"Don't judge me," Sekka said, and raised his hand. To Sabine, he said, "How do you say snake soup?"

Sabine looked at him, chop sticks poised.

"Trust me," Sekka said. "I've eaten worse."

"It is more a Cantonese dish," Sabine said. "Try *shé gēng*. They will know what you mean."

Had he or Sabine placed the order, Keel suspected the waitress might well have shaken her head, but something in Sekka's expression and his abrupt, yet accurate pronunciation of the words must have persuaded her that there was no mistake involved and that this particular customer knew exactly what he was asking for. Or it could have been that she planned on taking the order and then to watch from the wings, giggling along with her fellow servers, and probably some of the other observant customers, as the crazy *falang* made an idiot of himself.

It didn't take long for the soup to arrive, possibly

because the waitress couldn't wait for Sekka's come-uppance. After receiving the latter's curt nod of dismissal, she hovered momentarily before retreating to a safe distance to await the inevitable outcome.

Which never materialized.

"Not bad," Sekka said, after several spoonfuls. "He grinned at Sabine. "Want to-?"

"*Non, merci*," Sabine said, pushing her own plate away. "I would not," she finished emphatically in English.

Sekka shrugged, as if scornful of Sabine's reticence to try such a tasty morsel and turned his attention to finishing the bowl.

"What now?" Sabine asked when, an hour later, they emerged back onto the street, Keel slightly disappointed that Sekka hadn't won himself a round of applause.

"Back to the hotel, shower and change," Keel said.

"And then?"

"We hit the tables."

The steps leading up to the casino entrance were flanked by two huge lion statues, while the columns that supported the portico wouldn't have looked out of place propping up Rome's *Tempio di Portuno*. On the underside of the portico roof, in keeping with the statues decorating the outer walls, a large circular mural depicted a naked, long-haired warrior astride a winged horse, surrounded by flying cherubs.

After Sabine had her shoulder bag checked by one of two black-uniformed security guards, they made their way inside, past a metal detector screen, to be confronted by a chandelier-lit lobby, from where a wide, red-carpeted stairway swept towards the upper floor. With its polished marble tiles, fluted pillars, gilded busts and fresco-decorated walls, the interior would have done justice to any of Europe's grand palaces, or possibly a stage set for a camp Broadway musical.

The main gaming room was situated at ground level, located so that visitors were encouraged to pass by and linger at counters bearing numerous ivory and rhino horn products. One object caught Keel's eye: a plastic bag filled with a white flour-like substance. An attached label bore the images of two elephants and identified the contents as being a kilogram of pure powdered ivory.

The casino floor was big, the size of four tennis courts, with areas catering for a variety of diversions: Baccarat, Blackjack, Roulette, Caribbean Stud Poker and Tiger vs Dragon, while one corner of the room was given over to bank of slot machines, divided, like the tables, into those playable with either Thai baht or Chinese RMB.

Keel had guessed correctly that a black tie ensemble would have looked severely out of place so he and Sekka had dressed casually in jacket and slacks over open-necked shirts. Sabine, in her role as Sekka's paramour, had opted for a knee-length black dress and heels. She wore her hair down, a simple silver locket and chain about her neck, and the ivory bracelet on her left wrist.

"If I do not look at it," she said, as they left their rooms, "then perhaps I can pretend it is not there."

As they explored the gaming room, and as he studied the rest of the clientele, Keel wondered if the three of them weren't still a tad overdressed. The area was well attended and a lot of punters, men and women, were wearing just t-shirts, jeans and trainers. More Macao than Monte Carlo, Keel thought, which perhaps wasn't that surprising given Zheng's background.

The dealers were decked out in purple shirts and black waistcoats. Most of the chatter going on around them was in Chinese, suggesting the majority of visitors were tourists from across the northern border. Those that weren't were most likely from the Thai side of the river, which probably went for the smattering of Westerners, too. Curious backpackers, Keel supposed; most likely taking advantage of the GK ferry service to explore the resort and secure another stamp in their passports.

On a small stage tucked away in a lounge area and framed by red velvet drapes, a pianist tinkled away at a baby grand, while servers moved among the players offering soft drinks and hot beverages. A lot of people were smoking. Signs warned that neither alcohol nor picture taking were permitted. Several staff members, wearing black instead of purple shirts, were equipped with earpieces. Casino security, Keel assumed.

His eyes were drawn to the far end of the room to where two black-waistcoated employees were guarding the foot of a stairway that granted access to a mezzanine level containing a second gaming area. The pair were implementing what was obviously some sort of dress code. T-shirts and jeans were being turned away while those wearing smart casual were given leave to ascend. Sekka had spotted the process, too.

"Shall we?" he said, taking Sabine's hand.

The jackets and Sabine's dress would probably have done the trick, but the fifty-dollar note Keel slid into the stair-keeper's hand sealed the deal.

The top of the stairs opened up onto what was evidently a high stakes floor, where a second cashier's cage served those who didn't want to trek back downstairs if they needed a top-up. The air conditioning was doing its best to compensate but the atmosphere was heavy with the smell of tobacco fumes, produced mostly by young, chain-smoking Chinese males.

While Sekka and Sabine stood to one side, Keel bought two thousand dollars worth of tokens. As he handed them to Sekka, he thought it was probably just as well the efficient Mrs. Flint had given him free rein to access the HSBC account at will, otherwise he might have had a hard time justifying the purchase of two grand's worth of Blue Orchid Casino chips, as if acquisition of the two ivory pieces wasn't already sufficient grounds for inquiry.

The Thai and Chinese Baccarat and Tiger vs Dragon tables were heaving. Sekka and Sabine headed for the roulette wheel which was marginally less crowded. The dealers, Keel noted, were predominantly Burmese or Lao, though all were clearly fluent in Mandarin. He watched as Sekka placed half a dozen chips on red, saw Sabine clap her hands and smile when the colour came up. Sekka handed her some chips and she spread them around the board. Sekka stuck with red. The wheel spun. Sabine lost all her counters, Sekka won again.

"Welcome to Golden Kingdom."

The greeting had been voiced in English, though the accent also carried a faint whiff of Strine. Keel turned his head.

"How are you doing? Name's Bracken, Saul Bracken. Casino security."

435

Keel took the proffered hand and gave his name.

"A Brit, right?" Bracken said.

"That's right," Keel said, thinking that 'Brit' was at least marginally better than 'Pom'.

Zheng's security chief was dressed in navy slacks and a maroon jacket with a dark blue waistcoat. His hair was cut in a military-style fade: short at the sides, flight deck flat on top. He looked slightly more thickset than he did in the photo Cade had provided, but most of it, Keel judged, was probably muscle.

Bracken lifted his chin towards where Sabine was placing another half-dozen chips on the board. "Saw you come in. How's your man doing?"

"Too early to tell," Keel said.

"Interesting looking guy. What's his story?"

"Story?" Keel said.

"No offence meant," Bracken said quickly, holding up a placatory hand. "Only we don't get many black guys in here is what I'm saying."

"No problem," Keel responded. "Family's Nigerian."

"Yeah? You on vacation?"

Keel shook his head and nodded in Sekka's direction. "He does freelance work for Shell Nigeria. Been over in Bangkok for meetings with PTT; finished up sooner than expected and had some time to kill, so he opted for a little R&R before heading home. One of the PTT guys mentioned the SEZ. Figured we were close enough to come check you out."

"He likes a wager then?"

"Sure, who doesn't?"

"Gotta spend it on something, right?" Bracken smiled, then said, "You'll be ex-forces, yeah?"

"It's that obvious?" Keel said.

Bracken grinned. "Well, we don't get too many

436

civilians calling it 'R&R'. Plus it takes one to know one."

"Is that right?" Keel said, with just the right amount of feigned interest.

"Sixteen years ADF. Good times."

"Small world," Keel said. "How'd you end up here?"

Bracken, kept his eyes on the roulette table as he spoke. "Heard there was good money in the private sector. Decided to give it a try when I joined civvy street. Choice was either corporate security or your line of work: close protection. I went for corporate. Started out working for Crown. You heard of them?"

"The casino outfit? Sure."

"With them for a few years, learning the trade. Met the boss in Macao. He offered me this gig so I figured why not? Senior position, better pay. So far, so good."

"Crown..." Keel said, frowning. "Wasn't there a bit of trouble with them a while back?"

A shadow flitted across the security chief's face. "Yeah, not the best of times. It's why I got out."

Keel nodded and looked over to where Sabine was holding onto Sekka's arm as he played with a stack of chips, separating it into halves and quarters and clicking individual chips between his fingers, debating his next move. A small pile of chips sat on the baize in front of him.

"I reckon your guy must be up by now," Bracken said. "Attractive lady, by the way. Italian?"

"French."

"They married?"

"Just good friends."

Bracken chuckled and surveyed the room, before bringing his focus back onto the roulette wheel. "So, I heard you guys went shopping this afternoon."

Keel turned, deliberately hardening his expression.

437

Bracken held up his hands in a sign of mock surrender. "Small town, word gets around."

"And you don't get too many black guys."

Bracken smiled. "Like I said. So, what, they don't sell ivory in Nigeria?"

"Sure they do, but they're clamping down, trying to save the herds. Means he has to shop around. He's just bought a pad in the UAE so he's always on the lookout for stuff to put in it: furniture, art works, that sort of thing. Likes to attend auctions."

There came a two second pause, then: "So he's a collector?"

"Strictly amateur. Got a good eye, though. Knows quality when he sees it. Likes the finer things."

"I can tell." Bracken said, looking towards Sabine. "He a fair boss to work for?"

"Has his moments, but yeah, pretty good."

"Worked for him long?"

"A while, mostly on away trips. He has local help when he's on home soil."

"You ever had to step in? Protect him from the bad guys?"

You have no idea.

"Once or twice."

Bracken nodded absently, took another glance around the crowded floor, before turning back. "Reason I mentioned your shopping trip is that I wondered if you guys were going to be staying in GK long."

"Maybe, if he hits a winning streak. Why'd you ask?"

"You said your man likes auctions. "

"So?"

"So, it occurred to me if you *were* sticking around,

438

he might like to attend one we've got coming up. Could be right up his street."

"Yeah? How so?"

"Can't give too much away, but if your guy liked what he saw this afternoon and he's interested in adding to his collection, I don't reckon he'll be disappointed."

Keel nodded thoughtfully. "Have to ask, but is it legit?"

Bracken smiled. "Let's just say it's not aimed at the general public. More like a select clientele with a liking for the exotic. The boss'll be doing the honours."

"The boss?"

"Zheng, the guy who recruited me. He's the one who built the resort. It's his baby."

Keel waited a couple of seconds, as if considering his decision, then said, "Okay, well, you've got *my* attention. When is it?"

"Day after tomorrow. There'll be entertainment laid on as well. If your guy's into hunting, he'll fit right in. Unless he's one of those, whadda they call them...environmental protection pussies?"

"I told, he's from Nigeria," Keel said. "Hausa tribe. What do *you* think?"

"I think he might enjoy himself. What about you? You hunt?"

When it's necessary,

"Sure, here and there," Keel said.

"That case, hope you can join us."

"I'll pass the word," Keel said. "If it's a yes, how do I get in touch?"

Bracken drew a card from his pocket. "My cell number. Don't worry about transport. It'll be laid on. All part of the service."

439

Keel took the card. "Sounds good. I'll let you know."

"You bet. In the meantime, I got a casino to patrol, so I'll leave you to it." Bracken held out his hand. "Good to meet you, Thomas. Hope to see you again."

"Me, too," Keel said, as they shook. He watched Bracken walk away, waited until he was out of sight, then went to stand by Sekka's shoulder. "Time out. We've got a bite."

Sekka and Sabine collected up their chips and the three of them made their way to the lounge where the piano player was regaling his thinning audience with a selection from Debussy,

"So?" Sekka said, when they were seated and after Keel had caught the eye of a passing server and ordered three iced teas.

"We've been invited to an auction," Keel told him.

Sekka let out a sigh.

Sabine kneaded the ivory bracelet. "Will Zheng be there?"

"According to Bracken, he's running the thing."

"Master of Ceremonies," Sekka murmured.

"Something like that," Keel said. "There's entertainment being laid on, too. He asked me if you liked to hunt."

Sabine drew in a sharp breath.

"Hunt?" Sekka's eyebrows rose. "He say what?"

They paused as the server returned with the drinks.

Keel shook his head. "I'll frisk him for more info when I let him know we'll be there."

Sabine remained silent, though Keel knew what must have been going through her mind. Hunting an animal for sport had not been on the agenda.

"You think he knew our names before he made his

440

approach?" Sekka asked.

"Checked with the hotel, you mean?" Keel said.

Sekka nodded.

"It's what I'd have done. Though, he didn't question your nationality when I told him you were Nigerian."

"You mean if he *had* checked, he'd know I'm travelling on my Dutch passport?"

"Be my guess, but then maybe he figures you're doing it out of convenience, which would be correct. He'd probably tie it in with my telling him you were in the oil business. I mentioned that and his eyes lit up. Oil equals money and Nigerian oil usually equals corruption of some sort...allegedly. My guess is he sees you as a guy with money to spend, who isn't too bothered about the legalities. I doubt he'd have cast his invite, otherwise."

"And purchasing that ivory," Sabine said, having found her voice, "helped our...what do you call it...cover story, yes?"

"Hopefully," Keel said, "along with the visit to the roulette table. With luck he's reporting back to his boss, telling him there's a new whale in town."

"Whale..?" Sabine said.

"It's what casinos call a high roller, someone who gambles large amounts of money. If this was Vegas, they'd probably spot Joseph as a mark to cultivate in order to lure him back to the tables, by offering him a penthouse suite and a private limo, that sort of thing. In GK's case, it's been an invite to their auction."

"Makes me wonder how many other folk might be here for the sale, too," Sekka said. "You spot any likely candidates?"

"A couple," Keel said. "Maybe. There were three Chinese guys at the Baccarat table who looked

441

interesting. The one who wasn't playing spent a lot of time casing the room. Means he's probably doing the same job as me."

"And I heard two players at the roulette wheel talking about a *pāimài huì*," Sabine cut in. "It means auction in Chinese."

"One of them have a blonde hanging onto his arm?" Keel asked.

Sabine nodded. "One of the Ukranian girls."

She wasn't the first East European hooker Keel had spotted. Given the setting and their appearance - young, slender, long-legged and mostly blonde - they stuck out like sore thumbs. There had been a couple over at the Baccarat table, standing behind the two Chinese players, both of whom had been wearing headsets, marking them as professionals; probably taking orders from gamblers in China. Two piles of ten-thousand yuan card chips had sat on the table between them.

"So we'll assume they're around," Keel said.

Sekka took a sip of iced tea, the fixed Keel with a calm gaze. "Might as well make the call."

Keel nodded, fished out his phone and thumbed in Bracken's number. It took a couple of seconds for the response to come through. "Saul? Thomas Keel. I've spoke with my principal. We'd be happy to accept the auction invite."

"Ripper!" The security chief sounded genuinely pleased. "I'll have the details delivered to your room."

"And about the hunt," Keel said.

"Yeah? You up for that, too?"

"Possibly. My principal wants to know the type of game involved."

A chuckle sounded at the other end of the phone.

Then: "How's he feel about a tiger shoot?"
"Count us in," Keel said.

24

"A tiger?" Sabine said hollowly, the blood draining from her face, when Keel ended the call and relayed what Bracken had told him. "Was he serious?"

"Sounded like it," Keel said. "Seems they've got this new site up in the hills behind the resort; what they call their zoo. There used to be a menagerie down near the river, on the opposite side of the road from the hotel, but they were running out of cage room. Now that they've shifted location and expanded, they've got all sorts up there, not just tigers; bears and monkeys, too. It's probably where the little guy in the cage came from."

Sabine let out a low groan.

"It's like Cade told us," Sekka said. "They're farming animals for the pot."

"And medicine," Keel said, "and pelts. According to Bracken, folk get to pick the animal they want for parts, like choosing your dinner from a bunch of lobsters in a tank. They even run their own abattoir to cope with the demand. There's a full service; from killing to bagging and tagging, and everything's shippable."

Sabine stared at Keel in horror. "And you said yes?"

"Absolutely," Keel

"You can't mean it!"

"Going after a tiger? Of course not."

"Then why did you accept?"

"I accepted because according to Bracken, Zheng's going to be joining us on the hunt."

It was Sekka who broke the ensuing silence. "Where's the hunt taking place?"

"Golden Dragon Mountain. It's their name for the high ground at the edge of the zone. There's a five hundred acre enclosure up near the zoo. The idea is you pick your animal and they release it into the enclosure. They give you a gun and a guide and you get to be Jim Corbett for however long it takes you to bag your trophy. Once you've done that, the rest is taken care of. Like one of these pure cremation services, where the funeral firm takes the body and you get presented with the ashes, or in this case the bones, skin and teeth."

"*C'est barbare!*" Sabine hissed.

"That it is," Keel agreed.

"So how do we play this?" Sekka asked.

"Not sure," Keel said. "Maybe start with a recce: you and me, tonight."

"Sounds like a plan," Sekka said.

"What do we know about Cade's informant?" Sekka asked as he gazed down at the satellite images of the Golden Kingdom resort that Cade had e-mailed to them in Dubai.

They were back at the hotel, in Keel and Sekka's room. The information was spread out on Sekka's bed.

"Not a hell of a lot, other than she's female and worked in the casino."

"Until she disappeared off Cade's radar."

Keel nodded.

"Do we have a name?"

"Lulani Yang."

Sekka continued to study the photos. "I'm assuming she's how Cade got the information on the location of Zheng's compound and the new zoo site. Google Earth's no help. Street level detail only covers Vientiane and maybe a couple of other cities. Without this..." Sekka pointed to the hand-written notations, "...we'd be flying blind." He looked up. "You said Cade's asked us to look for her?"

"Not specifically, more like keep an eye open."

"Got a description?"

"Got a snapshot. It's from a group photo on the LCTW website."

"The what?"

"The Lao Conservation Trust for Wildlife. According to Cade, Yang's a member of the Trust's bear team."

Keel retrieved his phone, flicked a couple of buttons and held it out. The screen showed a young woman in a forest-green t-shirt emblazoned with the LCTW logo above her left breast. On either side of her could be seen the edge of an arm, indicating where the photo had been cropped. She wore no makeup and her hair was drawn back in a plait. Apart from a small horizontal scar on the right side of her forehead, just below her hairline, her broad face was unlined and set in a neutral expression, though a slight upturn of the lips hinted that a hesitant smile might be about to appear. There was a timeless quality to her looks, common to many Asian women. Possibly in her late twenties, she could just as easily have been a decade older.

447

"She volunteered to work undercover at GK and report back on what was going. The Trust works with ROUTES and TRAFFIC which is how she and Cade linked up."

"The Trust know she's Cade's informant?"

"Not sure. Cade was a bit vague about that."

"Do they know she's missing?"

"Don't know that either."

"Seems to me there's a lot we don't know," Sekka said.

"Wouldn't disagree," Keel said. He turned to Sabine who had remained silent during the exchange, noting that she had removed the ivory bracelet. "What are you thinking?"

"I'm thinking I should join you on your reconnaissance."

"Okay," Keel said warily, and waited, knowing an explanation was on its way.

"Two men and a woman together are less likely to attract attention than two men, who are not locals, and who might be considered to be acting suspiciously," Sabine said.

"*Acting suspiciously?*"

Sabine ignored the rejoinder. "That way, if we are stopped, I can pretend to be a *prostituée* you have hired for the evening."

"And that wouldn't be at all suspicious," Keel said drily.

"Plus," Sabine said, unfazed, "if you *are* planning on investigating the zoo, I can be useful. I have more experience with captive animals and their environment than either you or Joseph. I may see something that you do not."

Keel regarded her levelly. "Why do I get the feeling

that if I said no way, you'd end up following us anyway?"

"So it is agreed?"

Keel glanced down at Sabine's footwear. "As long as you ditch the heels."

Sabine gave him the look. "*Idiot!*" she said softly, but with a less than subtle eye roll.

They took the Fortuner. Keel drove.

Leaving the bright lights of the Casino and China-town behind them, it wasn't long before the tarmac petered out and the forest began to rise up around them, giving way to a more rugged, dirt-road surface. But then, just as they rounded a bend, the view changed yet again.

"At least they're not trying to hide it," Keel said.

The two huge carved figures sprang out of the shadows. Mounted on heavy stone plinths, and crafted into the shape of a rearing bear on one side and a snarling tiger on the other, they flanked a pair of solid wooden gates, above which, carved in Lao and Chinese calligraphy and English script, was the inscription: *Golden Kingdom Bear & Tiger Mountain Village.*

The gates were closed; not surprisingly, given the hour, and there didn't appear to be any signs of life in the immediate vicinity as Keel took the Fortuner past. Due to an impressively high wooden fence, it was also hard to see if there were any lights on inside the zoo's grounds.

They'd gone another two hundred yards when the Fortuner's headlights picked out an opening in the trees to the left, and the beginnings of what looked like a rough forest trail.

"There," Sekka said.

Keel swung the Fortuner off the road. The trail was indeed narrow, not much wider than the 4x4, but while the surface was furrowed and uneven, it wasn't bad enough to warrant use of the vehicle's traction control.

"We're on the zoo side," Sekka said. "Means there's got to be a fence somewhere ahead. We'd better dismount."

Fifty yards further on, Keel eased the Fortuner to a halt and reversed beneath the canopy. Turning the wheel, but remaining under cover, he edged the 4x4 forward so that it was facing the way they'd come, in case they needed to make a quick getaway.

Exiting the vehicle, they paused, and listened. All three of them had changed into dark, neutral clothing, and with the trees filtering the moonlight they were well camouflaged; more so than the Fortuner, but Keel was gambling that the odds of anyone wandering along the trail and spotting the 4x4 were relatively slim. It was a chance they'd have to take.

Other than the incessant buzz of crickets, the forest was still and silent around them, as if the rest of the inhabitants were being held in some sort of hypnotic trance. But, then, gradually as they waited, the birds and frogs began to take up the refrain and within seconds, the air was vibrating with night-time chatter.

Lit by moonlight, but hemmed in by shadows, it was an eerie five-minute hike to the fence. Studying it, they could see that here, unlike the section bordering the main gate, it was constructed from two materials. A stout, five-foot high wooden barrier formed the base, while the remaining fifteen feet were fashioned from stanchions supporting horizontal metal struts,

450

buttressed by a chain-link wire mesh, the top of which was folded inwards as an added precaution in case anything inside the fence decided to make a break for it.

What was immediately apparent was the glow from the lights within the zoo grounds. Set high on posts, they weren't particularly bright, but they were strong enough, nevertheless, to illuminate the structures arranged beneath them: rows of close-packed wire pens.

Sabine gazed at the barrier in dismay. "How do we get inside?"

Keel picked up a twig and tossed it at the wire mesh. When nothing happened, indicating the fence wasn't electrified, he said, "Work our way along. Find a weak spot."

Sabine regarded him doubtfully.

"He's right," Sekka said. "Someone will have screwed up somewhere along the line. They always do."

A primeval growl split the night, causing the three of them to freeze.

"Tiger!" Sabine hissed, staring through the wire towards the pens.

"No shit," Keel swore softly, as the short hairs returned to their dormant state across the back of his neck. While the eruption had seemed to come from perilously close by, Keel knew sound tended to travel further during the hours of darkness. Even so, it was a reminder that the other side of the wire was home to creatures that were quite capable of tearing a body limb from limb no matter what time of day it was.

Nerves taut, they resumed their passage along the fence line until Keel, who'd taken point, paused in mid-stride and said softly, "Bingo."

From the depression in the ground and the nearby mound of earth, it appeared as if some sort of drainage or irrigation channel was being dug. A hole had been cut in the fence to accommodate the ditch and, with the task half-completed, the gap in the barrier had been shored up with a raw-cut timber panel.

"So much for health and safety," Sekka murmured, as he moved the panel out of the way.

Keel turned to Sabine. "Decision time. You in or out?"

She looked back at him. The challenge was there. "Do you wish *me* to go first, or *you*?"

Keel nodded without speaking, turned back, and led the way through the breach. When they were inside the wire, Sekka eased the panel back into place. As he did so, a fresh series of growls and earthy grunts arose from the gloom, accompanied by a chorus of raucous shrieks.

"Macaques," Sabine whispered, and before either Keel or Sekka could stop her, she headed in the direction of the noise.

Keel let go a curse as he and Sekka set off in pursuit. As they approached the closest pen, he heard Sabine suck in her breath. Following her gaze Keel felt his heart sink. The caged bear cub back in Chinatown had been a depressing enough sight. This was worse.

Even in the semi-gloom it wasn't hard to see that the pens were small, perhaps four metres square, with featureless interiors. There was only the wire and a flat concrete floor set beneath a sloping tin roof designed to ward off the elements, but which looked severely inadequate to the task. A metal tray, half filled with water and set into the floor in a corner of the

452

cage, was the only source of nourishment. What made the spartan conditions more acute was the fact that several of the pens housed more than one animal.

It wasn't a zoo, it was a concentration camp.

And these weren't macaques.

Sabine stared at the tiger crouched at the back of the nearest pen. Belly to the ground, ears flattened against its skull, eyes glittering and teeth bared, it regarded Sabine with a mixture of hatred and fear, while emitting hisses and growls which, despite the animal's confinement, were still capable of chilling the blood.

"There are more tigers kept on farms than there are alive in the wild," Sabine said, her voice just above a whisper. "No one knows how many of them are killed each year. It could be hundreds. They slaughter them between the ages of two and three. The lucky ones are put down by injection. They electrocute or garrote the others using an elastic string."

She shook her head, her jaw clenched. "Some buyers are only interested in the meat, though they are careful not to damage the skin as that is all the other buyers may want. Teeth and claws are taken to make jewellery; bones are used to make the wine. They crush them and soak them in rice liqueur. It takes up to eight years to mature. The longer the maceration period, the more expensive the bottle. The cheaper versions contain material such as bone from dogs or pigs, or, sometimes, from bears and horses. They also use goat's blood, moss and cockroaches. There are said to be more than two hundred variants. I do not know if that is true."

Sabine held the tiger's gaze. The animal's ferocious expression had not faltered. "The Chinese believe the wine to be a powerful medicine. They use it to treat arthritis. The Chinese State Forestry Administration oversees the farms. Conservationists call it the Dragon."

Sabine smiled grimly. "It tells the world it is there to protect the wild tiger population. That is not true. Wild tigers are caught and killed and passed off as farmed tigers because the people who buy the wine say that wine made from wild tigers is more efficacious than wine made from tigers that are farmed."

Sekka said, "They don't just buy them in, they breed them as well, yes?"

"They take the cubs from their mothers when they are a few days old and hand-rear them. That way, the mother can be introduced to another male so that she can produce more cubs, perhaps as many as three litters a year. Wild tigers give birth perhaps every two to three years."

"There have been efforts to increase tiger populations, though," Sekka said.

Sabine nodded. "In 2010 there was a commitment made by the thirteen Asian tiger-range countries to double their tiger population by 2022. Nepal is the only one to have achieved that target."

As she spoke, Sabine moved to the next pen from which two sets of eyes glared back at her. "Most likely every one of these animals will have been born here, which means they will die here. Even if the farm was shut down tomorrow, there are not enough sanctuaries to take them. They do not know how to hunt and because of inbreeding, there is a danger they could carry disease, so they cannot be released into the wild. These animals will require human care for the rest of their lives, which will not be for very long, I

454

think."

The nearest tiger moved with frightening speed.

Keel had a sudden and startling vision of an open maw and yellow teeth and gleaming eyes as the enraged animal hurled itself at the wire mesh with a vicious snarl. Sabine leapt back in shock, as the beast reared above her, claws protruding through the metal strands, the wire mesh vibrating under the assault. Then, as abruptly as it had attacked, the tiger let out a low cough and dropped back onto all fours, tail swishing.

Immediately, Sabine moved back towards the wire and crouched down. Pursing her lips she began to expel air through her front teeth in a sequence of short exhalations. What emerged sounded like a cross between a clearing of the throat and a cat's purr. Astonishingly, after several seconds, the tension seemed to leave the tiger's body and, ears raised, it settled down on the floor, next to its cellmate, which, in all that time, hadn't moved. Keel couldn't tell if it was asleep or dead.

"It is called chuffing." Sabine kept her voice low. "Tigers use it to communicate. It is a sign of non-aggression. Mothers use it to calm their cubs."

Sekka's voice came from the shadows. "We've got bears in the next row."

Keel and Sabine were unaware that Sekka had left them. Sabine got to her feet and she and Keel went to join him.

The bear pens weren't much bigger than the ones holding the tigers and just as devoid of stimuli. The bears weren't small either, so space was still at a premium. Not that any of them looked active. Like the tigers, most appeared listless and showed little interest in the night-time visitors; pacing back and forth, heads rolling, a clear sign of stress and/or brain dysfunction brought on by captivity and sensory deprivation.

"Is any of this even legal?" Sekka asked.

Sabine shook her head. "It is against the law to hunt or capture bears in Laos."

"But this is China," Keel said. "Or as good as. Right?"

"And Zheng's protected," Sekka said. "So who's going to complain?"

Keel didn't respond. Bracken had told him the zoo was temporarily closed to visitors. From the evidence before them, seeing the conditions in which the animals were kept, it wasn't hard to see why. He was wondering if there were any of Zheng's employees on site, or if, in the absence of human watchdogs, there were any cameras running.

There didn't appear to be much in the way of security, other than the fence and the poor lighting; certainly no immediate signs of human activity. There had been security guards in the casino, but maybe Zheng didn't put as much store into guarding his menagerie as he did his gambling chips. In any case, who in their right mind would want to steal one of his animals, anyway? Nevertheless, it made sense to stay alert.

Sabine did not speak. Her gaze had shifted towards a low, single-story building over to the side. She frowned and then stiffened.

"What?" Keel said.

"There is something I need to check." There was a catch in her voice.

"Okay," Keel said, placing a hand on her arm. "But best wait a sec. Sher Khan here might have woken up the night shift."

"What?" Sabine looked momentarily confused.

"He's saying there might be guards who've been alerted by the noise," Sekka said.

Keel eyed the building. There were windows but no lights were showing inside and nothing moved in the darkness. As he scanned the area, Keel couldn't see anything that resembled a CCTV system, which could have been due to the zoo switching locations. Taking the half-dug irrigation ditch, or whatever it was, into consideration, it looked as if the facility was still under construction and maybe CCTV was part of the plan but hadn't yet been installed. File that under blessings counted.

After giving it a few more seconds, Keel tapped Sabine on the shoulder and he and Sekka trailed her to her target: a row of white-painted, waist-high metal containers aligned against the wall of the building. Storage receptacles, Keel supposed, but as he drew closer he became aware of a low, persistent hum.

"Refrigeration units," Sekka muttered.

The freezers were top loaders. Visibly steeling herself, Sabine stepped up to the nearest one and tested the lid. Finding it wasn't locked, she lifted it up. "*Enculés!*" she spat as an interior light illuminated the contents.

The cubs, Keel guessed, couldn't have been more than a couple of weeks old. Their tiny corpses entwined, they might have been asleep had it not been for the layer of rime that coated their striped fur. It was hard to tell how many there were all told, due to them being piled atop one another. At least a dozen, Keel guessed.

Sabine stared down at the dead animals and then

457

closed the lid. "I was in Bangkok when the Thai police raided the Tiger Temple and found the remains of forty cubs in one of the temple's freezers. When I saw these containers I wondered if I would find the same thing."

Sekka opened the second freezer. "Got bears in this one and some sort of...I don't know what it is."

"It's a binturong," Sabine said, the nerve along her jawline pulsing as she studied the frozen body, which was long and heavy, slightly larger than a Maine Coon cat, with a covering of charcoal grey fur, a thick bushy tail and a set of long wiry whiskers. "They are on the threatened species list."

"Be surprised if anything in here wasn't," Keel said. "And what the hell is *that*?"

The binturong lay on top of what were clearly the bodies of two moon bears: a cub and an adult male. Their pale chest markings were still visible beneath the layer of frost.

Sabine looked to where Keel was indicating. *"Merde,"* she muttered darkly, before sighing resignedly. *"C'est un robinet.* Ah, no... *un cathéter.* It is for collecting the bile."

"Jesus," Keel muttered as he gazed at the end of a thin metal tube poking out from the adult bear's lower abdomen.

"Bears that are farmed for bile are kept in cages so small they are unable to move." Sabine's anger was palpable. "Their paws are tied to the bars to prevent movement, while the tube is inserted and the bile extracted from the gallbladder. You can see here the adult's claws were removed to make it safer for the keepers. They also break the teeth, usually with a hammer. The *cathéter* is kept in place so they can drain the animal at will, which is what they did with this one, and someone has forgotten to remove it. Many farms breed bears so that they can have a constant supply. There are adult bears that will have spent their whole life in the cage, sometimes as long as thirty years.

"This one was lucky," she added, looking down at the smaller corpse. Tentatively, she reached out and eased open one side of the cub's mouth to reveal a ravaged gum line. "But they still broke its teeth before it died."

Sekka said quietly from the side, "Thomas."

Keel turned. There had been something in Sekka's voice, a note of warning coupled with despair.

The third cabinet contained the bodies of two adult tigers, what was left of them. It looked, Hawkwood thought, as if the cats had been run over by a steam roller, left out in heavy rain for a week and then placed in the unit for safe keeping, prior to their eventual conversion into rugs or stuffed ornaments. Their empty pelts were all that remained, their bones having been removed, presumably at the behest of Zheng's wine-maker.

But it wasn't the skins that had drawn Sekka's attention.

It was the third body.

"Oh, God," Sabine breathed, possibly unaware that she had spoken in English.

Like the tiger skins, the corpse was covered in a thin coating of ice crystals, at least the part that was visible. The bulk of it was concealed by the pelts, save for the right arm, which was in full view and dressed in a length of dark-coloured sleeve. Keel lifted the pelts aside to reveal the rest of the cadaver, which was

459

female and dressed in a casino worker's uniform.

Reaching down, Keel wiped a finger across the corpse's right temple, removing the layer of rime to reveal the scar. He straightened and stepped back. "Cade's missing asset."

"They *killed* her?" Sabine said, her voice echoing her disbelief.

"Explains why she went dark," Sekka said. "Can you tell how she died?"

Keel shook his head. Replacing the pelts, he closed the freezer lid. "And we don't have time for an autopsy. We go. Now."

Sabine stared at him, as if to countermand the abrupt directive but then, recognizing the look of dark intent in his eyes, she nodded.

Retracing their steps to the tiger cages, they were at the corner when a sixth sense made Keel look over his shoulder, in time to see a door opening in the building they'd just left. A figure appeared, silhouetted against the dim light radiating from within.

The windows, Keel realized, must have been fitted with some sort of blackout blind to prevent light from escaping, which made him wonder what activity was going on inside. As Keel watched, he saw the flare as a match was struck and the glow as a cigarette was ignited. A second figure joined the first and a second cigarette was fired up.

Move," Keel said, ducking into shadow, "In case they decide to stretch their legs."

Leaving the same way they'd arrived, when they had let themselves out through the break in the fence, Sekka levered the wooden panel back into place and they retraced their path to the Fortuner, where they sat without speaking, each of them absorbed in thought.

"Well, at least we know what we're dealing with," Sekka murmured from the rear seat, Sabine having joined Keel up front.

"Yes, but what do we do about it?" Sabine asked. "What *can* we do?"

Keel started the engine. "Teach them the error of their ways."

It was statement devoid of humour.

Heading back down the trail, when they arrived at the spot where the trail joined the road, instead of turning right towards the resort, Keel brought the 4x4 to a stop and rested his hands on top of the wheel.

"What?" Sekka said, leaning forward.

Keel said. "My turn; something I spotted earlier that might give us an edge."

Sekka frowned. "Care to share?"

"May not come to anything," Keel said. "Be easier to explain if and when we get there."

"All right." Sekka sat back. "Lead on, boss."

Sabine grunted and grabbed the dashboard as Keel hauled the wheel to the left, spewing dirt as he turned them on to the more solid road surface. There was no other traffic and no signs of habitation, and as they continued to climb steeply the forest grew thick and dark around them. It was only a minute or so later when a semi-circular patch of bare ground appeared on the outside of a bend on the driver's side of the road, along with a small, open-fronted wooden shelter that bore all the hallmarks of an in-country bus stop.

Keel pulled the Fortuner across the road and parked next to the shelter. Exiting the vehicle, he led the way to where a hand-painted sign written in several languages, identified the spot, not as a bus halt, but the start of the Golden Dragon Mountain hiking trail. A narrow path led off into the forest alongside it.

The sign was just readable in the moonlight, enough at any rate to make out a crudely drawn map, marking the trail loop in a series of dashes, and a list of the landmarks visible along its length, notably a viewing point and the ruins of what looked to be some sort of shrine or small temple.

Sekka eyed the sign and the path leading away from it, but said nothing as he and Sabine trailed Keel into the trees.

They had gone around two hundred yards when the path widened out and the ruin came into sight. It might have been a graceful temple once, but the undergrowth had long since claimed ownership. Segments of moss-covered wall and part of a pointed roof were all that remained. Remnants of what might have been an altar, or possibly a base for a spirit house, sat to one side, half hidden under a tangle of tree roots. A large, cracked, stone bowl lay on the ground next to it, while a few feet away, trapped by a patch of moonlight, a clay built, oven-like object which had probably been used to burn joss paper, sat covered in weeds. It was decorated with the carving of a small dragon,

It wasn't the ruin, however, but the ground in front of it that drew Keel's attention. The temple had been constructed on what was, effectively, a small plateau. A mosaic of broken, lichen-encrusted paving slabs, led away from the building only to end abruptly at the point where the ground plunged away sharply before merging into the darkened forest below. A jumble of debris just below the rim had formed a series of rocky outcrops that was dotted with bushes which suggested there had probably been a landslip at some time in the past, probably as a result of heavy rain.

Mindful of where he placed his feet, Keel crouched on the edge of the drop and studied the view spread out before them.

Cade had referred to the resort as an Oriental version of Las Vegas. It hadn't been hard to see why at ground level. At this elevation, the comparison was even more acute. The eye was immediately drawn to the brash array of neon on the casino roof, with the giant crown as the centrepiece. From there, the light show radiated outwards, as brash and as gaudy as a fairground attraction, creating a bright pulsating grid pattern along the streets of Chinatown, from the gift emporia to the restaurants in Food Street and a tangle of narrower alleyways, which, Keel guessed, probably housed the resort's massage parlours.

Beyond the resort, smaller moving lights indicated the passage of river traffic. Beyond those, the lights of Sop Ruak twinkled along the Mekong's west bank; the brightest feature being the *Phra Chiang Saen Si Phaendin,* which, illuminated from below, appeared to float above its surroundings like some alien being from a distant star system.

"Good vantage point," Sekka said.

Keel did not look up. "Hotel brochure mentioned a hiking trail. There was a photo alongside it. Didn't realize until we infiltrated the place that it showed part of the zoo. Meant it had to have been taken from higher up. Figured it was worth a dekko; see if we could find the spot."

Due to the nature of the terrain and the tight curves on the road, they'd probably only ascended five hundred or so metres. Sufficient, nevertheless, to have

463

been rewarded with a bird's eye view of the outbuildings and animal enclosures laid out below them.

Sabine, standing at Keel's other shoulder, followed his and Sekka's gaze. "It looks so peaceful."

"Hard to spot cruelty at a distance," Sekka said. He turned to Keel. "How much space do we need?"

Keel fixed his eyes on the area of open ground near to the bear and tiger cages. "According to Crow, safety margin's a hundred feet by a hundred feet."

"Not a lot to play with."

"No, but doable. Any case, I can't see us getting a better chance, so we'll take what we can get."

"Think Cade knows it was never going to be a dry run?" Sekka murmured.

Keel didn't reply. A short silence followed, broken when Sabine said softly, "Tomorrow, then."

Keel nodded. "Tomorrow. All in favour, say 'Aye'."

Neither Sekka nor Sabine offered a reply.

"Well, at least look on the bright side," Keel said.

"They both regarded him expectantly.

Keel smiled. "We'll have the element of surprise and they'll be giving us the guns for free."

25

It was two minutes after 9am, and the thermometer behind the reception desk was already pushing 26 degrees, when Bracken's driver met them in the hotel lobby. Chinese, mid-thirties, sallow-complexioned with slick-backed hair and clad in dark slacks and a short-sleeved white shirt, he greeted them with a polite bow and introduced himself as Huan before leading them out to the car park and a silver BMW saloon, where he directed Sekka and Sabine into the rear seats, leaving Keel to occupy the passenger side upfront. Servants' quarters, Keel thought, as he settled himself in. With the humidity rising as fast as the temperature outside, the air conditioning came as a welcome relief.

Keel made no attempt to engage their driver in conversation and both Sekka and Sabine remained silent during the ride. The zoo gates were still closed, but as the car drew near they opened to allow admittance. Passing under the two massive animal guardians, Keel just had time to catch a glimpse of the English wording on a sign at the side of the entrance that they had missed the night before - *Caring For Rare Animals. Protect The Blue Planet* - before the gates slid shut behind them.

There was no sign of anything approaching a ticket

office or a gift shop, Keel noted; which went some way to confirm that the word 'zoo' was indeed a misnomer and that Zheng had no intention of opening the place to the public. The facility had been constructed for no other reason that to breed animals for exploitation, as had been made clear by the nocturnal sortie.

Zheng's security chief was waiting for them in front of a long, low, pre-fab building which Keel recognized as the one from the night before, complete with the cold storage containers alongside.

"Good to see you, Thomas," Bracken said, holding out his hand, as Keel vacated the BMW.

"You, too," Keel said. Turning, he waited as Sekka and Sabine exited the vehicle, and then made the introductions. "Mr. Joseph Sekka and Miss Sabine Bouvier."

Bracken shook hands with both of them. "Welcome to Golden Kingdom. Call me Saul."

Bracken wasn't alone. With him were two competent-looking Asian males, both of whom, Keel assumed, from their olive green uniforms and black berets, were members of the zoo staff or, more likely, animal wranglers, to judge from the Magnum rifles they had slung over their shoulders. As well as the rifle, each of them sported a handgun in a waist holster; as did Bracken.

9mm automatics - Chinese-made, Keel guessed. In line with the ordnance he was carrying, Bracken had forsaken his casino wear for khaki pants with matching shirt and a maroon baseball cap complete with the letters GK sewn into the peak in gold thread. He threw a critical eye over his visitors' choice of apparel and appeared satisfied with their dun-coloured cargo trousers and shirts. Keel and Sekka were bare-headed. Sabine's hair was contained by her grey cap. Her bag was slung over her shoulder. Keel and Sekka were unencumbered.

"What say we kick things off with a look at some of those auction lots?" Bracken regarded each of them expectantly. "Give you an idea of what's on offer. How's that sound?"

"Sounds good," Keel said. He looked Sekka, who nodded.

"Excellent!" Bracken said, grinning, his Strine accent coming to the fore. "Right this way, folks..."

Keel had no idea what the value of the ivory arranged across the line of table tops might be. He knew only that it had to run into thousands of dollars, if not hundreds of thousands. The tusks - scores of them in total - were arranged in descending order of size from left to right; the biggest coming in at well over two hundred centimetres in length, with the shortest not much longer than a table knife. The colour varied; from burnt coffee to sandalwood, to ones with a paler, creamier tint. Many carried dark residue stains that might once have been spilled blood or decayed flesh.

It struck Keel, as he gazed at the display, that somewhere in the haul there had to be the tusks taken from the elephants at Salma. He stole a glance towards Sekka and Sabine. Sabine's complexion had lost some of its colour and look in her eyes told its own story. Sekka's expression had assumed a neutral pose, but Keel knew from past experience that anger was hovering very close to the surface and that Sekka was managing to keep his rage in check through sheer will power. Bracken was walking slightly ahead of them

467

and did not appear to have noticed his visitors' shift of mood.

Next in line were two trestle tables bearing a selection of rhino horn. Stacked alongside those were more than two dozen large hessian sacks filled to the brim with what looked like flattened brown sea shells or shards of sharpened flint.

"Pangolin scales." Bracken lifted out a handful and let them fall from his fingers back into the sack. "Primo stock. Should fetch a good price. But they're just the appetizer. Wait 'til you get a load of the main course"

A sideways glance at the tables reminded Keel of the video clips he'd seen whereby anti-poaching units, police, and customs officers showed off the contraband they'd collected following the interception of a smuggled cargo. He didn't dare risk looking towards Sabine for fear that it would cause Bracken to do the same, thus enabling the security chief to read the thoughts that Keel knew would be flooding her mind even more forcefully than before; the same thoughts he was experiencing and which Sekka would also be trying to quell: thoughts of utter helplessness allied to a desire to make someone pay for perpetrating such rampant cruelty.

The next room contained exquisite examples of worked ivory, far surpassing anything on offer in the Chinatown stores, in both size and quality; from processions of elephants carved from a single tusk, ornate landscapes, temples and flowering trees, to representations of the Buddha and fauna, ranging from tigers and birds of paradise to panthers and peacocks, along with a selection of fist-sized puzzle balls, each one more intricately fashioned than any Fabergé egg.

Keel knew ivory could still be traded legally,

depending on the age of the item and or the amount of ivory contained within it. Buying and selling one hundred percent ivory that was more than a century old – the definition of antique – could be considered a legitimate transaction. Dealing in anything younger could result in a hefty fine and serious jail time.

The problem, as Duncan Bryce had explained, was that poached ivory was often concealed within older stock. Once carved and sold on, it was almost impossible to trace. The carved items here looked pristine with no visible sign of aging, suggesting they were the end product of a recent poaching raid and that as well as being offered for sale at auction, they were there to illustrate the carver's expertise and to inform prospective bidders that decorative pieces could also be made to order.

Passing through a partition doorway into the next area, they were confronted by more tables, adorned with a collection of skulls and bones.

"Tiger?" Keel ventured.

"And lion." Bracken lifted his chin to indicate the nearest skull. "Most of it's farmed; the rest is from canned hunts. The stuff's freighted in from Jo'burg via Mombasa. It's one of the ingredients in TCM. Cheaper than tiger bone, so there's a bigger profit margin."

TCM, Keel knew, was traditional Chinese medicine. His eyes drifted further along the room to an array of animal skins. The majority were tiger but there were others laid out on a separate table, including ocelot and jaguar; the ones among them with lustrous grey and white patterning instantly recognizable as snow leopard pelts.

Bracken reached out and ran his palm across the surface of the fur. "Beautiful, right? Folk like to make them into waistcoats or use them as floor decoration. Bones are used in medicines along with lion and tiger. There's not a lot of wastage." He smiled and lifted his hand away.

"*D'où viennent-ils?*"

Bracken paused. "Sorry, what did the lady say?"

"She asked you where the skins came from," Sekka said in English, putting extra stress into his pronunciation to emphasise his Nigerian roots.

"Ah, right," Bracken's head came up as he threw Sabine what might have been a cautionary look. "Nepal mostly. Traders in Kathmandu arrange shipment into Tibet and the Chinese networks take over from there."

When neither Sekka nor Sabine responded, he nodded in acquiescence and said, "Okay, let's see what else we've got. If you're looking for a pick-me-up, we got just the thing." He lifted an eyebrow in Keel's direction. "You familiar with *yaba*?"

"Not personally," Keel said.

Bracken favoured Sekka and Sabine with a speculative glance, but neither of them responded. Sekka's aloof expression was back in place, while Sabine's interest was still concentrated on the snow leopard pelt.

Bracken turned back. "Me neither, but you wouldn't believe the demand for the stuff. Labs can barely keep up."

As if to emphasise the point, the security chief nodded towards what had to be hundreds of blue plastic baggies, each the size of a peanut pack, that were arranged in neat rows not unlike a counter display in a sweet shop. A Couple of baggies had been split opened and the contents emptied onto a plate. The tablets were the colour of a terracotta tile and the

470

size of an aspirin, and embossed with the letters WY.

"Myanmar?" Keel attempted to look interested.

"Shan State. The boss's old stomping ground before he came here. We got good contacts with all the suppliers. Same with the China White."

Bracken nodded to where half a dozen tables groaned under the weight of what might have been mistaken for bags of brown sugar, but which bore a large red, circular stamp comprising two rampant lions holding a globe between them, framed by Chinese characters and embossed with the words: *Double Uoglobe Brand.*

"Been using that logo since the first Indochina War back in the fifties," Bracken said. "Marks the H as coming from the triangle and that it's the real thing. Buyers reroute it from here through Thailand and Hong Kong.

"Triads?" Keel said.

Bracken offered a knowing smile and then spread out an arm. "And last but not least."

Keel thought, *Jesus.*

One crate had been opened to display the contents. The rest of the consignment was stacked on pallets like bundles of cordwood.

Chinese-made QBZ-192 carbines, the same make as Bracken's 9mm. They must have come in as a job lot, Keel presumed. They were a shorter and lighter version of the 191, which in turn had been a relatively new design, meant as a replacement for the old 95 assault rifle. Including the crate that was open, Keel counted fifteen boxes in all; five carbines to each crate. "They come with ammo as well?"

"Absolutely," Bracken confirmed. "And this ain't all of it. You want RPGs, personnel mines; we can get

471

those, too."

"Who bids for this stuff?"

The question was met with a shrug. "Who the hell cares? Long as they part with the cash. This part of the world there's no shortage of private armies; folk pissed off with being ordered around by their government or threatened by some local warlord."

"So, how's the bidding work?"

"Simple. People turn up in person; we give them an ID number and a private viewing like we're doing with you guys. Or else they can view on-line. Once they're satisfied the lots are authentic, they tender a sealed bid. Couple of days later the winning bidder's notified. Money's transferred electronically and the goods are couriered to their destination of choice. The ones with influence use diplomatic pouches."

"And no one knows who they're bidding against."

"Correct."

Keel turned to Sekka and raised a questioning eyebrow as if to enquire if the method was acceptable. Sekka nodded.

Keel turned back.

"Don't talk much, does he?" Bracken said softly.

"You get used to it," Keel said, in the same quiet tone. "Folk know soon enough if they've pissed him off."

"And the lady?"

"The same."

Casting another look in Sabine's direction, something moved behind Bracken's eyes. Keel wasn't sure what but for the first time a vague flicker of unease moved through him. His thoughts were interrupted when Bracken said breezily, "So, you wanna check out the wine? We make our own."

"Tiger bone?"

Bracken nodded.

Keel looked towards Sekka, but when there was no response he shook his head and said. "Doesn't look like it."

"Okay, no worries. Tell you what; let's go meet the boss man. He's keen to say hello."

Aren't we all, Keel thought.

The two uniformed wranglers were waiting outside. They straightened and fell into line a couple of paces to the side as Bracken emerged from the building with his visitors in tow and led the way towards the animal pens.

Of the three men waiting by the tiger cages, two wore the black uniforms and matching berets which, along with their hardware, identified them as GK security personnel, while the third was dressed more coolly, in a loose-fitting, button-down blue shirt and tan slacks, accessorized with a pair of burgundy deck shoes worn without socks.

A galvanised metal pail sat on the ground by his feet. His right hand held a piece of raw meat. A half-smoked cigarette dangled from his left hand. Approaching the nearest cage, he proffered the bloody morsel up to the mesh with his fingers, holding it at head height. He did not flinch as the tiger rose onto its hind legs and gripped the meat through the mesh with his teeth. Then, as the big cat sank back down with the prize in its jaws and retreated to the rear of the cage, he turned.

While some individuals never quite seem to match their photos, Zheng Chao did. His hair colour was definitely the result of chemical enhancement and close up, the artificial tightening of the skin around the corners of his eyes was just as evident, though possibly more noticeable in the flesh than the pigmentation in Lavasse's snapshot of him had suggested; while the grainy nicotine stains at the ends of his fingers, which hadn't been at all apparent in the photo, weren't dissimilar to the discolorations on some of the tusks on show in his storage rooms.

Placing the cigarette between his thin lips, Zheng drew tar into his lungs and exhaled slowly, allowing the smoke to drift past his face. "*Nǐ chídàole.*"

The cold tone as well as the detracting look he gave his security chief carried more than a hint of rebuke. Sabine, standing next to Keel, confirmed it by whispering softly from the side of her mouth, "He says we're late."

Bracken offered no reaction to his boss's curt observation nor did he give any sign that he'd picked up Sabine's aside. Instead, he turned to Keel and said smoothly, "Mr. Zheng welcomes you to Golden Kingdom."

"Pleasure's ours," Keel said, wondering if Zheng understood English. Cade's dossier hadn't been that specific, but given Bracken's nationality it was more likely than not that his boss did have some grasp. "Please thank him for his hospitality."

As Bracken looked to his boss, Keel let his eyes wander off to a point beyond Zheng's shoulder and the tops of the cages, up towards the thickly wooded hillside that led to the summit of Golden Dragon Mountain. A brief flash half-way up the slope, at the edge of a gap in the trees, caught his eye, but then it was gone.

As Bracken said amiably, though his eyes didn't quite match the humour. "Yeah, about that. There's been a change of plan,"

"Okay," Keel said. "Does this mean the hunt's off?"

"Not exactly," Bracken said. "Only, Mr. Zheng has a couple of questions that've been causing him some concern."

"No problem," Keel said, aware that Sekka had moved up to join him. "Fire away."

"Thing is," Bracken said. "The boss was wondering, like I was, what Miss Bouvier was doing here. Seemed a little odd to us that someone with her credentials would be keen on taking part in a tiger hunt."

And Keel thought: *shit.*

"Y'see..," Bracken continued, "...these auctions, we like to vet the attendees; those we don't know. You folk being last minute invites, we thought we'd take a look; see if any red flags came up. Turns out they didn't. Leastways, not with you and Mr. Sekka. Your lady friend on the other hand; well, imagine our surprise when we took a look on-line and that photo of her with some of her conservation pals at that conference in Dubai popped up; not just with her name - *Doctor Bouvier* - but her occupation as well: chief vet for Salma National Park."

Bracken stole glance towards Zheng, as if seeking approval to continue. Zheng took another casual drag on his cigarette. He stared at Keel unblinkingly. It reminded Keel of the look on a lizard's face just before it snatched a bug off a twig with its tongue.

"So naturally that made us think we should probably take another look at you guys." Bracken continued, his right hand dropping casually on to the butt of his pistol. "Only problem was, we still couldn't find anything. Nix. Nada. Zilch. Bells started ringing a lot louder, then, and so we asked ourselves: now what would a wildlife vet with links to conservation organizations, be doing visiting a place like Golden Kingdom in the company of two unlisted guys who might as well be ghosts, one of them ex-British army? R&R, my arse. Wild guess: I'm betting Mr. Sekka here sure as hell ain't in the oil business."

Keel remained silent.

"So, you all working for one of those save-the-world outfits?" Bracken's tone was mocking. "Big Cat Rescue, maybe? Animals Asia? I'm starting to think he ain't watching *your* backs." Bracken looked at Sekka as he said it. "You and he are watching *hers*. Probably while she sniffs around, looking to report back to the EIA before writing one of those freaking magazine exposés. Am I close? Shit, you people are unbelievable."

"If you had doubts," Sekka said, reverting to his own voice as there didn't seem much point in continuing the subterfuge, "why did you give us the guided tour?"

"Are you kidding? After the trouble you took, worming your way in? Would've been a crying shame not to." A smirk drifted across Bracken's face. "Any case, sport, whaddya gonna do?" He looked directly at Keel as he posed the last question.

Keel knew that any initiative they might have had was now lost. They needed to get back on track, and quickly. A weapon would help. Time to change tack and provoke Bracken into make a move. See what develops.

"We'll do what we came here to do," Keel said.

"Oh, yeah? And what the hell does that mean?"

"Means we're not animal rights activists and we're not here for a story." Keel lifted his chin towards Zheng, who still hadn't moved, though he was clearly interested in the exchange, which made Keel think that he probably did understand what was going on. "We're here for him."

It took a second for the statement to sink in. Then Bracken blinked. "Say, what?"

Zheng removed what remained of the cigarette from his mouth and rubbed it into the ground with the toe of his burgundy loafer. Sabine's hand started to slide into her shoulder bag.

"No!" Bracken snapped. Pointing at her with his left hand, his right hand curled around the butt of his pistol.

"*Bié.*"

Zheng's single-word command, clearly and calmly spoken, was enough to cause Bracken to pause.

Flanked by his two, now openly tense, minders, Zheng took a step forward. His expression seemed to be one of curiosity rather than aggression.

Keel said, "Tell me, Saul, the girl: Lulani Yang. Who killed her? Was that you?"

If proof were needed that Zheng had some command of English, it occurred at that precise moment. As his head swivelled towards his security chief, shock lanced across Bracken's face, and his gaze flickered towards a point behind Keel, to the storage building and the row of freezers parked outside.

"I'll take that as a 'yes'," Keel said.

Bracken's gaze snapped back. "How the fuck-?"

This time, when he went for his pistol, there was no order to stand down. Drawing the automatic, he aimed the muzzle directly at Keel's forehead.

"No auction for us, I'm guessing," Keel said. "Pity. Joseph was hoping to bag a bargain."

"You think?" Bracken cast a sideways glance towards his boss as if asking for instructions.

"*Shāle tāmen,*" Zheng said. The expression on his face and the dismissive, backwards swatting motion he made with his right hand as he went to turn away made any translation superfluous.

"All three of us?" Keel said. "Really? You think you can cover this up? People know we're here."

"Yeah?" Bracken gave a derisive laugh. "What people? And you see anyone else around? There ain't nobody here but us chickens. Plus we've cleared out your rooms and commandeered your vehicle. Anyone asks, as far as GK's concerned, you checked out and headed home."

"So how's this going to work?" Keel said. "Are we due for cold storage as well?"

He heard Sabine suck in her breath.

"Could be. We got plenty of freezers; plenty of room." Bracken smiled and jerked a thumb at the row of cages behind him. "Plus we got these guys, and they're *always* hungry. It's like having our own recycling plant."

"Protect the planet," Keel said. "Yeah, we read the sign." He looked towards Zheng, who had paused in his stride. "What about you, Fu? Got anything to add?"

"Maybe the cat's got his tongue," Sekka said.

Zheng stared hard at Sekka, before lifting his chin once more. His gaze was icy cold as he said in stilted English, "You all die."

"Hell," Keel said. "We're all going to die, eventually." As he spoke, he raised his hands. "But maybe not today, eh?"

478

"Wrong." Bracken grinned as the security guards brought their rifles to bear, and his finger tightened on the trigger. "Bye, sport."

The grin was still in place when a faint crack sounded and Bracken's left eye erupted from its socket in a ragged explosion of blood, grey matter, and jagged fragments of bone. Even as the automatic fell from his lifeless hand, Keel and Sekka were moving.

Wrong-footed by the report and the bullet's devastating effect, Zheng's minders and Bracken's wranglers were far too slow. Their first instinct had been to freeze and look for the source of the gunshot and to protect their boss, who'd automatically ducked down to avoid being hit by a follow-up shot. When they realized that the real threat might be coming from a source a lot closer to home, it was too late.

By which time, Sekka had disabled the first wrangler with a vicious reverse kick to the groin, driving him into his partner's side, tipping them both off balance, and Keel had scooped up Bracken's pistol.

Keel's first bullet took Zheng's nearest bodyguard in the throat. The bodyguard's colleague, sensing that he might have got his priorities in the wrong order, was halfway through his turn, when Keel's second shot hit him in the centre of his chest. He went down with the look of confusion still etched on his face.

"Go!" Keel said.

But Sabine was already in motion. Reaching Zheng in two strides and drawing the hypodermic from the inside pocket of her shoulder bag, she slammed her heel against the back of Zheng's left knee, forcing him the rest of the way to the ground. Then, with her weight pressed against his spine, she threw her left arm around Zheng's throat, removed the cap from the syringe with her teeth, and, before he knew what was happening, rammed the needle into his upper right arm and depressed the plunger. "*Cào nǐ zǔzōng shíbādài!*"

Behind her, Keel knew he hadn't been quick enough. Bracken's second wrangler, having recovered his balance following Sekka's assault on his pal, had drawn his pistol. Sekka was fast, but nowhere near fast enough to avoid a bullet from less than six feet away.

But as Keel brought his own pistol round in what seemed like agonizing slow motion, another far-off crack sounded and the wrangler's head jerked to one side. A crimson mist burst from his shattered skull, and as he fell to the ground, the blood began to pool beneath him.

The first wrangler was still doubled over in pain and having a hard time concentrating as Sekka picked up his rifle and plucked his handgun from its holster. He was unable to resist as Sekka drove the butt of the Magnum hard against his skull. He collapsed without a sound.

Now fully armed, Keel and Sekka crabbed to where Sabine was withdrawing the needle from Zheng's muscle.

"You have three minutes before he loses consciousness," she said as Zheng's eyes started to roll back. His body had already gone limp.

"Crow'll be here in four," Keel said.

He looked towards the nearby buildings. Other than Zheng, Bracken, and the security men, no other staff members had appeared, though that didn't mean there weren't any around, despite Bracken's remark about chickens, aka inconvenient witnesses. It was unlikely the two reports that had come from the hillside had

480

registered, but Keel's double dispatching of Zheng's minders had been a lot louder and could not have been mistaken for anything other than shots fired. It might only be a matter of minutes, possible seconds, therefore, before someone came to investigate and the site of four uniformed bodies sprawled on the ground leaking blood would tell their own story. And if that wasn't enough, within minutes it was going to get a hell of a lot noisier.

Because from the direction of the river, the heavy throb of an aero engine had just become audible.

"One minute," Sabine said as she checked Zheng's pulse.

Keel looked past Sekka, towards the approaching clatter, which was increasing in volume with each passing second until, with a juddering roar, the un-marked JetRanger powered into view, the wash from its rotors flattening the tops of the trees, creating a barrage of sound.

With the chopper hovering above them in dragonfly mode, the down-draught from the rotors pummelling the ground, Keel placed his mouth close to Sabine's ear. "We've got this! Time to go!"

Keel saw the doubt spread across her face and laid a hand on her arm. "You know what to do, and you know why! Move!"

For a second, it looked as though she was going to voice a protest, but then, with a glance up at the helicopter, she nodded and leaned in close. "Thirty minutes! After that the sedative will begin to wear off!"

Her instructions were only just audible, but Keel patted her shoulder to show he'd understood, and nodded to Sekka. Then, as Sabine let go, they took

Zheng's weight and watched as Sabine took off in a crouching run towards the fence line, her head held low.

As soon as she'd disappeared from view, Keel signalled Crow to bring the JetRanger down. The second the skids touched, Keel and Sekka hauled Zheng's inert form upright and, with an arm under each shoulder, they half-dragged, half-carried him towards the chopper's open door.

As half a dozen armed, black-clad figures appeared from the direction of the zoo's entrance gates.

"Company!" Sekka yelled, as they thrust Zheng's body across the rear seats.

"I see them!" Keel reached over and hit Crow's left shoulder. "Take us up! Go! Go!"

"Incoming!" Sekka screamed, and ducked as a bullet struck the edge of the door frame; though his warning was almost submerged beneath the rising engine note as Crow opened the throttle to increase rotor speed.

Someone, Keel assumed, had obviously cottoned on fast as to what was happening, having seen the bodies on the ground and their boss being manhandled through the JetRanger's doorway.

"You hit?" he managed to yell back in the second before Crow pulled up on the collective and the JetRanger rose into the air. Hanging onto the nearest seat strap and without waiting for a reply, Keel lunged for the back of Sekka's belt to drag him further into the cabin, as another slug seared through the canted doorway and buried itself in the bulkhead, narrowly missing the now fully sedated Zheng.

With the turbine screaming, Crow pushed the cyclic forward and rolled the chopper to the right in a tight climbing turn. Within seconds they were over the trees and out of sight from the guards on the ground. Keel wondered if or when it had occurred to the latter to stop shooting for fear of hitting their boss.

As Sekka checked Zheng's pulse, Keel grabbed a headset from the rear shelf and flicked the intercom switch. "You okay?"

Crow's voice came through loud, clear and angry. "Bastards hit the windscreen!"

The bullet had struck low on the right side, in front of the pilot's position. If there had been any more force behind the shot, Crow would probably have taken the hit. Fortunately, most likely due to a deflection, the perspex had only suffered scarring and not penetration.

"What do you want? Sympathy?"

"Screw you, too, mate. Sabine okay?"

"She's good. She's on her way."

"She'd better be." Crow looked out over the chopper's nose, at the trees passing below. Upon leaving the ground, he'd not steered directly due west, which would have been the shortest line home. Instead, he'd angled the chopper onto a more southerly track, on a heading that kept them above the forest and not over the resort complex. So even though the engine noise was substantial at low level, given the density of the upper canopy, the JetRanger's profile would be masked from people on the ground.

Interference from the authorities was also doubtful. With the nearest Lao Air Force base two hundred miles away at Long Tieng, it meant there was zero risk of flight interception, unless the Lao had aircraft capable of light speed. All things considered, Crow didn't think that likely.

Not that it would have mattered, for less than thirty seconds later, they were clear of the trees and the river lay before them.

Crow flicked the intercom switch. "Okay, guys, better get ready. Ride's about to get real interesting."

As soon as she had negotiated the break in the perimeter fence, Sabine took the syringe apart and buried the pieces in the earth beneath the trees. Then, brushing herself down, she jogged to the end of the trail, where, concealed by undergrowth in a spot from where she could observe the road, she recovered her breathing and settled down to wait. As she did so, she heard the beat of the JetRanger's rotors growing louder. She looked up, but the trees blocked her view. As the sound faded into the distance, she turned her attention back to the road.

Two minutes later, after two cars and a farm truck had driven past, her ears picked up the rattle of a motorcycle engine approaching at speed from further up the hill. She tensed and remained in her position as a helmeted male rider, wearing a semi-rigid backpack, appeared around the bend aboard an aged Honda 250. She watched as the biker slowed and eased his ride to the side of the road. Coming to a stop, he removed his helmet, to reveal his European features, comprising a sun-browned, grizzled-looking face, framed by un-kempt salt and pepper hair and a matching short-trimmed beard.

Shouldering her bag, Sabine stepped out from the trees.

The rider smiled. "Doctor Bouvier, I presume."

The accent carried a faint Northern Irish lilt.

484

"Mr. Donovan?" Sabine said.

The biker's eyes, she noticed, were almost grey in colour. "That would be me, but you can call me Harry. Grab this. Climb aboard." He held out a helmet that had been looped over his left wrist. "Bit of a squeeze with the backpack. You'll have to hold on best you can."

Removing her cap and stowing it in her bag, Sabine took the proffered helmet. As she slipped it over her head and mounted the pillion seat, the faint sound of the chopper's engine disappeared completely and a flutter of apprehension moved through her. Using the next few seconds to take some calming breaths, she waited until Donovan had re-donned his helmet and then took hold of the back pack, which was firmly secured around the Irishman's back and shoulders.

"You good?" Donovan asked, as he felt her settle.

"*Oui.* Yes."

"Okay, then hang on. We've got us a wee boat to catch."

"How we doing?" Keel asked. He looked down at the water, now passing less than two hundred feet beneath the skids.

"Peachy," Crow's voice was a rasp. "His nibs still sleeping?"

"He's good," Keel said. He looked past Crow and out over the JetRanger's snout. A couple more seconds and they'd be across the Mekong's centre line and in Thai air space. There was marine traffic below them but most of it was located up river, around the Sop Ruak landing stages and their counterparts on the SEZ side of the Mekong, with vessels thinning out the further they travelled from the ferry crossing points.

On the downstream side, Keel could see a convoy of slow-moving cargo barges and a scattered selection of small motor launches and assorted fishing boats. A few faces turned skywards as the chopper passed overhead.

The detonation, when it came, although partly veiled by the engine noise, was still loud enough to be heard, like a grenade going off in the middle distance.

As the chopper lurched, Keel grabbed a strap for support and looked back out of the open doorway. Thick black fumes were spiralling away from the tail section. "We've got smoke!"

"Roger that!" Crow yelled through the headset. "What's it look like?"

"Impressive!"

Keel thought he heard Crow mutter, "Bloody smartarse," as the helicopter began to yaw violently from side to side and he let go a curse.

Crow yelled again. "Going down!"

Keel and Sekka exchanged glances. Zheng was still motionless but his breathing remained regular, which, Keel reflected, was more than could be said for his own. Sekka, he knew, would be experiencing the same sensation. He looked out of the door. Their altitude had halved. Still straddling the centre line, they were now no more than a hundred feet above the water and less than four hundred meters from the Thai side of the river; a feature marked by a narrow strip of land pockmarked with mud flats and coarse vegetation, bordered on the inland side by a four-lane highway. On the far side of the highway, the terrain consisted of vegetable farms and patches of woodland.

Crow called through the headset. "Ninety seconds! You guys set? His lordship ready?"

486

"Set," Keel responded, thinking: *as ready as he'll ever be.*

"Okay. Heading in."

If the islet had a name, Crow had no idea what it was. It was the first in line and the smallest of three narrow islands that sat in a row some two hundred plus metres out from the Thai side of the river. Not much bigger than a soccer pitch, it was covered in a layer of rough grass and a few thick bushes, and separated from the next, much larger island, by a sixty-yard channel of sediment-stained water. Flight instructors would probably have called it the 'point of intended landing'. As far as Crow was concerned it was 'sandbar numero uno' and the flight path down to his intended target.

At seventy feet, Crow throttled back. At that height there was still sufficient elevation left to be able to turn the engine down further, disengage it from the main rotor blades and descend the rest of the way using autorotation. Crow didn't intend that to happen, not at first, anyway.

The smoke was still pluming from the JetRanger's rear end as Crow took the chopper down in a series of uneven slips until it was hovering thirty feet above the end of the channel between the small islet and its neighbour. Looking out through the perspex, he checked the positions of the nearest river vessels. Several were in sight, but none of them were in close proximity, save for a small, decrepit looking fishing craft drifting along the Thai side of the waterway.

Unstrapping his seat belt harness and removing his headset, Crow took a deep breath as he eased the cyclic back and forth to bleed off any remaining forward momentum and level the attitude indicator.

487

He hoped Keel and Sekka were ready. The next manoeuvre was critical and they wouldn't get a second chance.

Helicopters, unless fitted with floats, weren't equipped to ditch on water due to the skids being unable to provide a wide enough footprint, a factor not helped by rotary aircraft having a high centre of gravity due to the transmission, engine, and blade system being mounted above the cabin, which meant the moment the JetRanger's skids touched the water all stability was forfeit.

With the bottom of the skids now hovering only feet above the river, and with the mantra *'flare, pitch, level and cushion'* playing like a loop inside his head, Crow cut engine power, pulling back on the cyclic as he did so to execute the flare and pitch up the chopper's nose, careful to keep the tail clear of the water. As soon as he felt the helicopter level out and nudge the surface, he decreased rotor rpm and employed lateral cycle to tip the JetRanger onto its side.

The effect was immediate and twofold. The first effect was brought on by the weight of the water acting as a buffer, which prevented the blades from turning. The second, and more dramatic consequence, was that the JetRanger commenced its death roll. Within seconds, the helicopter was upside down, and flooding fast.

26

It took Donovan and Sabine six minutes to cover the
three miles to Mokkachok. The village lay to the south
of the SEZ, on the bank of the Mekong, at the end of a
dirt road, and, having elected, like Crow, to avoid the
direct route back through the resort and, instead,
follow a diagonal course to the river, Donovan had
pushed the bike hard. So much so, that there had been
several times during the ride when Sabine had come
close to losing her grip on the backpack, the only thing
keeping her in her seat. By the time Donovan brought
the bike to a stop by a rough wooden jetty on the quiet
outskirts of the village, it felt as though every bone in
her body had been shaken loose and then reset in the
wrong order. It was with a sigh of relief that she
dismounted and removed the helmet. Though, that did
little to subdue the feeling of worry that had dogged
her since leaving Keel and the others back in the zoo.

Taking off his own helmet, Donovan ran a hand
through his flattened hair. "You good?"

"*Oui.*" Sabine nodded, took her cap out of her bag
and put it on.

"Okay, then let's get the hell out of here."

There was a small hut at the top of the jetty, shaded
by trees. As Donovan trundled the bike towards the

open doorway, a wiry, and very brown Asian man, dressed in a ragged t-shirt, torn knee-length shorts, flip flops and a battered military-style bush hat, emerged from inside. Without extending a greeting, he took the bike from Donovan and pushed it into the hut. After securing the door with a padlock, still without uttering a word, he hurried towards the jetty beckoning for them to follow.

"This is Aroon," Donovan said, removing his backpack and transferring it to his right hand. "He's our ferryman. What you might call the strong, silent type; silent, anyway." Following Sabine's lead, the Irishman delved into one of the backpack's side pockets and extracted a cap of his own. He pulled the peak low over his forehead.

The boat was not moored to the jetty but drawn up close to the bank in the jetty's shadow. It was low and narrow, with a needle-sharp prow and a long-tailed engine. The centre of the boat was piled high with fishing nets. Aroon led the way down the bank and climbed on board. Donovan and Sabine followed quickly, avoiding the nets, and took their places at the bow.

Aroon was poling them away from the shore when Sabine's ears picked up a distant but familiar thrumming beat. Glancing at Donovan, she saw from his expression that he'd heard it too, but then, as Aroon yanked back on the pull cord, the sound was lost as the boat's engine burst into life with a throaty roar.

It had been enough, however, for Sabine's pulse to start racing, and as Aroon turned the boat around and they emerged from behind the jetty and out from the trees which, until then, had been blocking the view, her instinct was to look towards where she thought she'd heard the helicopter's engine.

The JetRanger came into sight almost immediately.

Close to a thousand yards away, it was hovering motionless above the water, close to the northern edge of an island around three hundred yards from the Thai shoreline. Sunlight glinted on its paintwork while tendrils of dark smoke were pluming out from the tail-rotor housing. Boats from both sides of the river were moving cautiously towards it.

Feeling an urgent tap on her shoulder, Sabine turned to see Donovan jabbing his thumb towards a point upstream. Following his gesticulation, she saw, among the now familiar river vessels, a brace of power craft moving out at speed from the Golden Kingdom landing stage. Another tap and she turned again. Donovan had his backpack on his lap. The main pocket was unzipped. Reaching inside, he lifted out the rifle scope and passed it to her, his expression neutral.

As Donovan instructed Aroon to raise the prop from the water to bring the boat to a halt, Sabine held the scope to her eye.

The power craft came into sharp relief. They were at least two thousand yards away but they were homing in fast. She could see black-uniformed men in each boat, all of them armed. Lowering the scope, she swivelled and looked again towards the JetRanger's position.

In time to hear the chopper's engine note drop away and to see that the skids were now touching the water and that the machine had started to list and then, in what seemed like a split second, she saw it turn turtle.

She gasped. It had happened so quickly, it took a

further couple of seconds for the vision to sink in, by which time Aroon had lowered the propeller back into the water and they were in motion once more.

Despite the boat's uneven passage, Sabine raised the scope and tried to focus on the sinking aircraft. Not being able to spot it due to the boat's jerky movements, she lowered the scope and searched with her eyes, and realized that she had not allowed for the rate of submergence. The bottom of the skids and the chopper's underbelly were all that remained above the water line, which showed that the downed machine was flooding at an alarming rate.

As she looked on in awe, the boats that had been moving towards the helicopter from all sides were gathering speed, anxious to offer whatever assistance they could. Sabine glanced back upriver. The GK boats had picked up momentum and were approaching more rapidly. She could see the churning wake of their inboards and their crews gesticulating wildly.

Instinctively, she turned her face away, while Donovan ducked his head as they surged by, though at the rate the launches were travelling it was unlikely their occupants were interested in anything other than the upturned aircraft, by which time Aroon had brought the boat close to the Thai shore and had powered down the engine. All Sabine's attention, however, remained concentrated on the activity downstream, to where more river craft were converging on the stricken machine.

Which was when a violent explosion blew what could be seen of the JetRanger's inverted fuselage into bright smithereens.

Zheng came awake slowly. It was a strange sensation. His eyelids felt as heavy as lead and it took several seconds before he was able to blink, let alone open his eyes. When he did eventually succeed, keeping them open became something of a struggle, no matter how hard he tried, and when he then attempted to move his arms and wriggle his toes, they felt just as heavy and uncooperative. It was like trying to float while weighed down by lead manacles clamped around his wrists and ankles. So overwhelming was the sensation that it was easier just to allow the drowsiness to take hold and to cease the struggle.

Gradually, however, after enduring several false starts, with no idea of how long it had taken, the tiredness began to dissipate and he was able to open his eyes to their fullest extent and to focus on his surroundings, which were just as confusing.

He saw that he was dressed in what appeared to be a white cotton nightshirt and lying in a bed in a room he did not recognize. The room was modest in size and functionally furnished with a desk, a chair and a wardrobe. There was a single window, with a half-drawn blind, through which sunlight slanted onto a linoleum-covered floor. A porcelain wash basin was affixed to one wall, flanked by soap and paper towel dispensers. The bed had white metal rails along each side and when he looked down he saw there was a tube attached to his left forearm.

Following the line of the tube, he saw it was divided into sections by a series of valves and clamps, all leading up to a drip chamber and above that an intravenous bag. Alongside the head of the bed was a patient-monitoring machine, from which thin leads ran down to small sensor pads on his chest.

He was studying the equipment in mild puzzlement when he heard the door open. He turned his head slowly. A bald, white-coated, Asian man entered the room bearing a clipboard. He did not smile when he saw that Zheng was conscious but offered a respectful bow, the sort a subordinate might offer a high-ranking executive or the leader of a clan.

"Zheng *Xiānshēng*," it is good to see you are awake. I am Wang *Yīshēng*. How are you feeling?"

The newcomer, who'd used Zheng's honorific title while identifying himself as a medical doctor, had spoken in Mandarin. Moving to the bed, he ran his eyes over the monitoring equipment.

Zheng looked around the room and found his voice, which emerged as a dry rasp. "Where am I?"

"You are in the Special Economic Zone medical facility." Stepping away from the monitor, Wang reached for a beaker of iced water that sat on a table beside the bed and held it to Zheng's lips. "Drink this."

Zheng swallowed, letting the liquid soothe the back of his throat before pushing the beaker away. "What am I doing here? *How* did I get here?"

As the doctor placed the drink back on the table, Zheng tried to sit up, but discovered he couldn't quite make it.

"Please, allow me," Wang said, laying his clip board down. Adjusting the pillow, he eased Zheng into a half-seated position. "I regret I do not know the full details; only that you were pulled out of the river and brought here. One of your men is outside. It would be better if he explains what happened. Allow me to fetch him."

Offering another formal bow, Wang left the room, leaving Zheng to gather his thoughts, which were running through his mind like termites in a nest. It was

494

a few minutes later, just as random snippets of memory were beginning to coalesce and arrange themselves into a vague semblance of order when the door opened and Wang re-entered. With him was an earnest-looking Chinese male dressed in the black uniform of a Golden Kingdom security guard. Removing his beret, the guard approached Zheng's bed, stood to attention, and bowed deferentially.

Zheng stared back at him, taking in the appearance of the uniform. Suddenly, it all came back to him: the African and his bodyguard; the woman; his security chief, Bracken, shot by an unseen gunman, and the panic and confusion as his guards failed to react; more gunfire; the woman running towards him; her arm around his neck; a sudden stab of pain, and then...he struggled to remember what had happened after that. There had been a loud roaring noise, he recalled. Thunder? Some sort of machine?

But, then, darker thoughts began to intrude, like snippets from a deep, disturbing dream, in which there had been blackness and a sense of being enclosed, of being trapped inside a confined space; as if he was trying to crawl through a damp, narrow pipe towards some sort of suspended light source; a feeling made all the more claustrophobic by an overriding sense of breathlessness, as if he was being smothered; as if he was...drowning? He remembered, then, what the doctor, Wang, had told him about being pulled from the river.

But how did he get there?

He realized the security guard was gazing at him expectantly and for a second he wondered if he'd voiced his thoughts out loud.

"I do not know you," Zheng said curtly. "Name?"

The security guard dipped his head in obeisance. "I am Gao Muyang, Zheng *Xiānshēng*. I was ordered to provide security while you are here."

Zheng absorbed the information. "Then speak."

The guard looked towards Wang, as if seeking reassurance.

"Do not look at him," Zheng snapped. "Look at me. Tell me how I got here." In exerting just that small amount of irritation he'd felt a tiny pulse of discomfort in the area behind his left eye socket. He tried not to wince.

The guard straightened. Then, as if wary of how Zheng might respond, he said hesitantly, "They took you."

"Took me? What does that mean? Who took me?"

"The *Fēizhōu rén* and the *Xīfāng rén*."

The African and the Westerner.

"Took me where?" Zheng sensed that there were several more dots that needed to be connected.

"To the helicopter."

Zheng frowned, and felt another tiny ripple of pain along his forehead as it occurred to him what the loud machine noise might have been.

"You were at the tiger village with Bracken *Guǐtóu*. We heard gunfire and the sound of a helicopter and when we arrived, the bodies of your guards and Bracken *Guǐtóu* were the ground and the *Fēizhōu rén* and the *Xīfāng rén* were carrying you on board."

"You were drugged, Zheng *Xiānshēng*," Wang broke in. "A sedative, to make it easier for them to transport you. We are awaiting the result of tests to determine what they used."

The woman, Zheng thought. She did it when she attacked me; the bitch! As if on cue, he became aware

496

of another, separate, area of tenderness, this time high on his bicep as he went to ease his right arm into a more comfortable position.

"The helicopter was damaged." the guard continued. "It landed in the river. We believe the pilot was trying to reach Thailand," he added.

"Thailand?" Zheng said. A frisson of unease moved through him as he thought of the ramifications had his abductors been successful.

"Yes, Zheng *Xiānshēng*. We had already launched boats, but the aircraft was sinking and it blew up before we got there."

Zheng stared at him. "Blew up?"

"Yes, Zheng *Xiānshēng*." Gao said. "We do not know how. Vessels were searching the river when we arrived. You were found by a fisherman who lifted you into his boat. He saw our uniforms and attracted our attention. We transferred you to our launch and brought you here. It is a miracle you are alive. Truly."

A thought occurred to Zheng. "When did this happen? How long have I been here?"

"You were pulled out of the water six hours ago." It was Wang who answered.

Zheng absorbed the information. His mind raced. "The *Fēizhōu rén* and the *Xīfāng rén*; what happened to them? Find out. I want them hunted down."

He wondered, idly, if Qinyang Lei had been told of his abduction. If so, had she been concerned for his well-being or had she scented an opportunity to take advantage of his absence? Either way, he had survived, which mean the priority was to seek out, if possible, and deal with the perpetrators accordingly.

Gao drew himself up. "There is no need, Zheng *Xiānshēng*."

Zheng's expression was glacial. "What do you mean? Are they dead?"

Gao shook his head. "No. They are alive." There was a pause, then: "We have them."

Zheng stared at his subordinate, then at Wang. His face hardened. "Leave us."

Wang bowed and left the room.

"Tell me," Zheng said.

"When we brought you back here, our other boat continued the search. They found the *Fēizhōu rén* and the *Xīfāng rén* on one of the islands. The *Fēizhōu rén* was unconscious. The other one had pulled him onto the shore. The pilot was not found. It is believed he drowned.

"The woman?" Zheng said.

Gao shook his head. "There was no woman, Zheng *Xiānshēng*. Perhaps she drowned also?"

Zheng re-ran the shootings through his mind. Whoever had killed Bracken had done so from a distance, which meant a sniper. So who else was involved other than the three people Bracken had brought to the zoo? There was only one way to find out.

"Where are they?" Zheng asked. He tried to keep the sense of anticipation out of his voice.

"They are here."

"*Here?*" Zheng's chin lifted.

"Yes. We are holding them. The *Fēizhōu rén* has regained consciousness."

"In this building?"

"They are under guard close by." There was a pause. "We thought you would want to question them and that it would be easier to bring them to you than for..."

Zheng held up a hand. He knew what the guard had

498

been about to say. That he, Zheng, might not have recovered sufficiently to be able to either make his way, or be taken, to where the foreigners were being held.

"Bring them to me, and send in Wang."

Gao nodded crisply, brought his heels together, turned, and left the room. Wang, who'd obviously been hovering outside, stepped back in.

Zheng indicated the chair. "I will sit. Have clothes been brought?"

Wang indicated the wardrobe. "Yes, Zheng *Xiānshēng.*"

"Then do not stand there like a stranded fish. Help me."

After hurriedly disengaging Zheng from the monitor and the intravenous drip, Wang retrieved the clothes from the wardrobe: a long-sleeved, collarless blue shirt buttoned at the throat, matching trousers and a pair of black canvas espadrilles,

It had been galling to Zheng that in his emerging state of recovery he'd neglected to transfer to the chair before Gao's entry into the room. In not doing so, he'd committed the unpardonable sin of allowing an employee to see him a hospital bed, hooked up to a machine in what could be only construed as a position of weakness, of vulnerability. He was not about to let that happen again, certainly not with the two men being brought before him. It was bad enough, having Wang help him into his clothes, without the indignity of being seen tethered to a heart monitor. He was Zheng Chao, not some decrepit ancient in need of life-support.

By the time multiple footsteps sounded on the other side of the door, Zheng was seated at the table.

The exertion had brought on a slight light-headedness, but fortified by a sip of water and fuelled by a visceral desire to administer retribution for the humiliation to which he'd been subjected, he ignored the dull throb in his arm, and prepared to exact punishment.

"Do you wish me to remain?" Wang asked. "I have some knowledge of English. Perhaps I can be of assistance?"

Zheng considered the offer. "Stand behind me. Do not speak unless I order it."

Wang nodded obsequiously. "Of course. Whatever you wish."

The door opened. Gao entered, turned, and beckoned.

Keel and Sekka were prodded into the room. Their clothes were stained with water and dried mud and their hands were zip-tied in front of them. A second, black-uniformed, Asian brought up the rear.

"Hello, Zheng," Keel said. "You're looking very dapper. How are you? How's the menu? Chow any good?"

Zheng said nothing, though a slight drawing in of the skin around the eyes and the corners of his already tight-lipped mouth indicated that some of Keel's words had registered, especially the 'chow' bit.

"Hospital food, eh?" Keel said. "Still, what can you do?"

A nerve flickered down the side of Zheng's left cheek. He lifted his chin. "You are hard men to kill." The accent was heavy and the words slightly stilted yet perfectly decipherable.

"I'll take that as a compliment," Sekka said. "Keeps us on our toes."

Zheng frowned. At that moment, it occurred to him

that despite claiming the chair so as not to present himself as the invalid, but to project his superiority, it was the two men standing before him who'd somehow gained the advantage, not only due to them looking down on him, but because neither seemed particularly cowed in his presence.

He viewed the ties around their hands. They looked secure enough, and Gao and his fellow guard had positioned themselves so that they could subdue the prisoners at any time. Maintaining contact with the desk in case it was needed for support, Zheng rose to his feet. He stared hard at Sekka and spoke in English again. "You would *mock* me?"

"Every waking moment," Sekka said.

Whether or not the phrase meant anything to him, and despite his condition, Zheng's right hand moved at such a surprising lick that it made Keel wonder if the man had martial arts training. Sekka's cheek took the full brunt of the back-handed strike, which turned his head a good forty-five degrees from the vertical. Keel heard Gao suck in his breath.

Sekka waited a couple of seconds before turning his head back slowly and deliberately and fixing Zheng with a look that would have stripped bark from a tree. "That's one."

Zheng, possibly not understanding the nature of the threat behind Sekka's statement, glared back at the man he'd just struck. "I am Zheng Chao! You will treat me with respect! *Cào nǐ mā!*"

"Now, why would we do that, Zheng?" Keel said.

Zheng's head swivelled. He fixed Keel with a look of such reptilian intensity that Keel half-expected the man's tongue to fork out of his mouth.

"I wouldn't piss on you if you were on fire," Keel

said. "I have no respect for any man who ordered the killing of an innocent young woman. At least, I'm assuming Bracken killed her on your orders. Lulani Yang? We never did finish that conversation. She's the one stuffed down the back of your freezer. Or did you forget?"

"Yes, I give order! She die because she ask too many questions."

"Ah, right," Keel said evenly. "I can see why that would make you angry. Must have put you in an awkward position, what with an auction coming up and all. So much to do, so little time, so forth. She was a distraction you didn't need, right? So you had your tame security guy do the dirty work before storing her away. What were you going to do with the body? Thaw it out and feed her to one of your pets? That's what you had planned for us, right? Probably still do. Yes, no?"

Keel saw Wang's eyes widen.

As opposed to Zheng's, which went even darker as he jabbed a finger towards Keel's face. "Yes, I feed *you* to my tigers! I feed *both* of you to my tigers! You will be alive when I do! You think you are smart! You fucking pieces of shit! I am *Zheng Xiānshēn*! I decide who dies, who lives! I am boss man here!"

As if drained by his outburst, Zheng fell silent, breathing heavily.

"Right," Keel said. "Good to know."

As he spoke, and before Zheng's startled gaze, Keel rotated his wrists, one against the other, spread his hands apart and allowed the plastic ties to drop to the floor.

As the realization of what his prisoner had just done speared its way into his brain, Zheng, screamed

502

at the two men in uniform. "*Shāle tāmen*! Kill them!"

Neither Gao nor his colleague moved. Zheng stared at them in stunned disbelief as they stood, feet apart, their hands behind their backs. Glancing to the side he saw that Wang hadn't moved a muscle either. He seemed to be waiting for something.

When Zheng spun back he saw that Keel was still standing there, as was Sekka. The only difference was that Sekka's hands were now free as well.

"You get all that?" Keel said.

Zheng blinked. He had not understood the question.

The door opened and Max Cade walked in.

"Every word," Cade said. "Every God-damned, glorious word."

"So," Keel said, indicating the now immobile Zheng who was staring around him as if he'd just been transported on to the lunar surface, "you want to put him out of his misery?"

"Be my pleasure," Cade said. "Zheng Chao, my name is Maxwell Cade, I'm here representing...well, let's just say...several agencies. You've already met my associates: Peter Wang, from the United States Treasury Department." Cade grinned at the now smiling man in the white coat, before nodding towards the two uniformed guards. "And these fine gentlemen are Senior Colonel Pravat Charoensuk, and Major Chai Son Ratanaporn from the Royal Thai Police."

At the mention of Royal Thai Police, Zheng's face seemed momentarily to lose colour and a look of confusion spread across his features. But then, just as quickly, a calculating gleam appeared in his eyes as, lifting his chin, he sneered defiantly. "I am citizen of the People's Republic of China. This is Laos." Adding triumphantly, "You people have no authority here."

Cade made no reply. Instead, he walked to the window and lifted the blind. As if released from a half-closed trap, the late afternoon sunlight flooded in. Automatically, Zheng's eyes moved to the view outside. It took a moment for the sight to sink in. When it did, his lips parted as his predicament became clear.

Seated in his dragon boat, the *Phra Chiang Saen Si Phaendin* - the Golden Buddha - seemed to fill the window frame. The sheer scale of the statue and its position in relation to the angle of view were enough to inform Zheng that the building in which he found himself was on the wrong side of the Mekong River.

"Guess you're not in Kansas any more, Toto," Cade said, and smiled. "He's all yours, Colonel."

27

"Still can't believe your cockamamie idea actually worked," Cade said, as he, Keel and Sekka gazed out over the river.

They were on the second floor terrace of Sop Ruak's Imperial Golden Triangle Resort. The terrace extended out from the hotel's restaurant and faced north-east, thus providing a breathtaking view over the confluence of the Mekong and its smaller tributary, the Ruak.

"Thank Richard Harris and Greg Challen," Keel said.

Cade looked nonplussed. "Who the hell are they? More buddies you roped in and didn't tell me about?"

"Not exactly. Harris was the doctor and Challen was the animal vet and technical diver who came up with the plan for the Tham Luang cave rescue a few years back."

"The kids' soccer team?"

"If it hadn't been for those two guys, none of them would have made it out. It was their idea to sedate the boys using ketamine and to bring them out using scuba gear. I thought it might be a way to extract Zheng. Harris and Challen administered xanax and atropine to the boys as well, to prevent them from panicking during the extraction, but that was because the boys knew what was coming. Zheng didn't, so we held off on giving him those."

"Well, shit," Cade said.

"Came to me when we chose the old Chiang Rai airfield as Crow's pickup location for the chopper. The cave rescue teams used the field as a staging post. It got me thinking that maybe we should add a few more items to the mission inventory."

"Using Crow's guy in Bangkok."

Keel nodded.

The drug had been delivered to the Intercontinental, the day they'd left for the airport, disguised as an 80ml vial of insulin, in case Sabine's baggage was searched.

"Can't have come cheap," Cade said. "That and the hardware."

"No shit," Keel said.

"Crow's guy know what you were planning to do with the chopper?"

"What do you think?"

"Ah, right," Cade said. "Better to ask for forgiveness than permission."

"There's been a lot of that on this gig," Keel said. "Good news is there's still some cash left in the kitty so he'll be well compensated. He'll get over it."

"Still a hell of a risk. Zheng could have croaked."

"Wouldn't have lost any sleep if he had," Keel said. "But it wasn't a long swim; hundred metres tops. Those school kids were two and a half miles from the surface when *they* were found. Their escape journey took hours. Zheng's took minutes. Truth is, we only *had* minutes. Twenty-five, thirty at the most before the drug wore off and he started to come round. It was a pretty close thing. We fitted him with a full face mask and a tank before we ditched; strapped him up, and

Joseph and I did the heavy lifting. Crow brought up the rear. Visibility wasn't great due to the sediment but Logan hung underwater lights off the side of the fishing boat to guide us in. Plus we were lucky. River's not flowing as fast as it used to, thanks to a bunch of dams the Chinese have built north of the border. "

"You've worked with Logan and Donovan before," Cade said.

Keel nodded. "A few times. I've got PADI certification and done a fair bit of diving but Mike's former SBS. He's got the serious qualifications and way more experience. It's what he did for a living, as near as."

"Donovan?"

"I didn't call on him for his aquatic skills, but he's been around a while. He's what you might call a jack of all trades."

"Shooter being one of them."

"You may say that, I couldn't possibly comment."

"Interesting accent."

"I hadn't noticed."

Sekka permitted himself a smile from the sidelines.

"I'm guessing he was the one who called in the chopper?"

"It was all in the timing. We had Crow park over here, on the outskirts of town. Soon as Donovan called him on the sat phone, he was off and running. And if you're asking, he used to ferry crews and rig equipment around the Indonesian oil fields. He's versed in underwater egress training."

"And how to make smoke..."

"Using one Enola Gaye canister and an electronic flick switch. We had to make it look good. Not that we didn't take a few rounds when we were making the

507

snatch, mind you. It was Mike who set the main charge on the chopper. Activated it from the boat, when he knew we were clear."

Cade turned to Sekka. "What about you, Joseph?"

Sekka fixed the American with a cool, enquiring gaze. "What? You thought black men didn't scuba dive?"

Cade grinned.

"So what happens to Zheng?" Keel asked.

Cade shrugged. "We got a few options. First thing we do is bleed him for information. Confirm trafficking routes, network personnel, location of drug factories, so forth. Find out how much influence Beijing has in the running of his organization. The Thais'll be all over him for that kind of intel. We threaten him with a stay in one of our black sites and he'll likely sing like a canary. Plus, once it sinks in that nobody's looking for him on account of they think he went down with the chopper and drowned with the rest of you, he'll realize we're his only friends and that cooperation's his best strategy."

"About that," Keel said. "I'm assuming a chopper doesn't ditch in the river every day of the week. What about the media? Anyone sniffing around? "

"Y'mean *News At Eleven*?" Cade let out a thin smile. "Thai authorities put the hex on that. Media was told to back off on account of it was a national security issue. Colonel Charoensuk told me the Chinese were kicking up a private stink, demanding the Thais investigate and to keep them in the loop, but they backed off when the Thais threatened to leak evidence that high-level bigwigs in Beijing were involved in Zheng's illegal activities. As for the Lao government, it doesn't want to upset its number one backer or risk

508

jeopardizing any relationship it has with Thailand.

"Wheels within wheels," Keel murmured.

"That about sums it up, yeah."

"Zheng will still serve time? Sekka said.

"Probably. Eventually."

"Golden Kingdom's still going to be there, though."

"True, but with what Zheng tells us, hopefully, we can find new ways of hurting the operation. Removing him and Bracken from the board ain't a bad start."

"Leaving his wife to run the place?" Keel said.

"Treasury's still got the hots for her but, yeah, that'd be my guess, unless Beijing figures she's become a liability and it appoints an overseer."

Sekka frowned. "Is that likely?"

Cade shrugged. "Who the hell knows? The resort's been good for them as a distribution hub. Brought in good money on Zheng's watch. They'll want to protect their investment, so they'll probably place her on some sort of probation. There's the Thai guy, Chantharat, but I can't see Beijing giving him the baton. They'd prefer one of their own.

"'Course, now we've taped evidence that Zheng ordered the killing of a Lao national, then maybe, just maybe the Lao authorities'll pull their fingers out. My thought is they'll go through the motions like they usually do and then things'll settle down and it'll be business as usual. I'm not even sure Zheng's people will have alerted the Lao police, given what they had going on behind the scenes and the goods you saw coming up for auction. They've probably got enough stuff on hand or on order to take over the damned province."

"Don't tell me they're still going through with the auction?" Keel said.

Cade offered a wry smile. "Told you before; we've always thought Qinyang Lei was a business partner more than she was Zheng's wife. She'll have customers lined up. You think a minor inconvenience like her hubby being kidnapped is going to stand in the way of making a fast buck? Shit, you believe that, you underestimate the whole of Beijing's business philosophy."

"That's not at all depressing," Keel said drily. "What about Zheng's pals: the Bach brothers? They're still in play."

"Getting rid of Zheng should put a serious dent in their operations. I reckon they'll lay low and take stock. How long for, I can't say. My guess is they'll be looking over their shoulders for a while."

"What about going after them?"

Cade made a face. "Thing is, if we bring the Bachs down, it's more than likely there are folk waiting in the wings to take over the routes; folk we don't have a handle on yet."

"So better to keep Van and his brother in place while you try and identify their replacements," Sekka said.

Cade nodded. "Freeland'll be keeping their ears to the ground, but, yeah. Maybe save them for a rainy day."

"Better the devil you know, right?" Keel said.

Cade nodded. "Something like that."

"Not a bad policy," Keel said. "They used it in Ulster during the troubles. Orders were not to take out known IRA commanders because they didn't know who'd be appointed in their stead."

"That work?"

Keel thought about Donovan's background. "Up to

a point."

Cade went quiet, then said. "We do go after the Bach boys, I don't suppose...?"

Sekka started to laugh as Keel shook his head. "Got a job, thanks. At least, I think we do. We've a couple of days to get back to Salma before René pulls the plug and hands us our P45s."

"What the hell's that? Sounds like some sort of sidearm."

"Severance papers."

"Ah, right. Gotcha. Well, good luck. The man's got any sense he'll keep you guys on. The doc, too, obviously. Hell, I bet she's more valuable to him that you are."

"Wouldn't disagree. Couldn't have pulled the thing off without her."

"You tell her that?"

"Oh, she knows," Keel said.

"Useful her being a vet."

"In both senses of the word."

Cade smiled, thumped his fists softly on the terrace railing and straightened. "Right, well, gotta go. Been a pleasure, gentlemen." He held out his hand. "Good to meet you, Joseph...again." As he shook Keel's hand, he said. "Until next time, Major."

"You think there'll be one?" Keel said.

"Way we keep bumping into each other? Wouldn't be at all surprised."

"That's what worries me," Keel said.

Cade grinned as he turned away. "You all take care, now, y'hear?"

"Always," Keel said.

Cade nodded and walked off.

He did not look back, but acknowledged the arrival

of the two men who emerged from the restaurant area and walked past him towards where Keel and Sekka were standing.

Harry Donovan raised a hand in greeting. The man with him wasn't carrying as many years, but his features were rugged and tanned and his untidy dark hair was streaked with grey. Like Donovan, he was dressed casually in a short-sleeved polo shirt and jeans. He smiled as he approached.

"Mr. Donovan, Mr. Logan," Keel said. "What'll you have to drink?"

They settled for beers and found an empty table in the shaded part of the terrace.

"How'd it go?" Logan asked as he took a sip from his glass. "Zheng spilling the beans yet? Your man Cade looked pleased."

Keel stretched out his legs. "They'll keep him under observation for a while; check his general health; make sure there are no after effects from the drug. He might have a few interesting dreams still, but after that, he'll be good to go."

"Having the doc on your team had to be a hell of a bonus," Donovan mused. "I never asked you what she said when you came up with the plan."

Sekka smiled. "That was the weird part. Once we explained the logistics, it took about ten seconds for her to come on board."

"Just as well," Keel said. "Hadn't been for her, we wouldn't have had a clue on what dosage we'd need to knock Zheng out."

"We figured it was probably less than you'd give an elephant," Sekka said, "but after that..."

Logan stared at Sekka for a while and then looked at Keel. "Why do I get the feeling he's not joking?"

"Speaking of which," Sekka said, as Sabine and Crow walked out onto the terrace behind Logan's shoulder.

"Started without us," Crow said, as Donovan and Sekka pulled up two more chairs. "Bloody typical." He winced as he sat down.

"How's the shoulder?" Keel asked and nodded at the sling around Crow's left arm.

"Police medic said it's bruised, not dislocated. I'll live. "

"Heck of a big bandage for a bruise," Logan said, and grinned.

"Screw you," Crow said. Lifting his chin to indicate Keel, he shook his head. "I bloody told him it'd been years since I did any underwater escape training. But did he listen..?"

Donovan leaned close to Sabine."Are they always like this?"

"*Constamment,*" Sabine said.

Crow had sustained the injury while exiting the helicopter, when he'd misjudged the angle during the final stages of the JetRanger's demise, and slammed the left side of his body against the door frame on his way out. Fortunately, his breathing mask had remained in place, allowing him to complete the swim, albeit in some pain. As a result he'd had to be hauled aboard the waiting fishing boat by the scruff of the neck and the back of his belt. Only when he worked out that he was still alive had he been prepared to accept the indignity.

Keel addressed Donovan. "You return the hardware?"

"Taken care of," Donovan said.

Keel nodded, satisfied. "That case, thanks again,

guys. I know it was last minute but I appreciate you stepping in."

"Wouldn't have missed it," Donovan said. "Besides, what are friends for?"

Keel raised his glass in salute. "I'll see your accounts are credited."

"No hurry," Logan said.

"I guess that's it, then," Keel said.

"If you say this was fun, we must do it again," Crow said, "you're a dead man."

"Nope, I was about to say drink up, the next round's on me."

"Thought you'd never bloody ask," Crow said. "Mine's a pint."

END GAME

"Call for you," Deschamps said, his expression speaking volumes. "My office."

It was a day and a half after the return to Salma.

Entering the office, Keel picked up the phone.

"See you kept your jobs, then," Cade said. "How's it going?"

"Whatever it is, Max, the answer's still no," Keel said.

"Not why I'm calling," Cade said.

Something in his tone made Keel tense. "Go on."

"Zheng's wife was taken out day before yesterday."

"How?"

"Shot, Long distance. Single round to the heart."

"Where'd it happen?"

"Give you one guess."

"The zoo."

"There you go," Cade said.

"Suspects?"

"Lao authorities aren't saying, and my Thai contacts haven't picked up anything on the grapevine...yet. Could've been the Chinese. Thinking she'd be picked up next and they were worried about extra fallout."

"Wouldn't put it past them," Keel said.

"Me neither. So, anyway, how are Crow and the doc? They back yet?

A small chill ran across the back of Keel's neck.

"Only I heard you and Joseph checked out of the hotel and they didn't," Cade continued

"So?"

"So, just wondering is all."

"The hell you were," Keel said.

A soft chuckle sounded at the other end of the line. "Yeah, well, anyway, just wanted to say be sure to give them my best when you do see them."

"Will do," Keel said.

"Appreciate it, Major," Cade said.

The line went dead.

"Tell René we'll be a couple of days late."

Crow's parting words when he and Sabine were seeing Keel and Sekka into the taxi that was to deliver them from the Bangkok Intercontinental to Suvarnabhumi Airport.

"Can't fly the chopper or the Cessna with this shoulder anyway and Sabine says she'd like to see a bit more of Bangkok, before she does head off to actually visit her old man. René was okay with her taking leave before, so another day or so tacked on won't make that much difference. If he wants to fire us, so be it. But you and I know that's not going to happen. Not if you speak to him nicely."

"Least I can do," Keel said.

"Yeah," Crow said, and grinned. "We know."

"Look after that shoulder," Keel said. "We need you back at base. And you," Keel said to Sabine, "Be gentle with him."

"I don't know what you mean," Sabine said.

"Yeah, right," Keel said, as he climbed into the cab.

516

Keel put down the phone. His mind went back to the exchange he'd had with Crow prior to the Dubai trip.

'Hell, I've seen her fire a tranquillizing dart. She can probably shoot the balls off a fire ant at two hundred paces.'

He thought, too, about Donovan telling him back in Sop Ruak that the 'hardware' had been taken care of and of the conversation he'd had with the Irishman when they'd discussed the yardage between the temple ruin and the tiger enclosures below. Four hundred and seventy, as near as made no difference.

The trick lay in compensating for having to fire down hill, when the line of sight and line of trajectory were almost parallel to the gravitational pull on the bullet. Most shooters in that situation tended to strike high. It took a good shooter to know what adjustment to make in order to hit the target; a really good shooter, most likely someone with military training, with, possibly, the additional skill of being able to aim, fire at, and bring down a moving target from a low flying helicopter.

And, lastly, there had been René Deschamps' response when his and Keel's discussion about Salma's new ranger recruits had brought to mind the policy of Germany's GSG9 anti-terrorist squads and why, when faced with a stand-off, their first targets were always the women.

Because they were always considered to be the most dangerous.

As he let himself out of the office, Keel wondered if that applied to vets as well.

In both senses of the word...

517

AUTHOR'S NOTE

The Salma Option is a work of fiction.

However...
In August 2012, a ranger patrol operating out of Zakouma National Park in Chad came across a set of tracks suggesting that poachers had entered the reserve. The next day, gunshots were heard, but due to poor weather, the rangers were unable to locate the source of the shooting. It wasn't until the next day that an aerial reconnaissance flight located the poachers' camp, along with the remains of a female elephant.

The ranger team raided the camp only to be shot at by one of the poachers, who, despite coming under return fire, was able to make his escape. Upon searching the camp, the rangers realized they had stumbled upon a major elephant-killing operation.

They confiscated food supplies, more than a thousand rounds of ammunition, satellite and cell phones, tools and horse medicine from Sudan. They also found evidence that the raiders were members of the Sudanese military, along with what appeared to be a note issued by the men's commander, granting them leave.

(The link between the poachers and the military was later confirmed by C4ADS, a non-profit organization which analyzes global conflict and transnational security issues; the Enough Project, which is dedicated to combatting genocide; and by Interpol. A spokesperson stated that due to the sanctions imposed on Sudan, resulting in the drying up of its oil revenues, the country was unable to pay its militia and paramilitary, thus it allowed them to 'loot, raid, or - in this case - kill elephants.')

With their camp destroyed and their equipment taken it was assumed the poachers were stranded in the bush with no means of support, and had, therefore, retreated back across the border.

Not so. A month later, the poachers returned and attacked the rangers' camp, killing five. The sixth, Hassan Djibrine, managed to get away. The seventh - the camp manager, Djimet Seid - was wounded and hid. He watched as the poachers helped themselves to the rangers' weapons and ammunition and made their escape.

Despite his wounds, Seid walked and swam twelve miles to the nearest village to get help. Upon receiving the news, the park managers wanted to launch an immediate search for the killers, and for Hassan who was still unaccounted for. Chadian officials, however, ordered the park staff to stand down because, seemingly, the Chadian government was worried for their safety.

Five days passed before anyone was allowed to fly to the ambush point, by which time the bodies had reached such a stage of decomposition they had to be buried were they had fallen. Hassan was never heard from again. He was presumed dead, possibly through drowning due to the onset of the rainy season having created vast areas of flooded landscape and waterlogged vegetation.

Receiving limited support from the authorities, the park personnel launched their own investigation, using information obtained from the phones found in the poachers' camp, including contact numbers, messages and photographs, which they duly passed on to the police.

The park managers distributed fliers featuring the people in the photos and offered a reward. Months later, a relative of one of the dead rangers, a travelling trader, received word that a member of the gang was hiding out in a village close to the Chad/Sudan border.

The trader, aided by border guards, seized the poacher, who turned out to be the individual who'd fled the scene following the rangers raid on the camp. His name was Soumaine. He swore he'd taken no part in the murders and had been recruited purely to look after the camp while the rest of the gang hunted for elephants. The Chadian authorities arrested him and delivered him to a military jail to await trial.

A month later, there was a prison break. Soumaine was one of the many inmates who got away. There were rumours that his escape had involved bribery and government involvement. He was never heard from again. The government dropped the case against him and neither he nor the remaining gang members were ever found.

I came across this story when I read *Poached*, journalist Rachel Love Nuwers' cracking account of her investigation into the world of wildlife trafficking. I'd been looking for an idea for a new adventure for some time and I thought the unsolved murders of the Zakouma Park rangers might form the basis for a story in which I could bring back the characters from my earlier, pre-Hawkwood novels.

It was during the course of my research that I came upon the links between the Chadian government, Sudan's Rapid Support Forces, and, more pertinently, the Janjaweed militia, and, perhaps, to my mind, one reason why the Zakouma killers were never brought to justice.

But then, maybe I was seeing a conspiracy were none existed and maybe it was just a series of coincidences. Either way, it made for an intriguing premise, prompting the question I'd asked myself whenever I was thinking of penning a new book: what if..?

As for the rest...

The Golden Kingdom Casino Resort and its founder are fiction in name only. Should anyone feel the urge to delve into the novel's background and familiarize themselves with the real locations and some of the individuals portrayed in the story, all they need do is Google: *Golden Triangle Special Exclusion Zone* and their curiosity will be rewarded.

In other instances I have used real names where I considered them to be appropriate and relevant to the plot. They include the conservation organizations mentioned; in particular the Bangkok based Freeland, which does sterling work, aided by the Thai police, in fighting wildlife crime.

As well as the Rachel Nuwer book referred to above (Rachel was the journalist who dressed up as the Eastern European hooker in order to infiltrate the real Golden Kingdom), I highly recommend two more publications which provided me with additional background detail. They are: *Killing for Profit* by Julian Rademeyer and *Blood of the Tiger* by J.A. Mills.

There are numerous websites devoted to wildlife conservation and the illegal trade in wildlife species; too many to list here. What set me on the trail of the Golden Triangle SEZ was the video produced by the EIA (Environmental Investigation Agency: eia-international.org) which takes you inside the real Golden Kingdom complex. It was made a few years ago but is viewable on YouTube under the title: *Sin City: Illegal wildlife trade in Laos' Special Economic Zone.*

At the time of writing, the resort is still in operation.

Information on the extracurricular activities of Sudan's Rapid Support Forces can be found on the Global Witness website: www.globalwitness.org/en/campaigns/conflict-minerals/exposing-rsfs-secret-financial-network

James McGee grew up in Gibraltar, Germany, and Northern Ireland. After periods of employment in banking and the newspaper industries, he spent 10 years as a supervisor with Pan Am Crew Operations followed by 15 years in the bookselling trade. He lives in Somerset.

As well as writing thrillers he is also the creator of the successful Matthew Hawkwood series of novels, set during the Napoleonic Wars.

Author's website: jamesmcgee.uk

*'Rapscallion...one of the best books I've read
in a long time'*
Coventry Telegraph

'A ripping yarn, fast-paced, violent and exciting'
HistoricalNovels.info

'McGee spins another rollicking yarn'
Yorkshire Evening Post

Rebellion...an epic tale. Hawkwood fans will delight'
Kirkus

*'Hawkwood is a complex and fantastically researched
character, enigmatic and completely engaging'*
SF Book Reviews

'Breakneck pace, brutal action and twisty plotting'
Reginald Hill

'A richly enjoyable and impressively researched novel'
Andrew Taylor

'Gripping stuff...I needed more!'
Goodreads.com

*'Love the way he weaves a story through a history
lesson. His hero is the 1800's version of Jack Reacher'*
Avidrdr, Amazon.com

Printed in Great Britain
by Amazon